THE
PARIS
SEAMSTRESS

NATASHA LESTER

FOREVER

New York Boston

Copyright © 2018 by Natasha Lester
Reading Group Guide copyright © 2018 by Hachette Book Group, Inc.
Cover design by Faceout
Cover copyright © 2018 by Hachette Book Group, Inc.

Forever
Hachette Book Group
1290 Avenue of the Americas, New York, NY 10104
forever-romance.com
twitter.com/foreverromance

First published in March 2018 by Hachette Australia
First American Edition: September 2018

Forever is an imprint of Grand Central Publishing. The Forever name and logo are trademarks of Hachette Book Group, Inc.

The publisher is not responsible for websites (or their content) that are not owned by the publisher.

The Hachette Speakers Bureau provides a wide range of authors for speaking events. To find out more, go to www.hachettespeakersbureau.com or call (866) 376-6591.

Library of Congress Control Number: 2018940376

ISBN 978-1-5387-1477-5 (trade paperback)
ISBN 978-1-5387-1475-1 (ebook)

Printed in the United States of America

LSC-C

10   9   8

For Ruby.
I promised that you could start reading my books when
you were twelve. It seemed so far away at the time. But
now you are twelve and you are my kindred spirit. I
hope you continue to love books and history forever.
Happy reading, my gorgeous girl.

PART ONE
ESTELLA

CHAPTER ONE

June 2, 1940

Estella Bissette unrolled a bolt of gold silk, watching it kick up its heels and cancan across the worktable. She ran her hand over it, feeling both softness and sensuality, like rose petals and naked skin. "What's your story morning glory," she murmured in English.

She heard her mother laugh. "Estella, you sound more American than the Americans do."

Estella smiled. Her English-language tutor had said the same thing to her when he ended her lessons the year before and joined the exodus out of Europe; that she had a better American accent than he did. She tucked the roll under one arm and draped the silk across her shoulder. Then she swung into a tango, heedless of the women's cries of, *"Attention!,"* cries which only goaded her to add a song to her dance: Josephine Baker's fast and frothy "I Love Dancing" bubbling from her mouth between gasps of laughter.

She dipped backward, before soaring upright too fast. The roll of silk skimmed over the midinette's worktable, just missing Nannette's head but slapping Marie on the shoulder.

"Estella! *Mon Dieu*," Marie scolded, holding her shoulder with overplayed anguish.

Estella kissed Marie's cheek. "But it deserves a tango at the very least." She gestured to the fabric, glowing like a summer moon amid the quotidian surroundings of the atelier, surely destined for a dress that wouldn't just turn heads; it would spin them faster than Cole Porter's fingers on the piano at the infamous Bricktop's jazz club in Montmartre.

"It deserves for you to sit down with it and start work," Marie grumbled.

Monsieur Aumont appeared in the doorway, drawn by the noise. He took one look at Estella draped in silk, smiled and said, "What is *ma petite étoile* up to now?"

"Injuring me," Marie complained.

"It's lucky you have enough flesh to withstand Estella's antics," Monsieur Aumont said teasingly and Marie muttered something under her breath.

"What are we making with it?" Estella asked, lovingly stroking the folds of gold.

"This," Monsieur Aumont replied, handing over a sketch with a flourish.

It was a Lanvin, a reworking of the 1920s La Cavallini dress, but instead of an oversized bow adorned with thousands of pearls and crystals, the bow was decorated with hundreds of petite gold silk rosebuds.

"Oh!" she breathed, reaching out to touch the sketch. She knew the delicate rows of flowers would look like a brilliant swirl of gold from afar and that their true composition—an undulating ribbon of roses—would only become apparent if one was close enough to the wearer to see it properly. There wasn't a military epaulet in sight, nor a gas mask case slung across the shoulder, nor was the dress colored one of the many variations of blue—Maginot blue, Royal Air Force blue, tempered steel blue—which Estella had grown to loathe. "If one day my sketches look like this," she said, admiring Lanvin's exquisite illustration, "I'll be so happy I'll never need a lover."

"Estella!" Marie reprimanded, as if no twenty-two-year-old should even know the meaning of the word, let alone speak it aloud.

Estella looked across at Jeanne, her mother, and grinned.

True to form, her mother continued to make tiny pink cherry blossoms from silk and didn't look up or intervene but Estella could see that she was pressing her lips together to stop a smile, knowing her daughter loved nothing more than to shock poor Marie.

"A dress is no match for a lover," Monsieur Aumont admonished. He indicated the silk. "You have two weeks to turn this into a golden bouquet."

"Will there be a remnant?" Estella asked, still holding the bolt of fabric tightly to her.

"They've sent forty meters but I've calculated that you only need thirty-six—if you're careful."

"I'll be as careful as a dream weaver making Leavers lace," Estella said reverently.

She took the silk away to be stretched over a wooden frame, held in place by rows of nails. A solution of sugar and water was applied to stiffen the fabric enough so that Marie could stamp circles out of it with the heavy iron cutters.

Once Marie had finished, Estella covered a foam block with a piece of clean white fabric, heated her shaping ball over a low flame, tested the temperature in a pot of wax, set the first round gold disk of silk onto the white fabric, then pressed the shaping ball into the silk. It curled up instantly around the heated ball to form one lovely rosebud. She laid the rosebud to one side then repeated the process, making two hundred flowers by lunchtime.

While she worked, she chatted and laughed with Nannette, Marie and her mother, as they did every day, until Nannette said quietly, "I've heard there are more French soldiers fleeing from the north now than Belgian or Dutch civilians."

"If the soldiers are fleeing, what stands between us and the Germans?" Estella asked. "Are we supposed to hold Paris with our sewing needles?"

"The will of the French people stands before the Boche. France will not fall," her mother insisted and Estella sighed.

It was pointless to have the argument. Much as she wished to keep her mother safe, Estella knew that she and her mother weren't going anywhere. They would continue to sit in the atelier and make flowers from fabric as if nothing mattered more than fashion because they had nowhere else to go. They wouldn't be joining the refugees streaming down from the Netherlands, Belgium and the north of France to the south because they had no family in the country to whom they could run.

In Paris they had a home and work. Out there, nothing. So, even though her mother's blind faith in France's ability to withstand the German army worried Estella, she had no reply. And was it so wrong that, inside the walls of the atelier, they could all pretend, for perhaps only a few more days, that if couturiers like Lanvin still wanted gold silk flowers made, then everything would be all right?

During their lunch hour, as they ate bowls of rabbit stew in the atelier's kitchen, Estella sat apart from the other women and drew. In pencil on paper she sketched out the lines of a long, slim skirt that fell to the floor, a dress with sleeves capped at the shoulders, a waistline with a thin sash of gold silk, a neckline cut into an elegant V and ornamented with lapels like those on a man's shirt—a touch nobody would expect on a floor-length gown but one that Estella knew made it both modish and matchless. Despite the skirt's close fit, it could still be danced in: it was bold and gold, a dress to live life in. And in Paris in June 1940, anything that promised life was welcome.

Her mother finished her stew and, even though there was still fifteen minutes remaining of their lunch hour, she threaded her way through the atelier to Monsieur Aumont's office. Estella watched their faces as they spoke quietly to one another. Monsieur, one of the *gueules cassées* of the Great War—men who'd had part of their faces destroyed, as he had, by flamethrowers, leaving him with distorted lips, barely a nose, a monstrous face that Estella no longer noticed and which he covered with a copper mask outside the atelier—was unabashedly vocal in his opposition to the Germans, or the Boche, as he and her mother preferred to call them. Estella had lately seen men coming and going from the atelier after they'd met with Monsieur on the stairs, men who were ostensibly delivering fabric or dye but whose boxes only the Monsieur ever unpacked.

And her mother—one of the 700,000 women left a widow by the Great War, her soldier husband dying not long after they were married, when Jeanne was only fifteen. Two people who had reason to hate the Germans and who seemed to speak too often in whispers, whispers that looked too serious to be of the romantic sort.

Estella bent her head back over her sketch when her mother returned.

"*Très, très belle*," Jeanne said of her daughter's illustration.

"I'm going to make it from the remnant tonight."

"And then wear it to La Belle Chance?" her mother asked, referring to the jazz club in Montmartre that Estella frequented still, despite the fact that since the French army had been mobilized last year and the British had fled at Dunkirk in May, there were few men to be found in the city; only those whose jobs in munitions factories exempted them from service.

"*Oui*." Estella smiled at her mother.

"I will be at the Gare du Nord."

"You'll be tired tomorrow."

"Just as you were this morning," her mother chided.

Last night it had been Estella who'd stood at the train station. She'd been the one handing out bowls of soup to the refugees streaming through Paris, some of whom had been lucky enough to arrive by train, many of whom had walked hundreds of miles to escape the Germans. Once fed, the refugees took up their trail again until they found a home with relatives, or else they continued on as far as their legs could carry them, as far as they could get from the war, across the Loire River where it was said they would be safe.

The day drifted by, rosebud after rosebud. At six o'clock, Estella and her mother joined arms and left, walking along Rue des Petits Champs behind the Palais Royal, past the Place des Victoires and Les Halles, horse-drawn wagons for transporting food standing in a line out the front now, not vans. As they walked, the realities that Estella had been trying to ignore beneath a roll of spectacular gold silk asserted themselves.

First was the eerie quiet; it wasn't silent but at this time of night they should be surrounded by seamstresses and tailors and cutters and models all finished for the day and making their way home. But there were few people walking past the empty ateliers and empty shops; so much emptiness where, once upon a time, even a month ago, Paris had been full of life. But when the *drôle de guerre*—the phoney war— ended on May the tenth as Hitler's army pushed into France, the rush of people out of Paris had begun. First the Americans in cars driven by chauffeurs, then the families with older cars, then those who'd been able to find a horse and cart.

But the June night was warm and soft and scented with lilac, the horse chestnut trees wore strands of pearl-like flowers and here and there a restaurant was still open, a cinema, the House of Schiaparelli. Life went on. If only one could ignore the cats that roamed the streets, left behind when their owners fled the city, the covered streetlights, the windows obscured by blackout curtains, all of which told a different story from the romance of summer in Paris.

"I saw you talking with Monsieur," Estella said abruptly, once they'd crossed over Rue du Temple and were enveloped in the familiar scent of decay and leather that was the Marais.

"He is coming with me tonight, as usual," Estella's mother said.

"To the Gare du Nord?" Estella persisted, unable to shake the feeling that, lately, on the nights her mother had been out, it was to do more than serve soup to refugees.

"*Oui.*" Estella's mother squeezed her arm. "I will start at the Gare du Nord."

"And then?"

"I will be careful."

Which confirmed all of Estella's suspicions. "I'll come with you."

"No. It's better if you enjoy whatever time there is left."

And Estella suddenly understood that all the talk about France standing strong was a fervent wish, not false belief, a wish her mother held for her daughter's sake. And, not for the first time in her life, Estella felt an overwhelming gratitude to her mother, who'd raised Estella by herself, who'd made sure she went to school, who'd worked hard to feed and clothe and shelter her, who never complained, who had such a small life, confined to the atelier and to her daughter.

"I love you, Maman," she whispered, kissing her mother's cheek.

"That's the only thing that matters," her mother said, giving a rare and beautiful smile, altering the contours of her face so that she looked more her age, which was only thirty-seven—not old at all. Estella wanted to stitch that moment into the night, thread it so tightly against the sky that it could never be unpicked.

Instead she watched her mother walk up Rue du Temple toward the Gare du Nord. Then Estella continued on to the Passage Saint-Paul, a tiny, dirty alleyway which led to a hidden entrance to the beautiful Église Saint-Paul-Saint-Louis, and on which their apartment was also located. As she pushed open the front door of the building, the concierge, Monsieur Montpelier, an old drunk of a man, grunted and thrust a note at her.

She read it and swore under her breath. It was the last thing she wanted to do tonight.

"*Putain*," the concierge hissed at her choice of words.

Estella ignored him. She'd scald his eyeballs later when she left in her gold dress but, right now, she had work to do. She hurried up six flights of winding stairs to the apartment and, even though it was June, put on a long cloak. Then she walked back the way she'd come until she reached the buying offices of one of the American department stores off the Rue du Faubourg Saint-Honoré.

Madame Flynn, who must have been one of the only Americans left in Paris, was, as Estella knew she'd be, alone in her office. On the desk in front of her was a stack of boxes labeled Schiaparelli. "Be as quick as you can," Madame Flynn said, turning her back as if she didn't know what Estella was about to do when of course the opposite was true.

Estella removed the dresses from the boxes and hid them under her cloak. Without a word to Madame Flynn, she hurried back down the stairs, along the street and up another set of stairs to the copy house where Estella moonlighted when the fashion shows were on. During the shows, sketchers like her could capture, on a good day, fifteen copies of haute couture dresses which she then sold to the copy house or American department store buyers.

The market in Paris and America for copies of Chanel, Vionnet, Lanvin, Callot Soeurs, Mainbocher—all the couturiers—was insatiable. Estella had always known she could earn more money working at the copy house. But she also knew that if she spent every day copying—stealing really—other people's designs then she'd never have the heart to create her own. So she only worked as a sketcher during the shows, pencil flying discreetly over the paper so that the *vendeuse* wouldn't notice she was doing more than mark the number of the dress that had caught her attention, scrutinizing the models wafting elegantly through the *salle*, capturing details: the number of pleats in a skirt, the width of a lapel, the size of a button—praying for the model to be a slow walker so that Estella didn't end up with unfinished sketches that she'd never be able to sell.

The Chanel show was always Estella's favorite. There, it was a true challenge to capture fifteen sketches. Although the lines were simpler, the elegance was so manifest that she had to work harder than ever to catch it; it was more than just fabric and buttons and zippers. Each dress had a soul. And, at Chanel, everything was quiet and serene. She lacked the cover of the circus atmosphere that prevailed at a house like Patou, beneath which one could easily hide their dirty work. No, at Chanel, the *vendeuse* had sharper eyes than a sniper. Each guest received a slip of paper to make notes on rather than a large program perfect for hiding sketches and Estella had to draw while appearing not to move her pencil at all.

She'd always convinced herself it was a game and now that the American buyers weren't coming over to see the shows because of the war, her income from the last season had been much smaller so she'd told herself she had to take the opportunities when they were offered. Then she could pay off a little more of the debt that she and her mother owed Monsieur Aumont for the English lessons her mother had insisted Estella take every day after school since she was six. Lessons which her mother hadn't been able to afford and for which the Monsieur had lent them the money—French women were not allowed to have their own bank accounts, and therefore couldn't borrow money from a bank. They couldn't vote either; they were an underclass, meant to sit unobtrusively at home and bake and breed.

Thus the war had come as a terrible shock for some, unused to doing anything besides dress as well as they could afford. Luckily, Jeanne

Bissette, through necessity, had brought Estella up to be more resourceful than most. Which meant Estella knew that, while Monsieur Aumont would write off the debt in an instant, it was a matter of immense pride for Estella's mother that they paid off every last cent. It would be impossible to do so without Estella's extra income.

It was the English lessons that had allowed Estella to do so well as a sketcher; none of the American buyers spoke French so they all preferred to deal with her. If she didn't respond to Madame Flynn's summonses, the debt would trouble her mother, a debt Estella had only added to during the year she'd spent at the Paris School, the French campus on the Place des Vosges of the New York School of Fine and Applied Art. There, until war had shut it down, Estella had formed a dream of one day seeing her own name on a fashion atelier, of having customers wear dresses designed by her rather than stolen by her. But it was at moments like this, with six Schiaparelli dresses stuffed beneath her cloak, that she knew it would never happen, that an American buyer like Madame Flynn taking a commission from a copy house to lend them a selection of dresses to duplicate was in poor taste and a designer like Elsa Schiaparelli would stitch Estella's eyelids shut if she knew.

Estella vowed this would be the last time.

But, right now, Madame Chaput was waiting for Estella to begin. The fitters took the dresses Estella produced from beneath her cloak and made patterns while Estella sketched and Madame Chaput noted what kind of buttons she would need and stole snippets of fabric from the seams where nobody would notice. Then Madame gave Estella the money for a taxi and Estella returned the dresses to Madame Flynn along with the commission Madame Chaput paid for having been given access to the dresses to copy. Estella knew the dresses would be on a boat to New York tomorrow—if boats were still sailing given the turmoil of the last few days—and that Madame Chaput would have models made up within two days, ready to sell to her line of loyal Parisians who wanted all of the haute but none of the cost of couture in their wardrobe.

Then Estella walked back to the Marais again, knowing she'd have to be quick if she was to sew her gold dress into being and still make it to the jazz club before midnight. Back at the apartment building, she filled a bucket with water from the tap in the courtyard. Under the gleaming eye of the concierge, who loathed Estella and her mother for their refusal to make obeisance to him and buy him port at Christmas, and who enjoyed watching the deprivation of those who lived in one of the many Parisian apartment buildings without running water, she hauled the bucket up to the top floor—the cheapest floor. She put some water into a kettle, set it on the stove and made a cup of coffee. Then she sat down at her sewing machine, took out her scissors and cut the fabric to the sketch she'd drawn at the atelier, wishing she had the luxury of a cutter who'd make the line of the dress as perfect as she wished it to be, knowing she'd never be a Vionnet who worked from scissors rather than sketches.

It took her an hour and a half, but when it was done she grinned; it looked exactly as she'd intended. She slipped the dress on and frowned at her scuffed shoes, but her skills didn't stretch to cobbling and she hadn't the money to buy a new pair of pumps. She threw on her cloak in case the evening grew cold later, eschewed the gas mask she was supposed to carry but made the one concession her mother asked of her—to carry a white handkerchief so that she could perhaps be seen by cars in the blacked-out city.

Once in Montmartre, she bypassed Bricktop's—she couldn't afford that—and entered a club that was decidedly less elegant but definitely more fun, where the Montmartre patois syncopated between saxophone riffs and where one man, a munitions worker no doubt, tried to squeeze past her a little too tightly. She fought him off with a hard stare and a few well-chosen words and slipped into a seat at a table beside Renée, one of Monsieur Aumont's daughters.

"*Bonsoir*," Renée said, kissing her cheeks. "Do you have any Gauloises left?"

Estella produced her last two and they both lit up.

"*What* are you wearing?" Renée asked with a bemused laugh.

"I made it."

"I guessed as much. It's not something you'd find on the racks at BHV."

"Exactly."

"Isn't it a touch...outlandish?"

Estella shook her head. Renée was wearing one of the Heidi-style dresses that had been hanging forlornly on the racks at Au Printemps as if they'd forgotten the way back to the mountains and she looked like every other woman in the club: demure, watered down, like the wine they were drinking.

"Why would we expect anything less from Estella?" Another voice, one with a smile inside it, carried over to their table. Huette, Renée's sister, leaned down to kiss Estella's cheeks. "You look *magnifique*," Huette said.

"Dance with me." A man rudely interrupted them. He smelled like the Pigalle at midnight—liquored, fragranced with perfume from the necks of the dozen other girls he'd already taken a turn with on the dance floor. A man reveling in the advantage of his scarceness, who would have, with his lack of manners, no chance at all were most men not away fighting.

"No thank you," Estella said.

"I will," Renée said.

"I wanted her." The man pointed at Estella.

"But none of us want you," she said.

"I do," Renée said, almost desperately, and Estella knew it was a sign of the times; a girl could spend all night without a dance partner and here was one before them, albeit coarse, but what did that matter?

"Don't," Huette said to Renée.

As Estella watched Huette put a hand on her sister's arm, a spontaneous act—one that told of how much she loved Renée no matter how irritating she could be—Estella felt a stab of yearning. It was followed immediately by an awareness of how silly she was; wishing for something she'd never have. She should be grateful that she even had a mother, rather than selfishly covet someone's sister.

The man pulled Renée to her feet, leading her to the dance floor, making sure to hold her as close as he could and Estella turned away, revolted, when she saw him press his crotch into Renée.

"Come and sing. We'll change the tempo to something fast so she can get away from him," Estella said.

Huette followed her over to the four old-timers who comprised the band, with whom Estella and Huette had spent many evenings playing piano and singing, putting their school music lessons to work. Estella's mother had learned to sing at a convent school she'd attended when she was younger and she'd always sung at home, adorning their apartment with music rather than useless gewgaws, and she'd passed on her love of song to Estella from a very early age. But while her mother's preference was for operatic hymns, Estella's was for deep and throaty jazz.

The musicians didn't miss a beat as they kissed Estella's cheeks and Luc, the pianist, complimented her dress in a patois so thick and dirty no ordinary Frenchwoman could have understood it. He finished the song then stood up to get a drink at the bar. Estella sat down at the piano and Huette joined Philippe at the microphone. Estella picked out the notes to "*J'ai Deux Amours*" and the crowd applauded appreciatively. As Estella played, she hoped everyone in the room had a love for Paris strong enough that it would save the city from whatever might soon befall it as the Germans drew ever closer. But Huette's voice wasn't high enough for the song so she bumped Estella off the piano and made Estella sing it, which she did.

Every patron in the club joined her for the final chorus, letting Estella believe, for just a few seconds, that everything would be fine: that Paris was too grand, too legendary, too brilliant to ever be troubled by a short and grotesque man like Adolf Hitler.

She stayed at the club for only a short time after that, laughing with Philippe and Huette and Luc until she became aware that they hadn't managed to save Renée, that she was leaving with the brute of a man who'd asked her to dance and Estella suddenly felt tired, far older than twenty-two, and more melancholy than ever.

"Time for me to go," Estella said, rising and kissing everyone twice on the cheeks.

Once out in the Paris night, she didn't walk straight back to the apartment. She wound her way through the dirt and dilapidation of the Marais, a dereliction all the more obvious at each of the *hôtels particulier*, once grand homes of the nobles that, no matter what had been done to them—their transformation into jam factories and the desecration of their stately courtyards beneath piles of cartwheels, pallets and lean-tos—still held their heads high. As Estella brushed her hand over the stone walls, the same way she'd caressed the roll of gold silk in the atelier, she wondered if the elegance imprinted in those walls—the same as the way a couture dress never lost the line that set it apart from pret-a-porter—would withstand Stuka bombings and an army of men in cold gray uniforms.

The Carreau du Temple was quiet as she passed, the fabric and secondhand clothes sellers all abed, ready to be up at dawn selling the discarded garments they'd found in the rubbish bins of those who lived over by the Champs Élysées. Indeed the whole area was quiet, Estella often the only one on the street as she strolled through her city, taking in things she'd grown used to but which were too beautiful to take for granted now that they might be lost: the fading brilliance of the red, gold, and blue painting over the *porte de l'hôtel de Clisson,* the building's curved medieval turrets framing the gateway like a pair of plump sentries; the symmetrical pavilions and grand arched passage of the Carnavalet.

Without meaning to, she found herself outside a house on the Rue de Sévigné, an abandoned *hôtel particulier* that her mother had often taken her to when she was younger, where Estella had played among the disused rooms, a place that Estella suspected was the location of her mother's meetings with Monsieur Aumont. But with the blackout curtains in place, the streets glazed a preternatural blue by the covered streetlights, it was impossible to see if anyone was inside. Not French Baroque like its neighbors, and eschewing symmetry and form, the house lurked in true Gothic style, the hunchback of the street. Its coroneted turrets should have put her in mind of fairytale palaces but instead they made her think of women held prisoner at the top of the tower, all escape routes cut off.

Impulse made her push open the wooden door that led into the courtyard, the statuary of the Four Seasons gazing imperiously down on her from the walls of the house, including a headless Summer bereft of his power. The gravel paths had not been swept and raked for many years but still formed a star shape, each spoke divided by hedges that had long since outgrown formality and now shot and twisted where they wished. Mint, probably once confined to an herb garden, waved its stems wildly, perfuming the air with the hot scent of danger. And then she heard it. The scrape of a foot over stone. Fear ran its teeth along her back like a zipper.

She turned. There, collapsed on a rickety bench, was Monsieur Aumont. The smell of blood and panic rose off his clothes and his skin.

"*Mon Dieu!*" she gasped.

He lifted his head and Estella saw a dark stain on the front of his shirt. "Take these," he whispered, passing Estella a small bundle, "to the Théâtre du Palais-Royal. Please. For Paris. Find *l'engoulevent*— the nightjar. You can trust him."

"Where is Maman?" Estella demanded.

"At home. Safe. Go!"

He slumped over again and Estella moved in closer to see how she could help him. She was able to lean him back against the bench, to see his pleading eyes. "*Go*," he repeated roughly. "For Paris."

Whatever she held meant nothing but danger. Yet it was important enough for him to have been injured seriously and also precarious enough for him to have added that one word—*safe*—when she'd asked about her mother. Had it only been an hour ago that Estella had been singing of her love for Paris? And now she was being asked to do something for her city.

Monsieur Aumont closed his eyes. Estella unrolled the bundle. Maps of a building drawn on silk. She could slide them into the pockets she'd sewn discreetly into the lining of her cape, pockets perfect for moving copied dresses around the city. But she was so conspicuous: a cape of blue-black velvet trimmed with silver beads over a shining gold dress.

"Go!" Monsieur Aumont whispered for a third time, through gritted teeth.

Estella nodded at last. Because now she felt the absolute truth of the words she'd sung at the club: her city was being violated and, perhaps, if she did as Monsieur Aumont was begging her to, she could prevent one more trespass on Paris's honor.

CHAPTER TWO

Estella hurried out of the courtyard and into the street, the maps whispering like rumors in her pockets, unable to stop thinking of all the stories she'd heard: Germans dropping poisoned sweets by air into the streets to make the children in the city ill; Germans dressed up as nuns to spy on the citizens of Paris; German parachutists landing in the city at night. Every person she passed she feared might be part of the Fifth Column, fascist sympathizers helping the Germans, who would therefore do anything to stop her from reaching the theater with her delivery. Still, she moved down Rue Beautreillis, past the ancient clock that hung rusted and unceasing, reminding Parisians that while their city might be immortal, they were not, and neither was she.

Then, hoping the circuitous route she'd taken might have allowed the city to draw its cape over her and hide her within its folds, she turned right and walked on to the Palais-Royal. Finally she reached the theater and thanked God for her dress which might be just fine enough to make it seem as if she belonged in a place like this.

She ascended the curving, plushly red staircase and, at the top, found herself in an intimate and opulent reception room—beautiful in any other circumstance—well lit by a chandelier so large and so dazzling that she drew her hand up to her eyes. Swagged red velvet curtains hung over openings that she assumed were entrances into the theater itself. The walls were papered in deep burgundy trimmed with gold; everything was accented in gold—the chandelier, the balcony railing above, the cornices, the trimming around the ceiling fresco, the bas-relief that arched elegantly over the door at the far end of the room. Women wearing dresses Estella recognized as Chanel, Lelong, Callot Souers lounged in a scattering of low red velvet chaises and men laughed and sipped cognac and calvados. She knew that, for many, life cavorted on and the parties and revelry continued but after what she'd just witnessed, entering the theater was like stepping onto the moon, or someplace else equally removed from the reality of a German army on the march into Paris.

The notes of a foxtrot rang out from a piano and a few couples began to dance, although there was hardly the space. Estella let the hood of her cape fall from her head, shook her long black hair loose and stepped into the room.

How would she know who or what the nightjar was? Her gaze swept over the women and then the men. She saw the eyes of one man, who stood in the center of the room surrounded by a circle of people, flicker curiously toward her in a manner different from the lascivious stares a handful of others were bestowing upon her.

It wouldn't do to quail, to act as if she didn't belong. She crossed the room boldly, cape flying behind her, dress concealing her shaking legs. She didn't need to push her way through the circle because it opened to allow her in, the confident attitude of her shoulders and head, an attitude she'd copied from the house models she'd seen at the fashion shows, gaining her admittance.

Once at the man's side, she kissed both his cheeks, smiled and said a loud, "Hello darling," her voice again copied from the house models who tried to seduce the husbands of rich clients, often with success.

"I'm glad you came," he murmured, sliding an arm around her waist, playing along so she knew she was right.

"I have an interest in ornithology," she whispered. "Especially *les engoulevents*."

Nothing betrayed that what she'd said had aroused his interest. "Shall we dance?" he asked, taking her hand and excusing himself from the crowd, leading her over to the couples swirling around in time to the music.

He went to undo the bow of her cape which was still tied at her neck but she shook her head, not wanting the maps to pass into the hands of the theater attendants. "I'd prefer to keep it on," she said.

Then she found herself in his arms, circling the floor, the damned music having slowed to a waltz and, given the time of night and the state of inebriation of most of the theatergoers, proximity was all that seemed to matter and she knew it would look out of place if they were at arm's length. As he stepped closer to her, she did the same until they were chest to chest, cheek to cheek. He was all hard muscle and tanned skin, as if he spent his time outside rather than in an office, his hair almost as dark as hers and his eyes brown. He was extraordinarily handsome and in other circumstances she might have felt rather more pleased at the situation she'd found herself in. He wasn't French though; his command of the language was impeccable and so was his accent but it was almost too schooled, too perfect to be his birth-tongue.

He was waiting for her to say something. And Estella knew from the way Monsieur Aumont had spoken, from the blood on Monsieur's shirt that he, and perhaps her mother, were involved in something far more dangerous than helping refugees at the train station and that this man was a part of it. She wouldn't have trusted him with anything except that Monsieur Aumont, who she'd known since she was a child, had said she should.

"I believe I have something for you," she said, switching to English.

That surprised him. "Who the hell are you?" he asked, also in English, his voice controlled.

"Nobody you know," she said, reverting to French.

"You're not very good at being surreptitious." He indicated the dress that she'd thought might spin heads, but that was the last thing she wanted right now.

"No one with anything to hide wears a dress like this," she said.

He tried to hide it but she heard it. A laugh.

"Nothing about this is funny," she snapped, the last vestiges of her courage almost giving out. She needed to get this done and then return to help Monsieur Aumont—please God let him be all right—and finally go home and hope like she'd never hoped before that her mother *was* safe.

"You're very prickly."

"Because I'm so goddamned furious," she retorted. "I need to hang my cloak somewhere safe. Where can you recommend?"

"Peter, over by the staircase, will look after it." All the while they danced and their faces continued to smile and nobody in the room except the man and Estella knew that things were not quite as they seemed.

Estella nodded and pulled herself out of his arms, untying the ribbon at her neck as she walked away, letting her hand rest for just an instant on the left side seam, assuming if he was the kind of man who took delivery of maps that were worth bleeding for, he'd notice her action. She had no desire to lose her cloak; it had cost her a month's wages to buy the fabric. But it was a small price to pay if it helped Monsieur Aumont. And her mother. And Paris.

She passed the cloak to the man indicated and hurried down the stairs, desperate to be home. She strode out into the night, away from things she didn't want to understand, things that scared her too much, things that made her realize the life she'd known, growing up in an atelier in Paris surrounded by beautiful things, was over.

The touch of a hand on her arm made her jump. She hadn't heard footsteps but somehow he was standing beside her, passing her a black jacket. "Put this on," he said. "You won't make it home alive at this time of night in that dress. Your cloak had blood on it. Is it yours?"

He moved a hand up toward her cheek and she flinched, but realized from the attitude of his hand that he hadn't been about to strike her, but to do something far more gentle—to check that she wasn't hurt. Her reaction made him move his hand away so swiftly it was almost like he'd never raised it.

"It's not my blood. It's Monsieur—"

He cut in. "It's best if I don't know his name. Can you take me to him?"

Estella nodded and he followed her, his knowledge of Parisian streets seemingly as good as her own, never questioning her route, walking quickly but casually beside her. As they went through the Passage Charlemagne and into the Village Saint-Paul, its crumbling whitewashed courtyards creating a maze that nobody would be able to follow them through, he looked across at her quizzically.

She spoke the first words they'd shared since they left. "Not much farther." Then, "Who are you?"

He shook his head. "It's safer for you if I don't tell you."

A spy. She had to ask, even though she knew he could have, once they were hidden within the walls of the parish village, shot her or stabbed her or whatever it was men like him did to those who got in their way. "Whose side are you on?"

"I haven't said thank you," he said, which wasn't really an answer. "But those papers will help the French people a great deal."

"And the British?" She pressed for more information.

"And all the Allies."

Suddenly the wooden doors of the house on the Rue de Sévigné stood before them and Estella slipped into the courtyard. She stopped when she saw that Monsieur Aumont had fallen to the ground.

She darted forward.

He stopped her. "I'll do what I can," he said. "He deserves a decent burial and he'll get one. I promise."

A burial. Oh God! What about...? "Maman," Estella breathed, the word barely piercing the true night of a blacked-out city.

"Go and see," he said.

"And Monsieur?"

"I'll look after him."

She turned, fear finally unbuttoning the coat of rashness she'd been wearing until then, seeing only her mother's face, praying that Monsieur Aumont had, in his final moments, been right. That her mother was truly safe.

"Get out of France, if you can. And take care."

She heard the words slip through the air, the calculating tone gone now, replaced by something almost solicitous, and she held them to her as she raced for home. *You take care too, Maman. I'm coming.*

Thankfully the concierge was snoring in his chair when Estella returned to the apartment and she didn't have to explain her wild-eyed appearance, or the fact she was wearing a man's tuxedo jacket over her dress. She curved around and around the staircase, going up and up until she reached the top floor. Relief slid over her like silk when she found her mother in the dark kitchen, sipping coffee. But the relief fell to the floor when she saw the whiteness of her mother's face and that her coffee lapped in the cup because of the way her hands were shaking.

"Tell me," Estella said from the doorway.

"I know very little," her mother whispered. "Monsieur Aumont is working for the English, I think. He never told me exactly. He couldn't. But he has so many cousins and nephews, all Jewish of course, in Belgium, Switzerland, and Germany; he was passing on information they sent to him. The Jewish people have no love for the Nazis, Estella. Nor does Monsieur Aumont. Nor I."

"And nor do I but does that mean you should risk your life?"

"What would you have me do? You've seen them. The children we've helped OSE spirit out of Germany and into France and on to safety, the ones we can give nothing more to than soup and a hug. Their mothers and fathers taken from them just because of their religion. If we can help them, shouldn't we?"

Of course they should and they had. To stand aside and do nothing was to give up Paris entirely, to give up on compassion, to agree that the world should be run by monsters.

"How involved are you?" Estella asked.

Her mother sipped her coffee. "Not very. I've done nothing more than keep Monsieur Aumont's confidence. And help him find, in the crowd at Gare du Nord, the person he's looking for. It's easy to over-look a red neck scarf, or a green beret when only one person is watching. He always meets me back at the station and walks me home after he's done whatever he has to do. But tonight he didn't come back."

"He's dead, Maman."

"Dead?" The word was like a dropped stitch, ruining the fabric of their lives. Estella's mother reached for her hand. "He can't be."

"I saw him. I delivered some maps for him."

"You did what?"

Estella tightened her grip on her mother's hand and told her what had happened. The house. The blood. The theater. The man. That he said he'd take care of Monsieur Aumont's body. "I think he meant it," Estella ended quietly.

"But now you're mixed up in it too," her mother said, terror bleaching her face of all color. "There are spies everywhere. And who knows how much longer until the full force of the Wehrmacht is here." Her mother took a deep breath and sat up straight. "You have to leave France."

"I'm not going anywhere."

"You are." Her mother's voice was determined. "You cannot stay here now. If anyone saw you tonight…" The sentence was unfinishable.

"Nobody saw me."

"If you've seen the maps, you could easily end up like Monsieur Aumont. And here in Paris you'll never be anything more than a midinette in an atelier. Like me. I'm sending you to New York."

"I like being a midinette in an atelier." New York! How ridiculous.

"No you don't. Look at that dress. A couturier makes dresses like that. We're in the middle of a war. Soon there won't be a fashion industry left in Paris."

"What would I do in New York?" Estella tried to keep her tone light, as if it was all a joke. But the image of Monsieur Aumont's body sprawled on the ground amid the weeds, the knowledge of how close her mother had come to danger, made her voice crack. "I won't go by myself."

"Yes, you will. Monsieur…" Her mother stopped, eyes flooded with tears. "Monsieur Aumont asked me, weeks ago, to take over the atelier if anything happened to him. Our *métier* is a dying art. I must keep it alive, to honor him. I didn't touch those maps tonight. You did."

"I'm not in any danger." *Get out of France, if you can.* She remembered the words the man had spoken to her as she'd left.

"That's what Monsieur Aumont thought."

Estella stood up and searched in the cupboard for a bottle of port. She poured herself a glass, and one for Jeanne, draining it quickly, unable to conceive of life without her mother. She'd been the one to first let Estella loose on a sewing machine when she was only five, who brought home scraps of fabric so that Estella could make ever more fantastical clothes for her cloth dolly, who had let Estella, during holidays and evenings when she had to work late, sit at her feet under the worktable making her own versions of flowers out of offcuts of material.

It had always been Estella and her mother. Estella and her mother walking to Les Halles every Saturday morning to buy food for the week. Estella and her mother praying in the church of Saint-Paul-Saint-Louis every Sunday morning. Estella and her mother lying in their shared bed side by side, some nights talking about what Estella had been up to at La Belle Chance with Huette and Renée, other nights falling into a dreamless sleep because Estella had been up sketching until late. There was nobody else. There never had been.

Occasionally, Estella would wish for a sister, so that she would still have the blessing of family once her mother was gone. But it was a futile wish. When Jeanne—God forbid—died, Estella would be on her own. And the absence of a father, beyond the fact that he'd died in the Great War, was the only thing her mother never spoke of.

Estella sat back down and took her mother's hand, searching for reassurance. "There are no ships," she said flatly. "Unless I can get to Genoa and that's impossible."

"Last week, the American ambassador placed an advertisement in *Le Matin* urging all American citizens to go directly to Bordeaux where the very last American ship would be waiting to take them to New York."

"I'm a French citizen. How does that help me?"

Her mother pulled away. She walked through their tiny apartment, which most people of sound mind would probably be glad to leave behind: the lack of running water and elevator, the six flights of stairs, the tiny rooms—only one bedroom, a kitchen-cum-dining room whose table was more often used for sewing than eating, a space for a sofa, nothing decorative, just the bare necessities of plates and cups and pots and wardrobes and, of course, the sewing machine. But it was all they could afford on their midinette's wages.

Jeanne picked up her *boîte à couture*, an antique beechwood sewing box, the most beautiful thing they owned. It was lithographed on top with an image of a stand of wild iris pummeled by wind, stems leaning away in a manner Estella had always thought of as dancelike and subversive rather than weak and bending to the storm's will. Her mother opened the lid, took out the needle cases, the silver thimble, the spools of thread, the heavy scissors. Right at the bottom, she found a document. "You have American papers," she said, holding something out to Estella.

"What?" Estella replied.

"You have American papers," her mother repeated firmly.

"How much did you pay for those? Nobody's going to fall for false papers, not now."

"They're genuine."

Estella rubbed her eyes. "How can I possibly have American papers?"

The pause stretched out until Estella could almost hear it fray and then snap as her mother said, "Your father was American. You were born there."

"My father was a French soldier," Estella insisted.

"He wasn't."

Silence dropped like heavy jute cloth over the room, making it hard to breathe. It was her mother's turn to drain her glass.

"I went to New York once," Jeanne finally said. "To have you. I never planned to tell you any of this but keeping you safe is the only thing that matters now."

Estella unfolded the papers and saw her name written inside. The papers supported, without question, her mother's story. "But how?"

Tears flooded her mother's eyes with anguish. "It hurts too much to talk about."

"Maman!" Estella cried, horrified at the sight of her mother in tears. "I'm sorry. I'm just trying to understand."

"Understanding isn't important now. You must leave Paris. The embassy's last special train departs tomorrow. I went to the embassy last week to make inquiries. Just in case. Then I wasn't brave enough to tell you. I didn't want to lose you. But now I have to."

"How can I leave you?" Estella's voice faltered, unable to imagine herself getting onto a train full of Americans, traveling through a country at war until she reached Bordeaux where she would get on a ship as an American citizen and travel to New York. Without Maman.

"You can and you will."

Estella's response was a sob.

"*Cherie*," her mother whispered, wrapping her daughter in her arms and tucking Estella's head into her chest. "Don't cry. If you cry, then I will too. And I might never stop."

The desolation in her mother's words undid Estella and she couldn't make herself obey. Instead she sobbed as she'd never sobbed before, thinking of her mother alone in the atelier, alone in their apartment, alone in their bed. Thinking of the years unspooling before them both, without one another, never knowing when, or if, they might see each other again.

CHAPTER THREE

Morning broke to the sound of Stuka bombers screaming over Paris, dropping bombs on the nearby Citroën factory. And Estella knew, as much as she'd hoped that her mother would change her mind, that the bombing would only strengthen her resolve to get Estella out of the country.

After a cramped and fraught morning in the bomb shelter, she and her mother hurried wordlessly to the Gare d'Austerlitz. Yesterday's early summer sky had been burned black and smoke hung thickly and rankly in the air.

"I hope they hold the train," her mother muttered while Estella hoped the opposite; that it had somehow managed to leave on schedule during the bombing and she would have no choice but to stay with her mother in Paris.

No one had knocked on their door in the middle of the night. Nobody had come looking for her. One young woman who knew so little wasn't important enough to attract anyone's notice, surely? Hard on the heels of that thought came the man's warning: *get out*. What if, by staying, she put her mother in danger? She shuddered at the thought and that was the only thing that made her keep up with her mother, valise and sewing machine bruising her legs as they rushed along. Most of the room in the valise was taken up by her mother's sewing box. Jeanne had insisted that Estella take it, and the sewing machine, and

Estella couldn't bear to think of her mother sitting in their apartment without either of those two things. But nor could Estella bear the hurt in her mother's eyes when she'd tried to refuse the gifts. So she took them, one part of her grateful to have two such precious items which would remind her of her mother every time she used them.

The Gare d'Austerlitz was so full of people it was almost impossible to move. The morning's bombing had sparked a fear so great it ran like wildfire through the city. If two hundred German planes could drop so many bombs so close to their homes then few people wanted to remain behind to see what would happen the next time the planes flew over. Abandoned suitcases and items of furniture, things that hadn't been able to fit on the trains, littered the floor—lamps and vases smashed to pieces, teddy bears with arms torn off, a grandfather clock unchiming.

It was hot, so hot; sweat ran down Estella's back even though she wore only a light summer dress. Her lungs snatched at air, the weight of bodies and the summer heat stealing it all away.

She could smell desperation steaming from pores, could see it made manifest in the way babies were passed overhead through the crowd to lie on a table by the train so they wouldn't be crushed, ready to be collected by their mothers when they reached the front of the pack. But Estella also saw those mothers step onto carriages of the train far from the table, assuming the babies had already been boarded, saw the train pull away and the mothers realize too late that they had left their children behind. Saw their hands bang at the windows of the train, their mouths open in soundless screams. Who would look after those children now? Estella wondered as she clutched her mother's hand.

"Here it is," Estella's mother said, leading the way to a less busy platform, keeping her eyes firmly away from the mothers who'd lost their children.

As they approached the train, one specially requisitioned for Americans, Estella felt guilty. She was an impostor; there was nothing

American about her beyond the accent with which she spoke English but that was an accident, an effect of having learned it from an American. Their train was busy but not so full that people were having to use the toilets as space to fit more on board, which she'd seen was the case on every other train. Here, the walls of the platform weren't covered in hundreds of chalk messages, leaving instructions to separated family members about where they were heading. There was only one possible destination for those lucky enough to be here: America. No tables of stranded babies.

The American men wore smart suits with polished shoes, and a few had wives with them dressed in lightweight summer skirts, gloves, hats, pumps. The French people on the opposite platform wore coats, three dresses, pullovers, all the clothes that wouldn't fit in their valises.

All too soon, Estella reached the man checking papers. Before she handed them over, she took her mother's arm. "Please tell me more about my father, Maman."

Jeanne shook her head firmly. "There isn't time. Be good, *ma cherie*." She kissed Estella's cheeks.

Estella wilted into her arms. "I'm always good," she said smiling weakly.

"You're never good," her mother mock-scolded. "And make sure you don't change. Always be who you are right now."

Estella's throat closed tightly, stopping up the words she wanted to say: *Thank you. I will never, ever forget you. Stay safe.* Her eyes dropped tears onto her mother's blouse.

"You must go," her mother urged, stepping back, tapping her daughter gently toward the train as if she was a child reluctant to go to school.

"I love you, Maman," Estella finally managed. "This is for you." She passed over a package, in which was a blouse made of the last pieces of gold silk, a blouse Estella had worked all night to sew. "Wear it whenever you're sad."

"Go." The look on her mother's face was one Estella had never seen, the mask of calm removed. What had been hidden was now exposed: all the love she carried for her daughter and the desperate fear too.

Estella made herself step onto the train. She leaned across a man—who told her to *Watch it!*—so she could follow her mother's departing back through the window. Just when she thought it was the last moment in which she'd ever see her mother, Jeanne turned back, eyes scanning the train, blowing a kiss and hugging the blouse, her last remaining piece of her daughter, close to her heart. Then Maman was gone.

Estella could only wipe her eyes, take her seat, replay that final glimpse of her mother and pray for a safe arrival in Bordeaux, where she was still terrified they'd turn her away. Even though her mother had said last night that her father was American, that she'd been born in America, it seemed impossible.

But she forgot about the mysteries of her own life as soon as they reached the countryside. At first, what she saw moved her. Groups of proud women, thousands of them, wearing trousers, eschewing delicate dresses as not up to the task of the march to safety they'd embarked on, hair tied back with patriotic scarves in red, white, and blue. Poplar trees stood tall beside them, lining the roads, mimicking the straight-backed women, their long shadows seeming to point the way to sanctuary. But as the train drew farther away from Paris, the hoped-for sanctuary did not materialize and Estella beheld a wretchedness far greater than her own, far beyond anything that could be imagined.

The chatter on the train ended when they came upon a fat column of thin people who'd been walking for many, many days from Belgium and the north of France and also from Paris. There was a woman carrying a cat, a child with a birdcage, an elderly man pushing a wheelbarrow full of children, a pram holding a frail old lady, a child clutching a doll, so many suitcases and saucepans and pets and bundles of blankets. So many women and children, only a handful of men. Some rode bicycles. Most walked. Cars with mattresses strapped to the top as protection from bombing were unable to move through the thick mass of people. Horses and carts tried to get beyond the column. Vans and lorries tooted, so overfilled with people Estella wondered how the windows didn't break.

As the train pushed on, Estella saw people lying down by the side of the road. People who didn't move. Old people who could not march so far with so little food. She began to cry again, hugging herself, knowing that if she'd seen this first, she would never have gone out last night wearing a gold dress. She remembered the day, not long ago, when she'd witnessed the stained-glass windows of the Sainte-Chapelle, swaddled in linen and taken out of the church for safe-keeping. She'd been shocked at what it meant: that the government believed Paris would be bombed, but also glad that the beauty of her city would be preserved, regardless. Now she saw how futile a gesture it had been: if the government had known the city would be bombed, then why hadn't they taken the people, wrapped them in sheets, and saved them instead of panes of lifeless glass.

The SS *Washington* wore so many American flags it looked like a strange advertisement for the country and of course it was; the flags were meant to leave nobody in any doubt that this was not a warship, that it should not be torpedoed or shot at, that it should be allowed safe passage to America, unlike so many other ships that had been sunk since the war began. Estella boarded openmouthed, unable to fathom that there was still time for cranes to winch the cars of the wealthy onto the ship, still time to make sure people took from France whatever they couldn't live without. Except for Estella, who was leaving behind the most precious thing of all—her mother.

The ship was only half full, which again surprised her—couldn't they have taken some of the desperate people she'd seen flooding through France, despite their lack of papers?—but then it was ordered on to Lisbon to pick up those who'd missed it at Bordeaux. So full was the ship then that cot beds were set out in the Grand Salon, the library, the Palm Court; even the swimming pool, drained of water, was now a bedroom. Despite all the people, the ship was quiet, as if they were ghosts, visible but soundless. Worry and fear were present on faces but remained unspoken, especially after they were told to sleep with their life jackets under their pillows. Every day came more news of loss. The Germans were kicking at the door of Paris. The government prevaricated, then fled too. Paris was covered in ash from the papers burned by government ministries to prevent the Germans getting their hands on them.

In the early hours of the morning on the eleventh of June, as they were steaming from Lisbon to Galway to collect yet more American passengers, Estella stood on the deck in the unearthly night, unable to sleep. Out beyond the ship it was dark but, where she stood, the sky dazzled with the glow from the ship's American flags which were fully illuminated, attracting attention rather than allowing them to slip past unnoticed. And she dazzled too, having put her gold dress back on as a surrogate for her mother's arms. She closed her eyes and imagined her mother wearing the blouse Estella had made for her, connected across the seas by a bolt of silk.

Always be who you are right now. Her mother's last words to her played over in her mind. But who was Estella right now, given she had no home, no job, no family, and a past full of lies and fabrications?

She felt someone appear at her side.

"Lucky Strike?" a man asked.

"Where did you get American cigarettes?" she asked the man, who was sandy-haired and amber-eyed and had a friendly smile, offering her something other than worry. She took a cigarette and breathed in gratefully.

"My parents brought cartons with them when they came to France last year. Despite how much we've all been smoking, we still haven't run out."

"Didn't they know we have cigarettes in France?"

"You're French?" he asked.

"Yes," she said firmly, proudly. "But I was born in America." The words seemed to hang like a flare in the night, stark, unsafe.

"Then you'll probably be offended when I tell you my parents think Gauloises are the equivalent of smoking soil."

"Whereas these are the equivalent of smoking air," she teased, smiling a little.

He placed a hand to his heart, mock hurt. "Are you saying the French are hardier than we are?"

"We have to be. Nobody's invading America." Estella flicked ash into the water, into the darkness that hid God only knew what horrors: U-boats, torpedoes. Nobody even thought about icebergs anymore.

"I'm Sam, by the way," the man said. "And I'm sorry."

"Estella. And you don't need to be sorry, unless you're planning to attack Paris too. What were you doing in France?" Estella asked.

"My father's a doctor, my mother's a nurse. They came over with the Red Cross. But now they're leaving."

"Won't people need the Red Cross more than ever now?"

"Yes, but my mother's ill. She was shot a few weeks ago by a soldier who accidentally discharged his weapon in the hospital and she has an infection."

"Will she be all right?" Estella asked, remembering that other people had mothers too, that others besides her were worried.

"She'll be fine. My father's embarrassed though. Feels like he's running away. But I suspect he's actually glad to have an excuse to leave. If Mother hadn't been ill, I think I would have stayed."

"Are you a doctor too?"

"No." He hesitated. "You'll laugh if I tell you."

"Then you have to tell me. Laughing would be a nice feeling right now."

Sam smiled. "All right then. In order to make you laugh, I can disclose that I'd taken a year off medical school to come with my parents to France but I was working as a cutter at the House of Worth. And the reason I came over to talk to you is because I've been trying to figure out who designed your dress. It's got the lines of a Vionnet and the modernity of a McCardell. Whoever designed it is someone I wouldn't mind cutting for."

"A McCardell?"

"Claire McCardell. An American designer."

"Well, she didn't design this," Estella said. "I did."

Sam whistled. "Where did you learn to make dresses like that?"

"My mother taught me to sew. I've been inside an atelier almost all my life. My *métier* was artificial flowers. And I went to the Paris School for a year. Since it closed down, I've been going to the markets in the Carreau du Temple every weekend, buying whatever I could afford of the secondhand couture they sell there. I'd take a dress home, unpick all the seams and sew it back together to see how it was done. Then I'd trade it for a new piece the following week."

"Then you'll know what I'm talking about when I say I'd rather cut fabric than cut people open. Here." He passed Estella another cigarette as she'd smoked hers quickly, the first she'd had in days.

"How does a medical student become a cutter at a fashion house?"

"Like you, my mother's always been a good dressmaker. I was the only child so I used to help her when I was younger. My parents have always nursed and doctored Manhattan's less well-off, so I spent a lot of time playing in the hallways of Italian hand-finishers and Jewish tailors and Polish cutters. I picked it up. Then, when all the men in Paris went off to join the army, there was a job. I got it."

"You must be very good to get a job at the House of Worth," Estella said. At the same time, a light pierced the night.

"What the hell was that?" Sam asked.

"I don't know." Fear roiled through her like the waves below.

The ship's engines were cut and the sudden silence of the sea, with only the slapping of water against the boat, was as terrifying as the loudest of all noises. The watertight doors of the ship closed. An alarm sounded. An announcement: all passengers were to be loaded into lifeboats.

"What's out there?" Estella asked, not really wanting a reply, remembering every ship blown apart in the water by the Germans over the past year.

"The Germans," he said, confirming her thoughts.

This is how it ends, Estella thought. At sea, surrounded by black water and even blacker night. Without her mother. Without anyone she knew, besides this man, Sam, with whom she'd shared no more than a few cigarettes.

How would it happen? she wondered, hand gripping her cigarette so tightly she could no longer smoke it. Would there be an explosion? Or would it be silent, the bomb slinking like a shark through the water, pouncing on them when they least expected it so they weren't even aware of dying. Goddamn the dark-haired man at the Théâtre du Palais-Royal—but for him, she wouldn't be here.

I love you, Maman, she thought.

"Come with me," Sam said.

"You should go to your parents," she said. "I'm fine." She tried to look composed, as if being alone on a ship that was about to be torpedoed wasn't the most frightening thing that had ever happened to her. She drew on her cigarette for courage as passengers thronged around them, the ship's officers shouting orders over megaphones, relaying the message that a German U-boat had the SS *Washington* in its sights.

"You'll be doing me a favor," he said. "They're loading the women and children first. My mother will be on the brink of hysteria and neither my father nor I will be allowed in the boat with her. Perhaps you could look after her for me."

Even as Estella suspected that Sam might be exaggerating his mother's nerves, she was glad of it. "All right," she said, following him as he pushed his way through the people on deck, searching for his parents.

They found Sam's mother being loaded, most unwillingly, into a lifeboat.

"Sam," his father said. "Thank Christ."

"This is Estella," Sam said to his mother. "She'll keep you company until we meet again."

"Sammy," his mother said, kissing his cheek. "I'm sorry."

"What for?" Sam asked with a puzzled frown.

"For not letting you do what you want. You should, you know, if…"

If we survive.

"I'm going to hold you to that," Sam said. "See you somewhere in the water," he said to Estella.

His words galvanized her. "You will," she said firmly. Because the one thing she must hold on to, no matter how evasive and slippery a thing it became, was hope. She couldn't let the Germans take that away from her too, like they'd taken it from the people whose bodies she'd seen by the roadside as her train passed by. She took her seat beside Sam's mother.

Everything was orderly, quiet, not at all how Estella thought such a moment might be. Nobody wailed or cried; in fact very few tears were shed. Perhaps that was what happened to people when the last week of their lives had been beyond terror; they'd seen too much and it had numbed them to ordinary ways of reacting. At least that was how Estella felt as she listened to the ship's officers say that the Germans had allowed them ten minutes to evacuate the ship, which would give them all a chance of surviving, of bobbing up and down in the middle of who-knew-where, of perhaps being rescued.

Estella reached out and took Sam's mother's hand in her own. She would do the same for her mother, and Sam's mother looked as if she might disappear into herself at any moment, shoulders hunched into her chest, neck sunk into shoulders, head bowed.

"Thank you, my dear," Sam's mother said.

She was using her other hand to clutch the silver-sequined and pink-beaded neckline of the dress she wore under her coat. Estella could just see that it was an excellent copy of Lanvin's cyclone dress, a glorious whirling two-tiered evening gown of gray silk taffeta, a dress meant for a ballroom, not a lifeboat in the Atlantic facing down a German U-boat.

"I suppose you think I'm a little mad, or extremely frivolous, wearing this at such a time," Sam's mother said apologetically, noticing Estella's gaze. "Sam's father certainly did. Gave me a stern telling off when I put it on."

She opened her coat slightly and Estella saw the decorative sequined pocket to the side, the inky ripple of fabric, dark as the night they were trapped in but shining too, like hope.

"If so, then I'm equally as mad," Estella said, indicating her own dress.

"It's a dress that makes me brave." As she spoke, Sam's mother straightened her back, neck emerging from her shoulders. "Every time I put it on, I feel like the best version of myself. Like I can be, for a night, the woman I always wanted to be. I don't suppose you understand that at all."

Estella felt the shine of a tear in each eye. When she replied, her voice was husky. "I understand exactly."

Because she did. In the same way that Sam's mother's dress gave her the courage to face a German U-boat with dignity, Estella's gold silk dress had transformed her nine days earlier, making her into the kind of woman who thought beyond herself and to a greater good, the kind of woman who would go on a fool's errand to meet a stranger at a theater because somebody she trusted had told her it was the right thing to do. And it had brought her some comfort earlier that evening when she'd stood on deck, thinking of her mother embracing the blouse in place of her daughter.

That a piece of clothing could do so much. That it had power beyond the fabric and the thread and the pattern.

Hovering above the black sea, in the lifeboats still strapped to the sides of the ship, yet to be lowered into the water below, with the risk of death closer than it had ever been, Estella vowed that if she survived this, she would follow her dreams rather than allowing them to be impossible. She couldn't fight in the war and she couldn't help Paris but she could make clothes and, with those clothes, she could make women feel stronger and bolder and more courageous, as they would need to be through these dark times.

All of this rushed through her mind as a finger of dawn stretched over the sky, and then another, like a golden hand unfurling. Then there was, strangely, a cheer. Estella felt the ship's engines throb to life, a roar of animation, and then movement, a thrusting through the water, heading straight toward the sun as if it were Xanadu and would save them all.

"What happened?" Sam's mother asked.

"I don't know," Estella said. "Perhaps we're safe."

"Really?"

"Yes," said Estella, wanting to believe it.

The message reached them that they were, indeed, temporarily safe, that the U-boat captain had let them go, had thought they were a different ship. But they were to stay in the lifeboats, just in case. The cheer that rose up from each of the lifeboats was deafening, stranger embraced stranger, and a collective smile lifted the sun higher in the sky.

They steamed on, aiming for that sun, Estella shielding her face from the light, shifting a little so her body might also protect Sam's mother.

"I'm Clarice, by the way." Sam's mother released her grip on her dress, relief uncurling her fingers. "I don't believe we've officially met."

Estella smiled. "Estella. I'm glad we got to exchange names."

"Rather than end up at the bottom of the sea. I wonder where Sam is."

Estella scanned the lifeboats on the other side of the ship and pointed when she saw him.

"How long do you think we'll stay in here?" Clarice asked, moving uncomfortably.

Estella remembered what Sam had said about his mother being unwell. "Not much longer, I hope. I don't fancy sleeping here for ten days," Estella said, hoping to distract Clarice. "Although a cot in what used to be the post office is hardly more luxurious."

"Why aren't you in a cabin?"

Estella shrugged. "There weren't any left. It's not as if I'm the only one."

"I insist on you sharing my cabin. George, my husband, can share with Sam."

"I'm fine," Estella protested.

"The post office in a cot is no place for a woman alone. Anything could happen to you."

Estella couldn't help laughing. "You realize that we're perched on the edge of a ship in the middle of the ocean with a U-boat somewhere behind us and you're worried about me sleeping in a post office?"

Clarice laughed too. "See, you'll be a good diversion for me. George is spending most of his time with the many sick people aboard and he refuses to allow me to help; says I need to rest and recover. And Sam's always off somewhere, smoking too many cigarettes. Lying in a cabin by myself worrying isn't helping me to get back on my feet. I'd love the company."

The ship turned away from the sun and the gentling of the light on their faces made the passengers around them relax, the camaraderie of having outfaced a U-boat washing over them all like sea spray. Finally, the ship stopped and they were allowed to disembark the lifeboats and stretch their legs on deck.

Sam and his father hurried over to Clarice and engulfed her in hugs. Estella turned away, as if that would help her to not miss her own mother. She heard Clarice tell both men about the new sleeping arrangements and she waited for them to demur but Sam just smiled and said, "Good. I'll be able to find you easily next time I need someone to smoke with at five in the morning."

"Are you sure you don't mind?" Estella asked.

"Mind? God no," Sam said. "If I have to read aloud another page of *Gone with the Wind* to stop her from getting out of bed, I'll be the one saying *I don't give a damn!*"

Everyone laughed companionably and Sam went with Estella to collect her valise and sewing machine from the post office.

"Do you think your mother will keep her promise once you're back on dry land?" Estella asked, remembering what Clarice had said to him about doing what he wanted if they survived.

Sam grinned. "I'm going to hold her to it."

"Will there be work for you in America?"

"More than I need. With Paris cut off by the war, this will be the year American fashion finally comes into its own."

"I hadn't thought of that," Estella said slowly. Of course Sam was right. The Americans wouldn't be able to come to Paris to fill their wardrobes next season, and there would be no copied sketches crossing the sea if this was the last American boat out of Europe. America would be severed from the influence of Paris fashions.

"What about you?" Sam asked. "Do you have a job?"

"I don't." Estella hesitated, then decided to come clean. She told him about her work as a copyist, how she'd earned $1.50 a sketch every season to pass on drawings to the American buyers in Paris, who'd then take them back to New York and make up "genuine" Chanel copies. "So I know some people in New York. Buyers and manufacturers. I'll see if they have a job for me, to start with."

"I can help too," Sam said cheerfully. "Start on Seventh Avenue. The great bazaar of duplication, where they'd copy your grandmother if they thought anyone would wear her. Otherwise known as the Garment District. You want to work as close to 550 Seventh Avenue as you can and definitely don't work anywhere below 450. And if that gold dress is any indication of what you can do, I don't see why you shouldn't have an atelier of your very own one day."

Estella smiled. That was a pronouncement she very much hoped would come true.

CHAPTER FOUR

Almost one thousand more people boarded the ship in Galway, so it carried twice as many as its capacity. Somehow, everyone made room for everyone else and Estella and Clarice shared their room with two elderly ladies who took the beds while Clarice slept in a cot and Estella on the floor. On the way, the news came through that Paris had fallen with barely a shot fired. Estella could hardly comprehend it, nor understand what it all meant.

Each day, she read *Gone with the Wind* to Clarice, which she rather liked, even if Scarlett had to make clothes out of curtains. At night she slipped out, senses feeling across the water for Maman, finding nothing, wondering what would become of the atelier where so many Jewish people worked, praying that Paris would not suffer its own Kristallnacht. She smoked too many of Sam's cigarettes and asked him to tell her everything he could about the New York garment industry, which wasn't as much as he would have liked, having not been able to indulge his passion freely in the years before he left with his parents for France.

It was with Sam that she first heard Charles de Gaulle speak over the ship's radio from London, speak words that the French government seemed too cowardly to say, words that made the tears pour unchecked down Estella's cheeks: "*...has the last word been said? Must hope disappear? Is defeat final? No!...Whatever happens, the* *flame of the French resistance must not be extinguished and will not be extinguished."*

Somebody cared. Somebody had given French people like her, who wept for their country, a dream to hold on to. Somebody would help her mother. She sobbed and Sam put a gentle arm around her shoulders, saying nothing, letting her take in de Gaulle's words, letting the flame flare a little brighter inside her heart.

Eventually she composed herself enough to thank him. "You've really been the best kind of friend."

"Glad to," he said, dropping his arm.

Three days later, New York came into view, suddenly and spectacularly. Passengers began to weep as Estella had wept on hearing de Gaulle. Estella grabbed Sam's hand and pulled him along, running to the front of the ship to get the very best view. In her rush, she'd forgotten to pin her hat properly and the wind picked it up and tossed it into the harbor, a lily pad of turquoise silk that bobbed delicately for a few seconds before disappearing into the wake of the ship.

"Hatless and homeless," Estella said with a wry grin, clasping both hands onto the rails and leaning out as far as she could.

"You'll fall in!" Sam laughed and tugged her back but she resisted, wishing she could reach down and touch the waters surrounding her new city.

"Is that the Empire State Building?" she asked, pointing at a spire that had nothing on the Notre Dame in terms of antiquity but was so very brash in its position as the tallest building in the whole of the world. Its ambitions had never been in question and she hoped she could be that brave.

"Sure is," Sam said.

After that, there was a flurry of docking and disembarking, of having papers checked and, once again, Estella was waved through as if she really was American.

"You'll come and stay with us tonight, my dear," Clarice said. "Have a proper bath. I still can't believe they rationed bathwater among nearly two thousand people and didn't once think how that would make the ship smell."

"My mother was given the address of the Jeanne d'Arc Residence by the American Embassy and I'm going there," Estella said, more cheerfully than she felt at the thought of striding off into Manhattan on her own.

It would be easy to accept Clarice's offer. Estella had refused to take more than the money needed for her passage from her mother because she'd known instinctively that her mother would need it more than Estella did. She couldn't afford to pay for accommodation for more than a week, and she was quite sure Clarice's home would be much more comfortable than the Jeanne d'Arc.

"Is that a nunnery?" Clarice asked. "I hope you don't mind my saying so but you seem a little too worldly for a nunnery."

Estella exploded with laughter, which made her feel better. It was still possible to laugh, even now. "Luckily it's not a nunnery. It's a women-only boardinghouse run by nuns. I'm sure they'll take me in."

It was what her mother had taught her to do. To stand on her own two feet. If Estella didn't tackle Manhattan on her first night headlong and independently, then she might let everything that had happened overwhelm her. In refusing Clarice, she sensed her mother's nod of approval, a closeness that she mightn't be able to hold on to in a big family home with people all around.

"Then I insist on you coming to dinner tomorrow," Clarice said. "So does Sam." She looked beseechingly up at her son.

"You know she'll make my life a misery unless you do," he said with a grin.

"We can't have that," Estella replied, smiling too, glad to know that she had at least one friend in the city and also very glad to have been given a way to keep the friendship going.

Clarice insisted on Estella sharing their taxi and on walking with her into the six-story brick building on West 24th Street to be sure she was given a room. It was spartan, but the apartment in Paris had been similarly plain and under-furnished. So it reminded her of home and brought her mother nearer to her.

After Clarice had left and before she'd even had a bath, Estella went into the small chapel attached to the boardinghouse, lit a candle, knelt on a pew and prayed, hoping that the fervor of her emotions would somehow make her pleas heard by Sainte Jeanne. *Please,* she whispered, *take care of my mother. Take care of my city. Take care of my country. Let no one die. Let the Germans be there for a week or even a month, no more. Let Charles de Gaulle save France quickly, before too many people get hurt.*

The minute Estella stepped onto the sidewalk the next day, she felt it: verve, energy, life. Paris had, she realized, been insentient for so long, holding its breath until all the animation had drained away. Whereas New York had the movement, the pizzazz, the *éclat* of a Lanvin fashion show. And there was much that was familiar. The streets near the boardinghouse were lined with buildings whose facades contained orderly and perfectly aligned windows, almost Haussmanian in style. There was a Metro, or subway, which she rode to Times Square. But there everything changed.

Coca-Cola billboards flashed beside those for Planters Peanuts, Macy's and something called Chevrolet. An advertisement for Camel Tobacco somehow blew actual smoke onto passersby, making Estella stop and stare so that everyone had to swerve around her, which they did without any real complaint. In France she would have, at the very least, been remonstrated with but most likely sworn at.

Peculiarly, amid this place of rushing and gaudiness and industry, there was a statue of a man and a cross—the words Father Duffy engraved below—as if he was worshipping at the altar of American goods. Perhaps they had no churches in New York, Estella thought, but prayed at street-side monuments like this one. She shut her eyes, erasing the image of her mother kneeling beside her at the Église Saint-Paul-Saint-Louis on Sundays. How could she live in a city un-adorned by steeples and stained glass and bells?

Then she opened her eyes, casting them around, realizing it was impossible to open them enough to take everything in. Here in Manhattan, one's vision was automatically drawn upward to the sights above, where buildings graduated in, like stepped pyramids piercing the sky. In Paris, the only thing of any height was the Eiffel Tower. But in New York, elevation mattered.

She smiled at last. This was New York. Bright, sparkling; the very place for a bold, gold dress. For the first time, despite the war and de-spite the awful contraction in her stomach every time she thought of her mother, she felt an exhilaration that made her walk on.

She crossed Seventh Avenue and saw a sight so familiar it made her smile broaden. Steam billowing out of windows from the irons, which pressed the garments before they were shown. But the steam was so far up above her head, on the twentieth floor, the thirtieth even, little wisps that joined the clouds, which meant that the clothes themselves must be made on all levels of the buildings. Imagine that. Sitting so high off the street while pressing, sewing, sketching, designing. The light would be good up there, she thought. Manhattan might be differ-ent, but that didn't mean it would be worse than Paris.

She decided to start with the offices of the manufacturers who'd bought sketches from her in Paris. If they didn't have a job for her, then she'd try the department store buyers. And she was especially pleased to see that the card of one of the manufacturers she knew, Mr.

Greenberg, bore the address Sam had told her to aim for: 550 Seventh Avenue. In Paris, it had meant nothing to her. Now it represented opportunity of the kind she needed to seize.

But her spirits did more than sink; they almost drowned when she reached Mr. Greenberg's office. He was pleased to see her. But he didn't want her to design.

"I need you in my comparative shopping department," he said. "The others get the details wrong, don't pay attention to the buttons or the seams. You always had an eye for what makes each dress different."

"Comparative shopping department?" she asked. It wasn't a phrase she'd ever heard and she wondered if it was particularly American.

"You go out to the stores—Bergdorf's, Saks, Forsyths—see what they're selling, especially anything that looks French, sketch it, give it to the cutter; then he makes it up."

"Pardon?" Estella replied, certain she had not, somehow, turned on the English language part of her brain sufficiently.

"Take your sketchbook," he shoved some paper at her, "and your pencil, and get me something I can make into a model. Damned war means nobody's got enough sketches. One dollar fifty a sketch. Same as Paris."

Estella turned on her heel, knowing she had to leave before she said something she shouldn't. That war wasn't simply a damned inconvenience; she'd seen dead people, people who'd done nothing more than try to move to a safer place, or people like Monsieur Aumont who'd tried to do the right thing when so many others were too frightened.

On the street, she was knocked sideways by a passing clothes trolley. "Damn," she muttered, feeling her ankle.

But it didn't matter how sore it was; she had to do what Mr. Greenberg asked if she wanted to pay for her room. If she wanted to eat, to buy a subway ticket back to the boardinghouse. She had to do something she'd sworn never to do again: copying. Why did nobody want anything original? Why was everybody here so in thrall to a few Parisian couturiers?

But those were unanswerable questions. Her purse contained just twenty American dollars. So she studied the map she'd been given at the boardinghouse and walked across town to Saks Fifth Avenue, glad she'd chosen to wear a dress she'd made herself, something smarter than she'd normally have worn to work at an atelier. She'd wanted to make a good impression on Mr. Greenberg but now she needed to pass as a woman who could afford to shop at Saks.

She adopted the walk and the posture she'd copied from the salon models and she breezed gaily up to Ladies Wear. The first dress she saw was a fake Maggy Rouff in beautiful black satin, dropping in a gentle flare to the floor. She checked the price ticket: $175! It probably sold for three times that much to a Maggy Rouff client in Paris. She wondered what price Mr. Greenberg would sell it for. Something lower than $175, she suspected. And here Estella was, at the bottom of a long chain of copies, making just $1.50 a sketch.

She surreptitiously made as many notes as she could until a sales clerk began to shadow her, then she slipped out to Bergdorf's, where the clerks were less attentive, and took down the details of another six gowns. After that, she walked back to Greenberg's to sketch them properly before the memory faded.

She soon discovered that Greenberg didn't have a designer working for him; he said it was the way of Seventh Avenue. Nobody had designers; nobody designed. They all copied Paris, and one another.

"America is industry; Paris is art," he told her. "Paris creates, we make." The cutter, he said, would make up the models from Estella's sketches.

"He might be able to cut fabric," Estella said, "but does a man in his

fifties know what women want to wear? I could design for you," she
offered. "I can bring in some sketches tomorrow."

"I can sell a genuine Chanel copy for far more than I can sell anything by an unknown," Mr. Greenberg said.

A genuine Chanel copy. Estella just managed to stop herself express-
ing her scorn at the oxymoron. Instead she sketched, thinking only
of the $10.50 she'd just earned, enough to pay for her room for the
week. It had been different, somehow, when the sketches she drew
were shipped over to America and she remained in Paris, far from the
scene of the crime. But now she was so far in the thick of it that it felt
like a blackout curtain had been drawn around her, shutting out all the
light she'd felt that morning on the streets.

Half an hour later, Mr. Greenberg interrupted her sketching,
scurrying in accompanied by a tall, blond woman. She was young like
Estella and appeared completely at ease in her sensationally curved
body.

"We need her dressed and in the showroom in ten minutes," Mr.
Greenberg said to Estella, as if this was a part of her job they'd already
discussed. "Buyer from Macy's is here. Pity we haven't got the models
for those made up yet," he said, pointing at Estella's sketches, "but
we'll have to make do with what we've got." He left the room and
Estella heard the sound of him greeting someone in the small reception
room.

"I'm Janie," the woman said cheerfully in an accent Estella couldn't
place. "House model. Only started last week but it's long enough to
know I don't want to work here forever. You?"

Estella started laughing. "I couldn't have put it better myself," she
said, "and I only started this morning. This," she said, pulling one
of the models off the rack, a siren suit she knew she'd copied for
Greenberg back in April, "is brought to you by Ms. Schiaparelli herself. Complete with kangaroo pockets, so you can escape into your

bomb shelter and take the kitchen sink with you, should an acorn chance to fall on us from the sky."

Janie giggled. "It's ridiculous, isn't it?"

"It's mad," Estella said. "Surely nobody would buy a siren suit in a city where there are no air raid sirens or shelters?"

"You'd be surprised," Janie said. "All you need to do is help me get each outfit on and off quickly or else there'll be trouble. He's been gracious enough to set up a curtain over there to protect my modesty."

Behind the curtain they went, Estella helping Janie into a dress, one she couldn't place. Then she realized it was another Maggy Rouff copy but whoever had cut it had made the skirt an inch too short and so the fullness wilted against Janie's legs as if she'd been playing out in the rain.

"The original swept the floor," Estella said. "I never liked it; too much faux-Victorian nostalgia, but at least it had purpose. Now it doesn't know what it wants to be." She stepped back and stared critically at Janie, thinking; this wasn't why her mother had sent her to America—to copy dresses. This wouldn't make Jeanne proud. Her mother, trapped in Paris by the Germans, deserved for Estella to make more of the chance she'd been given.

"Just a minute," Estella said, grabbing a handful of pins and deftly taking the hem up about five inches, keeping the fall of the skirt, and when she'd finished it looked jaunty, fun, as if it might just skip off by itself and take a turn on the dance floor.

"Gosh, it's like a different piece," Janie said admiringly.

"We're waiting," Mr. Greenberg's voice snapped.

Janie grinned. "Here we go."

As Janie walked toward the showroom, Estella could tell she was good at her job. That she had an innate self-assurance that would give any dress a shot of confidence. She peeped into the showroom and watched Mr. Greenberg jump from his chair as if Estella had stuck her pins into him rather than into the dress.

"Excuse me," he said to the buyer, only just achieving politeness, as he grabbed Janie's arm and walked her out the door. "What's this?" he barked.

"A dress," Janie said, innocent as a lamb.

"I fixed it," Estella said. "I don't know who copied it for you but they need a pair of spectacles at the very least."

"Skirts are not this short. Haven't been for years," Mr. Greenberg hissed.

"But they're moving that way," Estella said. "If you look at the lengths from the April shows and compare them to October, you'll see—"

"Skirts are not this short right here, right now, in America. Fix it!"

"No," Estella said, finding courage for the first time that day, unwilling to butcher what had once been something a designer had made with love and care.

"Then you're fired!"

"You owe me $10.50," Estella shot back. "Unless you want me to let the Macy's buyer in there know how you get your models."

He had no choice but to pay her, seething, hand shaking as he dropped dollar bills into her palm. "You ought to be careful, young lady," he said as his parting shot, "or you'll find it very hard to get another job on Seventh Avenue."

"In six months' time, all you'll be selling is dresses as short as this one and you'll wonder how you could have let me go," Estella retaliated as she picked up her purse and marched off, taking out her fury on the elevator button, trying not to think about what she'd just done. The elevator delivered her into the lobby and she paused there, wondering what to do next.

"Wait!" Janie called, stepping out of the elevator beside Estella.

As soon as Estella saw her, she couldn't help laughing. "Did you see his face!" she said. "You'd think I'd sent you out in your underwear."

"I think he'd have preferred that," Janie said wickedly.

They both dissolved into giggles and Janie slipped her arm through Estella's as they stepped onto the street.

If Estella had thought the streets were loud and busy before, nothing prepared her for Manhattan's Garment District at noon. Workers on their lunch breaks hurried along the sidewalk to take up every last seat at every café, men wheeled racks of garments back and forth across the street as if it were a subway track and, on the sidewalk, crammed into every available piece of curb space, trucks disgorged rolls of fabric, and boxes of buttons, zips, trims, and ribbons. Finished clothes paraded out of factories and into vans ready to be delivered to stores. Traffic was at a standstill: with all the parked delivery trucks blocking the way, nothing wider than a pedestrian could move along the street. Horns blasted ceaselessly, a Manhattan lullaby belting out its impatient chorus, accompanied by the rumbling of truck engines, the clatter of trolley wheels, the shouts of greeting from one delivery driver to another.

"I'm famished," Janie declared, leading Estella into a nearby café, where she proceeded to order a burger and coffee.

Estella craved the filling stews she was used to eating at the atelier at lunchtime but everything on the menu seemed made for speed rather than a leisurely repast. Another thing to get used to; that lunch wasn't to be the main meal of the day as it was in Paris. She ordered the cheapest thing she could find, given her now unemployed state—soup that came with a flimsy white piece of something that was supposed to be bread. One look at Janie's coffee told her not to bother.

"Where are you from?" Estella asked.

"Australia," Janie proclaimed. "I stole the money for my passage from my parents and ran away before I turned into an apple left on the tree too long. Brown and wrinkly and bitter as all hell, like everyone else in Wagga Wagga."

"That's a real place?" Estella asked uncertainly.

"You're a riot. Wagga's as real as I am. You're looking at the draper's daughter. I've been parading around in fabric since I could walk. A friend of mine decided to sail to England to work as a nurse. I skipped out to the port with her but I took the ship bound for New York instead. I've been here nearly a year. Long enough to know that place," she pointed at Mr. Greenberg's across the street, "is not for you or me."

"But what is the right place?" Estella mused. "I need money. I need a job."

"Me too. I've gotta pay the rent at the Barbizon, even though I almost have less freedom there than I did at my parents'."

"Well, I'm staying at the Jeanne d'Arc, which is the closest thing to a nunnery."

Janie grinned through a mouthful of burger. "Look at us both. Down on our luck. In a city that thrives on freedom but as far as you can get from it."

"I know. I keep thinking of Chanel and how she had to rely on a man's money to get her start. That's not what I want to do. And I definitely don't want to make any more money copying dresses for Mr. Greenberg."

"Everyone does it," Janie said cheerfully. "Scruples are as out of fashion as cloche hats. One of the girls from the Barbizon has a job where she's given money to buy dresses from the swanky made-to-measure fashion houses, which fellas with more cash than Greenberg copy. She gets to keep the dress as her pay. Models like me can earn a bit extra for passing on information about the clothes we've been fitted in at the manufacturer on the next floor down. I've even heard of delivery boys wheeling racks down Seventh Avenue being stopped and paid for a peek at their wares before they reach the stores."

"It's worse than Paris," Estella groaned.

"Tell you what," Janie said. "You can let a friend stay with you at the Barbizon in a cot that takes up half the floor space and it'll only cost you a dollar a night. You need three references and an interview for your own room, but to share for a while, we should be able to swing it."

"Three references? Is it a finishing school?"

Janie grinned. "The Barbizon Hotel for Women would like to *think* of itself as a finishing school. No men allowed, only the best women the city has to offer. And you're looking at Miss Sydney 1938. Winner of the biggest beauty pageant in the country. I brought with me three impeccably forged references from Australia and no one's gonna telephone down there to check, so I got a room."

"You steal money from your parents, you forge letters; anything else I should know about?" Estella asked with a smile.

"Just that you and me are gonna have some fun in this city."

"I know!" Estella said, standing up. "Let's go shopping."

"With what money?" Janie asked dubiously.

"We're not buying, we're looking. I want to know who to work for so we don't end up at another place like Greenberg's. There must be someone in America who actually designs their own clothes."

Into and out of Forsyths, B. Altman, Lord & Taylor, and Bloomingdale's they went, Janie attracting everyone's notice because she was so tall and so blond, like a giraffe that had metamorphosed into something as beautiful as its long eyelashes promised it could be.

Among the racks of dresses, many as bland and unoriginal and clearly copied straight from the Paris fashion shows as Estella had expected, were some with flair. "I think there are four categories," Estella said after a time. "Paris knockoffs, Hollywood imitations, made-to-measure, and sportswear. I like these ones." She held up two simple wrap dresses. Townley Frocks, the label read. "They don't look like much on the hanger, but I can see that the style means they'll adjust to most kinds of figures, and they're not knockoffs. Or this one—Clare Potter. Maybe we could work for either of them?"

"If they'll have us," Janie said.

"They'll have you," Estella said with certainty. "You're made for this. But I know someone who can help. And luckily we're due there for dinner tonight."

"*We're* due for dinner?"

"They're the kind of people who won't mind me bringing a friend."

As they walked across to Lexington and then up to 63rd, Estella told Janie about Sam. "I'm sure he'll be very happy if you come too," Estella said with a grin, nodding at Janie's beautiful face.

"Pfft," Janie scoffed. "I might be blond and leggy but you're as striking as the Chrysler at sunset. If he's already met you, I won't stand a chance, no matter how much flirting I do."

"We're just friends," Estella said. "So, believe me, you can flirt all you like."

The Barbizon Hotel for Women on the corner of Lexington Avenue and East 63rd Street was a beautiful building of salmon and rose-pink brick, flecked with emerald and black. Part Gothic, part Renaissance, it towered over its neighbors and Estella stared up in amazement at its crown. "I'm used to six-story apartment buildings," she said by way of explanation. "I can't imagine living up so high."

"You get used to it," Janie said cheerily as she led the way to the front doors. "In Australia, everything is single story but now I stand out on the terrace on the eighteenth floor and I barely notice I'm surrounded by sky."

As they stepped inside, Janie waved her hand at the wooden railings above them. "The lounge is up there; there's a stage and a pipe organ for concerts. They like to attract an artistic clientele—drama students, musicians, artists, models, as well as secretaries. There's a swimming pool, Turkish baths, a solarium, a gymnasium; more things than anyone could ever use. You need to get a pass to admit guests, so we'll do that now and I'll sweet-talk them into letting you share with me. If I say you're a refugee from Paris, they'll take pity on you."

Janie did just that, spinning a story about her friend who'd fled the Germans, experiencing unimaginable horrors, and who could not be left on the streets to suffer further. As Janie cajoled the matron, Estella watched young women like herself cross back and forth through the lobby with musical instruments, armfuls of books, even an easel. Everyone had something to do, everyone was purposeful and, what's more, they all needed clothes in which to *be* purposeful. If the clientele were largely artistic as Janie had said, they might just appreciate clothes that were designed, rather than copied. Which would mean making them to fit a working woman's budget. Estella's mind raced with a sudden sense of possibility.

Of course Janie succeeded in persuading the matron. And so, after they'd collected Estella's things and then freshened up, they caught the subway to Sam's parents' home. Clarice welcomed Estella with a hug and waved off all Estella's apologies about bringing an unexpected guest. Sam and his father both had to pick their jaws up off the floor when they saw Janie.

"You'll be pleased to know she's planning to flirt with you," she whispered to Sam, sotto voce, as his parents ushered them through to the drawing room.

"At least one of you will. I've given up on you." He grinned and turned his full attention to Janie.

Dinner was delicious and the evening passed quickly by. Clarice told Estella and Janie to go right ahead and quiz Sam about the New

York fashion industry—such as it was—and not to stand on ceremony and feel they must stick to polite but useless conversation.

"What about Tina Leser?" Janie asked. "I saw one of her playsuits at Lord & Taylor and I'd sell off my own mother to buy something like that."

"Tina Leser lives and works in Hawaii, so unless you're planning an island vacation, you can't model for her," Sam said.

"I wouldn't mind Hawaii," Janie said.

"You'd fit right in," Sam said, eyeing her body appreciatively.

Estella groaned. "Cut it out, you two."

Clarice shook her head. "My dear, I sometimes have to remind myself that you're French. Your Americanness is impeccable."

"My father was American," Estella said, testing out the words on her tongue rather than offering up the usual explanation of her English tutoring by an American. But the phrase sounded wrong, as if she really was fumbling with language. So she returned to her conversation with Sam. "You can flirt as much as you like with Janie when we've finished with the business."

"Where's your sense of romance?" Sam teased.

"I left it in Paris," Estella said, only half-joking.

"Sorry," he said, contrite. "Did you see the papers today?"

"No."

Clarice stood up and came back with the *New York Times*. On the cover was a picture of the Eiffel Tower, a swastika fluttering from the lacework of steel. "France signed an armistice agreement with Germany. They've divided the country into two zones. The free zone, below here." Clarice pointed at a map. "And the Occupied Zone, which includes Paris."

"Maman is in Paris," Estella said quietly.

"I'm so sorry." Clarice touched her arm.

Estella stared at the pictures in the newspaper: a swastika laid over the Tomb of the Unknown Soldier at the Arc de Triomphe, four cannons pointing down each of the main roads into the Place d'Étoile. She pushed the newspaper away. She tried to imagine her mother working in the atelier with Nannette and Marie but without Monsieur Aumont, making flowers to adorn the dresses of German women. Then realization hit her. Marie was Jewish. Given the stories Estella had heard, her heart twisted at the thought of what might happen to the women she used to work with. What might happen to her mother if she continued to help people the Germans didn't want her to help? "Do you think everyone will be all right?" she asked.

"I hope so," Clarice said.

Hope. That word again. How much hope existed in the world these days? Less than was needed? Or was there enough?

"Where should I start?" she asked, tearing the conversation away from things that hurt, away from the past and onto the future, to things that she had to do to make anything of the life her mother had given her. "With work, I mean," she added, in case she'd jumped too quickly from one subject to another.

"It doesn't matter where you start. It matters where you end up," Sam said.

"That's true," Estella said. And then it came out, the thoughts that had begun at the Barbizon, barely formed, ridiculous, yet also not. "Couture is all about clothes for some*one*. Whereas copies are made for no one; it's just the way things have always been done. What if I made clothes for everyone, for women like me. And you." She turned to Janie. "And the designs would make us feel like someone because they wouldn't be imitations. We could all work together. The three of us. For ourselves."

She stopped. They'd both laugh at her. She'd known them for hardly any time at all and, at best, they'd think she was foolish and overconfident. But her mouth opened again, the enthusiasm that had so infuriated Marie at the atelier—the enthusiasm that always drove her to speak up and to deliver deadly maps and dance tangos with bolts of gold satin—as unquenchable as ever.

"Once I have enough money," she added. "It wouldn't be straightaway. But when I've saved enough, I could design, Sam could cut, and Janie could model. If you like my designs, that is."

"Are you kidding?" Sam replied. "Have you seen the gold dress?" he asked Janie.

Janie nodded; Estella had hung it in Janie's closet at the Barbizon and Janie's eyebrows had arched so perfectly high in astonishment that they wouldn't need tweezing for at least a year.

"Sounds like a bloody good idea to me," Janie said. "At least I know you won't grope me in return for my modeling services, Estella. Although I don't mind if you do." She winked at Sam.

Sam exploded into laughter. "With a model like you, designs like Estella's, and cutting like mine, we'll leave New York speechless."

Clarice smiled and lifted her glass. "What would you call yourselves?"

"Stella," Janie said without hesitation. "Because we're aiming for the stars."

"Stella Designs," repeated Sam.

"Are you sure?" Estella asked at the same time as Janie said, "Brilliant! How can that fail?"

As she looked at the faces of her two new friends, friends who were also foolish and daring enough to want to throw in their lot with her, Estella laughed delightedly. She raised her glass. "To Stella Designs," she toasted.

CHAPTER FIVE

Estella found her next job with relative ease. Even though America wasn't fighting in the war, it had called up men for military service and so women were needed to fill positions in the fashion workrooms of Manhattan. She started at Maison Burano, an upscale New York couturier where she thought she'd be in the thick of things, rubbing up against ideas she could admire. But the couturier was so derivative in its styling that Estella thought they might as well hang up a sign out the front that read: "The American Home of Chanel."

Still, the work was easy, sewing dresses she'd sketched two seasons ago. Maison Burano made variations of the best-sellers, altering a neckline a quarter of an inch or changing a cuff, never straying from the basic shapes all American dressmakers had deemed were in fashion—based on what they'd seen in Paris—never once considering what women actually wanted to wear in New York City.

After only a month, the *première* was so impressed with her work that she allowed Estella to help at the client fittings, which was how Estella got into trouble. The *première* had been called out of the fitting room for a moment and, as Estella studied the tall woman in the dress before her, she couldn't resist making the sleeves less roomy, more sculpted, pinning them in, changing the line. Chanel had always wanted the woman to come first, to be noticed before the dress, and Estella believed that now, with the sleeves molded to the woman's elegant arms rather than camouflaging them, she'd achieved just that.

She stood back with a satisfied smile until the *première* returned, took one look at the sleeves and hissed, "Excuse us," to Estella.

"You seem to have made an error with the sleeves," she murmured once they were out of earshot of the client.

"Oh no," Estella said with genuine enthusiasm. "I've made an improvement."

"It's not your job to make improvements."

"But it looks so much better," she pleaded.

"It's not the fashion," the *première* snapped back. "You're a seamstress. How would you know what the ladies of the Upper East Side want to wear."

"I live on the Upper East Side," Estella retorted, which was true, even though she knew very well that the Barbizon Hotel for Women was not the kind of accommodation the *première* was referring to.

"I hope you have some money tucked away in your Upper East Side home because you no longer have a job here."

Just like that, Estella managed to get herself fired again. Nobody in American fashion had foresight. Nobody wanted to give anything new a chance. As she packed her things, she could hear the exclamations of the client. How much she loved the dress. Especially the way it flattered the arms, made them look so graceful. Could she order one in black and one in red?

"Of course," the *première* purred.

Estella waited for ten minutes for her to come back and apologize. But that didn't happen. Maison Burano sold two dresses with Estella's sleeves and Estella walked out the door with nothing.

Later, at the Barbizon, Janie was sympathetic. "Perhaps it's a blessing. Maybe now you'll find a place that appreciates your talents."

"I hope so," Estella said, although she doubted it.

That night, the night of her twenty-third birthday, she wrote to her mother again after Janie had fallen asleep, the tenth letter she'd written, all of them unanswered. She'd asked at the post office and they'd told her that letters might be getting through to Paris but they certainly weren't coming out. The Germans didn't want the world to know what they were up to. All she could do was curse the man she'd given the maps to in Paris for separating her from her mother and then spin a story of how happy she was, hoping that with every word she wrote, she might sustain her mother through whatever she was facing.

Janie had been lucky enough to gain employment as a house model at Hattie Carnegie, a made-to-measure salon, and Sam was cutting for a ready-to-wear establishment at 550 Seventh Avenue and seemed cheerful enough about it.

"It's a different set of skills to the House of Worth," he said to Estella and Janie one night when they all went out for a drink together. "I'm enjoying it. The clothes are awful, but I wonder if it's a better skill to have for the future."

"What do you mean?" Janie asked.

"What do you wear to work?" Estella asked her, knowing just what Sam was thinking. "It's not like twenty years ago, not even like last year, before the war. So many women work now. We don't have time to dress for the day, to dress again for home, and then again for dinner. We need clothes to wear to work, to wear out for a drink afterward; something that can be as wearable behind a desk as it can be on a date after work."

"Because you go out on such a lot of dates after work," Janie said dryly.

Estella laughed. "Married men and elderly tailors are the only men I meet at work so I don't have much opportunity for dating."

So she went back to Seventh Avenue for her next job because she thought Sam was right; ready-to-wear was a business that suited the times more so than couture which now seemed as much of an aberration—given that across the ocean men were dying—as newspaper pictures of Germans at the Ritz.

In a clothing factory, working with the seamstresses, she began to see that it might be possible to marry America's talent for mass production with her own original designs. She learned a hell of a lot about the need in ready-to-wear for fewer pattern pieces and cheaper fabric. She learned what each machine was for—the spreader to lay out each piece of fabric atop the other without stretch or wrinkles, the grader for changing the pattern to each different size. She heard about factor banks for the first time and began to understand the risks of a ready-to-wear business—that she would need loans from a factor bank based on an order from a retailer because it was usually ten weeks from the time an order was placed until the time it was paid for. An enterprise like Stella Designs would require her to save up a lot more money than she'd first thought.

She held her tongue for longer than she'd managed to at Maison Burano but when she was asked to sew a bias cut in a way that made the fabric stretch over the tummy and wrinkle at the hips, the ache in her jaw reminded her that she couldn't possibly swallow any more words.

Fired from three jobs in five months. Her résumé was so bad that, after being unemployed for a fortnight, she took the only job she could get: at a furrier, so far below 550 Seventh Avenue that it might as well have been Battery Park. The Fur District. And Estella's job was to be the drudge who swept the floors and hefted the furs and did nothing skillful at all.

"I worked in an atelier in Paris," she said sharply to Mr. Abramoff, the workroom supervisor. "I can probably sew better than you can." As soon as she said it she wanted to stuff a handful of fur in her mouth. Why, why, why couldn't she learn? "I'm sorry," she apologized.

In response, Mr. Abramoff passed her a broom. "Now you sweep."

Sweep the damn floor, she ordered herself. *It's a means to an end.* Money, which she needed if she was ever going to do anything about the dream that she and Janie and Sam had toasted to months before. Real life began at six o'clock at night, she reminded herself, when she worked on her own sketches, between smoking cigarettes at the Barbizon and chatting to Janie.

The furrier was even viler than she'd thought it would be. Workers doing one thing only: sleeves, or collars, never the whole garment. A head bent over a sleeve until it was finished, then another sleeve and on again, an endless parade of something more boring than any sheep on a sleepless night could ever be.

By the end of the day, Estella's arms ached from the weight of the furs and the constant sweeping but she still had a job and she just smiled at Sam and Janie when they went out for a drink that night. But after only a fortnight, she caught Mr. Abramoff looking up her skirt when she was bending down to collect scraps of fur and she suddenly understood why he was always so desperate for her to sweep.

She pushed the broom across a worktable laden with cut sleeves and collars and swept everything—pattern pieces, fur, and pins, onto the floor. Then she passed Mr. Abramoff the broom. "Since you enjoy watching the sweeping so much, you can have a turn yourself." She picked up her purse and stalked out.

"Four jobs in six months!" she moaned later to Sam after she double-kissed his cheeks—a habit Janie had now decided to acquire too, especially when handsome men were around—and sank onto the bed in Sam's new apartment at London Terrace in Chelsea.

A large, modern building of identical apartments that was really too square and angular and ordinary for Manhattan, its facade reminded Estella of the boulevards of Paris, all lined with symmetrical apartments too. She'd met Sam on his lunch break and he'd given her the key, told her to let herself in, that he and Janie would meet her there after work.

When Sam arrived, he made her a sidecar and sat on the chair while she lay on her stomach across his bed, as if she were in a sorority house, and bemoaned her fate.

"Do you regret walking out?" Sam asked, sipping a whiskey.

"Not for a minute!" Estella said emphatically.

"Then I have no sympathy for you."

Estella threw a pillow at him. "You could at least pretend."

"Why?"

"Because I have to trudge around tomorrow looking for a job. Again. At this rate, I'll have worked everywhere there is by the end of the year."

"There's one place you haven't worked," Sam said.

"Where? The moon?"

"No." He paused dramatically. "Stella Designs."

"But that's for later. When I have the money. I can't do that right now."

"Why not?"

Janie burst through the door with a grin on her face, arms laden down with magazines that they'd planned to spend the evening poring over, before they went out for a drink. "Get your glad rags on. We're going to a party."

"What party?" Sam asked.

"A proper get-dressed-up, swanky, putting-on-the-Ritz-style Christmas party down in Gramercy Park," Janie said triumphantly. "One of the ladies I was modeling for today left her bag unattended with a bunch of invitations sitting prettily on top. I helped myself."

"You stole party invitations?" Sam asked incredulously.

"Only three, so you can't bring a date. But you'll have us to escort," Janie said as if that should make Sam perfectly content. "I've been in New York more than a year and despite my best attempts at flirting, I haven't been anywhere near a society party. So we're going. I stopped off and got our clothes," Janie said to Estella. "I came to New York to find myself a husband and this will be the best place to do it."

"I thought you came to New York to be a model," Estella said in surprise.

"I don't want to model forever. A husband with an apartment on Park Avenue, a summer house in Newport, and the ability to start up a trust fund for our four children would be just about perfect."

"Really?" Estella said. "I had no idea..." Her voice trailed off. *That your ambitions were so conventional,* she didn't say.

"You don't plan to get married sometime soon?" Janie asked.

"No," Estella said. Truth be told, she'd never thought about it. Marriage seemed meant for others, not for her, not now. Not when there was so much to do, so much that she wouldn't be able to do if she married herself off to a man. "Would you really prefer that?"

"Who doesn't?" Janie said. "*Mademoiselle* magazine's latest survey said that only seven percent of women think you can actually have marriage and a career. It's one or the other and I'm planning for a wedding."

Estella didn't know why she was so surprised. After all, many of the women at the Barbizon who she talked to in the dining room were all looking for the same thing: a man to marry. And, she supposed, Janie was the epitome of those women, always wanting to dress well, always on the lookout for an opportunity to smile at a man who might ask her out to dinner, and coveting, apparently, the natural finale: a ring on her finger.

"If I started making my own clothes, where would I do it?"

Estella mused, in a tangential leap back to her earlier conversation with Sam.

"Right here," Sam said. "What's the point in having a perfectly good space in Chelsea, right next to the Garment District, that's empty all day long?"

"I can't work here," Estella scoffed.

"Why not?" Janie asked, lighting a cigarette and lying down beside Estella on Sam's bed. "You draw, Sam can cut for you at night, then you can sew during the day. When you're ready, we just need to hire a room for a private showing where I'll model everything and you'll have so many orders that you'll be able to take out your own lease at 550 Seventh Avenue."

"You wouldn't want me cluttering up your apartment," Estella said to Sam.

"Course I would. Besides, I have selfish reasons for wanting you to do it," Sam said cheerfully.

"Which are?"

"I want to cut that gold dress the way it should be cut."

"Do you really mean it?"

"Yes."

"So simple."

"I don't want to rain on your gold silk parade but," Janie searched through the magazines she'd brought and extracted one, "last year, *Vogue* ran a spread called 'Fashions America Does Best.'" Janie passed the magazine to Estella. "Play clothes, knits, and prints are, apparently, all we can do here."

Estella flipped through the pages. "But who designed these?" she asked. "There are no names."

"Nobody bothers to name American designers in the magazines. They're not important enough," Janie said.

"They don't name the designers?" Estella repeated.

Sam shook his head. "Nope. Claire McCardell has to see her clothes bear the name Townley Frocks. Ask anyone on the street and they'll tell you Chanel makes clothes. I bet they couldn't name a single American who does."

Estella stood up and began to walk in a semicircle around the bed. "Which means it's not just about making clothes. It's about making people believe that clothes made right here are every bit as good as Chanel's and deserve to have the designer's name attached to them."

"And it's about making them cheap," Sam added.

"Affordable," Estella corrected. "It's obscene to make clothes that cost hundreds of dollars when there's a war on anyway."

"Janie," Sam said, "have you got the one you were telling me about, where *Vogue* says there are four types of women? Leisured Lady, Globetrotter, Limited Income, and Businesswoman or something like that?"

"Here it is!" Janie said triumphantly, producing another magazine. She put on an exaggerated Upper East Side accent and read aloud: *"The Businesswoman works at the office with concentration and efficiency from nine-thirty to twelve-thirty. Twelve-thirty to two: has her hair done at Charles Brock's because she believes that a smart coiffure is one element of her success. While her hair dries, she has a manicure…"*

Estella snorted. "It doesn't sound like the Businesswoman has all that much work to do if she can take the afternoon off to get her hair and nails done. Are any of these people real? How many Globetrotters exist now there's a war on? I want the women who actually work. Like we do. Real Women, they should be called. I want to make clothes for them that are comfortable, stylish, and have a little unexpected beauty." Estella's thoughts tumbled out, forming as she spoke them. "The flowers I used to make, I want those to somehow be a signature of the label."

Janie raised an eyebrow. "That could work."

Maybe it could. All she really needed was her sketchpad, her sewing machine, and a whole lot of bravado. With Sam cutting for her, she'd be better able to reduce the number of pattern pieces, to work out how to get them off her drawing paper and into finished form affordably. And if Janie modeled them—well. Nobody would be able to resist. She just needed customers.

"I need to make it work pretty damn quickly though," Estella said. "Otherwise I won't even be able to afford my cot in your room at the Barbizon."

"That sounds like something we should toast to." Janie's eyes twinkled. "And the best thing about a party is the drinks are free." She brandished her stolen invitations in the air.

Sam laughed. "She's right," he said to Estella. "All you need is a dress. And I know you have a spectacular gold one somewhere."

"I brought it with me," Janie said, pulling it out of her bag.

"Then I'd best get changed." Estella ducked behind the screen in the corner and put on the dress.

Janie did the same, followed by Sam. Soon Sam was handsome in his tuxedo and Janie gorgeous in what should have been a severe black dress. It buttoned to the base of her neck and fell in a long, thin column to the floor. With Janie's blond hair, voluptuous figure, and red lips, she looked as if she were just waiting to be unbuttoned, which was the effect Estella had been hoping for when she designed it.

They clinked glasses, took a final swallow of their drinks, covered up their finery with their coats—Estella ruing the cloak she'd had to leave with the inscrutable man in Paris and wishing she could afford something nicer than her day coat to wear out at night—then Sam hailed a taxi for Gramercy Park.

The taxi pulled up outside a house that loomed in a familiar way over the street. The streetlamp was out so Estella couldn't see it very well but it made her shiver all the same and she pulled her coat tighter around her as if the December night had reached into her bones.

"Cold?" Sam asked.

She shook her head. "No. Just felt a ghost float past."

"Let's get into the lights and the champagne and there'll be no more ghosts," Janie said as she glided up the steps, winked at the doorman, passed over the invitations and had them all whisked through with barely a murmur. "Told you it'd be as simple as a Kansas model to get in here," she said.

The party was smoky, but not enough to obscure the many sparkling gemstones worn by the women and which Estella took to be real. She was glad of her dress, which made her feel a little more as if she belonged. It didn't take Janie long to find a man wanting to spin her around the dance floor, nor did it take Sam long to find a group of men playing poker and drinking whiskey, which he thought it was his duty to join. But he too was soon cajoled to join the dancers by a pretty brunette and then a redhead, before the brunette returned to claim him once more.

Which left Estella at the bar occasionally, and at other times on the dance floor as well, dragged out by a succession of young and ever drunker men who were all eager, although she kept declining, to show her the library, where she suspected reading aloud to her wasn't what they had in mind. After the fourth such suggestion, she switched to French, pretended not to understand, and drank far too much champagne.

Which was probably why, when Janie appeared at her side, Estella said, more loudly than she should have, pointing to a woman some distance away, "Look at that poor, ruined Lanvin copy. I sketched that very dress at a show last season. If I'd known what they were going to do to it, I'd never have copied it."

Janie followed Estella's finger across to a woman dancing in a dress with a handkerchief skirt, made out of panels of white and black silk, and a black bodice held up at the neck by a collar of pearls.

"They've scrimped on the panels to save money," Estella said. "It's meant to be twice as full. It looks like a butterfly one wing short of a set."

Janie laughed. "Any others?"

Estella twirled around and came face-to-face with a woman who had clearly overheard Estella's commentary and who wore a bud of a smile that looked as if it would take more than sunlight to open. "You're very sure of your opinions," the woman said, her tone far from friendly.

Estella could see why. The woman wore a copy too, a calamitous version of one of Estella's favorite Chanel gowns, one which was meant to skim the body like a lover's hand. The Chanel original was of black lace, flaring out gently into a long skirt, a bouquet of white linen camellias arranged over the right breast, concealing some of the cleavage exposed by the heart-shaped neckline. In this woman's version, the camellias were pinned too low so all you saw was the cleavage, the lace was poorly stitched to the lining so it rode up at one side, and the skirt collapsed to the floor, rather than falling gracefully down. The woman's defensive air indicated that she suspected Estella knew the dress did not possess the couture bloodline it claimed.

"I just wonder why so much energy is expended on something that isn't what it's supposed to be," Estella said, her tongue loose with champagne honesty, but trying to be kind.

"And what is your dress supposed to be?" the woman asked. "A little burst of sunshine?" The sneer was too evident to ignore.

"An original. Stella Designs. Come and see me when you're tired of imitations."

"Stella Designs. I'll remember that."

The woman stalked off and Estella couldn't help feeling as if she'd just made a huge mistake. That, once again, she should have buttoned her mouth one sentence earlier. She reached for another drink—gin this time—and Janie spun back out onto the dance floor.

Soon after midnight, Estella heard the words, "Alex is back," whispered around the party, accompanied by smiles from the women and the kind of frisson that an unexpected riff on a saxophone might bring. Estella wondered who could possibly cause such a commotion among people who seemed so hard to surprise.

"He's as enigmatic as Gatsby," one woman at the bar said knowingly to another, "and his origins are just as murky. I've heard tell that his father was a pirate on the Oriental seas." The woman tittered, then continued her tall tale. "I know being a lawyer pays well but he seems to have more money than one could legitimately earn. Add that to lethal charm and you can see why all the women in the room are quivering right now."

Estella smiled. A pirate with lethal charm was someone she should keep Janie away from. He didn't sound like the marrying kind. She cast her eyes around the room, searching for Janie, but couldn't find her. She walked around the perimeter, throwing a smile to Sam who had another young woman—blond now—comfortably ensconced on his knee, but Estella soon realized she was less steady than she should be. Home would be the best place for her. Janie was smart enough not to walk a pirate's plank.

She found her coat, drew it over her dress, then walked to the very edges of the room where she hoped to find the door. But the shadows beneath the pillars, out of the light of the double-story void, were disorienting. She could hardly see anything. It didn't help that the room whirled a little with her champagne vision.

"Alex!" a man called as he knocked against her in his rush, pushing her farther behind the pillar, spilling a little of his drink on her. "I heard the rumors."

"They're not rumors," another man, the mysterious Alex obviously, replied cheerfully. "I'm back."

"Until we run you out of the country again." The first man laughed grimly while Estella shook his whiskey off her fingers.

"With you chasing, I'll be in the country for decades," Alex said. "Excuse me." His voice was familiar. Unaccented, almost.

Before Estella had a chance to look up from brushing down her damp coat, she found herself swept into someone's arms, a very un-chaste kiss planted near her earlobe. "I found you," the same voice—Alex's—said.

Estella's mind raced.

Who the hell was he? It wasn't as if she made a habit of drunken and ginned-up nights at parties. It was too damned dark to see very much, just that his hair was dark and his lips were moving toward hers.

In a flash from a nearby cigarette lighter she caught a glimpse of two glittering brown eyes and the outline of a face that was *séduisant*, a word that she didn't believe had an exact English translation, handsome being too insipid for what *séduisant* implied and seductive being too obvious, too showy. No, this man was so attractive it almost hurt to look at him: attractive in a reckless way—as if he knew pre-cisely the effect his looks had on people—attractive in a way that was best avoided. But also memorable. Had she met him before?

The flare of the lighter was so quick that the impressions rushed over Estella in a moment. They were immediately plunged back into darkness before she could make out his features exactly, before she could trace back the path of a memory to discover where she might know him from.

Then this Alex began to kiss her in a way she hadn't been kissed for a very long time—in fact, she'd never been kissed like this—and be-cause it felt so good, she responded immediately, opening her mouth, searching out his tongue. One of his hands threaded through her hair so he could kiss her even more deeply and the other dropped to her hip, stroking the fabric of her coat, making the skin beneath burn.

The clawing of desire stronger than anything she'd felt before made her step backward, away from this man she didn't know but who she was kissing as if she knew him better than anyone. His gaze remained fixed on her face, which almost felt like standing naked before him, her skin peeled back and her heart on view. And she wasn't at all sure that she wanted this man to see her heart.

"Wait," he said softly, a whisper of a word, so gentle, like his hand had been as it ran down her back, but also hungry, wanting something from her that she felt certain he got far too often and far too easily, especially if he made a habit of kissing women like that.

His hand reached out and his fingertips met hers but that was all; a tantalizing and magical hiss of flesh against flesh before she turned away.

Meet me at Jimmy Ryan's tomorrow night, she thought she heard him say before the bodies of the dancers took her into their midst and the man, Alex, was swooped upon by voices both friendly and displeased. She stumbled once, twice, as if she were a sauced-up broad who couldn't hold her liquor when she was, in fact, just stunned, knocked out by a kiss.

She somehow found the front door, felt the same shiver as she ran through the Gothic arch and down the steps, hailed a cab but then realized she had no money. So she walked the long, long way back to the Barbizon, alone, lonely, images of her mother playing across her eyelids in a desolate stream.

When she arrived, she didn't bother to take off her dress, just fell onto the bed, curled on her side, and dreamed of being gathered against a man, naked, his arms wrapped around her, languorous and lovely with sleep.

When she awoke, it was morning and she curved her body back to feel the man but there was only emptiness and she recalled, in pieces, the night. The kiss. The man who was at once both familiar and strange, the realization that everything that had come after had just been a dream. A lump lodged in her throat, tears threatened her eyes.

Meet me at Jimmy Ryan's tomorrow night. Had that been a dream too?

CHAPTER SIX

Estella spent the next day with her head bent over her sewing machine making a dress to wear to a rendezvous she wasn't sure if she'd imagined. Janie telephoned to say she was going out after work with a man she'd met at the party and Estella thanked God; she didn't want to have to explain what she was up to. Not when she didn't even know herself.

She took one short break midafternoon to swim in the pool at the Barbizon, which she tried to do every day, enjoying the meditative sensation of stroking her arms through the water even though she wasn't a particularly good swimmer. She hoped it would relax her the way it usually did. But she timed it badly; she had the misfortune to bump into the matron as she entered the lift in her bathing suit, a simple white cotton affair consisting of a cut-off man's shirt that she'd bought for a bargain and denuded of sleeves. To this she'd sewn black cotton to cover her nether regions, resulting in a bathing suit that was streamlined, stylish, and so much more practical for swimming than the heavy, bloated dress-style suits that the other women wore.

"What are you wearing?" Matron snapped.

"I'm going swimming," Estella said.

"You will not parade around the hotel in that."

"I'm going to the pool."

"Cover yourself or you will need to find somewhere else to stay. This is America, not France."

"I know that," Estella retorted, before storming away to find the off-cut of black cotton in her room. She tied it at her waist to make a cover-up skirt. Which looked rather good, she had to admit, storing the idea away for later and cheekily blowing Matron a kiss to thank her for the idea when she passed by.

Then, at eight o'clock, she bathed and put on her new dress. Green jersey, long, slim skirt, with a sash that formed a halter-neck, crossed over the bust and then wound around her lower back to tie at the side. At first she'd imagined the ties would simply drape down, but at the last moment, she fashioned them into a blousy flower, like a peony. The dress was backless, a surprise that the classical front did not suggest. It was an homage to the draping and wrapping of Vionnet but using the kind of democratic fabric that someone like Estella could actually afford.

She darkened her lashes with mascara and reddened her lips. She left her hair down, its black waves falling down her back, secured on one side with a rhinestone clip shaped like a star. Her mother had given it to her for her sixteenth birthday. She touched the star, trying again to sense her mother's presence, to have the universe send her a message about whether her mother was safe but all she heard were the car horns of Manhattan.

Then, before she could ask herself what she was doing, she caught the subway to 52nd Street, having ascertained that Jimmy Ryan's was a jazz club in the basement of a brownstone that looked more conventional from the street than the music emanating from its belly would suggest.

"Two dollars," the barman said when she ordered a sidecar.

She winced and pretended to look inside her purse, knowing all too well that she couldn't afford to spend two dollars on a drink. "I left my money on the dresser," she said. "I'm so sorry." She pushed the glass away.

"On the house." The bartender winked.

"Thanks." She raised her glass, sipping gratefully. And then suddenly, by her side and looking so goddamned airtight she could almost feel her dress wanting to take itself off, she saw Alex.

"You came," he said, voice familiar from the party but from somewhere else too.

A memory blinded her. She crashed her drink onto the bar. The Théâtre du Palais-Royal. Dancing with a man mixed up in more than trouble; a man who, at the very least, dealt with death and secrets. Alex was the same damn man.

Before she could say anything, another woman entered the club, crossed over to Alex and slipped her arm through his, kissing his cheek. Estella's gasp was so loud she wondered how it didn't shatter glasses.

Because this woman looked so exactly like her that Estella could barely tell where she ended and the other woman began. Except this woman was an Estella of sometime in the future that she hoped would never come, an Estella with shadowed eyes. Estella, broken.

Alex took a step back as he looked from one identical woman to the other.

Estella wanted to shut her eyes, to run away, to never have seen the other woman—who the hell was she?—but she couldn't show a man like Alex and his lookalike paramour how bewildered and frightened she was. "Isn't this awkward?" she said hotly, tears stinging her eyes, before turning on her heel and leaving the club.

Out on the street when she thought she was safe, she doubled over, hands clutching a brownstone wall for comfort it didn't give.

Alex had kissed her last night because he thought she was someone else. It explained one piece of the puzzle. And Estella didn't care to solve any more; all Alex had brought her, from the first night she met him in Paris, was loss and suffering and heartache.

PART TWO
FABIENNE

CHAPTER SEVEN

May 2015

I declare the exhibition, *The Seamstress from Paris*, now open!"
The crowd gathered at the Met for the annual gala clapped and cheered and then began to file through to the exhibition rooms. Fabienne hung back, wishing it wasn't so crowded, wanting to spend time alone with every exhibit, feeling so proud of her grandmother that she thought she might burst. She realized she was standing beside Anna Wintour and she smiled stupidly, but her smile widened as Anna, who was also wearing Stella Designs, took in Fabienne's gown, nodded approvingly and murmured, "You have excellent taste."

The whole night held the elusive quality of a dream. From arriving at Fifth Avenue filled with gawking, celebrity-mad crowds (what a disappointment Fabienne must have been), to walking up a red carpet lined with cameras and stars, where she'd recognized Kate Hudson, Sarah Jessica Parker, possibly a Kardashian—she didn't watch much television so she couldn't be sure—and Hugh Jackman and Nicole Kidman, both of whom Fabienne had wanted to rush over to and befriend on the basis that they were all Australian.

If only Estella was here to see this, Fabienne thought. How Mamie would love it, the way people were exclaiming over the Stars and Stripes dress, in classic navy with a thin horizontal white stripe and a bold red star over the heart, or the red skirt—a one-off from 1943—that was beautifully embroidered with a tiny repeating pattern of three witches on a broomstick, or the blouses from 1944 printed with faded maps of Paris so that the streets looked like delicate crisscrosses, a subtle reminder of a city struggling to come back to the light. As Fabienne stepped closer to study the now even more faded map on one of the blouses, she tripped on someone's foot. To stop herself falling, she put out a hand, which connected with a man's back.

"I'm so sorry!" Fabienne gasped. "I was engrossed in the blouse."

The man had turned, as had the woman beside him, and they both smiled politely at her.

"It's incredible isn't it?" the woman said to Fabienne. "I'm trying to find the Arc de Triomphe which is why my foot got in your way. I'm sorry."

"Did you find it?" Fabienne asked.

"Just there. Bottom right." The man pointed and Fabienne couldn't help but notice his very handsome face: dark hair, blue eyes; a nice tuxedo—it looked like a Tom Ford—and a titanium Tiffany cuff peeking out at his wrist.

She snapped her eyes back to the blouse in the nick of time, before she was caught staring, and told herself not to covet another woman's boyfriend, especially a woman who'd been so nice. Fabienne smiled as she saw the tiny Eiffel Tower, then her eyes traveled along the Champs Élysées and onto the Rue de Rivoli, before stopping at the breast pocket over the heart where a cross was marked on the Rue de Sévigné in the exact spot where her grandmother's house, the house Estella would never live in, was located.

"Your dress is beautiful," the woman said, eyeing Fabienne with admiration. "Can I touch that flower? It looks so real."

Fabienne laughed. "Of course."

The woman's hand trailed gently over the petals of the black leather peonies that adorned Fabienne's shoulder. "They really are exquisite. You'd never think of leather and peonies, but that just makes them more fabulous." She sighed, staring over Fabienne's shoulder. "And look at that one. You could wear it now and it would still be fabulous."

Fabienne turned to see a gold dress, one of her grandmother's favorites. Estella had always said, somewhat cryptically, that it was a dress which had sealed her fate. "It would be," Fabienne agreed.

There was a moment of silence after that and Fabienne realized that she was a complete stranger taking up the couple's time. "Enjoy the exhibition," she said, moving off.

The next two hours passed by quickly as she toured the exhibits, unable to stop the thought: *how her grandmother would love this. How her father would too.*

She drank champagne and was introduced by the curator of the Costume Institute to people who left her a little starstruck. Mamie wouldn't have been starstruck, she reminded herself, and she tried to pretend that everyone else was as ordinary as she was. Around one in the morning, she decided it was time to leave; she'd seen enough to be able to give Estella a thorough rundown. She made her way outside and walked down the steps to catch a taxi, behind a couple who seemed to be having some difficulty. The man had his arm around a woman who was moving slowly, clumsily, as if she'd hurt herself, as if every step was agony.

"Can I help?" Fabienne asked, hurrying forward, unable to watch the excruciating movements without doing something, worried that the couple was about to topple off the steps.

"We meet again," the man said with a brief smile and Estella realized it was the couple she'd tripped over earlier.

"We do," she said. "What if I take the other side? Or shall I hail a taxi for you?" She touched the woman's arm when she saw her face:

pale, clammy, so vacant that she seemed to have withdrawn inside herself.

"A taxi would be great," the man said.

Fabienne ran down the rest of the steps and waved impatiently until a taxi pulled over, just as the couple reached the sidewalk.

"Thanks," the man said, giving her another polite smile, one that didn't touch his eyes, which were dark now with worry. He helped the woman into the car and, with that, the couple were whisked away into the Manhattan night.

"How much longer do I have to wait?"

Fabienne was woken in what felt like the middle of the night but as she blinked her eyes open, she realized it was light outside and that her woolly-headedness was a result of jet lag and a late night.

"She insisted on coming in." The nurse, who was pushing her grandmother's wheelchair into the room, apologized. "I held her off as long as I could."

"It's all right," Fabienne said, sitting up and leaning over to kiss her grandmother's cheeks.

"She's eaten and ready for the day," the nurse said before she left the room.

"Did you enjoy yourself last night?" Estella asked in that familiar voice, a voice unlike anyone else's, with its strange mix of French and American accents, an inflection that made it seem as if she didn't come from anywhere on this earth. Which was, Fabienne reflected sadly, how she looked. As if she were no longer part of the everyday, as if she'd already joined Fabienne's grandfather in heaven, as if even the fingertip hold she had on the world had finally slipped. And at ninety-seven years old, Fabienne supposed she was lucky to still have Mamie at all, and most especially lucky that, while Estella's body might have all but failed her, her mind was as sharp as ever.

"It was perfect, Mamie," Fabienne said. And she proceeded to tell her grandmother everything: what people wore, which clothes had been exhibited, who had come, what had been said, how much praise had been heaped upon Estella Bissette and her legendary Stella line.

Estella held out an opened envelope. "You were by far the most beautiful though," she said in a voice full of pride.

Fabienne slipped a photograph out of the envelope, which must have been delivered that morning by one of her grandmother's admirers from *Vogue*. It showed Fabienne on the red carpet in the extraordinary gown that Mamie had designed just for her—one unbroken length of silver silk that had been draped and spiraled around her body, with an enormously full skirt that wouldn't have looked out of place on a princess, a low neckline and capped sleeves that started at the edge of her shoulders, showing off her collarbones; and the black leather peonies, saving the dress from looking too princessy, fastened in a posy on the left side of her waist, another cluster sitting like a rosette above her right breast. The dress that had made her feel much less like a gauche Australian tripping over people's feet.

"I think you're biased," Fabienne said, smiling.

"Your father would have thought so too."

Fabienne reached out to take her grandmother's hand. "He would have loved to have been there last night." Then the tears, the tears that she'd hoped had finally stopped, clogged her eyes.

"Oh, Fabienne." Estella sighed. "I miss him too."

Neither spoke for several minutes and Fabienne knew that her grandmother, like her, was remembering Xander Bissette, Fabienne's father and Estella's son. The brilliant and loving man who'd never seemed old—his hair was still streaked with black even at age seventy-four—but who'd suffered a massive stroke just one month ago.

"Your mother didn't want to come to New York with you?" Estella asked.

Fabienne shook her head. "I think she was afraid of seeing you. You look so much like him. She's..." How to describe what had happened to her mother in the month since her father's death? "She's crumpled, can barely stand up straight anymore. I'm worried about her. Of course, she just buries herself in work, as always."

As Fabienne sat holding her grandmother's hand tightly in her own, she felt that same sense of attachment that she'd always had with Mamie ever since she was a child—much more so than with her mother—even though she only saw Estella once a year when Fabienne and Xander made the trip from Sydney to New York and then on to France every July.

"You look crumpled too," her grandmother said, sitting back in her wheelchair and assessing her. "Too sad for someone so young. And it's not just your father. Why didn't that young man of yours come with you?"

"We broke up," Fabienne confessed.

The young man in question, Jasper, had been her boyfriend for the past two years and he wasn't all that young—was thirty-seven in fact, eight years older than Fabienne. The day after her father died, she'd finally realized that her and Jasper's interpretations of love were different: that to him it meant someone to wear on your arm at the latest opening, someone consistent in your bed, someone with whom you didn't have to try very hard because they'd already chosen you and no longer needed to be wooed. Whereas for Fabienne, love meant an intensity beyond all feelings, an unbearable thrum in the air whenever the other person was near; it meant always wanting to slip your hand into theirs. Which she knew was probably a fantasy, that the way her grandmother spoke of love might be something Fabienne would never experience because it was meant for a time long past when things were different.

"Good. I never liked him," Estella said decidedly and Fabienne couldn't help laughing. "You should go to Paris," her grandmother continued. "Paris is the place where you find love."

"Mamie, people find love all over the world. I don't need to go to Paris."

"The love you find in Paris is different," her grandmother insisted. "Go for the weekend. Refresh yourself before you go back to Sydney and start your new job. You have nothing to lose by going."

"But I came all this way to see you," Fabienne said gently. Besides, there was something she needed to ask her grandmother about and she wouldn't be able to do it from Paris.

"I don't like to see you like this. I want to see the Fabienne you should be, the woman I felt you would become when I first held you as a baby. You haven't found that Fabienne yet." Her grandmother stabbed her finger into the air as she spoke the last few words, as if to underscore them, and Fabienne shivered a little at Mamie's intensity.

The Fabienne you should be. Who was that person? And how was she different from the Fabienne she was right now? Yes, she was sad, but her father had just died and she'd broken up with Jasper. What difference would a weekend in Paris make to any of that?

As she walked into the Théâtre du Palais-Royal, Fabienne knew that her grandmother was much wiser than she. She'd at last relented to Mamie's insistence that she take a weekend in Paris and she'd only been there a day and already felt better. Even the overnight flight hadn't tired her. Nothing ever tasted as good as French baguettes and French coffee eaten in one of the sidewalk cafés in the heart of the Marais, near her grandmother's house, where Fabienne and her father—rarely her mother—had holidayed so many times it felt as comfortable as pajamas, although that was possibly insulting to such a grand and ancient townhouse. And now she would spend the night in her favorite theater, a theater she'd visited so often with her grandmother that it never mattered what was actually playing; just being inside the intimate, lovely space was enough to make anyone feel a beauty that transcended time.

In fact, tonight, she hadn't even checked what was on and she discovered, to her surprise, that it wasn't a theatrical production but a film. A screen had been brought in to the theater to show a documentary about Jean Schlumberger, one of Tiffany & Co.'s celebrated designers who'd also, she read, served with Charles de Gaulle's Free French Forces in World War II.

She located the row shown on her ticket and realized she'd have to step over a couple who were already seated. She shuffled along but they seemed to be engrossed in conversation, the looks on their faces so grave that Fabienne waited a moment, reassuring the usher in French that she was fine, before she said, "*Excusez-moi.*"

They looked up at her and she recognized both their faces, struggling for a moment to place them.

"The Met," she said at exactly the same time as the woman did and they both laughed.

"At least I haven't tripped over you this time," Fabienne said.

"I'm Melissa Ogilvie. And this is Will." Melissa smiled and gestured to the man by her side.

Fabienne sat down next to Will. "I'm Fabienne Bissette."

"Bissette?" Melissa repeated. "We met at an exhibition of Estella Bissette's designs and you have the same surname. Surely that's not a coincidence?"

"She's my grandmother."

"Wow," said Melissa. "Hence your amazing outfits. I loved the dress you wore at the Met but I'm guessing it was a one-off."

Fabienne nodded. "She designed it just for me. It was so beautiful

I almost wore it to bed because I couldn't bear the thought of taking it off."

Melissa laughed again.

"Where are you from?" Will asked. "I heard you speaking perfect French to the usher and you obviously aren't American or you'd have been telling everyone at the Met who your grandmother was."

"I'm from Australia," she said.

"And you were born speaking perfect French?"

Fabienne shook her head and tried not to see how gorgeous he was. She didn't want to covet Melissa's husband or boyfriend or whatever he was. "My grandmother is very strong-willed and she absolutely insisted I be taught French from before I could even speak. She drilled me in French verbs and obscure vocabulary every time I visited her. For which I'm very grateful now, although I probably wasn't at the time. And we came to Paris every summer. Estella has a house in the Marais."

"I've been dying to have a wander around there," Melissa said.

"It's the most beautiful part of Paris. You should definitely spend a day there. How long are you here for?" Fabienne asked.

"Just the weekend," Melissa said. "My brother here is on a mission to take me somewhere new every month." She paused and looked at Will.

Fabienne tried to smother her pleasure at discovering Will was Melissa's brother.

Will shook his head at his sister but she kept talking anyway. "I have ovarian cancer," Melissa continued. "Terminal. And I know Will thinks I should just keep it to myself and not depress us all but that's the way it is. So, as long as I'm well enough, he's escorting me to places far and wide each month."

Melissa placed a gentle hand on Will's arm and Fabienne saw his face constrict with a terrible sadness.

"Thanks for helping us the other night," he said to Fabienne. "That's the other reason I knew you weren't American. A true New Yorker would have just stepped over us rather than hailing us a cab."

"I hardly did anything," Fabienne said, wishing now that she'd done more, feeling that her gesture in the face of terminal ovarian cancer in a woman as young as Melissa—she appeared to be in her mid-twenties—was so insignificant as to not be worth mentioning. And she knew, because her own mother had set up one of the first women's cancer clinics in Sydney, just how swift and vicious ovarian cancer could be.

"I get back pain from time to time," Melissa said. "It can be debilitating. And it obviously decided I'd been having too much fun and the only way to remind me of my limitations was to cripple me with such force that I left the gala looking like a drunk."

"Everyone must say *I'm sorry* to you," Fabienne said. "So I won't. Instead I'll say I'm glad you decided to come to Paris. My grandmother believes that Paris can be more therapeutic than the best of medicines."

"I'm glad we came too," Melissa said.

Will put his arm around his sister's shoulders and kissed her gently on the cheek. Fabienne's throat ached and her eyes teared up.

Luckily the lights of the theater dimmed at the same moment so she was able to wipe her eyes before anyone noticed. Except that she felt Will pass her something and she saw it was a perfectly pressed and folded white linen handkerchief. What man still carried such an item? Her grandmother would be delighted. "Thank you," she whispered.

Fabienne couldn't concentrate on the film. All she felt were two contradictory impulses: the crack in her heart for Melissa, who she barely knew, but who seemed so spirited and full of life that in any other circumstance she would have made a wonderful friend; and an intense discomfort at sitting beside Will, an acute awareness of every small movement he made. Since her father had died, all of her feelings seemed keener and more raw and she tried to put it down to that. But she knew it was because she found Will Ogilvie, with his classic good looks, his obvious affection for his sister, and his folded pocket handkerchieves, very alluring.

At intermission, Fabienne hung back a little, wanting to leave the Ogilvies to their time together, but Melissa leaned across and said, "Have a drink with us. At least that way I'll get what I actually ordered, rather than whatever the barman can interpret of Will's terrible French."

Will laughed. "You told me the fish last night was delicious."

"I was trying to interpret the menu," Melissa said conspiratorially to Fabienne, "and he told me a dorado was a kind of beef!"

Fabienne laughed. "A sea-cow perhaps."

Will smiled at her and her stomach clenched.

Stop it, she told herself. *You're behaving like a teenager.* "What would you like?" she asked, glad of an excuse to step away to the bar. "It's on me," she said as Will took his wallet out of his pocket.

"Gin and tonic," said Melissa. Will frowned at her. "I can have a drink. It's not going to kill me," Melissa said to her brother with grim humor.

"Liss," he said darkly.

Fabienne slipped over to the bar to avoid a sibling tiff. She realized she hadn't waited for Will's order so she got him an Aperol spritz like her own.

"It's great," he said when she handed it to him with an apology. "Cheers," he toasted. "To new friends."

"Do you work for your grandmother?" Melissa asked Fabienne.

"No. She wants me to. She begs me to every year, in fact. I do work with fashion, but in a different way. I've just been appointed," Fabienne smiled, loving saying it aloud—still not used to it as it had only come about last month—"Head Curator of Fashion at the Powerhouse Museum in Sydney. It's my dream job," she confessed.

"Congratulations," Melissa said, clinking her glass against Fabienne's. "But why don't you want to work with your grandmother?"

"Liss," Will interjected. "You're being nosy." He turned to Fabienne. "She thinks she can get away with whatever she likes because everyone feels sorry for her. Just tell her if she's being a pain."

"It's fine," Fabienne lied. Her reasons were not something she'd ever shared except in the most secret place inside her head. "I suppose I'm scared," she said hesitantly. "Of not living up to expectations. My grandmother is a true force of nature. And she's been successful for so long. I don't want to be the one to step in and screw it all up." She winced as she finished. She was oversharing. She'd only just met these people and now they knew more about her than most people did.

"I understand that," Will said softly.

"He does," Melissa added. "I practically had to force him to take the job he has now. Head Designer at Tiffany & Co. He didn't want to destroy the legacy either. As if there was ever any chance of that," she scoffed.

"Head Designer at Tiffany," Fabienne repeated. "Hence your interest in the film. What a job."

"It's pretty amazing," he said with a grin.

"And it has very good benefits," Melissa replied, stretching out an arm adorned with a breathtaking diamond bracelet.

The bell sounded to call them back into the theater. As they walked down the aisle, Will placed a hand lightly on the small of Fabienne's back to allow her to step in first and she felt her whole body come alive in a way it never had before.

CHAPTER EIGHT

The next morning, Fabienne tried on and discarded three outfits, swearing when she realized that was all she'd brought with her; a rendezvous with a handsome man being the last thing she'd thought of when she'd packed. In the end she settled on a playsuit, a vintage Stella design from the 1950s, in faded navy, which she embellished with a red scarf around her neck and red lipstick. Then she set off to meet Melissa and Will at the Hôtel des Invalides.

It had been Melissa's idea that they meet up; she'd said she wanted someone with expert knowledge to show her around the Marais. Fabienne had admitted that she'd promised her grandmother she'd go to an exhibition at the Musée de l'Armée at Les Invalides—a bizarre request, Fabienne had thought at the time, but given Estella was ninety-seven she was prepared to allow for some strangeness—and Melissa had said they'd tag along and could all head off to the Marais afterward.

Les Invalides was a stupendous building, and Will said he'd never been inside, so Fabienne hoped that seeing its magnificence would at least prove worthwhile even if the exhibition did not. She met them out front and Fabienne kissed both Melissa's cheeks, having lapsed into French ways as she did so easily when in Paris. Then she felt she must do the same with Will. As she leaned toward him, she caught the scent of citrus, amber, and the sea, like a Riviera holiday. "Sorry if this isn't how you'd imagined spending your day," she said.

"It's the perfect way to spend the day," he said and he smiled at her in a way that made her believe he meant it.

"What's the exhibition about?" Melissa asked.

"Estella said it was something about the war, which is not a part of her youth that she ever talks about. That's why, when she insisted I come, I thought I should." Fabienne consulted the brochure.

"MI9: The Secret Ministry of the Second World War," she read aloud. "MI9 was formed as an inter-service intelligence section in December 1939 to facilitate escapes of British prisoners of war, and to help those who succeeded in evading capture in enemy occupied territory to return to Britain. It was a lifeline to escapers and evaders in World War II, although its existence was unknown to most outside the military, and its actions saved the lives of thousands of British servicemen. This exhibition honors the French people who worked with MI9 to form escape lines across France, as well as those who helped evaders stay out of enemy hands. It also honors the men of MI9 who worked with the French people to cause immense irritation to the Germans as escapers and evaders slipped through their fingers and returned to active duty to fight once more."

"That sounds cheery," Will said.

"You guys should definitely go and do something else," Fabienne said.

"I'm joking," he replied, walking on in. "Let's see what it's all about."

Although Fabienne couldn't understand why her grandmother had insisted she go to the exhibition, it only took half an hour for her and, she thought, for Will and Melissa, to become so engrossed that she felt they'd all be, not glad—that wasn't the right word to use about something so haunting—but grateful that they'd come.

Fabienne translated some of the plaques for Will and Melissa that were in French, explaining that it was considered a soldier's duty to escape, that escape tactics were taught to the men before they set off for war, and that escape committees were formed in prisoner-of-war camps to send messages to MI9 and to receive escape supplies and invent escape plans, many of which worked. They marveled at the buttons that hid compasses and the other crazy inventions: air force boots that turned into peasant shoes, blankets with patterns marked on them so they could be cut and stitched into civilian clothes, hacksaws hidden in fountain pens, the first silk map of Colditz Castle where inveterate escapers were sent, a map which helped many men escape the inescapable fortress. But they became sober when they saw a list of those who had died while helping Allied prisoners and downed airmen to flee back to England.

"It says that any MI9 agent caught, or any French man or woman found helping Allied soldiers to escape, was sentenced to death. Or sent to a concentration camp, from which few returned," Fabienne read. "Whereas the Allied soldiers they assisted were just sent to a POW camp."

"They were so young," Melissa murmured, hand resting on a cabinet in which the "Pat" escape line, a passage across France through which escapers and evaders were ferried, was mapped out and the fate of one Andrée Borrel, a twenty-two-year-old Frenchwoman who worked the line, was described.

Fabienne winced, hearing something in her words, a note of extreme empathy, which made her think that Melissa herself must have heard those same words repeated to her over and over again. So young. Too young to die. Which of course she was. As was Andrée Borrel, betrayed, captured, and taken to a concentration camp where she was given a lethal dose of phenol in July 1944, just one month before France was liberated.

"It's hard to imagine people being so courageous," Fabienne said and she felt Will come to stand beside her as she spoke. "Helping others for no reward whatsoever, but in the hope of achieving a greater good. I wonder if people like that exist anymore?"

"Doesn't it make you wonder what you would have done if it'd been you?" he asked. "Whether you'd have just looked after yourself and stayed out of everyone's way? Or if you'd have done whatever you could, like they did?"

"I'd like to think I'd have done the right thing," Fabienne said quietly. "But seeing that I'm not even brave enough to take on my grandmother's business, I guess that's unlikely."

"That's a different kind of bravery," he said. "That comes from love: love of your grandmother and her legacy. The other kind, the kind they had is…" He stopped, looking for the right word.

"Heroic," Fabienne finished.

"Yes," he said. "I don't think we have many true heroes these days." He rested his hand on his sister's shoulder as he spoke.

Fabienne moved away a little, wanting to give them that moment together. She examined a row of photographs, headed: The Heroic Men of MI9. She scanned their faces, most of them younger than her. Then her eyes froze on one particular name underneath a photograph: Alex Montrose.

Her surprise was audible; she tried to turn her gasp into a sneeze. And she suddenly knew why her grandmother had pressed her to come to this exhibition. It was because of Alex Montrose, a name Fabienne hadn't heard of until three weeks ago. The same name was branded on a piece of paper that she held in her purse, a piece of paper she'd found when she was clearing out some of her father's things after his funeral.

Estella didn't know she'd found the paper. But on insisting Fabienne attend the exhibition, Estella must have wanted Fabienne to know something of Alex Montrose. Which meant that, in the few hours she had in Manhattan on Monday before her flight to Sydney, she would go to see her grandmother again. She would ask Mamie about the piece of paper she'd found. Alex Montrose was somehow important in Fabienne's and Estella's lives and she must discover why.

It took them the entire Metro ride to throw off the quietude that had settled on them in the museum. But once they exited at Saint-Paul and lost themselves in the narrow streets and beauty of the Marais, they regained their spirits.

Fabienne took them to lunch at the Marché des Enfants Rouges, with its delicious food and handful of rickety tables near the old Carreau du Temple. Then they wandered through two of the *hôtels particulier*—the Carnavalet and the Salé, stopped for coffee, and strolled through the maze of courtyards of the Village Saint-Paul—once Fabienne had remembered how to find her way in. It was now home to an eclectic assortment of antiques shops, galleries, cafés, vintage treasures, and beautiful objects and Melissa loaded Will down with a growing pile of shopping bags. They finally arrived at what Fabienne had always thought was the area's pièce de résistance, the Place des Vosges.

"Oh, it's beautiful," Melissa cried as they turned off the Rue des Tournelles and came upon the square, lined on each side by redbrick and blond-stone apartments and townhouses with blue-black slate roofs, all symmetrical and made more beautiful by the repetition of the facades, the lines, and the elegance. Vaulted arcades of cool stone cast them back in time while the modernist art galleries situated beneath kept them firmly in the present. In the middle was the park, a little enclave of green and statuary, where many Parisians sat on blankets, picnicking.

"It really is." Fabienne beamed, glad that Melissa liked it too.

Fabienne felt the back of Will's hand brush hers as he shifted toward her to avoid a pedestrian. He glanced down, but didn't immediately withdraw his hand. The Fabienne of just two days ago would have moved away so that she didn't appear to be more interested in him than he might be in her but the Fabienne she was that day left her hand where it was. And the simple act of the back of his hand touching hers felt as sensual as silk on skin.

"Let's have a picnic!" Melissa said, clapping her hands together like a delighted child and looking pleadingly over at her brother as if she expected him to demur. "I'm not tired. In fact I feel better than I have in a long while. Fabienne's grandmother is right; Paris *is* very therapeutic."

"My grandmother's house is just around the corner," Fabienne said. "I'll go get a blanket and plates and glasses—it's a champagne evening, don't you think?"

Will laughed. "Is it ever not a champagne evening in Paris?"

"No." Fabienne smiled at him. "I'll stop at the boulangerie on the way back—there's also a fromagerie on the street we've come from—and get some food."

"Why don't I get the food?" Will suggested. "I'm sure I can order bread and cheese."

"God knows what we're going to end up eating if you get it," Melissa teased her brother. "Maybe just point to things and don't speak."

Melissa hurried off to squeeze into a tight space on one of the benches to wait and to escape Will's rejoinder. Fabienne pointed Will in the direction of the shops and then dashed off to the nearby Rue de Sévigné to get everything she needed. While she was there, her phone buzzed. The message read: *Hey Fab, I need a date for a dinner next Saturday. You up for it? Or are you still not speaking to me? Jasper*

She considered ignoring the text. *Are you still not speaking to me?* It made her sound petty, as if they were having a disagreement that she was causing to drag on when in actual fact she'd made it pretty clear that they were done with. And he'd only shrugged, as if he couldn't be bothered with the effort of expending emotion on Fabienne, which was a pretty accurate summary of the last couple of years of their relationship. *No Jasper, I'm not up for it*, she texted back and ignored the next buzz from her phone.

When she returned, she couldn't find Melissa. Nor Will. She stepped farther into the park, thinking perhaps they'd set themselves up in a picnic spot, but they definitely weren't there. Her heart sank. Perhaps taking them to a war museum hadn't been such a good idea.

"Sorry I took so long. Seems everyone else wants bread and cheese too."

She whirled around and came face to face with Will, who had a baguette and a bag of cheeses in his hands. "I can't find Melissa," she said worriedly, his sister's whereabouts overriding the relief that he hadn't run off to his hotel.

"She called me," he said. "Apparently she felt tired and caught a taxi back to the hotel. I told her to wait for me, that I'd take her back, but she said that if I tried to, then she wouldn't leave and I'd have to put up with her being tired throughout the entire picnic. She's too stubborn to argue with so I let her go. I think…" he paused, "it might be her not so subtle way of letting me spend time alone with you. Which I hope you don't mind."

Fabienne blushed. "Remind me to thank her for meddling."

Will laughed and slid his hand into hers. "Where shall we sit?"

And Fabienne, smiling so hard it almost hurt, replied, "What about over there?"

They chatted as they ate and Fabienne found out more about him: that his mother had died in her mid-thirties of breast cancer, that Melissa had inherited a rogue gene. That she'd planned to have a preventive mastectomy and hysterectomy when she was thirty but the cancer had caught her years before that.

"That's awful," Fabienne said quietly.

"It is," Will said.

"Are you close to your father then?" Fabienne asked. "I imagine you must be if he was all you had." In a way, Fabienne had often felt as if her father was all she'd had. Her mother, whose oncology work at her clinic was all-consuming—as it should be, given that lives were at stake—had always been less of a presence in her life than her father had been.

"My father," Will said, and his voice had changed to a rougher, harder tone, "had other things to amuse himself with. He found solace in women, not his children. Liss and I saw more of our housekeeper than we did of him."

"No wonder you and Melissa are so close."

"Liss was twelve when our mother died. I was seventeen. By the time I was twenty-one, our father had bought himself another apartment so he could 'entertain' without—what he called—my disapproving stares. He visited us once a week until I told him not to bother. We haven't seen him for years."

"That's so sad," Fabienne said, catching a glimpse in his eyes of the hurt boy who'd taken on his sister's care at such a young age and who would be devastated, ripped apart, when she too died.

"Much too sad for a Paris night with beautiful company and the best champagne I've ever drunk." He lifted the bottle and refilled her glass and his.

"Paris evenings really are like none other," Fabienne said, knowing he wanted to change the subject.

She lay on her back on the picnic rug, unable to fit in any more bread or cheese. Around them, the sky was still light even though it was nine o'clock, the sound of laughter and children playing in the fountain drifted around them like a lullaby, twining with the music that someone nearby had thought to bring with them. The square seemed to hum with the simple joy that radiated from everyone at spending a glorious night outside with family and friends.

Will leaned back on his elbows, shifting a little closer to her. "I should get back and see how Liss is."

"Of course you should." Fabienne sat up, brushed off her playsuit and began to put things into the picnic basket. "I hope she won't be too tired after today."

She stood up, as did he, and then he leaned toward her, taking the picnic basket from her hand, and setting it down on the ground. The music floating across changed to "The Nearness of You," a bluesy jazz number that spoke all of her thoughts.

He slipped his arms around her waist and murmured, "Please tell me to stop if you don't want this."

At the same time as she registered the thought—*don't stop!*—she realized he was kissing her, that one of his hands was on her back, the other tangled in her black hair, and she stepped in as close as she could, wanting more than anything to feel the nearness of Will Ogilvie.

CHAPTER NINE

Fabienne was packing her suitcase the next morning when her phone rang. She leaped on it when she saw Will's name on the screen. "Good morning."

"And good morning to you."

Was it possible that he sounded even sexier this morning than he had last night? She conjured up the memory of that kiss, the kiss she had replayed all night, a kiss that couldn't go anywhere because they were in a public park and he had to get back to his sister, a kiss that had made her whole body ache. "How's Melissa?" she asked, snapping back to reality.

"Still asleep. I know you're flying out soon but do you have time for a coffee before you go? Liss'll probably sleep for a bit longer so I have an hour or so."

"Sure," she said. "If you think you can stand the hipster factor, Ob-La-Di is nearby and has good coffee."

"It can be as hip as it likes," he said softly. "I'll only be looking at you."

Fabienne felt her stomach flutter. "Will…" she said. *Don't make me fall in love with you*, she wanted to say. *I live in Sydney. You live in New York. Don't be the nicest man I've ever met.* Perhaps it was just because she was in Paris. She'd fallen under its spell, become a cliché, was having a weekend fling without the sex.

"I'll see you there in half an hour," she said.

She finished her packing and walked up to Rue de Saintonge, where she saw Will waiting on the footpath. She waved and he solved the problem of how she should greet him by leaning over and giving her a gentle kiss.

Of course the temptation was just to stay there, but she was aware of the harried waiters with trays of coffee and the tiny footpath so she broke away. "Mmmm. I think we should stop that before we get thrown out for causing an obstruction."

"Shame though," he said, smiling at her, and leading the way inside.

Over coffee, he asked about her new job and she told him that it was what she'd been working toward since she left university. "It's the crème de la crème for an Australian curator with an interest in fashion," she said. "Like being offered a curatorship at the Met. I start on Wednesday and I should be nervous but I'm too excited to feel anything besides a desperation to get in there and start planning my first exhibition. Is that how you felt when you got the job at Tiffany?"

He nodded. "Once I decided to take it, I did. But Liss was right, it took me about a week to accept because I was terrified of screwing it up. Then once I'd agreed to do it, that all fell away. Jean Schlumberger has always been an inspiration to me and to be able to see all of his work in the archives and be a Tiffany designer like he was is pretty incredible."

"The Tiffany Head of Design, no less," she said, smiling at the way he'd described himself, as if he was just one of many designers. "Does jewelry design work like fashion design? You start with a sketch and go from there?"

He nodded. "I think it's probably much the same. You have an idea of a theme for a collection, you sketch out the pieces, get them made up, some of them work, some of them don't, and after lots of trial and error, you have a collection."

"So simple," she teased.

"Do you sketch as well? Fashion, I mean." He signaled to the waiter for more espresso for both of them.

"I do. My father taught me. He was so talented, was supposed to take over the business from my grandmother. He'd been immersed in fashion design since he was a boy and he had such a feel for it."

"What happened?" asked Will.

"He fell in love," she said, telling the story that everyone swooned over when her father used to relate it. "He went to Australia for a summer holiday, for inspiration. He'd designed just one collection for Stella and it was a sensation. An iconic fashion moment. The press said he had the potential to be even better than Estella. But in Australia he met my mother at a party. She was an oncologist and she'd just set up a clinic specializing in women's cancers. Of course she couldn't up and leave and go to New York, not when women's lives depended on her. So my father gave up everything for her instead. Back then there was no internet, no way to work overseas. So his are the shoes I'd have to fill, the lost potential I'd always feel I had to compensate for. It seemed easier not to try, I guess."

"It was a big move for your father."

Fabienne tried not to read anything into his words, tried not to ascribe to him any particular thoughts on the trickeries of long-distance relationships and the inevitable sacrifices that were involved. "He always said it wasn't love if you wouldn't give up everything for the other. Otherwise it was just a flame, not worth the candle it was lit upon." *And every time he said that, he'd look at my grandmother and she would turn away and her eyes would be full of tears and I would think it was because he'd moved so far away from her but now I'm not so sure,* Fabienne thought but didn't say.

"Your father was very poetic."

"And an utter romantic. I miss him." The words fell out before she could stop them, her voice wavering a little as she spoke.

"Did something happen to him?" Will asked, reaching out for her hand.

"He died last month. A stroke. Nothing's been quite the same since."

"I know what you mean," he said and she knew that he did, that nothing in his life would have been the same since his sister had been told she was dying. The prospect of death changed everything, made all the ordinary rules of restraint and politeness fall away, made beautiful moments into precious keepsakes, made the future, once taken for granted, seem extraordinary.

Church bells sang through the morning, ringing in the hour, and Fabienne realized she'd been so engrossed in their conversation that time had flown by, that she hadn't once looked around the café at the beautiful Parisians sipping coffee or taken in the hipper-than-hip decor. Will Ogilvie had arrested her full attention.

"I have to go," she said reluctantly. She searched through her handbag and extracted a card. "You have my phone number but here's my e-mail address too. New York and Sydney aren't that far away via e-mail," she added lightly, as if the distance was a paltry thing, wanting to emphasize that she didn't expect grand gestures like her father's, which belonged to a less prudent past.

"And here's mine." Will passed her a card. "I'm glad you bumped into me twice," he said, smiling as he stood up.

"Technically, I only bumped into you once. The second time I said excuse me before I pushed past you." *Light and easy*, thought Fabienne. They were doing such a good job of light and easy. Until they reached the footpath and a cab pulled over then he put her suitcase in the trunk and she said, "I think I have to kiss you again before I go."

She stepped into his arms, lips brushing his. How was it possible for a kiss to be so heady, for the hard muscles of his back to feel so good beneath her hands, for the press of his body against hers to feel like something she could lose herself in forever?

"Fabienne," Will murmured eventually. "We need to stop otherwise I will do everything I can to persuade you to stay here for one more night and then you'll miss your plane."

The way he looked at her was more than enough to convey exactly how he'd like to spend that one more night. She moved back reluctantly. As much as she wanted to, she couldn't stay. She had a six-hour layover in Manhattan, which she needed to use to ask her grandmother some questions, and then she was on the last possible flight to Sydney in order to start her new job on time.

"Thanks for a perfect weekend," she said and then she climbed into the taxi and closed the door before temptation won out over sense.

On the way to the airport, she saw that he'd sent her a friend request on Facebook, which she accepted. She spent the next ten minutes scrolling through his profile and looking at all the pictures of him, of which there weren't enough. Then she received a text from Melissa, which read: *Will's just arrived back looking like the cat who ate the canary. I take it you two have been getting along. I'm glad. He hasn't smiled like that in a long time. I've stolen your number from him so we can keep in touch. I hope you don't mind. x*

Fabienne texted back: *I don't mind at all. I'd love to keep in touch. So glad I met you both. x*

And then one from Will: *I miss you already.*

So do I, she texted straight back. *So do I.*

For once, the plane was on time and as soon as she'd landed in New York and cleared customs, Fabienne took a taxi to her grandmother's house in Gramercy Park. She unlocked the door and let herself in, listening. No movement, no sound; her grandmother must be in bed.

She hurried upstairs and found the nurse propping Mamie up onto the pillows. Fabienne kissed Estella's cheeks, the thinness of the skin like a translucent gauze crumpled into folds, not able to withstand the everyday wear and tear of living for much longer.

You can't die too, Fabienne suddenly thought, for the first time genuinely shocked by Mamie's fragility. Of course she knew her grandmother was old, that she was ninety-seven, couldn't walk, had to go everywhere in a wheelchair, rarely left the house except if Fabienne or the nurse pushed her awkwardly over the gravel paths in Gramercy Park. But she suddenly seemed finite, whereas Fabienne had always thought of her as immortal. Perhaps that meant she shouldn't ask, that she should let her grandmother keep whatever secret her father's birth certificate implied. But Fabienne knew she couldn't do that. With the death of Xander, Fabienne's father, Estella had become the last thread connecting the past and the present and if Fabienne didn't ask now, she knew she never would.

"Paris seems to have agreed with you," Estella said, eyeing Fabienne in a way that made her blush. "What happened there to make you look like that?"

Fabienne picked up her grandmother's curled hand, smoothing out the fingers, tracing over the veins that ridged the skin like skeins of purple wool. "I met someone," she said.

Estella lifted Fabienne's chin and her gaze took in the smile Fabienne was unable to hide, the flush of red on her cheeks, the way her eyes tried to duck and dodge Mamie's stare. "He must be quite someone," Estella said.

"He was," Fabienne said. "He really was."

"Was? Or is?"

"He lives in New York. Ours is destined to be no more than an e-mail correspondence, or a series of flirtatious text messages."

Estella cackled. "Ahh, the text message. I wonder how I ever survived or loved without it? But surely you can see him again?"

"In a year's time when I'm back in New York? It's not the way to have a relationship. Besides, we didn't really talk about it."

"Young people never talk about what matters," Estella scolded. "Everyone's too busy protecting their own hearts to do what's best for them. I sometimes think you all need to go back seventy years and see how we used to get along when we had no other way to communicate besides speaking to one another. To a time when courage was saved for things that mattered, rather than simply being open about your feelings. It might do you all a world of good."

Perhaps it would, thought Fabienne. And so she opened her purse and unfolded her father's birth certificate, then held it out to Estella.

"What is it?" Estella asked, reaching for her glasses and peering at the paper.

Fabienne's finger pointed to the words. Estella Bissette was not named as Xander's mother. And Fabienne's grandfather was not named as Xander's father.

"Who are Alex Montrose and Lena Thaw?"

PART THREE
ESTELLA

CHAPTER TEN

December 1940

Estella knocked on Sam's door half an hour after fleeing the club. "It's Estella," she called.

She heard movement inside and the door opened. Sam, in his striped pajama pants, rubbed a hand across his eyes. "To what do I owe the pleasure?" he yawned.

"Do I need an excuse to visit my friend?" she replied, trying for glib but falling several feet short. She pushed past him before he could see her face. But he obviously heard her tone.

"What happened?" he asked.

"I..." she began, but faltered, stopping by his dresser, back turned to him.

She heard him sit down on the edge of the bed and put on his pajama shirt. Then he patted the space next to him. "Come here," he said.

Estella sank onto the bed beside him and he slipped his arm around her shoulders. She rested her head against him, eyes fixed wide open as if that would stop the stupid tears from falling.

Sam reached behind him. "Lucky Strike?"

Estella nodded and he took two out of the pack, put them in his mouth, lit them and passed one to her. She inhaled deeply then exhaled blue smoke into the gray light of the apartment.

"What time is it?" he asked, collapsing back onto the bed and closing his eyes. "I need to lie down."

Estella couldn't help laughing. "I love that you're the only man I can trust to say that to me with no expectations."

He laughed too. "I never have expectations of you, Estella. You always shatter them." He wriggled back up onto the bed so his head was on the pillow.

Estella scooted up the bed, leaning her back against the wall. "I went to a jazz club. I met a man..."

"Did he hurt you?" Sam raised himself up as if he might leap out into the night and track down any assailant of Estella's.

Estella took a long drag on her cigarette. "He didn't hurt me. Not physically. But he was with a woman who looked just like me." She shook her head. "That's an understatement. She *was* me, Sam. Exactly. Not just a close resemblance, or similar hair. It was like looking in the mirror and watching myself step out of the glass."

Sam whistled. "But how? Why does nothing normal ever happen when you're around?"

"I don't know," she whispered.

"Come here," Sam said and Estella curled in beside her friend, his arm resting chastely around her. "You look as if all the ghosts of Manhattan had escaped their graves and come chasing after you. Even in the middle of the ocean with a German submarine minutes away from torpedoing us, I've never seen you scared before."

"I'm not scared. I'm terrified."

He didn't offer any platitudes, thankfully. Estella couldn't have borne them. He just held her, not asking any more and she was glad he knew that she didn't want to talk about it and also that she didn't want to be alone. Glad that he didn't try to persuade her that she'd imagined everything because that would have meant remembering the woman aloud; running over every contour of the woman's face in her head was bad enough without putting her too-similar features into words.

Eventually, even though she knew he'd been trying to fight it for more than an hour for her sake in case she changed her mind and needed him to listen, he fell asleep. But Estella didn't. She sat on the bed in the green dress she'd made for a rendezvous that had turned into the worst kind of catastrophe, Alex's face and the woman's face a stubborn chimera before her.

She was up at dawn, trying noiselessly to escape when she heard Sam's voice. "Quick getaway?"

She smiled ruefully. "I obviously haven't had enough practice at sneaking out of men's apartments. After rudely waking you last night, I wanted to let you sleep. Sorry."

"Don't be." Sam sat up, his blond hair a disordered mess, his face soft as a child's from sleep, his eyes fixed on her. "Are you going to find out who she is?"

This time, Estella had an answer. "No. I'm going to get my sewing machine, bring it here and spend the day working. I'll have sketches ready for you to cut tonight. If…" She paused. "If you're still willing to help."

"Of course I am. But do you think it's the right thing to do?"

She knew he meant about the woman, not about working on the designs. But she pretended to misunderstand him. "It's the only thing to do," she said.

With her sewing machine and sketchpad, Estella returned to Sam's apartment and drew clothes that were less about fuss and frippery and more about ease; easy to put on, easy to move around in, easy to care for. Clothes that had style, clothes that understood exactly what a girl might get up to when wearing them.

She started with the bathing suit, drawing it properly. It was a suit to swim in, rather than just splash about in, the white shirt style of the bodice making it look almost too chic to be confined to a swimming pool. Then onto clothes meant for work. Each design carried just a single embellishment in the form of a flower: a thin spray of pink blossoms softening the dark collar of a suit, a white silk lily just visible on a white cotton shirt, a gold rose pinned to the shoulder of a black evening dress.

At the end of the day, she leaned back and surveyed the desk. Most of them she probably wouldn't be able to use but, out of experimenting, of following where her pencil took her, she had some designs that she thought might work.

The next thing she needed to do was to visit the fabric manufacturers; she had to find a jersey in black and one in silvery-gray, the colors of the water the ship had sat upon when facing down the German U-boat as the light shifted from night to dawn. Tomorrow she'd go back to the Garment District and visit every fabric manufacturer until she found one who could do what she wanted. White cotton would be easy but the silvery-gray less so. Plus, she wanted two other colors: a deep green that wasn't too bold for work but that could also take a woman out to a bar or a dinner after work, and a pale gold, like the triumphant dawn they'd sailed into after the Germans had let them go, a color that might make a woman feel confident, unique. A color that would set the wearer apart, but which would still make her feel as if she belonged.

She was thinking this as she stepped out onto West 23rd Street in the early evening, intending to return to the Barbizon. Someone stepped in beside her and she knew, without looking, who it was. A man with hair as black as her own, and dark eyes to match.

Her mind raced; she could keep walking but Alex would, no doubt, stick fast. She could run, but where would that get her? It wasn't as if she could run away from the vision scored in her mind of the woman from Jimmy Ryan's. Every time he turned up, her life fragmented like the pieces of a kaleidoscope, re-forming into something that looked similar on the surface but hurt so much more.

"I have no interest in talking to you," she snapped. It was impossible to tell if her words bothered him; he wore the same inscrutable expression she remembered from Paris.

"Don't you want to know who she is? Who you are?" he asked.

"Clearly not as much as you do," she said. "Did she send you here?"

"No."

"Then what business is it of yours?"

His expression hardened and she thought he was probably not a man to get on the wrong side of but she was so angry she couldn't help being blunt.

"Look," he said, "the house you took me to in the Marais belongs to a Jeanne Bissette. I had to check after we met in Paris to make sure all our tracks were covered. Is she any relation of yours?"

Estella stiffened. There was no possible way her mother could own that house. Her mother earned a seamstress's wage, had no money to speak of, couldn't possibly have anything to do with a once-noble home. "You're mistaken. It's an abandoned house, like so many in the Marais. Nobody owns it."

"No. *You're* mistaken."

His voice was flat, unemotional, stating a fact as plain for all to see as the snarls of pedestrians around them. Why was he lying to her? How the hell had she gotten mixed up with him? And what *was* she mixed up in?

"Meet Lena. Tomorrow night."

Lena. So that was her name. "No."

"I'll keep turning up like this if you don't."

"Goddammit! How would you feel if it had been you?" Estella bit her lip, clamped her mouth shut, not wanting those words said, words that made her vulnerable because they showed just how agitated she was by the events of the night before. Her entire life had shifted out from under her and now she stood dangling over the void of everything she'd ever believed about herself. First the revelation that Estella had an American father and had been born in New York. Now the preposterous idea that her mother owned the house in the Marais? And a woman who looked like Estella was here in Manhattan.

"I'm sorry," he said and his voice had softened.

All part of his charm, she supposed. The lies, the brusqueness hadn't worked so now he was resorting to the age-old tactic of seduction. One woman who looked like her wasn't enough; he wanted two. But maybe if she went along tomorrow night and had the meeting he might leave her alone. "Where?"

"Café Society. In Greenwich Village."

"Café Society," she repeated, raising an eyebrow. Of course he moved in society, unlike Estella. That much had been plain in Paris.

"It's not the way it sounds. It's jazz like you've never heard it before."

"I'm from Paris. I've heard better jazz than anything you can imagine."

"Well, even if you don't want to come for me or for Lena, come for the music. At least that way you'll be able to tell me who was right about the jazz."

A tiny smile touched her lips but she smoothed it away before he noticed.

"I'm taking your silence for a yes. Café Society—ten p.m.," he said before he walked away.

Estella was deliberately late. Spectacularly dressed. Shielded and bulwarked with her gold dress, ready to deflect anything she didn't want to know about. Which she suspected would be quite a lot.

She took Sam and Janie with her for protection, Janie squealing with delight when she heard where they were off to. "It's known as the wrong place for the right people," Janie said by way of explanation. "And everyone wants to go to the wrong place."

"I don't," Estella said shortly. "I just need you to reassure me that she looks similar to me but not identical."

"You probably drank too much," Janie said.

"I'd had one sip!" Estella protested before she saw Alex coming from the opposite direction. They met at the top of the steps to the club.

"This," she said to Sam and Janie, "is Alex. Paramour of my looka-like."

Alex raked his hand through his hair. "Pleased to meet you," he said to her friends. Then, to her, "This is already going badly."

"Did you expect it to go anything other than badly when you invite me to a club and you turn up on the arm of a woman who looks exactly like me? Are you so incompetent at kissing that you can't tell one conquest from another?"

Estella could see Janie and Sam eyeing each other and then Janie shrugging as if to say: *I've no idea what she's talking about*.

Alex winced. "I seem to remember that you didn't behave as if I was a complete stranger either."

"You thought I gave you special treatment at the party?" Estella laughed, as if she wasn't at all concerned about what she would find inside the club. "Perhaps that's just how I am with every man I meet." Which was a lie, but he didn't need to know that.

She walked down the stairs before she became any cattier, a disposition she'd never thought she possessed but Alex seemed to bring out the worst in her. She found herself in a basement club where the jazz reminded her of Paris and where the mix of patrons—black and white, well-dressed and louche—was unlike New York's usual inclination for segregation by class and skin color. Some people danced, some people listened to the music, and others talked in groups around tables. On the stage, Billie Holiday, who Estella had heard of but never seen perform, began to sing "Strange Fruit."

"I'll find us a table," Sam said, ushering Janie forward, leaving Estella and Alex to bring up the rear.

Estella strode over to the bar and smiled at the bartender. "Sidecar. Best make it extra strong."

"He giving you trouble?" the bartender asked, eyeing Alex.

"Nothing I can't handle. Besides, he's paying for the drinks." She winked at the bartender and left Alex to settle the bill. As she turned away she walked straight into a woman. Lena.

Estella took a large sip of her drink and pushed on a smile that could've lit up Broadway. "I'm Estella," she said to Lena. "I don't believe we've met, although I feel as if I see you in the mirror at least a dozen times a day."

"Only a dozen?" Alex remarked sardonically.

Estella couldn't help laughing. "Touché," she said. "I'm not really that vain."

"I'm Lena," the woman said, smiling the kind of smile one gave out of politeness, rather than any notion of gladness.

It made Estella shiver. She watched Lena bestow the same smile on a couple who waved to her, a man who said hello, another one who smiled at her. It seemed people knew who Lena was, but her poise and the way she was dressed indicated that she knew her way around moneyed society.

"My friends have found a table," she said, indicating Janie and Sam who were watching with mouths open. She walked over to them and sat down. "I take it from your expressions that I wasn't exaggerating."

"If anything, you underplayed it," Janie said. Then she dazzled her smile at Alex. "I didn't have a chance to say so outside but it's lovely to meet you."

"And you," he said. "You're Australian?"

"I am," she said, flashing him a Janie-special smile. "I'm a model. I'm not the type to nurse wounded soldiers. I'm the type they dream about instead."

Estella rolled her eyes. Janie was the most brazen creature she'd ever met. Sam laughed and Alex smiled. Only Lena didn't react. *She's colder than the North Pole*, Estella thought, wondering what Alex saw in a woman so devoid of emotion. Not that she cared. She studied Lena unobtrusively and the only difference she could see between them was that Lena was slightly heavier and curvier than Estella.

"I thought, given your reluctance to discuss how you and Lena might be connected, you'd want to have this conversation in private," Alex said to Estella, glancing across at both Sam and Janie.

Estella shook her head emphatically. "Privately would mean just Lena and me. If she gets to have you here, then I get to have Sam and Janie."

"I know!" Janie exclaimed. "You're twins. Kidnapped at birth. Heirs to a fortune."

Estella laughed, even though Janie's joke rattled her unaccountably because it reminded her of how much she didn't know: an American father, American papers, a house in the Marais that Alex said was her mother's. She took a long sip of her drink. "That's the most ridiculous thing I've ever heard," she managed to say.

Alex passed Lena a cigarette, which he lit for her in the way lovers do, and Sam tugged Janie's hand. "Let's dance," Sam said and, despite her misgivings, Estella let them go. They didn't need to suffer an uncomfortable night too.

After Sam and Janie departed for the dance floor, Lena stared at Estella. "Your dress is beautiful," she said.

"Thank you," Estella stammered in surprise. "I made it. I'm a designer."

"I haven't heard of you," Lena said smoothly.

Estella flushed. "I'm just starting out. I hope to have samples ready to show in a few months."

"How are you funding yourself?" Lena asked, in that same unruffled voice.

Estella's cheeks went even redder and she looked around for Sam and Janie, but Janie was twirling from one beau to another and Sam was buying a woman a drink at the bar. "You don't need much besides a sewing machine and some samples to get started in fashion."

Lena eyed her appraisingly. "You've heard of the Fashion Group?"

"I might be broke but I'm not stupid," Estella said. Of course she'd heard of the Fashion Group, a collective of some of Manhattan's most influential women in fashion, including Dorothy Shaver from Lord & Taylor and Carmel Snow from *Harper's Bazaar*.

"Elizabeth Hawes, one of the members, makes dresses for me. You might like to meet her."

Did she want to owe Lena anything? Estella was desperate to demur but meeting a member of the Fashion Group wasn't something she could afford to say no to. "I'd be very grateful," she said, knowing that there it was, the thing that made her the most deficient at the table. Lena clearly had money; her clothes and jewels dripped with it. Alex, for all that he must be a spy, had suits tailored so impeccably that they must come from the best bespoke service. And then there was Estella, a poor French refugee who didn't even know who her father was. Nor how she'd come to be sitting beside another version of herself.

"Who are you?" Estella blurted.

Lena gave a small and mirthless smile. "That's a very good question. For all intents and purposes, I'm Lena Thaw. Godchild and distant relative of the Thaw family. Have you heard of them?"

Estella shook her head.

"They're a family of lunatics."

"Lena," Alex said gently and Estella watched them, how Alex was protective of Lena in a way that didn't sit with the man she thought he was, as if Lena was a fragile gem, like a topaz, prone to breaking.

Outwardly, Lena didn't seem as if she needed protection, except if you looked deep into her eyes, which was the only place where Estella could see a difference between the two of them. Lena's eyes were ancient, a muddied blue like a once clear lake that had been dirtied beyond repair.

"Lunatics?" Estella repeated. "Enough of the drama or my heart might fail from the suspense."

"The Thaws are Pittsburgh coal tycoons," Lena continued, her words dripping with a world-weary sarcasm that was painful to listen to, suggesting that she was so cynical about life that she'd ceased to dream. "Their son, Harry Kendall Thaw, is my godfather. 'Uncle,' he likes me to call him. I was born in August 1917 and foisted upon the Thaw family by an unwed young relative who was only fifteen. The Thaws were so very kind in taking me in and then giving me to Harry to raise once he was let out of the asylum in 1924. Harry's a convicted murderer who was eventually found not guilty of his misdeeds by reason of insanity. He's cruel, depraved, deranged, and obsessive. Luckily, he moved to Virginia once I was off his hands. I think that about sums me up." Lena leaned back into Alex's arm.

"I'm not sure Estella is going to get a lot out of that explanation," he said.

They were toying with her, giving her half answers to big questions, dragging out something that should be so simple. All they needed to do was to tell her who Lena *really* was, then Estella would know that they couldn't be related because their stories didn't connect. Estella had never heard of any of the people Lena had mentioned. Except that she was also born in August 1917. She finished her drink in one long swallow that didn't render her as insensible as she'd hoped.

"Why is this anything to do with you," she demanded, rounding on Alex. "Actually, I don't care. I'm going to dance."

But before she could find someone to partner her, Alex was beside her, swinging her around, and she had to move with him or else be knocked out by the couples encroaching on either side.

"When I told you to leave France, I didn't expect to see you here," Alex said.

Estella couldn't tell if his words were apology or accusation. "I caught the last American ship out of France. The SS *Washington*. The one that almost got torpedoed. You might have heard of it," she said bitingly, as if that was his fault too.

"I didn't know it was you," Alex said. "At the party, when I kissed you, I thought you were Lena. Which makes me an idiot. I'm sorry."

She spun away and then back to him, as required by the dance. Was he really sorry? "You're a spy," Estella said, testing him to see what else he might disclose.

"You know I can't answer that."

"Or a map thief?" Estella said. "Which title would you prefer?"

"You're still as prickly as ever," he said.

Estella felt Lena's eyes on them.

Perhaps Alex felt it too because he hurried on. "I was in France for government work, yes. And this is not something you can repeat, but since you know half of it already, maybe it's better if you know the real story rather than coming to your own half-baked conclusions. Monsieur Aumont was helping the War Office. I was...facilitating the exchange of papers."

The way he spoke, hard and remote, should have made her angrier but she remembered that he'd cared enough about the consequences of his work that he'd come with her to find Monsieur Aumont, that he'd told her he'd look after his body. That his response to seeing Monsieur Aumont was not like Estella's—that of someone who'd never seen a dead body before—but of someone who'd seen too many.

"What were the maps of?" she asked.

He didn't answer straightaway and she thought he'd avoid telling her but then he said, "Maps of Oflag IV-C. Otherwise known as Colditz Castle. A prisoner-of-war camp in Germany where Allied prisoners are held."

A long silence stretched before them, and the music changed to a slower song but she didn't even notice, her body moving to the music unconsciously, following his lead. "You're helping prisoners of war to…what? Escape?"

"Nobody wants to be left in German hands until this damn war ends."

"No." There was nothing more to say. He hadn't actually confirmed her supposition but nor had he denied it. But he'd made it harder for her to hate him when he was doing something so dangerous to help her country.

"I'm a lawyer," he added. "I work for international companies like the Chase National Bank so I divide my time between here and London."

"And France."

"Occasionally."

"Are you English?" She still hadn't been able to place his accent.

"It's a long story," he replied, then smoothly changed tack. "Do you know how your mother came to own the house in Paris? Because it's the same as…"

Estella drew away before he could finish. Every thread of her body felt unpicked but somehow he thought he had the right to hold on to his own questionable dignity? "No longer than the story of how a woman who happens to be my doppelganger is sitting over there, surely? And you seem so very keen to have that story told."

"She's got to be more than your doppelganger."

She caught Alex's eye before she turned away and what she saw there, a concern, a solicitude for someone—surely not her, it must be for Lena—almost made her drop her anger like a pair of rolled hose. Why were he and Lena trying to forge some scant facts into a bond? If what Alex had said was true—*she's got to be more than your doppelganger*—then he was implying a relationship between Estella and Lena that transformed her mother into a stranger. And Estella wanted more than anything for that not to be true. So she would not help Alex and Lena tear away the fabric of the stories she and Lena had been told because that would leave her naked and with nothing.

Instead she would pretend she could still sit across the worktable at the atelier and that her mother would smile at her, reach out her hand and say: *everything is just as it was* ma cherie. *There is you and there is me and that is all that matters.*

CHAPTER ELEVEN

At the front desk of the Barbizon the next morning, a note from Lena waited for Estella. Lena hoped that Estella would come to her house at half past nine. Then Lena would take her to meet Elizabeth Hawes. Estella showed it to Janie.

"It might not be so bad," Janie said. "Lena looks as if she knows people who matter. Did you find anything out last night?"

"Just that it's a huge coincidence that I look like Lena." Estella picked up a pair of scissors and searched diligently over her seams for loose threads that might need trimming. But she didn't find any.

Janie raised one eyebrow. "And I'm the president's mistress. Are you kidding? You've gotta be related."

"What does it matter if we are?"

"Aren't you curious though? I would be."

"Isn't there a saying about curiosity killing cats?" She finally met Janie's eye.

"Lucky you're not a cat." Janie grinned as she left the room in her robe and headed for the bathroom.

Estella knew she'd be more curious if it didn't implicate her mother in some way. But, despite her reluctance, Janie was right; Lena did look as if she knew the right people. Which would be immensely helpful if Estella was to make anything of Stella Designs.

So she tidied her hair and caught the subway to the address in

Gramercy Park that Lena had left for her, realizing now that the party Janie had stolen the invitations to had been at Lena's house. Despite having a mad, murdering uncle, Lena hadn't done too badly for herself if she could afford a place in Gramercy Park.

Estella emerged from the subway into a brilliantly cold and blue winter's day. A smile dropped onto her face when she saw the sun. She'd meet Elizabeth Hawes, take whatever help she could get from her, work feverishly on her collection, and aim to show it in the spring of 1941. It was a plan, a plan that made her feel good, a plan with certainties attached to it unlike the many uncertainties presented by the evening before.

But as she swung into Gramercy Park East, her smile was quelled by the grip of nausea in her stomach, by the fingernails of terror sweeping over her neck.

She was standing outside the house it had been too dark to see on the night of the party. But now she could see it too well. And Alex's words, the ones she'd cut off, played over: *Do you know how your mother came to own the house in Paris? Because it's the same as...* Now she knew what he'd been about to say: *it's the same as Lena's.*

As well as Estella having a double in Lena, the *hôtel particulier* in the Marais on the Rue de Sévigné had a Manhattan double and Estella was standing right before it. Lena's house was an exact replica of the one Estella had been in with Alex the night her world turned upside down.

She stared at the massive arched portal. In daylight, the house was so out of the ordinary for New York that it seemed impossible she wasn't drunk or dreaming. The portal led to a courtyard through a carved wooden door—which must have been open on her previous visit—and was even flanked by *chasse-roues*, the guard stones that used to protect the walls from the damage inflicted by carriage wheels curving in too close. Redbrick trimmed with blond stone, a blue-gray slate roof, a courtyard garden with swept gravel paths and the scent of mint freshening the air, the Four Seasons sculpted onto the facade of the townhouse—Winter looking hunched and despairing, Summer's head affixed, his gaze brutal.

The door swung open. Lena frowned when she saw Estella's face. "You need a drink," Lena said.

Estella followed her inside and saw that the interior rooms were identical in size, shape, and location too, their perfect condition showing off the splendor that the Marais townhouse must once have possessed. The friezes on the wooden ceilings sparkled with resplendent color rather than neglect and Estella could now see that the stencils were of flowers and pearls and cupids, something that had been impossible to discern in the faded pigments of the Rue de Sévigné's ceilings. And there was the vaulted staircase, buttressed by a spectacular void underneath, in which Estella had kissed Alex.

In the parlor, Lena made Estella a sidecar. "Drink up," she said.

Estella drank gratefully even though it wasn't yet ten o'clock. "I don't suppose it's the best thing to do before meeting a member of the Fashion Group."

"But nor could you have gone looking as if you might faint at any moment. Surely you're not nervous. You don't seem the type."

Estella shook her head, trying to find the words, wondering if she should keep it to herself. But it was so momentous, so large and terrifying and altogether peculiar that she had to say it. "There's a house in Paris that is an exact copy of this one. And when I say exact, I mean like us. As in there's no possible way the two houses aren't somehow related."

"So you've conceded we must be related."

That same implacable tone. It gave nothing away. Estella had no idea how Lena felt about any of it. Whether she was as unsettled as Estella or if she didn't care a bit. Instead of answering, Estella said,

"This house must be a copy of the one in the Marais though because that was built in the seventeenth century."

"My uncle built it the year I was born," Lena said.

"The mad, murdering one?"

"The very same." Lena smiled a small smile and Estella wondered if that was all she ever gave of herself, that slight curl upward of each lip, the barest glimpse of white teeth, a smile so guarded it would take an entire army to break through.

"I've never heard of your uncle," Estella said, as if that was proof of something.

"And I've never heard of your mother."

"Which leaves us with nothing besides speculation." Estella stared up at the painted wooden beams on the ceiling. "I need to meet Elizabeth Hawes. I need to focus on immediate problems, such as how to gain a foothold into New York's fashion industry, problems that are solvable, rather than the vastly larger and ever more complex riddle of who we are to one another."

"Then let's go and meet Liz," Lena said.

Which they did, in an elegant townhouse on the Upper East Side, where an equally elegant lady ran her eyes over Estella's dress before she took in her face. "Your design, I imagine?"

"It is," Estella nodded. "I've read your book," she continued, referring to the exposé of the fashion industry that Elizabeth Hawes had published two years before, detailing the ins and outs of copying Parisian designs, and the practices of Seventh Avenue factories and Upper East Side made-to-measure businesses with such candor and humor that it had created quite a buzz. Hawes no longer ran her own made-to-measure business and Estella wasn't sure if that was by choice or whether Manhattan society hadn't taken too kindly to the truth-telling. "I worked as a sketcher in Paris too."

"Did you enjoy it?" Elizabeth asked.

"It was a way to pay the bills. A way to become a better designer. Paying bills and designing are both skills I need."

"They certainly are. Despite the fact that one has to sell one's soul, it was the best training I ever had." Elizabeth eyed Estella appraisingly. Then she smiled at Lena. "I think I'd like to chat with Miss Bissette for longer. You don't mind?"

"I hoped you would. I'll be back in an hour." Lena kissed Elizabeth on the cheek, which proved to Estella that Lena must have some warmth hiding somewhere inside her if she was capable of friendships, and left.

"Judging by the look of your dress," Elizabeth said, standing up and coming over to finger the oversized white collar of Estella's dress, an elongation and elaboration on a man's tailored shirt, with a white silk lily in the buttonhole, "you're designing sportswear. I don't mean that as an insult. But you'll know, if you read my book, what I think are the issues with designing sportswear."

"I do. But that was before the war."

"Tell me, what do you think of the monastic dress?" Elizabeth asked, referring to Claire McCardell's famous dress, the first-ever American design to have become much-copied.

"I like the intention," Estella replied honestly. How much should she say? What if Elizabeth loved the monastic dress and Estella's opinion proved only how ignorant she really was? McCardell was a member of the Fashion Group, alongside Elizabeth, after all. But holding her tongue had never been her strong suit and, just as it had gotten her into trouble before, so it probably would now.

"It's easy to move in, and it's washable," Estella said. "But it's also very plain and its strength—its shapelessness—means it doesn't suit all figures."

"What would you do that is different?"

It was impossible to tell whether Elizabeth agreed with her or not, whether Estella was digging a hole for herself right through to the subway with every word. "I'd keep the same price point—make dresses for somewhere between twenty and thirty dollars from washable fabric. But McCardell's dresses don't make you want to tear them from the hanger and drop them over your head; they're functional but not beautiful. Despite the war, I'm still predisposed to beauty. So I'd add the tiniest of embellishments. In Paris, my *métier* was making the artificial flowers for couture designers. I want my clothes to have just a little touch of something fun and stylish to set them apart. Like the lily," she finished, pointing to the flower on her dress; it was also plain and made of an affordable fabric but it was cut closer to the body, which meant a slender figure like hers wasn't overwhelmed in fabric as it might be in the monastic dress.

Elizabeth Hawes didn't reply immediately. Then she said, "You know it takes two years for a Parisian trend to become a trend on Seventh Avenue. Or it used to take two years," she amended. "What you were used to seeing in Paris last year won't make it to a Manhattan office building until 1941."

"I remember you said that in your book."

"But with the war on, how will anyone know what the women in Paris are wearing?" Elizabeth mused. "How will the buyers know what's an experiment and what's a copy of Lucien Lelong? Will it make them more conservative? Or less?"

"I heard that Claire McCardell has just succeeded in having her own name on the labels at Townley Frocks," Estella said. "And the *New York Times* has finally started naming some American designers. Surely, if there are enough of us saying 'this is fashion, these are clothes you can work in, play in, go out to dinner in,' then people will start to believe it? They'll ignore Schiaparelli's ridiculous suggestion that American women aren't elegant enough for there to ever be a fashion center here. They'll start to see that not *all beautiful clothes are made in the houses of the French Couturières.*'"

Elizabeth laughed as Estella quoted her book at her. Estella took it for encouragement and plowed on. "I saw your Paris showing in 1931. My mother took me to it."

"What did you think?"

If she lied, Elizabeth would be able to tell. How to phrase what Estella wanted to say in a way that captured the sense of that show, but without being insulting? "We thought it was like what the Statue of Liberty is to the Eiffel Tower. French-inspired," Estella continued, "but with more self-importance."

Elizabeth laughed again. "I couldn't have put it better myself." Then her face became suddenly serious. "You know that the Great American Design movement that Lord & Taylor began in 1932 fell flat on its face?"

"And you think I will too?" Estella's eyes fell away from Elizabeth's face and into her lap. Did that mean it had been a waste of time coming? That everything she'd hoped for in a boat in the middle of the Atlantic was proving as elusive as the end of the war?

"On the contrary. Maybe now its time has come."

"Really?" Estella's head lifted to meet Elizabeth's eyes.

"Fashion is one of a very few industries where women can have influence and power, albeit within a male-centric space. The manufacturers are all male, the magazine owners are male, department store executives are male. They run the business; we do the designing. So there's a constant battle between the authority our design abilities and our understanding of the customer grant us and the tendency of men to want to put their stamp on everything because they hold the purse strings."

Estella frowned. If this was a pep talk, it needed work.

Elizabeth sipped her tea, then continued. "I'll never forget *Fortune* saying that success in style, designing, or in the sale of cosmetics implies little or nothing. That Elizabeth Arden is not a potential Henry

Ford because what she does isn't a career in industry; cosmetics and fashion being weekend hobbies rather than industry. It's branded on my brain; the article concludes by saying that '*Elizabeth Arden and her kind, in other words, are not professional women.*' Never forget those words. You have to be ten times as good at what you do than any man ever is at what he does."

"I can't believe they said that!" Estella slapped her teacup on its saucer. "Actually, I can. I've always been disappointed in Chanel and all the other female couturiers who got their start by being some-one's mistress. But how can I blame them? Is it even possible to do anything without first sleeping with a man for his money? Even if it was, you'd still be seen as 'not a professional woman.' Men seem to only want us in our negligees in their beds rather than doing some-thing that matters."

Stop, Estella told herself as her mind caught up to her mouth. *For once, just stop*. The conversation had taken an upward turn. Now, who knew.

"You're very outspoken." Elizabeth paused, then smiled. "As you've read my book, you'll know that outspokenness is a quality I admire. I'll do what I can to help you. You don't need much to start making clothes. But publicity and trade customers can be decidedly trickier. That's where I come in. We'll start with an introduction to Babe Paley, a fashion editor at *Vogue*—your aesthetic is more *Vogue* than *Harper's Bazaar*—and also to Marjorie Griswold, Sportswear Buyer at Lord & Taylor. And perhaps you'll show all the naysayers that American women do have the courage to be fashionable in a way that suits them rather than in a way that suits French women."

Estella couldn't help herself. She flew at Elizabeth, kissed both her cheeks and said *thank you* so many times that Elizabeth was forced to tell her, in no uncertain terms, to shut up.

When Lena collected Estella, she had a patron, plus a way to earn some money to fund her business. Elizabeth Hawes had suggested she approach André Studios, a subscription fashion service, for which Estella could sketch copies. The copies were then sold to manufacturers who didn't have designers or comparative shopping departments—which meant most of Seventh Avenue. It would be an easy job. Nothing Estella hadn't done a hundred times before. Something she'd do until she had her samples and could show her own designs.

"Sell a bit more of your soul; it makes the bits you're left with all the more precious," Elizabeth had said, smiling a little, before she saw Estella off.

"Thank you," Estella said to Lena once they were in the car. "I really mean it."

"Glad to help," said Lena, smooth as always, responding as if Estella had just thanked her for the loan of a cup of sugar rather than a lifeline. "Why don't you have your showing at my house? I assume you don't have another venue?"

"I don't even have dresses to show, let alone somewhere to show them," Estella said. "But I can't use your house."

"Why not?"

Because I don't know you. Because I'm scared of what you mean. "I don't..." Estella paused but there was no way to say it delicately. "I don't think I can afford somewhere like your house."

"My house is free. I think you can afford that. But can your scruples?" Lena raised an eyebrow at Estella. "Design me a dress in exchange. A one-off. It's the ideal payment."

Estella wanted to say yes. But if she did, she was committing herself to Lena, to knowing her, to finding out more. Then she looked across at Lena and saw something so sad about Lena's eyes, a kind of emotion Estella knew she never wanted to feel, which made her say, "I would love to have the showing at your house."

"Work out what you need and then come and see me and we'll

go through the details. Perhaps you could aim for a late spring showing?" Then Lena hesitated. "Try to come before New Year. Please?"

Was 1941 really so close? In all the confusion of the past week, Estella had lost track of time. Her mother had been living under German rule for six months but Estella had heard nothing from her. She would try again to send her a letter, to ask who her father was, to say that she'd met Lena. Then, if she heard nothing more, she'd go to see Lena and, with her, try to piece together the mystery of who they might be to one another. Because what if Lena *was* her sister, a sister Estella had always wanted. Surely that was worth finding out?

So she made up her mind. It wouldn't be before New Year, but she would see Lena again. First, she had to give her mother this one last opportunity to explain.

The New Year passed with no word from her mother. Estella decided she would wait until mid-January before she gave up. Before she delved into things that hurt with Lena, a woman she didn't know, instead of with her mother, a woman she'd thought she'd known best of all.

To keep herself occupied, she worked at André Studios each day and, every night, she went to Sam's apartment and sketched and sewed, determined to make enough dresses for a showing in the spring, while he cut and Janie modeled.

One freezing night in January, while Sam cut the designs Estella had worked on earlier in the week, she emptied a bag of groceries onto the kitchen table and used the single burner and tiny oven to make a chocolate cake. She knew if she didn't do something, she'd hover over Sam while he was cutting and annoy the hell out of him. The cake was one her mother had taught her to make and Estella thought of it as the best comfort food she'd ever eaten. And she wanted the smell to waft through the apartment, to remind her of winter nights in Paris when she and her mother would eat cake and drink coffee, huddled by the fire, happy. It was a way to hold on to those memories while she still could.

The door buzzed while Estella was melting chocolate and she let in a beaming Janie.

"I only have an hour," Janie said. "I'm meeting Nate at the 21 Club."

"That sentence requires a great deal more explanation," Estella teased, scraping her finger around the mixing bowl and licking cake batter off her finger.

"Nate is the man I met at the party in Gramercy Park," Janie announced.

"Is met another way of saying kissed?" Sam inquired. "It didn't seem to me that there was a lot of meeting going on at the party."

Janie put her hands on her hips. "I don't have time for meeting. I'll be twenty-four this year, which is ancient. I need to cut to the chase."

Estella shook her head. "Janie, you'll be gorgeous for at least another hundred years."

"For that," Janie smiled, "you can find me something to wear. I saw you whipping up a silver number the other day and I think silver and my hair color would be magic."

"They would," Estella agreed, "but it's not quite finished."

"So hop to it!" Janie said.

"I know you're only half-joking," Estella mock-grumbled, putting the cake in the oven and sitting down at the sewing machine.

"When you get a workroom," Sam said to Estella, "you should put Janie in charge. She'd frighten the freckles off a Midwesterner."

"A Midwesterner," Janie scoffed. "I'd frighten the freckles off an Australian, and that's saying something."

Janie chattered on, amusing them with anecdotes about Nate, who did something in a bank, who'd sent her flowers, and who Janie thought had "catch" written all over him.

A short time later, Estella stood up and handed the dress to Janie. "Here's your rod. Hope your fish is worth catching."

Janie kissed Estella's cheeks. "He's worth at least a free dinner at the 21 Club. And I asked him to bring a friend for you. So you'd better get dressed."

"I have work to do. I can hook my own beaux."

"Really?" Janie raised her eyebrows. "Where are all these beaux? Hiding under the bed?" Janie shucked off her shirtwaister shamelessly, so used to dressing and undressing in front of others that she couldn't have cared less who was watching although Sam did have the manners to turn away.

"You know she'd rather you watched," Estella joked and Sam laughed.

"Get dressed," Janie ordered. "We have a date to go to."

Estella knew there was no point arguing. But she could at least set some terms. "I'll come. But I'm going to leave at ten so I can still do some work tonight."

"You might find you don't want to leave at ten," Janie said and Estella wondered, as she changed her dress, if Janie was right. If her mysterious date would turn out to be someone she'd be happy to see again.

While Estella brushed her hair, Janie fished a copy of *Women's Wear Daily* out of her handbag. "Did you see that?" she asked, pointing to a picture of a "kitchen dinner" dress, a Claire McCardell design complete with attached potholder.

"I hope that's supposed to be ironic," Estella said grimly. "I see the point she's making, that the dress can go from work to the kitchen and back out to the dinner table but couldn't she have attached a…I don't know…a…"

"A box of rubbers?" Janie supplied.

Estella doubled over laughing. "You're terrible!" she said. "But yes, you get my point, although I was thinking of something more like a typewriter. All the women at the Barbizon are artists, musicians, actresses, secretaries. Not just the makers of dinner."

"A typewriter would be much less fun," Janie grinned.

They caught a cab to the 21 Club and Estella's heart sank the minute her date, Eddie, said, "You sure are a looker." He proceeded to regale her with a comprehensive rundown of baseball, which he said she'd need to get to know now that she wasn't French anymore.

"I'll always be French," Estella said stiffly. Even though she had no idea what being French meant anymore in a world where swastikas hung from every hotel, monument, and municipal building in Paris.

Rather than think of France, she studied Nate, who seemed perfectly benign. He wasn't as well off in the handsome department as she'd thought he'd be, but he clearly thought Janie was also a "looker." He joined in the baseball talk with enthusiasm but had the manners to glance over at Janie occasionally to top up her wine, to ask her how her meal was—a meal that he'd ordered for her—and to ask her if she was cold, or if she wanted champagne instead, or to remark that he bet she'd never tasted lobsters so good before.

No, Estella wanted to interject, *our lives were so dull before you came along*. We couldn't order our own champagne or work out for ourselves if we were cold or make a decision about the lobster without first checking with you.

But Janie didn't seem to mind. She smiled and asked Nate to tell her more about the Yankees, whoever they were. Estella excused herself, knowing she was descending into grumpiness, hoping to recover her humor in the ladies' room.

Janie went with her. Once out of earshot, Estella said dryly, "I didn't realize you were so interested in baseball."

"I couldn't care less about it," Janie said gaily as she reapplied her lipstick. "But men love it when you ask questions. It makes them feel important. Which makes them happy."

"Does he ever ask you anything in return?"

"Why would he?" Janie shrugged. "I put on a dress, parade it around, take it off, put on another one." She snapped her compact closed. "You could still make dresses when you're forty. But my face is my fortune. Nobody will pay me for it when I'm forty." Janie swept toward the door.

Estella caught her arm before she left. "I'm sorry. You're right. You should do whatever you have to do. But I might go back to Sam's and do some work. I think that's my fortune, not Eddie. Do you mind?"

Janie hugged her. "Of course not. Besides, Eddie's been ogling the legs of the lady at the table next to ours. He's not the right man for you."

Estella laughed. "Thank you. My legs feel shunned but my ego is still intact. I'll see you tomorrow."

Once back at Sam's flat, she answered Sam's question about her date by cutting herself some chocolate cake, rolling her eyes and saying, "If I never hear the word 'baseball' again, it'll be too soon."

She changed out of her dress and into a pair of black rayon-crepe trousers that she'd made up in memory of the refugee women trudging across France. The matron at the Barbizon had censured Estella again when she'd seen her wearing them the week before.

"Women do not wear slacks in the public areas of the Barbizon Hotel," she'd said as she caught Estella crossing through the foyer.

"Then I'd best get myself out onto the sidewalk," Estella had replied, hurrying away with a grin. It had earned her a formal reprimand so she'd left the trousers at Sam's knowing she couldn't afford to lose her cheap accommodation.

Now, she lapsed into quietness, getting up from the kitchen table every now and again to see how Sam had to alter the design slightly so that it could be cut in a more economical way, letting her pencil sketches come to life on the wooden mannequin they were using to trial the designs.

"If we cut this on the bias," he said of one, "then it can be slipped over the head and you can save money and time on fastenings." Or, "If you alter the line of this skirt slightly, I can cut it a little off-bias and it will hang evenly but keep its fullness and you'll save on pattern pieces." And so the night wore on until Sam yawned so much that she told him to get some sleep.

"Stay as long as you like," he mumbled as he collapsed onto the bed and fell asleep in an instant.

She'd finish one last dress, she decided, then she'd take the train back to the Barbizon, go in the service entrance to avoid being caught breaking curfew, and sleep for a few hours herself. She turned the wireless on low, in time to catch Charles de Gaulle speaking from England, urging the French people to fight, to do whatever they could to resist the Germans, to never, ever give in.

As she listened, she felt so strongly the distance she'd put between herself and her mother, herself and her homeland, only able to sit here and hope and wish and pray, unable to do anything besides make dresses. What was her mother doing right now? Was she listening to de Gaulle too, in secret on a wireless hidden somewhere in the apartment? Was she thinking about Estella? Was she, did she ever, think about Lena? Did she even know about Lena? She must, surely.

Then she heard a light tap on the door. She looked across at Sam, but he hadn't stirred. It had to be Janie. Something must have gone wrong on her date if she'd come back here.

Estella tiptoed over to the door and opened it with her finger on her lips to warn Janie that Sam was sleeping. Except it wasn't Janie. It was Alex.

CHAPTER TWELVE

God she was beautiful. Alex kept the thought strictly locked away, far behind his eyes, as he watched her finger drop from her lips. Her face, so easy to read, moved through shock, annoyance, and anger, and he read her move to close the door just in time, stopping it with his shoulder and stepping into the apartment.

He took in the bed, shoved over to one side, the man sleeping in it, face turned away from the door. Alex couldn't stop the movement of one eyebrow upward; he hadn't realized she had a lover. But why shouldn't she? Everyone else did. A sewing machine, fabric sprawled immodestly across a kitchen table, a rack on which hung two dresses. The lack of her in the room besides those things. She either didn't stay here often or the man in the bed preferred she keep her belongings elsewhere. He was just glad he'd been able to find her here, rather than at the Barbizon, which would have challenged even his abilities to get inside secure buildings.

The wireless crackled and de Gaulle's voice concluded its speech. Good. She listened. She hadn't put France out of sight and out of mind. Because France needed everyone to care if the British were ever going to defeat Germany at a game the Allies were scrambling to play.

"I suppose I needn't ask how you found me?" she said in a chilly voice, the distance of a hundred miles between them. "I imagine it's the first thing they teach you at spy school; to hunt down unwilling parties to interrogate."

"I didn't come to interrogate you."

"How did you meet Lena?" she asked abruptly.

How to answer that question without adding a million more miles to the distance that already separated them? "I met Lena six months ago. Here in Manhattan. Not long after I met you."

"What are the chances," she mused, "of you meeting both of us in different countries within a few weeks?"

Alex couldn't help it. He gave a small laugh.

The tiniest hint of a smile touched the corners of Estella's mouth, making her, if possible, even more beautiful. Even that minute suggestion of amusement added stars to her silvery-gray eyes. But a movement from the man in the bed removed her smile before it became indelible.

"How hard does he hit?" Alex asked about the man he assumed was her lover.

"I can wake him up and find out if you like," Estella said.

Alex gave another muffled laugh. "Perhaps if we talk over there," he indicated the table, "then I won't need to."

"Cake?" Estella asked, holding up a plate of the most deliciously fudgy-looking chocolate cake Alex had ever seen.

He nodded and she cut two slices and poured two glasses of whiskey, mixing her own into a sidecar. He chose the cake over the drink, taking an enormous bite. It took him a moment before he could speak. "That is possibly the best food I've ever had after midnight."

"I used to make it at least once a week. It was my regular snack after I arrived home from a night out in Montmartre."

"You made it?"

"I can do other things besides look the same as the women you sleep with."

Alex's laugh was a gasp. "I take it back. You're more than prickly. France would have had more luck if they'd used you on the Maginot Line for their defenses."

It was the smallest of sounds but it was definitely a laugh and it had definitely come from Estella. "Point made," she said and this time she tossed him a real smile and he caught his breath. She was stunning. Completely, utterly bewitching and he needed to get his head back in order—and definitely not drink the whiskey—if this was going to end up anywhere other than him kissing her.

"I'm not kissing you again, by the way," she said.

For the first time in a very long time he felt himself blushing. Did she read minds too? "Glad we've established that, and the fact you can smile if you want to."

"What about we make a deal? I'll stop being prickly if you stop flirting."

"I'm not flirting."

"You can't help yourself. You don't even know you're doing it." Her smile vanished.

Shame. He knew what it was the instant it seized his gut with its unfamiliar fist. He was behaving appallingly and he had to stop. He swallowed the whiskey, despite his vow not to, and put on the impassive face of the man who'd faced much more difficult and dangerous situations than Estella, the man so used to not being who he really was that he could no longer be Alex Montrose no matter how hard he tried to find a way back to him.

She noticed the shift in his demeanor. "That's better," she said quietly.

"And you're making a lot of assumptions about Lena and me."

"A man doesn't kiss a woman the way you kissed me unless he's sleeping with her."

"No." He paused. *Unless he has slept with her. Once.* Past tense, not present. "I thought you might want to read this," he said, passing her a newspaper article, and helping himself to more of the cake. "I know Lena didn't explain a lot the other night. It's…hard for her to talk about Harry. But this might tell you who he is."

He watched her eyes skim over the words Lena had shown him months before.

June 26, 1906

    Harry Thaw Kills Stanford White in Jealous Rage Over Actress Wife

    Harry Thaw's trial for murder has the plot of a dime-store novel. More sensational revelations were made in court today, leaving even the hardiest reporters gasping, ensuring this trial will remain fixed in the nation's headlines for weeks to come.

Below that piece of breathless reporting were photographs of three people: Thaw himself, or, as the newspaper called him, the "millionaire slayer"; the murder victim, an architect by the name of Stanford White; and Thaw's wife, Evelyn Nesbit Thaw, an actress whose marriage to Harry the previous year had, according to the newspaper, caused its own sensation. Estella rolled her eyes and Alex knew she was wondering what any of those people had to do with her. But she read on anyway.

    Harry Kendall Thaw, millionaire assassin of Stanford White, the world renowned architect, told his own story of the killing in court today. Jealousy, hate, and revenge were his motives. According to Thaw, White ruined his wife, Evelyn Nesbit, prior to their marriage by luring her into a secret loft adorned with a red velvet swing, and a bed where he drugged her and stole her maidenhood from her.

    At a subsequent meeting with White at a Manhattan party, Thaw said that Nesbit, "my poor delicate wife, shivered and shook when confronted with the sight of the scoundrel White.

Now, he won't be able to ruin any more homes. White deserved all he got."

What White got from Thaw was a public execution; Thaw strolled up to White during a performance at the rooftop theater at Madison Square Garden—a Stanford White project no less—and shot him in the head while the performers on the stage sang "I Could Love a Million Girls."

But was Harry Thaw as guilty of violence toward Nesbit as Stanford White? Another witness, a friend of Nesbit's, in the most shocking testimony, claimed that she tried to rescue Nesbit from Thaw's clutches in Paris two years earlier. Thaw had, she said, beaten Nesbit repeatedly until her skin was blue and then locked her in a room while he went out to solicit women. Nesbit was kept a virtual prisoner by Thaw in Paris and she believed that Thaw would eventually kill her. His actions were those of a brute and a madman, the witness stated.

But Thaw explained away his behavior as a simple attempt to extract the truth from Nesbit about what Stanford White had done to her.

What sort of woman could prompt such jealousy-fueled acts of rage? Evelyn Nesbit is an infamous beauty, a Gibson Girl, an artist's model, a performer. She has attracted the attention of many a New York gentleman from the time she was only fourteen, including that of John Barrymore, Stanford White, and Harry Thaw. During Barrymore's courtship, which ended in a proposal that she turned down due to the actor's lack of funds and White's interference, Nesbit underwent at least two emergency appendectomies, which were rumored to have been a cover for other operations meant to save her from disgrace, and had to take at least one trip to Paris to recover.

*Today's claims of Thaw's predilection for violence are not
the first to have been made. Earlier in the week, a Manhattan
brothel madam said Thaw took pleasure in beating her girls
with a jeweled silver-capped whip…*

Estella put the newspaper down. "I need a drink." She finished her
sidecar. "What happened to him in the end? I'm not sure I can read
any more."

"To Thaw?"

She nodded.

He produced another article with more garish headlines by way of
explanation. "He had a history of drug-taking and erratic behavior
which meant that he was able to plead not guilty by reason of insanity.
But he only served a few years before another team of lawyers proved
he was no longer insane and arranged his release—don't forget he had
a lot of money. Evelyn filed for divorce then."

"If what the paper says is true about what he did to her in Paris,
why did she ever marry him in the first place?"

Alex shrugged. "I guess she was young. Young people do foolish
things." Which skated dangerously close to the truth of his own past so
he pointed at the article to bring the conversation back to Harry Thaw,
and thus to Lena. "Before the Thaws took in Lena, Harry whipped
and abused a boy almost into unconsciousness in late 1916. He was
found insane and locked up again. But it only took him seven years to
prove his sanity this time and to be released. At which time he took on
the care of Lena from his mother."

"He doesn't sound like much of a father figure," Estella said with a
frown.

"He wasn't," Alex replied shortly, wishing to God that Lena would
just tell Estella what Harry had done to her, certain it would arouse
her sympathy. But Lena had expressly forbidden it. So he was doing

what he could, without betraying Lena's confidence, to make Estella understand at least part of it. Because, like everyone else, he had no real idea of what any of this meant, of how it might connect Lena and Estella.

She stood up suddenly, surprising him. He'd relaxed too much with the whiskey and the goddamn cake. He sat up straighter, waiting.

She leaned her back against the wall and studied him in return. "Tell me about you."

He reached over and switched off the lamp. "It's bright in here for two in the morning. And no, I'm not turning off the light in an attempt to seduce you." It was better without the lights. More places to hide. "What do you want to know?" he asked.

"Where are you from? How did you become a spy? And who are you spying for now?"

"Is that all?" he replied, pretending to joke but she didn't respond. He supposed he owed her some information. He folded his arms across his chest, making sure to keep his face blank. "I'm from everywhere and nowhere," he said lightly. "Born in London, son of a diplomat. I've lived in France, London, Shanghai, Florence, and even Hong Kong. I went to university here in New York, which gives me cover of being American; if I was in France as an Englishman I'd be interned. Whereas America is still neutral. I chose my job because I can speak more languages than most, because whispered conversations and politics are in my blood, and because it pays me a lot of money. And that's about all I can say. Now, what about you?"

Estella turned to the window and stood with her back to him, looking out on the real witching hour of New York, the slice of time between true night and morning. When she spoke, her voice was expressionless and he listened hard for a change in inflection that would point him to the truth that would naturally lie somewhere between what she would say and what he heard.

"Apparently my father is American. I have American papers. My mother was abandoned as a baby and raised by nuns in a convent; they taught her to sew. She had me when she was only fifteen, told me that my father was a French soldier in the Great War, that he married her one day, and died the next. But if I have American papers, then none of what she told me is true."

"You know as little about your background as Lena," he said slowly.

"Which might not mean anything." She turned a little, her face silhouetted by the streetlights, the same face he'd seen walking through the door at the Théâtre du Palais-Royal, the same breath-stealing, gut-punching, groin-stirring silhouette that he hadn't forgotten at all. The face and the body that he thought he'd found in Lena until he'd realized, after just one night with her, that she didn't have the spirit he remembered from Paris.

"Or it could mean everything," he said.

"Why are you so interested in this?" she snapped. "It has nothing to do with you. Is it for Lena? Do you love her?"

They were the worst possible questions to have to answer. And she misread the silence.

"She loves you but you don't love her," Estella surmised. "You have quite a reputation, you know. The people at Lena's party spoke of you as if you were as easy as a child's puzzle."

On any other occasion he would have laughed and shrugged. So, the whole world thought he was a womanizer. What did it matter? He *was* a womanizer. He was a man without a life, with a house in three countries, all of them hardly lived in, rootless, moving from one assignment to the next, living in the shadows, dealing with the kind of men she could never imagine existed. But, somehow, it mattered what she thought and she was staring at him as if she could see far inside him, to the person he used to be. As if she'd found what he'd thought was lost, leaving him, for the first time in his life, utterly discomposed.

"I'm here because I got you into trouble in Paris," he said. "I'm here because Lena deserves a proper family and maybe you're it. I'm here because..." *I want to do one decent thing in my life* was the part he couldn't bring himself to say.

He stood up. "Talk to Lena," he said abruptly. "Think of her for just one minute. Go and see her like you said you would. She needs you. She's infamous because of Harry Thaw's cursed legacy—and his money—which means she's either treated like a curiosity or a momentarily diverting *objet*. She has no friends." He stopped. Lena would be furious if she knew what he'd said about her, despite the fact that it was true. "You needn't worry about me hunting you down again," he finished brusquely. "I'm going away." Then he left before he got involved in something that, as Estella had said, didn't really concern him.

For the rest of the night, Estella replayed Alex's words in her head: *I'm here because Lena deserves a proper family and maybe you're it. Think of her for just one minute.* He'd shamed her. Made her see that, whatever was happening, it wasn't just about Estella and her feelings. It was about Lena, another human being who had feelings too. And she'd promised Lena she would go and see her, but she hadn't. It was time.

On her very next day off work, Estella took the subway to Gramercy Park, emerging into a foul day, rain beating down upon her head, the wind trying to tear off her coat. But even the weather couldn't disguise the fact that it was a beautiful neighborhood, the square lined with gracious and ornate apartment buildings and townhouses. The park stood in the center, its locked gate keeping out anyone besides the residents who held keys, the black iron railings saying more about the exclusivity of the area than any number of butlers ever could.

Lena's townhouse crouched like an unloved child on the street, res-

olutely determined to hide its sadness behind its grand facade but it
seeped out anyway. Estella shivered and knocked on the door.

An older woman, thin and tall, like a Dickensian schoolmistress answered. "You must be Estella," she said, with a warmth at odds with
her spare figure. "Lena asked me to give you this."

It was a note that said: *I don't know if you'll get this but I've had to
go away for a while. I hope you'll see me when I return. You can still use
the townhouse for the showing. My housekeeper, Mrs. Pardy, will help you
with anything you need. Lena.*

Estella crumpled the note in her fist. Alex had said he was going
away. Now Lena had too. Most likely for a lovers' rendezvous, leaving
her with all the questions and none of the answers. Which she knew
wasn't entirely fair. Lena had asked her to come before the New Year.
But she hadn't.

"Come in," the woman who must be Mrs. Pardy said. "I'll get tea
and cake for us."

"Thank you," Estella said.

She followed Mrs. Pardy down the hall, marveling at the way
tasteful furniture, and walls lined with modern art—spanning Frida
Kahlo's exuberant use of color to the mind-bending trickery of
Magritte—could transform the house she'd known in Paris as cold,
neglected, even cursed, into something quite breathtaking. The entry
void was magnificent, rising up to draw the eye to the inlaid and
painted wooden ceiling. The furniture was Art Deco, sleek, polished
metal, wood, and stone, the lines softened by the paintings and the use
of luxurious fabrics for the drapes and sofas. Lena, she had to admit,
had excellent taste.

Mrs. Pardy threw open the doors to a cozy room that, in the
Marais house, had felt compressed by spiderwebs and disrepair. She
invited Estella to sit, disappeared and emerged a few minutes later
with a plate of pastries so similar to the ones Estella used to buy to

go with her morning coffee that she almost felt as if she was back in Paris.

"This is delicious," she said, picking pastry crumbs off her dress and smiling at Mrs. Pardy.

"Lena said you were French and I've always loved working with pastry."

Estella put down her plate. Lena had thought to tell her house-keeper about Estella. She was as complicated and twisty as Alex, like a hedged maze in a French château: lovely to look at but terrifyingly complicated once inside. "That was kind of her," she said. "How long have you worked for her?" A nosy question, she knew.

"Four years. Ever since Lena turned nineteen and took this house as her own. There's nowhere I'd rather work. You'd have to search high and low for a mistress as good as Miss Thaw."

"Really?" said Estella, unable to keep the surprise from her voice.

"Of course. She might be quiet on the outside but I prefer to think of her as restrained. Not like other ladies of money who can't wait to spread it all around like butter."

"Yes." Estella nodded. "She is restrained. It's very good of her to let me use the house. Are you sure she won't mind?"

"She'd be most upset if you didn't. She gave me strict instructions that I was to pay you a visit if you didn't come by the end of the month. Shall I show you around?"

Estella wolfed down the last of her pastry and stood up.

"She suggested the models use this parlor for changing their out-fits," said Mrs. Pardy, gesturing to the room they were in. "Then they can walk down the hall to the front sitting room which looks over the park. It's a lovely room."

A lovely room. It was a gross understatement. Mrs. Pardy opened a door and Estella stepped into the loveliest room she had ever seen. Sure, she'd grown up in a two-room apartment on the top floor of a rundown building in a rundown part of Paris, where there was no running water and a shared toilet on the landing, so her points of comparison weren't strong. But she'd also been in hotel rooms in the Ritz to hand over sketches to American buyers and those rooms had been wonderful. As was this one, with a view of the park that made it feel like a glasshouse, a row of windows looking out over lawn and leaf and shrub.

Over the fireplace hung another Frida Kahlo portrait, or rather a double portrait: two Frida Kahlos sat in chairs, their hearts exposed. From each heart ran a thread of vein joining one woman to the other. Estella couldn't help but study it, wondering what it meant. Did Lena know that Estella had existed prior to their meeting or was it some force of sheer coincidence that had caused her to buy a painting of two identical women joined by the most tenuous, but also the most sacred of bonds: blood.

"That picture gives me the willies," Mrs. Pardy admitted. "Can't bear to see their hearts sitting on top of their dresses like that, for all the world to see."

"It makes them fragile," Estella said.

"It makes them macabre."

Estella forced her eyes away from the picture. "The room is perfect."

"That's settled then. Miss Thaw left a list of people she thought should be invited. I'll arrange to have invitations posted to them when you're ready."

"Thank you." Estella felt horribly guilty for the way she'd delayed meeting Lena again. Lena had thought about which rooms Estella should use, had left her a list of names. But why had Lena run off?

"It's my pleasure." Mrs. Pardy beamed. "I like the house to have people in it. I'll prepare some tasty treats for everyone to nibble on. We want them to be well fed and happy so they'll buy lots of dresses."

"That would be wonderful," Estella said, laughing. "I feel almost too lucky to have this."

"Nonsense, my dear. The skill and ability to put together a collection of dresses doesn't come without hard work. Why don't we meet each week in the lead-up to the showing? Then you'll be assured that everything's going smoothly. Now, before I forget, Miss Thaw wanted you to see this."

Mrs. Pardy led the way upstairs to what Estella imagined was meant to be a bedroom. It was empty, save for a long table that Estella recognized as the twin of the kitchen table in the house in the Marais. The one before her now had an antique air about it whereas the one in the Marais had only the neglect of age visible in its surface. A piano— a Bösendorfer, the same as the one in an upstairs room in the house on the Rue de Sévigné—stood beneath a cathedral window that looked over the park, where bare tree branches waved to Estella, welcoming her.

"Miss Thaw said you could work here if you wanted to," Mrs. Pardy said. "That you'd have more room than you do at present."

"It's far too much," Estella protested.

"The house will be empty for three months or so. There'll be no one here besides me. I'd like the company. It's a house that doesn't do well when left alone. It becomes…" Mrs. Pardy hesitated. "It starts to feel bedeviled." She smiled a little. "Listen to me. Being a fool."

"No. I understand exactly." It was how the house in the Marais had always felt to Estella, as if it had, once upon a time, been a happy place. That happiness sometimes leaked out of its walls, making its neglect all the more haunting. As if it was trying to recover a time in the past that had been long forgotten. "What I don't understand is why Lena's being so generous."

Mrs. Pardy smiled. "People don't think it because she's so reserved but Miss Thaw is one of the kindest people I've ever known. And there can be no doubt that you two are related in some way. I've never seen two people so alike. Miss Thaw has no real family. Perhaps it's her way of welcoming you in, of saying that she'd like to know more about you."

As Alex had forced her to, Estella again saw the situation from Lena's point of view. Growing up without any parents, with a guardian who was, from Alex's account, notorious and dangerous, couldn't have been easy. How would you become anything other than reserved if you'd known so little love? Estella felt her heart contract with remorse; she'd been so abrupt, rude almost, to Lena and here was Lena offering her a work space, giving her everything she wanted when Estella hadn't offered anything more than suspicion.

"If you're in contact with her," Estella said, "please tell her thank you very much. That I'll repay her in dresses."

"She'd love that."

"She's away for a few months, you said? That'll give me plenty of time to make some things for her."

Mrs. Pardy nodded. "Yes. A pity; I thought she'd found a man who interested her. Seems I was wrong."

"She's not gone with Alex?"

"No, she's not gone with Mr. Montrose." Mrs. Pardy sighed. "Shame about that. I think if she could just fall in love..." She stopped. "Well, falling in love is a good thing for anyone, isn't it?"

"I suppose it is," Estella said.

As she left the house, with a box of pastries in hand, forced on her by Mrs. Pardy, she reflected that she was the wrong person to ask such a question of. Her mother, as far as she knew, had never been in love with anyone. Estella had slept with two men in Paris, neither of whom she loved, and had only done so in an attempt to assuage her latent curiosity about this emotion that had been documented in so many books, in movies, in art, everywhere. She might have been almost torpedoed by a German U-boat, might have witnessed the poor and the starving and the desperate flooding out of Paris and away from a sinister enemy, might have somehow helped an Allied spy smuggle maps out of Paris, but she'd never been in love. And she mightn't ever be, not now. She had no time for love. She had a show to get off the ground.

CHAPTER THIRTEEN

Alex couldn't get out of London fast enough, despite his superiors' protestations that he stay out of the field, that he was more good to them alive in an office than dead in France. "Depends on your definition of alive," he said, before being dropped by a Lysander into a field in France.

This is it, he thought, as he pulled the ripcord and his parachute only half-inflated. Flying, in a way no man was ever meant to fly, through the sky and down to the ground.

Luckily his welcome crew were there. Luckily the farmer had made a fresh haystack that morning. Luckily, he landed in it. But he didn't know any of that until much later. Months later, when he'd recovered from being knocked senseless and breaking his arm and his leg, when he emerged from the Seamen's Mission in Marseille, a rallying point for resisters, to discover that the war hadn't ended, that it was raging as brutally as ever.

He finally got to Paris, via Toulouse, and made his delivery to Estella's mother. Not that he took it himself; he asked another of his operatives, Peter, to take it for him to the mailbox, just one of many scattered throughout France. He knew he couldn't risk getting any nearer to the mother of a woman he couldn't shake from his mind. He didn't want to do anything to put her in more danger.

The parcel contained three things. First, a letter from him, unsigned, imploring Jeanne Bissette not to continue in Monsieur Aumont's footsteps, not to use her apartment as a safe house for downed airmen because he knew her daughter would be furious if she found out her mother had put herself in any kind of jeopardy, and that Alex had known about it. He expected though, if Jeanne Bissette was anything like her daughter, she'd burn the letter and ignore him.

The second item was a stack of German money, enough to buy liquor on the black market to keep the concierge in the building drunk enough that, if Jeanne continued to help the Allies, she could at least do so knowing the concierge would be too sozzled to notice. The third was a letter from Estella to her mother that he'd purloined, knowing it would never get to Paris via regular mail. He wished he could wait for a response but that would be one risk too many.

All through France's length, from Paris to Lyon to Marseilles to Perpignan, he delivered similar parcels—money, cigarettes—to the *passeurs* and couriers. They were all women, like Jeanne Bissette, women who held together the resistance movement in France, which nobody would suspect, but that was their great strength. It was up to him to make sure that everyone who risked their lives had the means to do so. But Estella's mother was the only person to whom he delivered letters from a daughter.

The Gramercy Park workroom was paradisiacal. So much light came through the windows in the early mornings as Estella sat at the big old table—it had become her workbench—for a couple of hours before going to work at André Studios. She sewed the pieces that Sam had cut the night before, making the most of the sun and the quiet, feeling warm, safe, almost as if she were in a trance, as if she somehow belonged in the room, as if the room was cheering her on. She even spoke to it aloud at times, holding up a finished dress and saying, "What do you think?" If she strained her ears, she could just hear a rustle of approval from the drapes, could swear the Tiffany pendant lights glowed a little brighter, that the windows curved outward into a smile.

In the evenings after work, she and Sam would go to Gramercy Park and Mrs. Pardy would bring them delicious food, stopping to eat with them sometimes, and Janie would join them before she went out with Nate. It was a time of joy, she and Sam laughing over creations that didn't quite work out the way she'd hoped, and never getting discouraged because Sam would just say, in the gentle way he had, "Try again. It'll work next time."

And if it didn't quite work the next time, then it might work out the time after. He was an expert cutter and she said to him, late one night after they'd been working solidly for six weeks, "How is it possible that, of all the men on the ship, I happened to stand on the deck and smoke cigarettes with the one who could help me the most?"

He smiled and put down his scissors. "I don't know if 'happened' is quite the right word. I'd seen you on the ship and thought you were probably the most striking woman aboard. I figured if I was going to be sailing across the Atlantic for two weeks, it'd be best to do it in the company of someone like you."

Estella laughed. "Were you planning to seduce me before the U-boat interfered?"

"No. I just wanted to talk to you. To see if you could possibly be as beautiful as you looked from far away."

Estella found herself blushing. "Don't," she said, unsure where the conversation was going. She and Sam were uncomplicated friends and that made everything so much easier. She could be in a room alone with him at midnight and there were no expectations. She could accept that he was giving up so much of his time to work with her simply because he enjoyed it; she didn't need to be fearful that he wanted something in return.

"But then I realized what a slave driver you were and now I don't see anything in your face other than a woman passing me design after design, along with rolls of fabric, and telling me to 'cut this as fast as you can!'" he joked and the mood shifted back to one Estella felt more comfortable with.

"I don't really do that, do I?" Estella asked. "I'm sorry. You probably want to be out like Janie is, finding someone who's much nicer to you than I am."

"I'm teasing. I like doing this. There'll be time to go out later. Besides, I have ulterior motives."

"Oh?"

"I want this to work. Then I can quit my job making copied made-to-measure."

"The minute I can pay you what you deserve, you will have a job, not as a cutter, but running my workroom," she said smiling and Sam smiled back.

It was a moment when Estella thought she could actually do this. That a buyer or two would come to the show, would like what they saw and would place orders. Then she could give Sam and Janie real work and Stella Designs might become a label to look for when women went shopping for clothes.

On Saturdays, Estella still went to Gramercy Park early, creeping out of the Barbizon so as not to wake Janie, who often came in after midnight. Saturday was her sketching day, when she could transfer the pictures in her head into pencil lines on paper, which she would then watercolor to capture the details of the way a skirt should pleat, or how a sleeve should fall. Finally, she'd annotate them with particulars about buttons or belt buckles or fabric.

Her hand was sweeping pencil freely over her sketchpad, always moving because that was how she worked best, when she felt something, a gaze, that made her heart literally stop; she felt the skipped beat like a punch to the chest. A man stood in the doorway, well dressed but exuding a coldness so visceral that Estella buttoned her arms over her chest.

She stood up. Mrs. Pardy couldn't have let him in because Mrs. Pardy took Saturdays off. But Estella had left the front door unlocked for Sam and Janie, neither of whom would be arriving for a couple more hours. Which left Estella alone in a room with a man who seemed to be feasting on her discomfort, his eyes alight now with a kind of lunatic brightness, his mouth curling upward into a smile that gave Estella no joy.

"So," he said, "there really are two of you."

He must know Lena. "And you are…?" she asked.

He stepped into the room and picked up one of Estella's final sketches, pencil lines filled in with watercolor, the fabric sample affixed to the page. "What a hive of industry this is," he said.

"I'd prefer you didn't touch those," she said stiffly.

He picked up another. And another. Dread anchored in Estella's stomach more heavily than it had when she'd been in the middle of the ocean, facing down German torpedoes. At least then she'd known who the enemy was and the likely consequences. Now she knew nothing, especially not this man's intentions, nor what he was capable of.

"Could I have those please?" Estella put out her hand, keeping her voice neutral, not wanting to betray how much she didn't want him to tear them up or to come any closer or to even speak in his high-pitched voice, like a dangerous child who knew no limits.

"You're not very trusting. Another way in which you take after my charge."

His charge. The blood recoiled away from her extremities, forcing the flow to her heart and lungs where she needed it most to survive this conversation. "You're Harry Thaw," she said.

A smile that was two parts derangement, one part cruelty. "Yes."

Estella cursed herself for having spent so much time trying to ignore the larger problem of who Lena was and who Estella was in relation to Lena that she hadn't bothered to find out anything more about Harry Thaw. Did his predilection for murder and whipping and beating extend only to his wife and those who'd slept with his wife or was he indiscriminate about who he shot and tortured?

She wanted desperately to run through the door and down the stairs and out onto the street, to scream, *Help me!* Instead she waited, eyes on her designs, on his hands holding them, willing him to put them down, to go, to never come back. "I thought you lived in Virginia," she said, voice shaking only a little.

"I heard there was something in Manhattan worth seeing." He put the sketches down. "Where's the lovely Lena?"

"She's gone away."

"Where to?"

"I don't know."

"She keeps secrets from you too, does she?" He lit a cigarette and as the smoke twisted over to Estella, she knew it wasn't tobacco.

"Or are you the secret?" he continued. "You must be; there's no other explanation for your existence."

"I'm busy," Estella said, forcing politeness into her words, not wanting to anger him in any way. "If I can help you with something?"

"I don't know whether you can," he said, blowing a long stream of chokingly sweet, pungent smoke into the room. "But now that I've seen you for myself, I'll let you know, sooner or later, what you can do to help me."

And then he turned around and strolled out.

"Oh God!" Estella gasped when she heard the front door slam. She couldn't move, her limbs were bloodless and her hands shook as she pressed them down onto the table, over her designs, as if that was the only thing she needed to keep safe. As if she hadn't just endured the most sincere and appalling threat of her whole life.

She sat down with a thud. It seemed as if, from the way he'd said, *there really are two of you*, that she'd been a surprise to him, that he hadn't known of her existence until someone had told him Lena had a double and he'd come to see for himself. She supposed that going to meetings with Elizabeth Hawes and nights out at Café Society meant that word had got out.

Where the hell *was* Lena right now? And Alex? They were the only people she could talk to about Harry Thaw.

Estella walked slowly down to the kitchen, stopping to bolt the front door. She made a cup of coffee. Then she waited, standing silent and still in the kitchen for half an hour until the caffeine hit her veins and her breath evened out. *Forget about Harry Thaw*, she told herself. *And then hopefully he'll forget about you.*

The next month was all about research. Estella watched women step off trains and run for busses, she watched them sit down together at lunch, and she watched herself bending down to measure a hem, sitting for long periods at her sewing machine—her equivalent of a typewriter—noted what women wore out at bars and clubs whenever Janie succeeded in dragging her and Sam away for a night out.

American women had a very different aesthetic from French women, she began to understand. Not for them the finishes and furbelows that so many Parisians craved. In fact, like Estella's gold dress, which she hadn't realized was such an unusual piece of clothing for a woman in Paris, American women preferred simpler lines, for the gloss and polish to be embedded in the fabric and movement of the dress, rather than something overlaid and forced upon it.

So Estella drew and erased and tossed away and redrew and erased and watercolored and screwed up paper and drew and painted some more. She sewed and she fitted Janie and she had Janie send in to

Gramercy Park some other models who Estella paid with her André Studios earnings, and who exclaimed over the clothes and made Estella feel as if perhaps people would buy them. She ignored all of the larger problems, which she was so good at doing—such as her lack of staff or a workshop, that she didn't have a spreading machine or a bonding machine, which she'd need if she ever wanted to make up orders in any quantity—reasoning she'd deal with those issues after the show, if buyers placed orders.

At last she was ready. She had twenty pieces. Elizabeth Hawes, who'd sent her a list of names to add to her invitation list and with whom she'd met on two more occasions, had said twenty would be the ideal number. Two bathing suits to start with, accompanied by matching wrap skirts, two trouser suits—Estella wasn't sure which was the more daring, the bathing suits or the trousers—four day dresses, two skirt suits, two playsuits, four evening dresses and four dresses that she thought could do for work, home, and an evening out. Twenty pieces would be manageable to manufacture, she hoped, until she could make enough money to find premises to rent, to buy more fabric, to start up an atelier that didn't run out of a bedroom in a mansion in Gramercy Park.

She sent the invitations out and the buyers and the press said they were coming. Which meant it was time to show Manhattan what Stella Designs could do.

The day of the showing was bleak. Steel-gray clouds over slick black pavements and the gunmetal glint of skyscrapers searching for sun.

"It's not an omen, is it?" Estella asked Janie as they dressed.

"Course not," Janie scoffed. "An omen would be walking into Gramercy Park and finding someone had stolen all your models."

Estella laughed. "Or maybe that would be a good thing. At least it would mean somebody wanted them."

"That's the spirit."

Spirit. It had forsaken her. All Estella could think right now was that this was her one and only chance and everything rested on it. If the showing was a failure, then Janie would marry Nate and move out of the city. Sam would never have the job he wanted and would be so disappointed in her he would take his friendship elsewhere, to someone more deserving. Estella would be stuck at André Studios for her whole life, feeling her talent and her soul snipped into ever smaller pieces. Her mother would know that she'd wasted the opportunity she'd been given to become more than a midinette in an atelier. And Lena, whoever she was, would see Estella as someone who'd promised much but delivered naught. Estella would be alone, the scraps of dreams collecting at her feet like snapped threads.

The thoughts played over in her mind as she caught the train with Janie to Gramercy Park, where Mrs. Pardy let them in with her customary beam on her face, the much needed sun on such a gray day. "I've made coffee to get you started," she said. "And pastries."

Janie groaned. "You're playing havoc with my figure, Mrs. P."

"Nonsense," Mrs. Pardy said. "You're the kind of girl who can eat anything and it never shows. You should enjoy it."

"I intend to," Janie said, diving on the plate and choosing the largest pastry.

Estella took one sip of coffee and didn't bother to sit down. "Right, let's start. Mrs. P, we'll take a look at the front parlor and see what needs to be done there. Janie, can you get everything ready in the dressing room?"

"Sure can." Janie waltzed off to organize racks of labeled clothes.

In the parlor, the first thing Estella saw when she opened the door were the vases scattered around the room, things of brilliance in themselves: orb-shaped, with speckled aquamarine enamel making them shine like a tropical sea. Then she saw the flowers arranged inside the vases: lustrous peonies in bright pink which, against the green-blue of the vases, was lively, bold, and enchanting. "How did…who did…?" Estella stuttered.

"I had so much housekeeping money left over with Lena being away that I thought the flowers would be a nice touch," Mrs. Pardy said.

"They're beautiful," she breathed. "But I can't let you do that. You've been feeding me and Sam and Janie and I'm sure that we all eat more than Lena does. You can't have that much money left over."

"Which is exactly what I knew you'd say. But I wanted to thank you for my suit." Mrs. Pardy gestured at the elegant sapphire-colored suit Estella had made for her and which Mrs. Pardy had declared she might never remove.

Estella smiled. "Thank you. The room looks magnificent."

And it did. The color of the vases was a perfect match for the greenery of the park outside, the pink flowers sat like stunning and delicate gowns, even the gray light of the sky gave the room a softer quality than sunlight might, meaning her samples might be able to shine.

After that, there was no time to think. Only to ensure that Sam, who'd called in sick to his workplace, as Janie and Estella both had, was as happy as she was with the way the models looked, that Janie and the other girls knew who was to wear which piece of clothing and in what order they had to line up.

Then it was half past two and Mrs. Pardy thrust a glass of champagne into Estella's hand, which she sipped with something like pleasure, feeling the bubbles tickle her nose and tease her face into a smile, pushing her earlier worries away. "Here's to you two," she said to Sam and Janie. "The best friends anyone could have. And to Mrs. Pardy." They all toasted and sipped and Estella added, "And to Lena. Who's been more generous than I can quite believe."

They drank that toast too and Sam smiled at her and brushed a stray curl from her cheek. "You should be proud of yourself too."

Before she could reply, the sound of footsteps made her turn and then flinch at the sight of Harry Kendall Thaw.

"Mr. Thaw," Mrs. Pardy said austerely. "What can I do for you?"

"I'm here for the show," he said.

Estella steeled herself. "I don't believe you're interested in women's fashion," she said.

"I'm not interested in women's fashion. But I'm very interested in you." He smiled mirthlessly at Estella, and Sam put a hand protectively on her back.

"This," said Estella, forcing out the words, "is Lena's—or was Lena's—guardian. Harry Thaw."

Janie eyed him the way only she could, with her typical Australian brashness, leaving no one in any doubt about what she thought. "You like to ogle the models do you?" she asked.

But Janie was the one left openmouthed when he replied, "I don't limit myself to ogling."

The silence that followed was gawping, like that of the clowns at an amusement park with their noiseless mouths stretched wide and waiting.

"Estella," Sam said, his hand still at her back now tight with discomfort.

"It's fine," she said stiffly. "Take a seat, Mr. Thaw." She had no other option. She didn't have the physical strength to throw him out and nor did she want a scene of that kind right before the showing. And perhaps he owned the house. She knew so little, nothing really about Lena, so she had no way to fight against him.

"Can you keep an eye on him?" she whispered to Sam as Harry settled himself in one of the best seats near the front.

"I will," Sam said grimly.

The first guests arrived so Estella had no more time to think of

Harry Thaw. And Lena's and Elizabeth's guest lists proved to be quite remarkable. The buyer from Lord & Taylor had come, as had the buyers from Macy's, Saks, Gimbels, and Best & Co. the *New York Times*, *The New Yorker*, *Vogue,* and *Mademoiselle* were all represented by editors or writers. Elizabeth Hawes swept in, kissed Estella's cheeks and introduced her to a friend she'd brought along, Leo Richier, who owned a cosmetics empire and whose eyes sparkled when Estella showed her the program and mentioned that the black gown she'd made for the finale would most definitely suit her.

There were also several other ladies Estella had never met, ladies who must be the arbiters of taste for Manhattan otherwise Lena and Elizabeth wouldn't have invited them. But they all looked so glamorous and rich that Estella knew immediately that they were wrong for her; they didn't need the kinds of clothes she'd made because they didn't work. They had drivers and spent the morning getting their nails done, giving the housekeeper orders for lunch, pouring a drink for their husband at dinner. Most of them stared at Estella and then moved off into hushed circles, glancing at her often, and it wasn't until she heard them mention Lena's name that she realized it was her appearance, her similarity to Lena, that was giving them all the entertainment they desired. She cursed herself for not having thought of that before; of course people would wonder. Just as she herself wondered.

But she greeted and talked and directed and handed out programs as if everything was fine and as if, the whole time, she couldn't feel Harry Thaw's eyes on her as he sat, not speaking to anyone, poised, watching. He was the subject of many a whispered conversation too, many a glance, many a subtly pointed finger. Estella had time to think, fleetingly, of how Lena must feel carrying his name, attracting the same kind of fascinated scrutiny wherever she went.

She was running through the program with Babe Paley from

Vogue, who was the only person in the room who didn't seem to think that Harry Thaw or Estella's resemblance to Lena was the main attraction, when she heard a voice say, "We meet again."

Estella looked up and into the face of a woman who did indeed look familiar and she struggled to place her for a moment, eyes widening when she finally did. Lena's party in this very house. The woman in the awful Chanel dress who Estella had told to come and see her one day. And now, here she was, and she didn't look as if she'd come to be pleased.

"I work for *Harper's Bazaar*," the woman said. "Diana Goldsmith. Wonderful to be officially introduced. I've never forgotten our little chat."

"Well, today you'll see what can be done without Paris copies," Estella said determinedly—she was already in desperate trouble so she might as well try to save her scruples—but Diana walked off and sat in a chair next to Harry Thaw as if she somehow knew that was the last place Estella wanted her. Estella tried in vain to catch Sam's eye to see if he could steer Diana away from Harry but one of the fashion writers was simpering at Sam and had his full attention.

It was time to begin, no matter that nothing was playing out the way she'd dreamed it would. She set the needle on the phonograph and asked everyone to take their chairs. Then she slipped to the dressing room to watch Janie and the other models glide out, admiring the way Janie could walk as if she was skating on ice, so elegantly lithe, clothes seeming to float on her skin as if they'd been put there by magic.

The show itself didn't take long, under an hour, enough time for twenty outfits to be paraded down a hall, into the drawing room for three turns, then back out again, with a quick change into the next model. Estella straightened sleeves, smoothed back pieces of hair, fastened buttons, ensured shoe buckles were tight. Every now and again she could hear a strange noise from within the parlor, like a cackle, the kind of cackle that narrator in *Rebecca* might hear in her Gothic mansion late at night but there was no reason why anyone would be laughing, so she tried to pretend it was a bird, or the phonograph record sticking.

When it was time for the last two outfits—evening dresses—Estella slunk back into the parlor while all eyes were on the gowns. The silhouettes were as different from the mid-nineteenth-century look that was so pervasive right then and also so infantilizing that Estella heard at least one or two exclamations.

The gowns were almost the exact opposite of the other: Janie, with her blond hair and extraordinary figure wore the black velvet, an off-the-shoulder dress with a strap circling the top of one of her upper arms, a cinched-in waist and full skirt that dropped away in thick, sensual gorgeousness to the floor. She wore black elbow-length gloves and she looked timeless, ageless, a beauty who could have stepped out of any portal of history. The other model wore a dress which was more of the time: Estella had taken on the trend for lamé and purchased a length of sparkling silver that tinkled through her fingers like pirates' treasure. She'd designed a plunging neckline that draped in Grecian folds over the breasts, was sashed at the waist, and then fell, without clinging—because clinging and lamé were never meant to be paired—in gentle folds to the ground.

The models looked spectacular and Estella felt herself smile for the first time. She looked over at Sam, who smiled back, and she mouthed, "Thank you," at him. She could never have done it without him, the lamé especially, which needed the best cutter in the world to make it behave the way she'd wanted it to.

But then she heard it again; that strange cackle, like a groan, almost spectral. It was coming from Harry Thaw. He was laughing—no, not laughing, moaning—with glee, with merriment utterly unfit for a parlor in Gramercy Park at a fashion showing. Estella knew it was the sound she'd heard earlier, that while she'd been putting months of work onto the backs of the models, Harry Thaw had been sitting in here convulsing, attracting the stares and whispers of everyone in the room. Diana from *Harper's Bazaar* stood up and walked out, a look of utter disgust on her face.

Estella's heart dropped so far down she thought she heard it hit the floor. Of all the contingencies she'd planned for—a sick model, a dress splitting its seam, nobody turning up—she'd never imagined a madman might turn her show into a farce.

She swept into the room and, in the loudest and most serene voice she could muster, said, "Thank you so much for joining us today to see the first collection of Stella Designs. I'd love to talk to you about how we might work together, so please stay and enjoy the champagne."

Throughout her short speech, Harry Thaw continued to howl, a hysterical wolf in the throes of full-moon madness. Immediately Estella had finished speaking, the ladies all stood and kissed various cheeks, declined offers of champagne and swept, en masse, toward the door, eager to be away from the brush of lunacy.

Harry Thaw stood too and, without a word to Estella—but what did he need to say? He'd well and truly won—he left too. Within five minutes of the show finishing it was just Estella, Sam, Janie, Mrs. Pardy, and Elizabeth Hawes standing speechless in the room with the scent of failure clinging to the open and undrunk bottles of champagne, the uneaten pastries, the bent and embarrassed heads of the peony flowers.

"You tried," Elizabeth said sympathetically.

"I've a good mind to hunt him down, seduce him and slice off a certain piece of his anatomy when he's amid the throes of passion," Janie said.

"I think even that's too good for him," Sam replied darkly.

"Dammit," was all Estella could say.

Never had anything hurt so much. The love and devotion she'd sewn into each gown now felt like a tawdry thing, a cheap gimmick. She'd squandered Janie's and Sam's and Mrs. P's and Elizabeth's time, she'd spent all her money; everything she'd feared before the show had now come true. It was just Estella and her rack of worthless dresses, destined never to be worn, as useless as all the hopes she'd clung to, alone in New York City.

She strode out of the parlor, down the hall, through the front door, across the street to Gramercy Park, the quiet haven that nobody could enter without a key. She unlocked the gate and made it to the nearest tree, where she felt her back slide down the trunk, splinters ripping through the fabric of her dress and tearing into her skin. But she didn't feel any physical pain because nothing could hurt more than her heart rending. She sat on the cold ground, rainwater soaking her dress, heedless, and she stayed there until the tears finally stopped and she was able to go back into the house and tell her friends that it was all over.

PART FOUR
FABIENNE

CHAPTER FOURTEEN

May 2015

Inside the Gramercy Park house, the replica of the house she'd just left in Paris, a similarity Estella had always explained away as the folly of relatives long past, Fabienne held out the birth certificate to her grandmother.

"Where did you get that?" Estella asked.

"In Dad's desk," Fabienne replied.

"So he knew." Mamie shrank back into the pillows, eyes closed, as if Fabienne had somehow diminished her. "All this time."

"Knew what? I don't understand why your name and Grandpa's name aren't on Dad's birth certificate."

Her grandmother didn't reply.

Fabienne's breath caught as she saw the evidence everywhere of, not just old age, but a body at the end of its time, a body not meant to last for so long, a mind that Fabienne had thought indefatigable, worn out by the loss of her husband, the loss of her son, the loss of her friends, clinging on to life for who knew what purpose?

"I don't want you to die," Fabienne said suddenly, picking up Mamie's hand and holding it to her lips. "You're too precious to lose."

"It's my time," Estella said. "I can feel it coming for me. I keep trying to ward it off but I know it's a battle I won't win. I want to last long enough, you see," her grandmother opened her eyes and fixed them on Fabienne, "to convince you to take over the company. It wouldn't suit anyone but you."

"Oh Mamie," Fabienne said. "There are so many better qualified people than me. People who wouldn't make a mess of it."

"Everyone messes up at least once. I did, when I first started. It was my biggest learning experience."

"You never told me about that," Fabienne said.

"Too many stories. Never enough time." Estella smiled fondly at Fabienne.

"Like this story." Fabienne pointed to the piece of paper.

"Like that one." Her grandmother's eyes closed again, and the silence felt as heavy as velvet, weighing them down, drawing them beneath its thick weave. "I will tell you that story, I promise. I need to work out how to tell it though." Her grandmother looked up at Fabienne abruptly. "I want to tell it right. To do justice to Lena. And to Alex."

Fabienne watched in horror as her grandmother's eyes flooded with tears, as her voice cracked on the name Alex, as a look so stark and sad passed over her face, a shadow of whatever had happened in the past suddenly finding form. "You don't have to…" she started to say, frightened, knowing that if she'd understood the pain she'd cause, she'd have thrown the birth certificate away.

"It's best if you start at the beginning," Estella interrupted. "In the bookcase over there, on the bottom shelf beside *Gone with the Wind*, there's a book. Take it and read it and then we'll talk some more."

After that, Fabienne had to return to the airport. She slept on the plane so she'd be at her best for her first day at her new job. She also managed a few hours in bed in her apartment but had to drag herself out when the alarm went off. From there, the day passed in a blur of coffee, of smiling determinedly through fatigue, of trying her best to demonstrate to everyone—especially her boss, Unity, who'd been appointed in the month while Fabienne was finishing up her old job and who had not, therefore, chosen Fabienne herself—that she had an expert knowledge of fashion history.

She left work in the evening and fell into bed as soon as she arrived home. All too soon it was two o'clock in the morning and she sighed as she checked the time on her phone again. She'd been lying awake for an hour, clearly still on New York time. She thought about checking her e-mails but knew that would only wake her up more, then realized she'd fallen asleep before calling Will to thank him for the flowers he'd sent to her at work. She propped her head up on her hand, found his name in her contacts list and before she could talk herself out of it, hit the FaceTime call button.

The screen flickered and there he was, in suit and tie and so gorgeous she wanted to rub her eyes to make sure she wasn't still asleep and dreaming him into being.

"Hey," he said, phone in hand, "let me shut the door."

Fabienne's heart spun a little at the thought that she was the kind of person with whom a closed-door conversation was best.

"That's better," he said, sitting down. "How are you? What time is it there?"

"Two in the morning," Fabienne admitted. "I wanted to thank you for the flowers but by the time I popped in to see my mother, then waited for it not to be too early to call you, I'd fallen asleep. But now I'm wide awake. So thank you. They're beautiful."

"Just like their owner then," he said softly and this time her heart turned a cartwheel. "Are you blushing?" he teased when she didn't reply.

"Are you flirting?" she replied, smiling.

"Yep," he said. "Shall I stop?"

"Hmmm," she said, pretending to think about it. "No, I quite like it."

"Besides," he said, raising his eyebrows, "you can hardly accuse me of flirting when you're calling me from your bed."

She laughed. "You're right. I'm too tired to get up and sit on the couch like a normal person to make a phone call but not tired enough to go to sleep."

"I don't mind," he said. "Receiving a call from you in your bed is definitely the best thing that's happened to me all day."

Now he really was flirting and Fabienne felt her whole body flush, the same way it had done when he'd kissed her and told her he'd like her to stay one more night in Paris.

"How was your first day?" he asked.

"Great," she said. "I need to plan next year's major exhibition so I've had to dive straight into things, which is the best way to learn. I'm thinking of doing an exhibition on adornment and decoration. Clothes with flowers, feathers, embroidery, lacework, leather work, sequins, and jewels. The old *métiers*. Estella started work in an atelier that made the flowers for haute-couture dresses and I've always loved the way she kept using flower-work on her clothes."

"You wouldn't want to be lent a late-nineteenth-century evening gown worn by Mrs. Cornelius Vanderbilt that has Tiffany diamonds sewn onto it would you?"

"Are you kidding?" gasped Fabienne. "There isn't really such a thing is there?"

"It's in the archives here," he said, smiling at her obvious excitement. "I came across it earlier in the year when I was looking at some of Tiffany's Gilded Age pieces. I'm sure it would like a trip to Australia. I'll see what I can do."

"That would be amazing. But only if you're sure you don't mind following up on it for me. You probably have better things to do."

"I don't."

A silence followed, a silence in which Fabienne yearned to reach out into the screen and run her hand across his jaw, to kiss him again. A silence in which she could feel his eyes trace her cheekbones, and then her lips.

"I don't expect anything," she blurted. "From you I mean." Oh God, why had she said that? But now that she'd started, she needed to clarify what she meant. "It's just that I know we're two people who met one weekend in Paris. That I live here and you live there. I know you'll want to get on with your life and I think that's right. That you should. And I'm not saying this because I don't like you or anything, I do really like you but I know it's kind of impossible…" *Shut up, Fabienne*, she told herself. She definitely should not call people at two in the morning. The filter part of her brain that would ordinarily stop her from embarrassing herself like this was obviously the only part of her that was napping.

"I feel like I should say the same. That I don't expect anything from you." Will rubbed his jaw and glanced to the side as he spoke, as if he was embarrassed too. "I don't want to stop you from doing anything you want to do just because of a weekend with me. But all the same I want to see you again, to find out where this might go. If you do." He looked back at his phone and Fabienne cursed the physical limitations of FaceTime.

"Don't you have a line of girls in Manhattan who you could actually see every evening rather than a girl who only comes to New York once a year?"

"I checked to see if it was possible to go to Sydney for a weekend. It's not."

"You checked?" Fabienne thought that was probably the most romantic thing anyone had ever done for her. "I have no leave owing to me because I've just started this job," she said.

"And I've been taking long weekends every month to escort Liss around the world so I haven't got any leave either."

"So it really would be once or twice a year."

"And phone calls in between."

"Is it enough?"

"No. But I'd rather have that than nothing."

"Will," Fabienne said softly. *You are the nicest man I've ever met*, she wanted to say. And what if he really was? What if she said no to him now, told him he should forget about her and she looked back at this moment later with the clear sight of experience and saw that this had been love and she'd been too polite to recognize it? "If you were here right now I'd kiss you," she ventured.

"If I was there right now I'd like to do more than kiss you."

Fabienne laughed. "You're flirting again. Which means I should go."

He smiled ruefully. "You're probably right. Sleep tight. And sweet dreams."

"They will be," Fabienne said. And they were.

The next day at work, Fabienne found an e-mail from Will when she arrived.

Dear Fabienne, it said. *I am pleased to confirm that, should you require a Poiret Gilded Age gown decorated with Tiffany diamonds for your forthcoming exhibition, Tiffany & Co. would be delighted to lend it to you. In order to make the arrangements, please contact our archivist, Tania Fowler, who has been copied into this e-mail. Regards, Will*

Immediately after was another e-mail: *I really wanted to say it was good to talk to you and that we should make a habit of it. I'll call you tonight. Will x*

Fabienne beamed, too much obviously, because one of her researchers, a young woman named Charlotte, who had a straight fringe, a sharp-cut bob, and intelligent glasses raised an eyebrow at her as she came into the room. "Someone looks happy," she said.

"I am," Fabienne said. "I've just secured us the loan of the only gown in the world that was made in a collaboration between Poiret and Tiffany and has real Tiffany diamonds on it. It'll be a fabulous centerpiece for our exhibition."

"That is a coup. How did you manage that?"

"I met the Tiffany Head of Design while I was in New York. He offered me the dress."

"Is he as gorgeous as everyone says he is? I saw a profile of him in *Vogue* a few months ago and almost resorted to being a teenager and pinning his picture on my bedroom wall."

Fabienne cursed her fair skin, which showed every blush. "I didn't really notice. I was talking to him about work," she lied.

Charlotte laughed. "Of course you were! I can tell by how red your cheeks are that you noticed nothing about him besides his professional qualifications."

Fabienne smiled. "Isn't it time for our meeting?" she asked. "Get everyone in here. We've got an exhibition to plan."

"Yes ma'am," Charlotte said teasingly. "And I promise not to ask you any more about it in front of everyone."

"Thank you."

The meeting went smoothly. Lots of ideas for the exhibition were put forward, the team went away with phone calls to make, and Fabienne and Charlotte spent the afternoon in the archives looking through some of the pieces they thought would work, imagining how they might fit together as an exhibition.

Later, when she returned to her apartment in Balmoral, which she'd rented in a hurry after she moved out of the place she'd shared with Jasper—but which she fortunately loved—she knew she had to make herself stay awake. Otherwise she'd fall straight to sleep and find herself staring at the ceiling at two in the morning again. So she made herself a coffee and took out the book her grandmother had asked her to read. Its cover was worn with age, the binding splintery, the cardboard swollen, the pages as fragile as a 200-year-old bridal veil. It bore the words: *The Memoirs of Evelyn Nesbit: The Girl on the Red Velvet Swing.*

Fabienne turned to the first page.

My name is Evelyn Nesbit and more words have been written about me than the Queen of England, such is my notoriety. You think you know me: the girl in the newspaper, the girl whose husband murdered her lover in plain sight at Madison Square Garden, the girl whose virtue was taken from her on the infamous red velvet swing. But you don't know me, not really. This is who I am.

Evelyn Nesbit was, without question, an ambitious girl. Why shouldn't she be? She had the kind of looks that would unroll the socks from any man's legs.

I discovered that when I was just twelve years old and my mother sent me to collect the unpaid rents from the men who took rooms in our boardinghouse. The men would invite me in, ask me to wait while they searched their wallets, and command me to come and take the money from their hands. They all thought they were so clever, toying with a twelve-year-old girl gifted with a face and figure that were too much for anyone to handle.

The artists soon discovered this too as I sat for them for hours and earned one whole dollar for doing nothing more than posing in a chair and having my image preserved in oil or watercolor or charcoal. Of course they soon wanted to know what I looked like unclothed and, as we needed the money, I acquiesced. As much as my mother denied it, the results are there for all to see in Church's and Beckwith's portraits of me.

Then there was modeling—is there a product that I haven't lent my face to? Toothpaste. Cold cream. Even becoming a Gibson Girl

*was nothing, a way to earn money, a way to grift some more, a way
to keep Mama in the manner to which she wanted to be accustomed.*

*It wasn't until the theater called that things began to happen. Although I suppose many of you would think I was so corrupted by
then that what came after could only be called my just deserts. But I
was still an innocent then. Until John. And Stanford. And Harry.*

Fabienne looked up from the page more confused than ever. Who
was Evelyn Nesbit and what the hell did she have to do with anything?
She switched on her iPad and typed the name into Google, where she
found a story of, as Evelyn's memoir suggested, murder, rape, abuse,
lunacy—a gothic story that had more in common with a penny dreadful than the questions she had asked of her grandmother. Then she
typed in the name Lena Thaw and found only the briefest of mentions
in Harry Thaw's Wikipedia entry.

"Excellent," Fabienne muttered as she read. "The person named on
my father's birth certificate was the ward of a lunatic murderer."

Then she tried Alex Montrose. Nothing besides the same description she'd read at the exhibition, which she read properly now, having
been too stunned at the time to finish it properly. She gleaned only that
Alex Montrose had originally worked for MI6 but had become a liaison between that division and MI9 when the former began to feel
that the latter's activities might encroach on its remit. He'd worked
mainly with the escape lines set up across France to spirit Allied forces,
especially escaped prisoners of war and airmen who'd crash landed,
back to England to reinforce the numbers of the undermanned RAF
and army. He'd ensured that the escape lines were staffed with loyal
helpers, organized money and supplies for all the *passeurs* and couriers
on the lines, interviewed those who successfully got away and gathered
intelligence information from them.

Fabienne's fingers twitched over the keyboard. *Lena Thaw*, she typed, *and Alex Montrose*. Nothing. Then: *Estella Bissette and Alex Montrose*. Almost nothing. Just a blurred picture at an American Fashion Critics' Awards night in 1943 showing them standing in a circle of people. That they'd chatted at a party gave her no good reason why his name should be on her father's birth certificate.

So she rang her mother, despite being almost certain she'd be no help. Her mother lived in a world peopled by her patients, not her family, even though she was seventy and could have given up working a long time ago. Fabienne had been a terrible accident; her parents had decided never to have children because they needed only one another. Her father had long since forgiven Fabienne for her sudden appearance into the world but Fabienne wasn't sure her mother ever had.

It took some time for the receptionist to locate her mother. Once she was on the line, Fabienne casually mentioned that she'd found some papers when she'd packed up her father's things, his birth certificate among them.

Her mother didn't react. She just said, tiredly, "Keep them if you want."

"Do you want them?" Fabienne asked.

"Your father is in my heart. I don't need papers to remember him by."

Which implied that Fabienne shouldn't either. In the great battle of who Xander loved more, Fabienne's mother needed always to win. Fabienne was usually happy to let her. "How are you?" Fabienne asked.

"As good as I'll ever be without your father around. Some days I think I should just take enough morphine to finish me off."

"Don't say that," Fabienne said sharply. "I'll come and see you tomorrow after work."

"Not tomorrow. You look too much like him. It hurts to see you."

Fabienne hung up the phone.

Was that really love, she wondered, not for the first time? The wish only to die when the other did because living became unbearable? Her grandmother had soldiered on for seventeen years after Fabienne's grandfather died. Did that mean she didn't love him? Or that she'd found a way to survive without him?

Fabienne sighed. So many questions. More riddles than answers. When she spoke to her grandmother on the weekend, she'd ask for more of the story.

Restless, she stood up and tried to tuck the book onto her shelf. There wasn't room. She pulled out the nearest stack of books and realized they were her old sketchpads, things she hadn't looked at for so long.

She sat on the floor, back leaning against the wall, and opened the cover of the first one, cringing when she saw the crude sketch of a dress marked out in pencil, blemished by the heavy-handed mark of an eraser. On the next page was a sketch she'd watercolored like Estella had taught her, more detailed, adequate, she supposed, but lacking any true flair. It was followed by drawings of figures with legs too short and faces too small, the unequal proportions ruining any dress she'd attempted to place on them. Once she'd finished criticizing every sketch in the first book, she opened the second, where the bodies were at last in proportion and she'd done away with heads as being irrelevant to the clothes anyhow. And then the third, where she was surprised by her own evolution as a sketcher, able to see how much she'd changed her ideas, her style, and even her ability, especially by the fourth book. One or two she even liked.

She jumped when her phone rang and snatched it up when she saw Will's name on the screen. "Hi there," she said, as the same uninhibited smile spread across her face the way it did every time she even thought of him.

"Hi there yourself," he said, smiling back.

"Where are you today?" she asked, noting the background wasn't the same as yesterday.

"Running late for work," he said. "I'm still at home even though it's already eight in the morning. Liss had a rough night and I was up with her so I overslept."

"Is she all right?"

The smile disappeared. "She's asleep now. Which is good."

"I didn't realize you lived with her."

"She's always had our parents' apartment. I have a place down in SoHo but I moved back in here this year to keep an eye on her."

When Melissa was told she was terminal. Fabienne heard the subtext and wished she could reach out and coax a gentle smile back onto his face, tell him that everything would be all right. But it wouldn't be. Her mother's work meant that she knew exactly what would happen to Melissa. That it would be painful and torturous for both the Ogilvies.

"The doctor told her yesterday that the tumor in her brain has grown." *That it's near the end*. Again Fabienne heard the words he couldn't say.

"Please give her my love," Fabienne said. "I have nothing else of any use, although that's probably useless too."

"She said you'd e-mailed her. It made her happy. So thank you. Anything that makes her happy is great." His hand rubbed his jaw in a gesture she was beginning to see was characteristic. "I'm being maudlin so let's talk about something else. What's all that stuff?" he asked, pointing at the books on Fabienne's lap.

"My old sketchbooks," she said, blushing a little at being caught in the past. "I haven't looked at them in years. They're as bad as I remember them," she said, smiling a little, wanting to mock her futile introspection.

"You should see my early sketchbooks. Full of garbage. But I always found that the only way to unearth the good stuff was to get all the garbage out first. I bet they're better than you think they are."

"Maybe," Fabienne shrugged, eager to shift the conversation. "Will you still take Melissa away at the end of the month?"

"If I book it, then there's hope," he said simply. "We're going to Hawaii. She needs sun and fresh air."

"Hawaii," Fabienne breathed. "That sounds great. I've never been."

"Melissa caught me checking out how long it takes to fly from Sydney to Hawaii," he said casually. "Apparently it's about nine hours. Doable for a weekend if you just take a day off."

"Are you asking me to come?" Fabienne asked incredulously.

"I am." He stood up and talked quickly as he paced. "I'll let you know where Liss and I are staying and you can stay at the same hotel if you want to but if you think you'd like some space, you don't have to. I always get Liss one of the best rooms because, you know, she might as well take the luxuries while she can and I just make sure I'm nearby on the same floor in case she needs me. But you can be anywhere you like; it's totally up to you."

Fabienne laughed. It was the first time she'd ever seen him flustered and God he was gorgeous. "I wonder if Hawaii would be more fun if I shared a room with someone?" she mused. "Since I haven't been there before, it might be nice to have someone very close by to show me around." She stopped speaking because he'd stopped walking and the way he was looking at her made her flush again, a flush that spread from the ache in her stomach, right through to her fingertips.

"Are you serious?" he asked quietly.

She nodded. "If you want to."

"Are you kidding? I've dreamed of you every night since Paris. Sharing a room with you in Hawaii would be…" He flashed a grin like the one that had been on her own face when she proposed the idea. "Something I can't wait for."

She suppressed an overwhelming urge to squeal. "It's only a month away. I'm sure it'll fly by."

"God I hope it does," he said.

CHAPTER FIFTEEN

Needless to say, Estella was delighted when Fabienne telephoned and told her she was going to Hawaii to meet Will. And she didn't mince words. "Good," Estella said. "Young people are so arrogant about time. You seem to think there's an infinite amount, an excess, that age will never come for you. It will. And you also think that love…" She stopped abruptly.

"What?" Fabienne asked.

There was a long pause. Fabienne almost asked again, but then she heard Estella sigh.

"You think that love is an emotion created and sold in movies," Estella said. "It's not. It's the most real thing of all. And it deserves more reverence than it gets. You have all the freedom in the world to love these days but nobody seems to grasp that. Generations past would shake their heads at you, not taking advantage of the things they couldn't. Loving can hurt spectacularly, but it can also heal. So I hope you're sharing a room with him."

"Mamie!"

Estella laughed and Fabienne couldn't help laughing too. How many ninety-seven-year-old women would say that to their granddaughters?

"I had the nurse find me a picture of him on the internet," Estella said and Fabienne knew her eyes were twinkling with mischief. "He's very handsome. I certainly wouldn't book my own room if I was going to Hawaii with him."

"Okay, I'm sharing his room. That's enough about me and Will." Fabienne paused, not wanting to spoil the moment, but knowing she had to say something. "I started reading Evelyn Nesbit's memoir."

"And I suppose you have more questions than ever?" The mischief was gone from Estella's voice.

"I do."

"Evelyn Nesbit," Estella began, then stopped. She sighed. "I suppose there's no way to say it that won't be surprising. Evelyn Nesbit and John Barrymore are my grandparents."

"Your grandparents?" Fabienne repeated, trying to work out how on earth a showgirl and an actor, both from America, could possibly be Estella's grandparents.

"They were in love, before Evelyn was taken under the abhorrent wings of Stanford White and then Harry Thaw. She fell pregnant to John twice: the first time she had an abortion, disguised as an appendectomy. It made her so ill that, the second time, she had the baby in France, away from newspapers and prying eyes. She gave the baby, my mother, to the nuns to raise. The house on the Rue de Sévigné was Evelyn's; she bought it with the money men bestowed on her. It was her love nest, the place where she and John were at their happiest. Until Evelyn's mother decided that John's pockets were too empty and, with Stanford White's persuasion, that she could sell her daughter to a higher bidder. Evelyn gifted the house to my mother but something happened to her there and she could never live in it. I thought I could break the curse but…" Estella stopped.

"I don't even know what to say," Fabienne stuttered. "I had no idea why you gave me the memoir to read but I certainly wasn't expecting that. I suppose I should be grateful, given everything it says about Harry Thaw, that he isn't your grandfather."

A long silence extended through the phone, Fabienne's mind working to understand the fact that her great-great-grandmother was someone so notorious, that her great-grandmother had been abandoned to be raised by nuns and that, out of it all, had come Estella. That if the house in Paris had been Evelyn's, who had built the replica in which Estella had always lived in Manhattan? And none of it explained the names on her father's birth certificate.

"Are you all right?" Fabienne suddenly asked, aware that Estella hadn't spoken for some time.

"Just a little tired," her grandmother said. "Anyway, that's where the story starts. If Evelyn and John hadn't happened, then…" Estella paused. "I'll tell you more of the story when you're back from Hawaii. Hopefully you'll be in so blissful a mood that whatever I have to say won't upset you too much."

"Why would it upset me?" Fabienne asked warily. "And what does any of that have to do with Dad?"

Her grandmother yawned. "As I said, I'll explain everything after your romantic rendezvous. I promise."

Then she hung up the phone and that was that.

Fabienne's bags were packed, her body waxed and fake-tanned, and her bikini purchased as the taxi drove to the airport, so slowly that Fabienne wanted to leap into the front seat and drive herself. Instead she reminded herself that it didn't matter how slowly he drove, the plane would still take off at the same time and it would still be about twelve hours until she saw Will and Melissa again. Until she was able to close a door behind her and Will and kiss him. She forced herself to look out of the window and at the black walls of the tunnel. Fantasies in the back of a cab were not helpful.

She thought instead of Melissa; Will had wondered if it would be the last trip he'd be able to take her on, had said that the last month had been hard and she knew in his understatement lay a truth that would be difficult to face when she saw Melissa again. They'd been corresponding by text and e-mail most days and it broke Fabienne's heart to see what a spirited woman Melissa was, to think of the life she could have had, to think of what it would do to Will when her body shut down.

Her phone rang, surprising her when she saw Estella's number on the screen. "Mamie?" she said.

"Sorry, Fabienne, it's Kate."

Mamie's nurse. Fabienne's heart contracted. "What is it?" she asked.

"Estella's just been taken to the hospital. When I came in this morning she was unresponsive. I think she may have had a stroke."

"Oh no!" Fabienne squeezed her eyes shut. "I'm coming. I'm on my way to the airport now in fact. I'll change my flight and I'll be there as soon as I can. Is she all right?" *Please God let her be all right. I know she's old but you don't need her. You have enough people. You have my father. You're taking Melissa. Leave my grandmother alone.*

"She's alive," Kate said simply.

She's alive. Fabienne would focus on that, would pray to God that Estella hung on long enough for Fabienne to get there.

She rang the airline and changed her flight. Then she called Unity at work and told her she needed a few more days off. Unity wasn't pleased but Fabienne assured her that she'd work while she was away, that she'd be in e-mail and phone contact, that it'd be just like she was still there. She could tell Unity didn't believe her but Fabienne didn't care. She wasn't going to leave her grandmother in a hospital on the other side of the world all by herself.

She checked her watch. Will and Melissa would be in the air. She texted them both, explaining what had happened and apologized. To Will she said, *I'm so, so sorry. I wanted this weekend so much. I hope that we can make it work another time. I really do.* Then she hesitated and wrote, *Love Fabienne.*

Fabienne sobbed as she sat by Estella's bed, holding her hand and doing all of the other pointless things that people did at hospital bedsides, including telling her grandmother, like she'd told her father only two months ago, that she wasn't allowed to die. Even as she'd said it to her father, she'd known she couldn't make it true, that nobody would ever recover from the pallor of his skin. And now her grandmother looked the same as he had, or worse even, because her body was already so desiccated.

The doctors told her that her grandmother had had a stroke. They would have to wait and see how much damage it had done. She would be kept sedated for another twenty-four hours. Fabienne should come back then.

What if she dies while I'm not here? Fabienne wanted to ask. But after much persuasion from the nurses, and their reassurance that they'd call if there was even the slightest change, Fabienne dragged herself back to her grandmother's house to shower, put on fresh clothes and eat. She changed the sheets on her grandmother's bed, bought peonies for a vase by the bedside table, plumped the pillows and made the room look so inviting that Estella would have no choice but to return.

Then she read the message Will had left: *I'm sorry too. I hope your grandmother is doing okay. Call me if you can. Love Will.*

Love Will. Yesterday the words would have been enough for her to laugh with delight. Today they hurt. Love and hurt, hurt and love. The two seemed to go together far too well. What was the good in loving Will when she lived so far away? What was the good in loving her grandmother if it hurt this much to face the thought of losing her?

Not long after Fabienne returned to the hospital, a nurse touched her shoulder. "Here are your grandmother's things."

Fabienne opened the bag. Estella's nightgown sat neatly folded at the bottom. On top was her watch and the Tiffany key Fabienne's grandfather had given Estella on her seventieth birthday, which she'd always worn around her neck. But there was also another chain, with a medallion or a pendant attached to it. Fabienne recalled always seeing a glimpse of another silver chain glinting beneath Estella's collar and she reached into the bag for it. The medallion was made of silver, crudely carved with three witches on broomsticks. Fabienne turned it over. There was nothing written on the back. It was the strangest thing. Not lovely at all, and clearly of no monetary value, unlike the diamond-studded Tiffany key it had sat beside. Why would her grandmother have worn it every day of her life?

A memory stabbed through the confusion. She'd seen a cloth patch bearing those same witches at the exhibition at the Musée de l'Armée in Paris. What had the plaque beside it said? She closed her eyes, straining to remember something she'd paid little attention to at the time.

Then Estella stirred. Her hand clutched Fabienne's. Her eyes jerked open, not delicately flickering, not gradually moving from death to life.

"Mamie!" Fabienne moved to press the buzzer to summon the doctor.

Her grandmother shook her head. "Love," she whispered.

"You don't need to talk," Fabienne said. "Let me talk."

"So much to say."

And so little time. The unspoken words echoed in the room.

"Two kinds of love," Estella said, her voice almost transparent in its thinness. Fabienne couldn't quite make out the rest of what she said; it sounded like, "…had both…lucky…"

"Grandpa loved you so much," Fabienne said, remembering the way Mamie had looked at Fabienne's grandfather when he lay dying.

Fabienne had seen her heart breaking, not in shards, not piece by piece, but in one long rent, too large to ever stitch back together.

Estella smiled, her words stronger now, rushing over Fabienne who tried to shape them into some kind of sense. "Love like a toile," Estella said. "The pattern on which one's whole life is shaped. But nobody sees the toile, or knows it ever existed. Nobody understands that, without it, nothing can be fashioned."

"Mamie…" Fabienne began but her grandmother spoke again.

"And love like a spool of thread, running on, strong enough to pull everything together." Estella studied Fabienne. "You don't understand, do you?"

"I'm not sure," Fabienne said slowly. She opened her hand, in which the medallion lay. "What is this?"

Estella reached out for it and closed her hand tightly around it. "Don't wait for anything, Fabienne. It all goes so fast." Then Estella fell asleep, hand embracing the silver pendant, face a tracery of longing.

CHAPTER SIXTEEN

Hours later—Fabienne checked her watch and couldn't believe that she'd been sitting for eight hours by the bedside—her grandmother stirred again. She opened her mouth. A noise came out, like a moan, which seemed to surprise her grandmother as much as it surprised Fabienne.

"Have some water," Fabienne said, raising the end of the bed a little and passing Estella a glass with a straw. Her grandmother sipped. Then she moved her mouth again and it issued another groan, a malformed word.

"I'm getting the doctor," Fabienne said, grabbing the call button.

Estella gripped Fabienne's arm. Her eyes were huge, pleading, struggling to make Fabienne comprehend the incomprehensible. Fabienne felt her stomach turn over, nausea rising into her throat at her inability to soothe, at her fear of exactly what her grandmother's lack of speech implied.

The nurse arrived and Fabienne was bundled out of the room, told it would be at least a couple of hours before they'd finished the tests they needed to do. She went to the cafeteria and bought a tea, unable to forget that awful expression on her grandmother's face, like a child without the language to explain to its mother that a dragon lay just behind, breathing fire down their necks. The over-brewed tea made her nausea worse and she threw it in the rubbish bin. Through the door, she saw a familiar head of dark hair, a chin more stubbled than the last time her cheek had brushed against it, a flash of blue eyes.

"I hope you don't mind me coming to see you," Will said.

Rather than answer she wrapped her arms around him. She tried not to cry, blinked her eyes open and shut, open and shut, cheek pressed into his chest, one of his hands threaded into her black hair, holding her close to him. And then, because it would be so good to think about somebody else for just a moment she whispered, "How's Melissa?"

"Tired. More tired than she should be."

It was her turn now to run her hand up behind his neck, to bring his head down to rest against her forehead, to hold him so hard that she hoped he would know she understood.

"Talk to me about something normal?" she said when she at last drew back.

"Something normal." He thought for a moment. "Sometimes I think I forget what normal is," he admitted. "Do you have time to sit down?"

Fabienne nodded and they found the least sticky of the cafeteria tables and sat on plastic chairs with cups of a questionable substance masquerading as coffee, which Fabienne made herself drink.

"I'm supposed to be designing the new collection," Will said once they'd settled. "Tiffany produces a Blue Book each year; people covet it. They save them and old copies sell for thousands on eBay. The new collection is showcased in the book; it's a big deal. But for the first time in my life I don't have an idea to design the collection around. Is that normal enough? Or still too depressing?"

Fabienne gave a small smile. "I'd say that's normal enough. It's the one good thing about curating rather than designing; I only need one idea to focus each exhibition. It's not quite as tricky as coming up with an idea for an entire collection of jewelry that the whole world is waiting for." She frowned. "Wow, I just totally increased the pressure for you, didn't I? Some help I am."

Will smiled too, and reached out for her hand across the table. "You didn't. Because it's not the pressure of expectation that's bothering me, I don't think. It's just hard to come up with ideas for beautiful pieces of jewelry when Liss is so sick."

"What normally inspires you?" Fabienne asked, pushing doggedly on with the conversation so that one word—*sick*—wouldn't set the fear in her stomach twisting and turning again at the thought of what the doctors might be discovering as they examined her grandmother.

"It's hard to say. Usually just something I see or hear. It might be anything from a painting to a song to a leaf, even." He sighed. "I'm sure something will come eventually. It kind of has to. But I also know ideas don't like being forced."

Fabienne sipped her coffee, grimaced, and pushed it away. "No, they don't. I always used people as my inspiration when I sketched. I'd draw a dress that I thought, in my immature teenage mind, would be perfect for Estella, or for her best friend, Janie, or someone else I loved. God, if they'd ever seen the sketches and known I'd designed it for them, they'd probably have been horrified." She'd managed a smile when she'd begun to speak but the minute she said Estella's name, it quickly turned watery and now she felt herself blinking back the fresh rush of tears.

Will slipped his finger under her chin and kissed her softly. "I bet they would have been honored." He studied her. "And I think you've just given me an idea."

"Really?"

"Really."

"Well, at least this day has one good thing in it." She rested her head on his shoulder, feeling his hand stroke the nape of her neck in a way that, momentarily, made her feel a little better.

"I'm glad I came to see you," he whispered against her ear.

"Me too," said Fabienne. "Me too."

"She's had another stroke," the doctor said to Fabienne later. "And now she has aphasia. Which means the part of her brain that controls speech is damaged. We can't tell yet whether it's permanent."

Now there really were no words. Just her grandmother's eyes on her, pleading with her to fix it, to make it better, to let her say all the things she hadn't yet said. After an hour or so of pointing and gesticulating and making that awful moan, Mamie began to cry and Fabienne did too.

"I'm so sorry," Fabienne whispered as she stroked the fine strands of her grandmother's once abundantly beautiful black hair.

It took a long time to calm Estella down. When at last the tears had dried, Estella's hands reached up to her neck, eyes growing large, tears threatening once more when she felt nothing there.

"It's here," Fabienne said, removing both the key and the medallion from her handbag, unsure which one Estella wanted.

Estella clutched the medallion and then motioned at Fabienne's handbag as if urging her to take out something else. Fabienne held it open for Estella, who rummaged through, pulling out every piece of paper until she eventually found Fabienne's father's birth certificate.

Estella unfolded the paper. Then she pointed to the medallion and her finger moved from it to Alex Montrose's name. Back and forth, each time becoming more emphatic.

"Is it his medallion?" Fabienne asked, warily.

Estella nodded, something more than frustration showing in her eyes for the first time all afternoon.

"Why do you have it?" Fabienne asked. "And why have you kept it for so long? Who is he? And Lena, who is she?" Now Fabienne's eyes blazed with frustration. Of course Mamie couldn't answer any of the questions. That was the point. They'd waited too long and now nobody might ever know.

Estella closed her eyes and within seconds was asleep, the effort and vexations of the day having worn her out utterly.

Fabienne stared at the birth certificate, stared at the medallion, mind replaying her grandmother's words about love: that she'd had two kinds. Fabienne had supposed she'd meant some kind of youthful infatuation but if she was talking about it now, when she was being robbed of life, for it to have been an infatuation didn't make sense. And none of it explained why Estella's name, why Fabienne's grandfather's name, weren't on her father's birth certificate. What if it was true? That Estella wasn't Xander's mother? Then, despite the fact that they both had black hair, Fabienne wasn't related to Estella at all. Which was a thought too awful to contemplate.

Days passed. Through each of them, Fabienne sat by her grandmother's bed, texting Will and Melissa or talking to them on the phone, and reading aloud to her grandmother. Eventually the doctor said she could take Estella home if she wanted to. If she felt it would be a more comfortable place for Estella...

To die.

And so Fabienne rode in the ambulance back to the house in Gramercy Park. She made sure her grandmother was comfortably settled into bed. She moved her grandfather's picture close by, propping against it the medallion her grandmother seemed to treasure.

Estella had been sedated for the move and didn't stir. The nurse said she'd be unlikely to wake until morning. Which is how Fabienne found herself downstairs, sketching clothes, finding solace in drawing pencil lines onto paper, letting the confusion of her thoughts take shape in the lines of dresses. They weren't very good, but she didn't care. It was meditative, the movement of pencil over paper, the appearance of something she hadn't intended to draw forming in front of her through her subconscious.

She drew for hours, into the night, stopping for nothing. She even took out her grandmother's watercolors and painted each one, messing up the first few as she was so out of practice, but gradually recalling how to work with paint and water to transform the sketches into dresses with movement and dimension.

At around two in the morning, her hand stilled. Her head shot up. Time unpleated before her, opening up a gap into the past and she could feel something falling into it, leaving the present and going back, far away, to a time Fabienne could never reach.

She raced up the stairs to her grandmother's room. "No, no, no!" she cried as she ran over to the bed.

One entire world had ended. Not just a life. A world of bravery and courage and things that mattered.

PART FIVE
ESTELLA

CHAPTER SEVENTEEN

July 1941

For weeks after the disastrous showing, Estella got up every morning and went to work at André Studios. She sketched copies without comment, dutifully and well, doing only as she was asked. She read the first of the newspaper reports of the showing, which were no more than gossip columns speculating on her relationship to Lena and which mentioned, right at the end, that she made clothes. She stopped reading them after that. She did not sketch anything of her own. She did not sew. At nighttime she dreamed because that was the best place to have fantasies, in the dark where nobody could see them.

She returned the first of Elizabeth Hawes's telephone calls and thanked her for her assistance, apologized for letting her down and said, "I think you were right. That all the beautiful clothes are made in the houses of the French couturiers and all women want them."

"I wrote that two years ago," Elizabeth said bluntly. "Things are changing and you know it."

"Yes," Estella said. "Things are changing. I've learned not to be so overconfident. That unthinking optimism only turns out badly."

And so she existed in the life she'd dreaded. Without her mother. In a strange land. Doing a job she detested. But she'd spent all her money, and scattered all her contacts with Harry Thaw's maniacal giggles.

What she did have, she could count on one hand: a cot bed in a room at the Barbizon; Janie's and Sam's friendship, which seemed unshakable despite everything; twenty clothing samples that she couldn't bear to look at. What she didn't have was a list far too long for anyone's hand: her own atelier, her own designs sold in stores, a reason to do more than survive, a safe homeland, a mother who hadn't lied.

In spite of his gravest misgivings and only after trying everything else he could think of, Alex found that he needed Estella's help. One night in late July, after he'd returned to New York, he told Lena what he hoped to do and she nodded. A small gesture, bleak, hopeless, but that was Lena. A person wafting through life with no expectation of happiness or pleasure. Which was why he also had to help both Lena and Estella sort out their own mess.

Luckily for him, it turned out that Estella's friend Janie was dating a big-shot banker who was having a society party the following night to which Lena had been invited. Janie would be there with her friends—Estella and that man, Sam, who Alex still hadn't been able to properly place in Estella's life.

"You can come as my date," Lena said and he didn't know if she was being bitter or pragmatic.

He chose to believe the latter and, when he collected her the following evening, she looked as stunning as ever in a gown made for her: silvery fabric that showed off her cleavage and a strand of spectacular pearls around her neck that he knew would never get the same attention that the body they adorned would.

"You look incredible," he said as he kissed her cheek. He felt her shift a little so the kiss fell on the corner of her mouth.

I'm sorry, Lena, he wanted to say but then Lena smiled and said, indicating the dress, "It's one of Estella's. She made it for me."

"She's very good."

"She is," Lena replied, voice inscrutable.

When they arrived at the house on the Upper West Side, Alex saw Estella as soon as he entered the ballroom; she wore a black velvet dress the same color as her hair and she looked like midnight come to life. The gown had a strap that sat just below one shoulder; the other shoulder was bare and her creamy white skin beckoned a hand to run down the line of her neck. He breathed in sharply and Lena noticed.

"She looks beautiful," Lena said.

"Like you," he replied.

Lena moved away, drawn into a crowd of people who kept her like a pet for her infamy, just as they kept debauched Hollywood stars and Broadway showgirls for the frisson. He heard the rustle of gossip as fingers pointed subtly at Estella and at Lena, wondering about the likeness, eager for the latest installment in the legend of Lena's notorious life. He frowned, seeing Lena's back straighten into a false confidence that belied the way he knew she would feel about the whispers. At the same time as he made up his mind to join her—to shield her from the murmurings—she shook her head at him, which he should have expected. Lena always liked to fight her own battles.

So Alex turned his attention back to Estella, hoping she wasn't aware she was the subject of rumor and speculation too. He watched her sip champagne and pretend to listen to a man who was flirting with her as appallingly as a schoolboy. Her eyes roamed the room and settled upon something that seemed to please her because she smiled a little and lifted one eyebrow and Alex could see that Sam was the recipient of those facial antics.

Estella made as if to move away and the callow youth bellowed loudly and enthusiastically at her, "Come find me when you finish powdering your nose."

"She's above your pay-grade," Alex muttered as he strode over, lighting a cigarette and drawing on it deeply before taking his place next to her at the bar. "Sidecar?" he asked and she nodded.

"You've reappeared from wherever you vanished to. And Lena too, I see," Estella said.

"Where's Lena been?" he asked.

"How should I know?"

The barman passed them their drinks.

"You look…" He stopped. There wasn't a word in the entire English language that would do. "*Exquise*," he finished in French, which somehow seemed a closer approximation to what he meant.

"*Merci*."

"Do you miss it?" he asked abruptly. "Speaking French? Being French?"

"I'm still French, aren't I?" she asked lightly but her eyes had darkened from dusk to almost night.

"Do you still feel French here in Manhattan?"

"I don't know what I feel," she said and the pining in her voice, for what he didn't know—wondered even if she knew—made his next words come out in entirely the wrong way and in entirely the wrong moment.

"Here," he said, passing her a paper, a facsimile of one he'd found in Paris. The *matrice cadastrale*, or land ownership document; it showed that Evelyn Nesbit had sold the house on the Rue de Sévigné to Estella's mother for the queenly sum of just one franc.

Estella's face turned bloodless. She looked at him as if he was the most hateful man in the world and stalked off, out the front door.

He caught up to her on West 77th and let her walk on for a minute to let off some of the steam he'd once again caused.

"Can we stop?" he asked, but she didn't reply.

"Please?" he put a hand on her arm which was a huge mistake because it was like putting his finger into a blazing fire. That even touching the skin of her upper arm could make him feel that way was shocking. But she stopped walking and he schooled himself to be composed, pretended she had a gun in her hand and it was his job just to get out of there with his wits, if not his life.

"Why are you doing this?" she whispered and her voice held so much pain that it even made his stony heart feel something.

So that you don't turn out like me and Lena: ruined people, skeletons lacking heart and soul. "For Lena," he said instead.

"You do love her?" she asked.

He nodded, because he did, just not in the way she thought. And if pretending to love Lena was what it took to get her to listen, that's what he'd do.

"Where did you get that?" she asked quietly, glancing at his pocket as if it contained something dangerous and explosive which of course it did.

"Can we go somewhere and talk?" he asked. "Standing on street corners is all very well but not for this conversation."

Estella lifted her head. "Your house," she said, laying down a challenge. "I'll talk to you at your house."

The pause that followed stretched on and on. She somehow always managed to pick the one thing to say that made him acutely uncomfortable, giving him no choice but to forestall her, thus coming off as even more hateful than she already thought he was.

She turned away when he didn't answer. "I knew it," she said. "You poke around in my life but keep yours as well protected as Wolf's Lair."

He forced himself to say his next words because she was right and they both knew it. "Okay," he called after her. "I'll take you to my house. It's quite a drive."

"It's only nine o'clock. I'm sure we have time," she said in that same provoking voice.

He led her back to his car and drove northward, out of the city. She didn't say anything, just watched Manhattan slip past, and then the green of upstate, the flow of the Hudson, the slow unrolling of city into paradise. Not that much of it could be seen in the dark but flashes of light every now and again showed just enough to make it clear that they were encroaching on a pastoral scene.

"What did Harry Thaw do to Lena?" she asked suddenly.

"I think you should ask Lena that," he said. "It's her story to tell. Or not."

She was quiet again and he was glad she didn't push. But her next question was, "What's your story then?"

"I told you," he said glibly. "Son of a…"

"Diplomat. Yes, I know what you told me. But there's a hell of a lot more to that story than what you said. I want to hear it."

She folded her arms determinedly across her chest and looked at him with those dazzling eyes, brilliantly silver. Ordinarily if he was in a car like this with a woman like that he'd be working out a way— no, he'd have already found a way—to talk her out of her dress. He frowned. Perhaps he ought to tell her some of what she wanted to know. At least it would send his thoughts along a more decorous line.

"My father was a diplomat," he began and held up one hand at her impatient click of the tongue. "If you want me to tell you, I'm going to do it my way."

She nodded, granting him permission to continue.

And then it came out, so much more truth than he'd ever told anyone. "He pimped me out, for want of a better expression," Alex said flatly, eyes fixed on the road ahead, not wanting to see her face as he spoke. "I was a gun for hire for every crook, thief, rogue, and swindler in Rome, Paris, Hong Kong, Shanghai, and Berlin from the time I was twelve to the time I was seventeen. We were moved every year because the British government knew something was rotten but all they could pin on my father was the smell, not the carcass. I ran drugs, I ran guns, I ran government secrets: everything illicit you've ever heard of and more."

Estella shifted in her seat. "That's not what I was expecting you to say," she said, somewhat apologetically. "I thought it would be a story of…" She hesitated.

"Boy born into money and prestige behaving badly?" he suggested. "It is, in a way."

"Just not quite the way I'd thought."

"Shall I stop?"

"No. Tell me why you went along with it. You're not the sort of person who seems easily pushed around, even as a boy."

If he'd been hoping for a reprieve, he wasn't getting one. "Because of my mother." He stopped then, the words cutting too close to agony, to feelings he'd become so expert at excising from his heart. But then, unbelievably, beneath Estella's now gentle gaze, he kept talking.

"She had tuberculosis," he said. "Had been unwell for years. She was in pain and my father didn't care but I did and he knew it. He told me he wouldn't buy her the medicine she needed, wouldn't pay for the doctors, unless I helped him out with his sidelines. So every time I passed on information or jewels or weapons or drugs I told myself I'd just bought my mother another day of care."

"I'm sorry," Estella whispered, stretching out her fingers toward him and then withdrawing them. "You're right. It's none of my business."

He was able to let it go because they'd finally arrived at his home in the Hudson Valley, just past Sleepy Hollow, a house he'd bought for himself three years earlier, and where he'd barely lived for more than three months across those three years, a place nobody knew about. Until now.

He pulled up at the front door and climbed out, walking around to open her door but she'd already done it, her heels sinking into the gravel, her mouth dropping open at the sight of the house, at the points of light from the closest town shimmering on the satin ribbon of the river that lay far down below. The classic facade before them, fashioned from the region's cream-colored fieldstone, was suddenly lit up and Alex knew the housekeeper must have heard them and turned on the lights.

Estella swore softly in French. "It's very impressive. No, it's beautiful."

And it was, he knew. It was why he'd bought it. A place that felt like a castle in the air, a sanctuary where the real world had not yet found a way in.

"It's like looking at a gown fashioned by a master," she said, eyes traveling over the house, "where every stitch, every pleat, every fold has been made with the kind of devotion I feel when I sit down to make a dress." She blushed. "I'm raving. Sorry."

"That's how I feel too. But less poetically."

He smiled at her and, for only the second time since he'd met her, she smiled back and he felt that maybe it would all work out. That he could help her and Lena find out what bound them, that it would unshackle Lena—who was the innocent victim of a cruel man just like his mother had been. That Lena might find the love she craved with Estella, who must surely be Lena's sister.

Then the front door opened and the housekeeper, the plump and always smiling Mrs. Gilbert, waddled down the stairs and kissed his cheek.

"One day, you'll give me some notice that you're coming," she said, scolding him in a way that nobody ever did. "How long are you here for this time?" she asked.

"Just the night, I think?" He looked questioningly at Estella who frowned. He realized his mistake and added, hastily, "This is Miss

Estella Bissette. She needs her own room made up. Perhaps in the east wing." He added, so that Estella perfectly understood his intentions, "My room is on the opposite side of the house."

"Good," Estella said and all the camaraderie of before dissolved like a Nazi politician's promise.

"Come with me, dearie," Mrs. Gilbert said, beckoning Estella through. "I'll show you where you can freshen up and I'll put out some dinner for you in the sitting room."

"Thank you," Alex said, letting his housekeeper take Estella away, making sure they were well upstairs before he made his way to his own room. Once there, he splashed his face with water, feeling the scrape of stubble on his hand, took off his bow tie, undid the top button on his shirt, contemplated changing into something more appropriate for a late dinner and then thought, what the hell. It wasn't as if he was trying to make any kind of impression on Estella. Which was just as well because he could see, in the mirror, that he looked tired, as if the strain of his head injury and the following months of dodging Germans and bedding down an escape line for evading airmen in France had finally, just as he was able to unwind on a week's leave, caught up with him.

He threw his jacket onto the bed, rolled up his sleeves and readied himself to face whichever version of Estella he might find downstairs. She wasn't there when he arrived, which gave him a chance to pour the whiskey and make sure Mrs. Gilbert had lit the fire and set the food out on a low table by the sofa.

Then she swept into the room in that way she had, but didn't realize. He wondered if she'd picked it up from the models she'd sketched—as if she was making a grand entrance. She was still wearing the amazing gown, but no other adornment or jewelry because she had no need of it, just black hair, gray eyes, black dress.

"Hungry?" he asked, indicating the food.

"Yes," she said and piled her plate high, sitting down on the floor, back against the sofa, her dress pooling around her like the night sky grounded at last.

He helped himself to a plateful too and sat in a chair before the fire.

They ate quietly for a few minutes. "You look tired," she said.

"I am." He sipped the whiskey, letting the familiar burn tease his throat, relax him at last.

"Were you in France?" she asked.

He nodded.

"What was it like?"

He knew she'd be able to tell if he lied. "In some ways it was like nothing had happened," he said. "In other ways, it was…" He paused. "Worse than anything I've ever seen."

"How?"

"The Germans are making life very difficult for anyone they think is working against them. The communists especially. And those who haven't done anything other than be born Jewish. Every time anyone acts against the Germans, they shoot French hostages in retaliation. How can anyone resist when they know one single act of protest costs a hundred lives? But, unbelievably, the parties still happen and the women still dance and the men still drink and unless you stand quietly in a room, you almost can't feel the terror. But it's there on every street corner."

"Is my mother…" Her voice was so low he almost couldn't hear it.

The question he'd been dreading; all he had were reports from the field but sometimes they were wrong. He hoped, this time, they were right. "I understand she's alive. I can't go to her apartment to check on her. Any link to me could easily put her in danger."

"How did you get the *matrice cadastrale* then?"

"From the *mairie*."

"You think Evelyn and Harry are my parents. Mine and Lena's." Her voice was barely audible.

"God no!" He hurried to reassure her. "They'd divorced by the time you were born. By all accounts, Evelyn hated Harry by then."

The fire crackled into the silence.

"Estella." It was the first time he'd said her name aloud and the sound of it on his tongue was a provocative thing. "All I know is that you must be Lena's sister. Evelyn Nesbit sold your mother a mansion, albeit crumbling, for just one franc. And Lena, a woman who looks just like you, was raised by Harry, Evelyn's ex-husband. It's too much for coincidence. But it doesn't make Evelyn and Harry your parents."

"You forgot to mention that Lena's house is the double of the one in Paris if you wanted any more evidence with which to damn my mother and whatever she did twenty-four years ago."

Her tone was that of someone who'd had everything they'd ever known stolen away, like his had been the day he found out his mother was dying. How could anyone's mother ever die, he'd wondered back then? Mothers were the gold light in a gray day, the gentle hum on an otherwise too-silent night, the scent of violets when all else was rank.

"I'm not damning your mother," he said, as gently as he could. "But with all of those connections…"

"We must be twins. But how? Who's my father? And is my mother really my mother?" Her voice broke on the final sentence and then she pressed her lips closed and he knew she didn't want to cry in front of him.

Alex sat down on the floor, leaning his back against the table so that he was facing her, rather than beside her.

"I don't know," he said. And then, "You can live with secrets if you have to. I've been doing it all my life."

She stared at the fire, her eyes too shiny to be holding anything other than tears. "What happened?" she asked abruptly.

And he knew what she was asking: what happened to *your* mother? There were so few people he'd told this story to, beyond his boss when he was recruited into MI6, before he moved across to MI9; talking about oneself was generally a waste of time. You discovered more when you let others do the talking.

"She died on my seventeenth birthday," he said, using every bit of his training to keep the words smooth, emotionless, but that only made them sound all the starker. "I stole the cash I was supposed to take back to my father that night after I'd run an opium exchange and I hid in Hong Kong for two weeks. Then I stowed away on a ship which landed in New York and I was taken to Ellis Island. I had British diplomatic papers so they called the British Consul. They did some digging, found out who my father was and then they knew they had me. They were kind enough to offer me their 'support and protection' in exchange for information about everything my father had done. Or else they'd send me straight back to him."

He shifted a little, put down his plate, picked up his whiskey and made himself finish. "My father shot himself the day they went to arrest him. I told the Consul I wanted to stay in New York and they sent me to law school because I was valuable: I spoke Chinese, French, German, Italian and I'd played in more back alleys and knew more about criminals than anyone fresh out of Sing Sing. Law school here gave me the perfect cover; international lawyer is a better entrée into society than British spy."

She didn't say anything immediately, just stared at the fire. He watched the fire too; it snapped and spat, and he wished he hadn't sat quite so close to it because now he was warm and drowsy from the whiskey and the release of confession. But he didn't want to fall asleep because to sit here talking to her all night would be almost the best thing he'd ever done in his life.

He knew now, really knew, that she was a different person entirely from Lena. Looks were all they shared. The morning after the first and only time he'd ever slept with Lena a year ago, he'd known—

and she'd known too—that whatever they'd both been searching for in one another's arms, neither had found. That Lena wasn't the woman he'd been looking for. But he owed Lena, wanted to show her that she wasn't only the broken, slutty, drunk person beneath the polished facade who she pretended to be.

"Those might be things you've done," she said. "They're not who you are."

He felt himself stiffen. He was suddenly aware of how near she was to him; if he stretched out his hand, he would touch the soft skin on her arm again. If he leaned over a little, he could graze his lips against hers. It took all of his willpower to steady his breathing and then he made himself say it because practicalities and logistics were always the best distractions. "I need you to come to Paris with me. Lena's coming too."

He wasn't expecting her to laugh. But she did, the sound like a rip in the night and he realized he'd said it all wrong.

"What am I, the chaperone?" she asked incredulously.

She stood up, in one smooth, lithe movement and he dared to reach out a hand to stop her.

"I need your help," he said, knowing he had to keep her in the room so that she wouldn't steal his car keys and drive herself back to Manhattan, which he knew she was more than capable of doing. "I've got an agent with a broken leg stuck in Paris and no one can find him. He was hurt in an operation gone wrong and then taken by a friendly Parisian to the Village Saint-Paul, which is a great place to lose somebody; it's such a bloody rabbit warren we can't find the right building. The Parisian managed to get a note to one of our mailboxes, which gave us a few details of the location, but then he didn't turn up to the rendezvous with another of my agents to show him the way in. My man says he can see a shuttered-up bookstore from the window, a pile of carriage wheels, and what he thinks might once have been a forge."

"I remember there was a bookstore in the Village. I'll draw you a map."

"Can you draw a good enough map that somebody will be able to find him?"

She hesitated. "Probably not," she admitted. "But I'm not going with you."

She said it as if she loathed him, as if she doubted his motives. But there was no possible reason in the world for him to ask an untrained person to go with him to a war zone unless he was desperate. No one in MI9 or MI6 could fathom the Village Saint-Paul. Their handful of local operatives had tried and failed, saying that unless one had grown up near the Village Saint-Paul, it was impossible to navigate. Estella and her mother had lived just streets away. She'd taken him through the Village that night in Paris. He couldn't ask her mother because word had reached him that she thought she was being followed.

Which left Estella. A woman who despised him and who was now saying things that made him furious.

"How do you lose a man?" she asked scornfully. "What kind of people do you have working for you?"

"The best kind," he snapped. "French women mostly because, in case you hadn't heard, there are no men left in France and English spies aren't too well treated there. Those women have everything to lose and nothing personally to gain except a hope that their country might one day be returned to them."

She still looked at him with doubt.

This time, anger seized him, hard and cold like the French winter he'd just been through, deadly. Each word he spoke was as precise and brutal as a sniper's bullet. "There are women younger than you opening their houses to Allied airmen on the run, taking them in, feeding them, passing them on to the next safe house, knowing that all it takes is one slip of the tongue and they're dead. All for the sake of

France. I don't care about seducing you or whatever you think I'm asking you to come to France for. I care about their lives. And then there are the women who smile at the Germans and sit on their knees at Fouquet's, eating steaks and wearing couture dresses while the rest of Paris freezes in threadbare clothes and starves. Which would you be, Estella, if you'd stayed?"

It was blackmail of the worst kind but wasn't that all he was good at? "Forget it," he said brusquely. It was mad of him anyway.

"Why do you want to help him so much?" she asked and he could see the tremor in her hands, hear the falter in her words, the swallow of a tight throat resisting tears.

"He's one of my best agents," he said, laying out the whole truth for her. "He saved my life a few months ago when I jumped out of a plane and my parachute didn't open properly. He got me where I needed to go while I was out cold. I owe him."

"Why can't you tell me more?"

"Because if you know any more, you put everyone's lives at risk. You have no idea what the Germans do to people they think are colluding against them, nor how they extract information from those they arrest. The less I tell you, the safer everyone is."

He could see her taking in what he'd said, that he wasn't being evasive as some kind of game. That it was the best way to keep people alive, to protect those whose actions had put a gun at their backs, that he didn't want her to be responsible for pulling the trigger. Her breath was ragged; he'd got her attention.

"I'll come," she said. It was her turn to reach for the whiskey. "And just so you know, I would never sit on a Nazi's knee," she added quietly.

I know you wouldn't. Instead he said, "Thank you." Then he stood up before she could leave the room. "I asked Lena along to chaperone you," he said. "Not the other way around. So you'd feel safe from me.

And because you want to run a fashion business, which means you can't have anyone questioning your character. Nobody should think you've gone to Europe with me unchaperoned. Having Lena accompany you will keep your reputation intact."

Then she stood up and ran upstairs, leaving behind more than just her scent, sweet and musky like gardenias and spice on a hot summer's night. She left behind the devastating and also unbelievable knowledge that he had managed to, somehow, fall so far in love with her that he didn't know if he'd ever be able to find his way back out.

CHAPTER EIGHTEEN

F lying boat," Sam said the next morning, with the same disbelief Estella's voice had carried when she'd discovered exactly how she, Alex, and Lena were getting to Paris. "Do you think you'll come back alive?"

"I don't think the flying boats are the worst danger," Estella said.

"You're going to a war zone with a man you hardly know…"

Her stomach turned over and the sidecars and whiskey of the night before made her feel nauseated, sweaty, fearful. *You're going to a war zone with a man you hardly know.* But what she did know, she realized, was that, despite his reputation, his womanizing wasn't directed at her. Lena must have tamed him.

Lena. Who'd grown up with Harry Thaw while she, Estella, had not. Through some accident, through some quirk of fate, she'd had her mother, while Lena had had Harry. Like it had done all night as she'd lain awake in her bed at Alex's home outside Sleepy Hollow, terror squeezed her heart. What if Jeanne Bissette wasn't her mother? By going to Paris, Estella would have to ask her mother that question.

Before her panic became too overpowering, Estella thought of the man stuck in Paris, hiding from the Germans. The agent Alex had said was one of his best. The agent who could help so many of her countrymen and -women if he was free. Estella must go to Paris. Her fists clenched. Once she'd helped Alex, she would take Lena to see her mother and they'd ask her to tell them everything. Otherwise, Estella's fear of whatever secret her mother had kept from her would haunt her for the rest of her life.

"I'm also going with a woman who might be my sister," Estella said to Sam now. "She's there to protect my reputation. I'm doing some translating for Alex; his French is shocking." It wasn't true of course but it was the story he'd asked her to tell—that he had legal work to do for some American clients in Paris and she was there to help him with the language. "And I can see my mother. That's worth anything." And it was, no matter what she learned. Her final words were sober and Sam squeezed her hand.

"Besides," she said, forcing a smile, "I seem to remember traveling out of a war zone last year with a man I hardly knew and look how well that turned out."

"Come here," Sam said gruffly and she stepped in closer and found herself enveloped in an enormous hug. "Estella," he began.

At the same moment, the door to Sam's apartment flew open and Janie rushed in, holding out her hand. "Look at this!" she shrieked. "I'm engaged. Nate asked me to marry him. And I said yes. Isn't it huge?"

"It really is," Estella said, leaning over to examine the proffered finger, then reaching out to hug her friend as if she could, without words, say everything she wanted to which was: *Don't get married. Stay exactly who you are.* But nobody ever stayed who they were.

"We should toast," Sam said. "This is the last time we're all going to be in the same room for a while." He poured out three whiskeys in water glasses and passed them around.

"What were you about to say before Janie barged in?" Estella asked him.

"Nothing." He raised his glass. "To your adventures, Estella."

"What are you doing?" Janie demanded.

"I'm going to Paris."

Janie laughed.

"I really am," Estella said. "In a Pan-Am flying boat."

"Why the hell would you do that?" Janie asked with disbelief.

"It's a long story," said Estella.

"It really flies?" Estella asked for possibly the tenth time that morning, shouting so that her voice would project from the rumble seat and into the front of the car where Alex and Lena sat as they drove to wherever flying boats departed from.

"It really does," Alex replied.

"But isn't that just the teeniest bit exciting?" Estella said. "Have you been on one?" she asked Lena.

"I haven't," Lena said and she turned and gave Estella a small smile.

"See!" Estella said triumphantly. "You're excited too. As for you," she said to Alex, "you've probably been on them dozens of times and are so jaded by the whole experience that you'd rather us just be there already."

"Dozens of times?" he replied, in a mock-boastful voice. "Try hundreds."

Estella laughed. So did Lena, and then Alex.

They soon arrived at the Marine Air Terminal at LaGuardia and Alex ushered them inside. Estella watched him talking to two men in military uniforms, who both laughed with him and seemed to know who he was.

While they waited, Estella turned to Lena. "Thank you for coming."

Lena's eyebrows lifted a little in surprise. "I'm happy to."

Then Estella made herself ask. "Will you come with me to meet my mother while we're in Paris?"

Lena shook her head. "I don't think so."

Estella reached out and took Lena's hand, the first time she'd ever dared touch her. "Harry came to my fashion show. He came to the Gramercy Park house another time too. He's everything you said he was. A monster. I grew up with nothing but love; I can't imagine what it would have been like to grow up with him. So I want you to meet my mother. I want us both to talk to her. I think..." She hesitated, unsure if this was pushing Lena too far. "I think there are things you would like to ask her, just as I have questions for her too." Then she let go of Lena's hand and waited.

Instead of replying, Lena searched through her handbag and passed Estella a book. The title—*The Memoirs of Evelyn Nesbit*—was emblazoned in red on the cover, along with a sensational picture of a red velvet swing. "I thought you should read this," Lena said. "It might fill in some of Harry's background better than I can."

She didn't look at Estella as she spoke but Estella heard something fragile in Lena's voice and she understood that Lena really meant it might fill Estella in on things Lena found too difficult to say. The moment of vulnerability touched Estella but she knew if she acknowledged it, Lena would freeze over once more. "I'll read it on the plane," was all Estella said.

Lena turned away from her, as if she was watching Alex walk back over to them, and, while her face was obscured, said, "I would like to meet your mother."

Estella tried not to let out the breath she was holding, tried not to let that one poignant sentence make her cry. Once the tightness in her throat subsided, she said, "Then you will." And added, "I'm sorry I was so awful to you when we first met."

Estella thought she saw Lena reach up her hand to her eyes. "You're the last person who should be sorry," she heard Lena say before Alex reached them.

He led them down a gangplank that stretched out over the water to where the flying boat was perched, like a large and lazy bird, atop the water. Estella saw the way Alex kept his hand just behind Lena's back, helping her down the gangplank, then handing her into the airship. He turned to do the same to Estella, reaching out his hand to take hers.

"I can manage," she said.

"I know. But I'm trying to show you I have some manners," he said.

"All right then. I don't want you to think I have none," she said.

She slipped her hand into his and saw his face stiffen, as if she'd done something wrong. She didn't know what it was and could hardly wait for the three seconds to pass until she'd stepped into the flying boat and could remove her hand from his. Perhaps she'd held on too tightly and he thought she meant something by it. Perhaps he thought she was attracted to him, just like every other woman he encountered. She'd do her best to make sure she gave him no such signals for the duration of the flight. She'd be polite and reserved and speak only when necessary.

Her resolution left her the moment they were inside. "It's like a palace," she said, taking in the linen tablecloths, the crystal glasses, the wood paneling, amazed that something so luxurious and capacious could be hidden inside an airship. "It's almost as lovely as…" She stopped, uncertain if Lena knew of her sojourn at Alex's house in the Hudson Valley. Something about the way he was looking at her made her say, "Your home, Lena."

"We should move along," Alex said. "We're down the end. In the bridal suite."

"You're joking," Estella said. "There's a bridal suite?"

"Can you think of a better place to spend your honeymoon?"

The truth was, Estella had never once thought about a honeymoon, let alone having one while suspended over the Atlantic Ocean. "You won't want me staying in the bridal suite with you," she said.

"I think Alex will be able to control himself," Lena said dryly, walking ahead.

"I'm sure I can talk to the, whoever—somebody—and have another seat arranged," Estella said.

Alex took Estella's arm and propelled her forward. "Can you please keep going. We're holding everybody up. I promise not to behave like a man on his wedding night with anyone for the duration of our time in the bridal suite. Happy? I fly back and forth a lot. So they give me the best seats when they can. I'm going to France because the Chase National Bank and the American Hospital in Paris need some legal help and you're my translator and Lena's your chaperone. The bridal suite is big enough that I can work on the way over."

"Oh," Estella said, understanding that everything was about his assignment in France, nothing more. "Of course."

"Have a seat," he said brusquely at the very last room. "I'm closing the door for my own privacy, not because I have any evil intentions."

"Of course you don't," Estella stuttered. "I never thought you did…"

Her voice trailed off. She determined to sit down and be quiet. But the suite was spectacular. "I'm speechless," she said, looking around.

Lena smiled and Alex looked at Lena and said, "Will you say it or will I?"

"Go right ahead," Lena said.

"You're never speechless, Estella," Alex said.

"Well, pardon me for being unable to be blasé about my first voyage in the bridal suite of a flying boat," Estella said crossly, sitting down in the nearest chair. "I almost think it would take someone blowing this up before you reacted at all."

"We're not that bad, are we?" Alex teased.

But Estella didn't want to be placated. "Yes," she said. "You are."

"I bet if I told her it cost $675 each she really would be speechless," Lena mused and Estella stared at her in horror.

"$675? That can't be true."

"Lena," she heard Alex say in exasperation.

She turned to him. "You spent $675 to put me on a flying boat to France?" Whoever they were getting out of the Village Saint-Paul must be even more important than she'd realized. None of this was a game. Which would explain Alex's demeanor, his lack of excitement. It was a job. A dangerous job, one that he must be desperate to accomplish, one that he must have used all other resources for and failed, if he'd asked her to help.

Alex didn't reply. He sat down in a chair, unfolded a newspaper and began to read. Lena closed her eyes. Estella pulled out the book Lena had given her, read the first line—*My name is Evelyn Nesbit and more words have been written about me than the Queen of England, such is my notoriety*—and braced herself for what Evelyn would have to say about Harry Thaw. She put the book aside half an hour later when her stomach began to churn from the horrors revealed, most of which she already knew from the newspaper articles Alex had shown her, but hearing from the victim, who used a childish and breathless tone to recount the various cruelties, was so much worse.

Not long after, an impeccably made sidecar appeared at her side. "Peace offering," Alex said.

"Isn't coffee more appropriate for this time of day?"

"It's already nighttime in Paris," Alex said.

"I suppose that's true," Estella said grudgingly as she put the book down and sipped her drink. A sudden roar of engines jolted her upright and she jumped to her feet. "Are we starting?"

"Taking off, you mean?"

"Look!" Estella remembered Lena had her eyes closed so she said again, more quietly, "Look!"

Out the window, water rushed past, waves created by the movement of the flying boat over the water lurched up onto the glass, and she was moving faster than she ever had in her life. The whole ship vibrated so intensely she wondered if it might burst apart from the force, from the noise. Then she felt the boat tip to one side and she grabbed hold of the wall at the same time as Alex put one hand on her back to steady her.

"Sorry," he said, ripping his hand away. "I promised to behave myself."

Estella relented. This was the experience of a lifetime; she might as well relax her hackles. "It's fine," she said.

Suddenly the flying boat was no longer a boat but an airship and she was suspended in the sky, surrounded by blue, soft clouds floating within arm's reach.

Alex stepped in closer to her. "Look over there. You can see the Chrysler Building. And you can just make out the Statue of Liberty."

Estella smiled up at him. "It's amazing."

"It is," he said, and for the next couple of hours, while Lena slept, they stood shoulder to shoulder in the bridal suite of a flying boat, staring out the window, not speaking, reveling in the wonder of passing over the ocean, of migrating, birdlike, from one country to another, of soaring into the blue, of almost touching the sun.

I'm coming, Maman, Estella thought as her palm lifted to touch the window. Looking out at the blue promise of sky, Estella knew that, as well as wanting to ask her mother about Lena, she wanted, more than anything, just to feel her mother's arms wrapped tight around her once more.

The flight was long—twenty-seven hours Alex had told her, including a stop at a place called Horta in the Azores, which she'd never heard of—but Estella couldn't settle enough to sleep. She tried once or twice but after an hour she'd be up and about and back at the window, staring out, suddenly realizing, in a way she hadn't on the ship from France, how vast the world was, how small she was, how insignificant her place in everything. As she watched, she imagined dresses in all of the colors of the sky: an optimistic morning-blue, an almost white, gold-shot midday hue, the deeper blue of the afternoon, the violet-gray of dusk, the silvery ripple of early evening and then the fathomless inky black of night.

She pulled out her sketchbook and began to draw, unworried by the relentless moan of the engines, the sudden lurches, the ceaseless vibration that Lena said rattled her teeth and which had made her ill several times. Estella had helped her as much as Lena would let her, which wasn't a lot. Lena was asleep now, pale, looking childlike and artless in a way Estella had never seen.

She glanced across at Alex once or twice, marveling at the transformation that came over him in sleep. His face looked even more handsome in repose because it was unarranged, that schooled, expressionless countenance suddenly relaxed, open, not hiding anything. She smiled as she watched him, knowing he'd hate for her to see him like that, enjoying having the upper hand on him for once even if he didn't know it. Estella wondered for a moment how she looked in sleep, what worries left her, what dreams blessed her face with an expression different from that which she wore in life.

She lost all track of time, glad to think of nothing other than her pencil on the paper, glad to discover that, while her first showing might have been an unmitigated disaster, she still loved to draw. And that, even if nobody else thought so, she could draw designs she believed were worthy of adorning a woman's body.

The sound of movement made her lift her head; Alex had woken and was checking on Lena, who seemed utterly diminished by the flight. "What can I bring you?" Estella heard him ask.

"I don't think my stomach can take any food right now," Lena said. "Coffee?"

"No. Just sleep." Lena smiled at Alex.

He touched Lena lightly on the shoulder and it occurred to Estella that she'd never seen any gesture pass between them that moved beyond close friendship—like Estella's with Sam—and into passion. She'd never seen him kiss Lena, never seen him embrace her the way a lover would, never seen him do more than touch her back or her shoulder or her arm, never seen him reach out to her out of need or hunger or want. She felt her hand move up to her own lips, lips Alex had most definitely kissed, and she wondered how Lena could be so restrained when she had the chance to feel, every day, the way Estella had when she'd kissed Alex.

She realized Alex was staring at her with curiosity written all over his face, was watching her hand on her lips. "Sorry," she said, startled. "I was daydreaming."

"I hope it was pleasant," he said dryly and she felt herself blush from her forehead right down to her toes. "Are you hungry?" he asked.

"I am," Estella said. "Starving in fact."

He put his head through the doorway and, within a few minutes, a steward brought in a tray of food.

"Should I take some over to Lena?" she asked Alex.

He shook his head. "She doesn't want anything."

"What time is it?"

Alex checked his watch. "It's almost four in the afternoon in Paris," he said.

"So we're having afternoon tea," she said, grinning at the plates of lobster, cold smoked salmon, spears of asparagus, the steaming tureens of soup.

"Sorry, I forgot to order scones," he said, dropping seamlessly into a very aristocratic English accent, and she laughed.

"You know, you're actually quite funny when you try," she said.

"Don't tell anyone," he said conspiratorially as he sat across from her. "Besides, they'd never believe you."

"I suppose being funny isn't in the spy handbook."

"It isn't, as a matter of fact." He pointed to her sketchbook. "They're beautiful."

She went to put her hand over them but he sounded so sincere she was touched. "Thank you," she said. "I don't know if I'll ever make them up though."

"Don't let Harry stop you. That's what he wants."

"Well, he got what he wanted. I don't think I'll do another fashion show any time soon. I can't afford to." She helped herself to the lobster, then offered him the plate but he shook his head.

He sipped his coffee. "If I didn't think I would offend you so utterly that you'd throw yourself out the window, I'd offer you the money you need."

"Well, it's a good thing you have the sense not to," she said, closing her sketchbook with a snap. "I'm not a charity project you can fly around the world and splash money on when you feel like it."

"And that's exactly why I didn't offer." He smiled at her and she caught a glimpse of what she'd seen when he was asleep, of the man who might once have emerged from the skin of Alex if only his mother hadn't died, if only he'd had a different father.

"I'm being prickly again, aren't I?" she said, smiling a little too.

"Nobody would ever dare call you prickly, would they?" he said.

"Not if they want to live a long life."

They were both quiet a moment after that, enjoying a rare moment of conviviality.

"I should let you get back to it," he said at last. "Tell me, do you ever sleep?"

She laughed. "I forgot that you always tend to see me after midnight. But yes, I do sleep. Just not well or for long stretches."

"I know what that's like," he said. Then, "Estella." He stopped.

"What?" she asked, fear pressing against her throat at the way he was looking at her, as if he was about to hurt her and was trying to find the right words with which to do it.

"France is a very different place from how you left it. Be prepared for that. And thank you for coming."

Estella chewed on a mouthful of delicious lobster, as well as the fact that he'd thanked her. "What happens next? Can you tell me that much at least?"

"We land in Lisbon, then take a train to Perpignan, then on to Marseilles. The flying boats can't land at Marseilles anymore because of the Germans, which makes the journey take twice as long as it should. We need to push on, to get to Paris as soon as we can, before..." He stopped and she knew he must be thinking about the man he needed to help. "I have Ausweis for us all, passes that allow us to cross the demarcation line into the Occupied Zone. Your pass has your name on it. You don't have to pretend to be anyone other than who you are, which is always easiest. And you're French, so being a translator for me, the incompetent American, shouldn't raise an eyebrow."

"So you're American now?" Estella asked.

"Of course. If the Germans knew I was British, I'd be interned. That's another secret you have to keep." Alex shook his head. "I'm sorry. I know it's all half-lies and untruths. But I don't want to put you in danger."

"Oh, and you'd care about that," she joked and was utterly taken aback when Alex said, very low so she almost didn't hear. "I would."

Because she looked like Lena. He cared about Lena, and, by extension, Estella. Although after her earlier realization about their lack of intimacy, she wondered for the first time what exactly was the nature of his care for Lena. He had once said that he loved Lena though.

She shrugged. It wasn't a line of thought that was worth pursuing. He'd kissed Estella once by accident and she'd enjoyed it, more than enjoyed it; she'd been utterly capable of removing her clothes and his at that moment. But he'd only kissed her because he thought she was Lena. So, despite the fact she hadn't witnessed any obvious affection—which probably meant he was more discreet than she'd given him credit for—he and Lena were some kind of oddly entwined item. He thought of Estella as Lena's annoying sister. All of this was for Lena; he wanted to find proof for Lena that she had a sister—one family member who wasn't a lunatic—and Estella was simply a means to the end of that, and of finding his agent.

"I don't seem to remember you telling me before we left that lying would be part of my job," she said somewhat testily.

"Because then you'd never have come." He grinned at her, that god-damned heartbreaking grin that she knew women across the country must fall for because it was so seductive, so charming, and she made herself look away because he didn't need any more women prostrate under his spell.

He picked up his coffee and walked back to his seat. She reopened her sketchbook, her pencil flitting over the pages, adding in another detail, loosening or lengthening a line, changing the fit of a sleeve. Within an hour there was nothing left to fix; everything was perfect. Yet the only breathing she could hear was Lena's. Alex's face was as blank as it always was, betraying the fact that, while his eyes might be closed, he no longer slept.

CHAPTER NINETEEN

Alex slept a little on the train, as did Estella he noted with relief. Half an hour before they pulled into Marseilles, he leaned over and whispered in Lena's ear. Judging by Estella's sharp glance, he could tell she thought he was whispering sweet nothings and she moved to stand up and walk away but he held out a hand to stop her. Lena simply nodded at what he told her, for which he was grateful.

Then he sat beside Estella and spoke quietly. "If anything happens en route or in Paris," he said, "get yourself to Lyon or Marseilles. Go to the Vieux Port, or stay close to the cafés. Someone will pick you up."

She stared at him. Before she could say anything, he opened his traveling case and passed an acetate box to her and one to Lena. It was small, easily fitted into a coat pocket or a purse. He watched as Estella flipped open the lid and rifled through the contents, which he could list by heart: malted milk tablets, Benzedrine tablets, sweets, matches, chocolate, surgical tape, chewing gum, tobacco, a water bottle, Halazone for water purification, needle and thread, soap, fishing line. She held up the razor. "What's it for?" she asked.

"It's magnetized," he said. "You can use it as a compass if you have to. Sorry, they didn't have anything more feminine."

Estella shook her head. "Not the razor. What's the box for?"

He reached across, took the box from her and slid it into her purse. "It's an escape box," he said shortly. *Of the best kind*, he didn't say.

Made by MI9 for the British air force and their agents. "Don't put it in your valise. Keep it on you at all times. You can last a couple of days with that. Trade the tobacco if you don't want to smoke it."

"Trade the tobacco?" Estella repeated incredulously.

"Estella," he said sharply. "Just leave it." He'd tried to choose the best time. On the plane and it would have rattled her. But he knew that no matter when he gave it to her, it would make her ask questions. If only she could be like Lena and hide away her box as if it were a powder compact.

"I'm sorry," she snapped. "Maybe next time you want to pass me something so out of the ordinary you could give me a little warning."

And even though she might hate him even more than she already did for what he was about to say, he had to say it. "You have to stop questioning me. Otherwise I'll have to send you back to Lisbon. I need your help but not at the risk of everything else. Trust that whatever I say and do, it's for a good reason. It's your job, for the next week, just to nod and agree with me no matter how much it irritates you. Can you do that?"

He kept his voice tightly controlled but he could still tell that he sounded annoyed. She was the weak spot in this plan. He hated having to act like this with her, like the autocratic intelligence officer he had to be in order to keep everyone alive.

He felt like an utter bastard when she bent her head to hide the flush of embarrassment on her cheeks. "I can," she said quietly.

"Thank you," he said, an edge to his voice that sat at the far end of courtesy. "There are no cars in France anymore. We're catching the train to Paris. I need to stop at the Seamen's Mission first, then we'll go."

"The Seamen's Mission?" Estella started to ask. Then she closed her mouth and picked up her valise. "Doesn't matter," she said.

Once the train stopped, he left to see Peter Caskie at the Seamen's

Mission, one of the many stops a downed airman might make on the long and secret journey across France. He distributed money and tobacco for the couriers, so much tobacco—it had become a more reliable currency than any paper money. He gathered intelligence, made sure nobody on the escape line thought anything was amiss, that no Germans were aware of its existence. He arrived back at Marseilles station just as the train shot steam into the air.

Then began the long trip from Marseille to Paris, which he hoped would take no longer than a day and a half, what with all the checks they'd be subjected to, which made what used to be a simple journey far from smooth. At five in the morning the next day, as the sun began to rise, he moved over to sit beside Estella; Lena had been asleep for hours and he thought she'd be more comfortable if she could lie down on the seat. Even though Estella looked the most exhausted of them all, she was still awake.

He didn't speak to her, just tilted his head back on the seat and closed his eyes, needing to rest for even ten minutes; that would be enough or else he'd have to start on the benzedrine and he tried to save that for only when absolutely necessary. He awoke with a jolt some time later—night had passed and sunlight was seeping into the sky—feeling something land on his thigh. It was Estella's upturned hand. She'd fallen asleep and, while oblivious to the world, her body had turned toward his and her arm had shifted.

He stared at her hand, at the nimble fingers that he'd watched caressing paper with a pencil, transforming lines of lead into stunning images, studied the tips of her index finger and thumb, which were marked, he saw now, with tiny wounds—needle marks perhaps—a side effect of the work she did. In sleep, her hand looked tranquil and lovely and he remembered that the French seamstresses were reckoned to have *doigts de fée*—fairy fingers—and all he wanted to do was to reach out his own hand and link it with hers.

He shook his head; what was the matter with him? He'd never in his life wanted to just hold hands with anyone. But, right now, he knew he'd be completely happy to feel her palm against his, to know that she cared enough about him to hold his hand. Of course, she was only here because he'd persuaded her in the worst possible way. If he did so much as reach out a finger to lightly touch her, she'd snatch her hand away, say something biting and wouldn't speak to him again for the rest of their time in France.

So it was better just to sit in the carriage of a train on an early morning in France, watching the sun gently lift into the sky. It was better to simply endure the torment of her hand resting on his thigh, knowing that if she was aware of what she was doing, a moment like this would never happen.

After passing through Lyon, Alex slipped out from under Estella's hand, not daring to pick it up and place it on the seat, just letting it slide away from him as he pulled out the bread and cheese and wine he'd bought in Marseilles. They were about to cross the border and food would help them keep their wits.

"I'm starving," he heard Estella say as his rustling paper bag woke her.

He passed her bread and water and sat down next to Lena, nodding at the window. "You should take in what you can of France now," he said to Estella. "It's different in the Occupied Zone."

The train ran along the escarpment of the Côte d'Or, the valley of the Saône spread out in front of them, flashing gold off the leaves of the grapevines, reminding him of the dress Estella wore the first night he met her. The river drifted along beside the train, a belt of blue, unraveling gently, and the grapes and the water and the undulations of the country were glorious, one peaceful moment on this whole fraught journey. An idyll, where one could forget the war raging around them.

"Oh," he heard Estella say as she turned her eyes to the view.

They ate, eyes fixed to the pastoral scene outside, souls feasting on it the way their mouths did on the bread. When he was done, he rested back, legs stretched out before him and Lena smiled at him. He saw, as he always did, the damaged soul lying beneath her eyes and he tucked a strand of hair behind her ear, a gesture meant to show her that he did care.

He realized Estella was watching, that to her it would look like the action of a lover. And even though, in the deepest part of him, he didn't want her to think that he and Lena were lovers, he was glad she did because that was another barrier between them. Without such barriers, he knew that he would—if his past was anything to go on—only hurt Estella in the end and he couldn't bear the thought of doing that.

Eventually he had to turn to business. "I'm supposed to stay at the Ritz," he said. "But it's crawling with Germans and I'd rather you two not be so close to the Wehrmacht. I'll go in and out of the hotel from time to time to keep up appearances but, Estella, I hoped we could use the house in the Marais. I had it chalked outside as a *maison habitée* months ago, which you have to do if you don't want the Germans commandeering your home. So it's safe. You shouldn't go to your mother's apartment yet, just in case." *Just in case you get caught helping me steal an agent with a broken leg out of Paris,* he didn't say.

She opened her mouth and he could tell she was about to protest, that he was in for another of their neverending battles. Then she nodded, surprising him. "Whatever you think is best. I don't want to put Maman in danger."

It wasn't until they emerged from the Metro that Estella comprehended what Alex had meant when he said it was different in the Occupied Zone. The Metro had been overstuffed, carrying the kind of wealthy and coutured women who would never, before the war had rid the country of cars and fuel, have deigned to sully themselves on the trains. There were also women who belonged to a breed Estella had never seen before: thin, dresses almost translucent with wear, legs bare, shoulders turned in, heads dropped so low that it was as if they wanted to hide inside themselves. The stink of unclean bodies made it hard to breathe. Estella didn't ask questions. But when they reached the Rue de Rivoli, she stopped still.

"I know," she heard Alex whisper. "Just keep moving. Ask me whatever you want when we get to the house but don't stop on the street."

So she kept moving, knowing only that when she'd asked Alex if things in Paris were bad, she'd never expected this. A group of German soldiers marched along the Rue des Rosiers in their steel-gray uniforms, bulldogs on leashes racing ahead of them, and Estella watched everyone steer a wide path around them, keeping their eyes down. So many shops had closed and others—the cobbler owned by Monsieur Bousquet, the buttons and trims shop owned by Monsieur Cassin, the tableware shop owned by Monsieur Blum, all Jews—bore a red poster, advising that, by decree of the government, the businesses had been placed in the hands of a non-Jewish administrator.

What of Nannette? What of Marie and all the other women Estella used to work with? What of Maman? Estella was trying so hard to quell the agitation she felt, trying so hard not to think too much of her mother. Because, while she hoped for an embrace and tears and laughter, she feared what she might actually find in their old apartment on the Passage Saint-Paul.

Outside her favorite boulangerie, a long line of people queued, their faces gray, arms hanging thinly from the sleeves of their dresses, all women, hardly a man to be found. Except German soldiers.

As they neared the boulangerie, Estella saw a familiar face. She called out, "Huette!" and ran across the street.

A girl who was too skeletal to be Huette turned, the smile on her face the most substantial thing about her. "Estella! How did you get here?"

Estella embraced her friend, unable to cover the shocked gasp as her arms wrapped over the bony plates of Huette's back. Huette had always been well proportioned, curved where she should be, but now her skin hung from her, the layer of fat between it and the bone gone. And that same smell from the Metro rose rankly from her friend. "Oh, Huette," she said again. "What are you doing?" she asked, so glad of the sound of her native tongue back on her lips.

"Queuing for food," Huette said. "It takes all day. We arrive at five in the morning and stand here for hours. Sometimes we get bread. Rutabaga. Chicory for coffee. The last time I had meat, the cherry trees were in blossom."

"Rutabaga? But that's for cows. I have food," Estella said, remembering the coffee, the chocolate Alex had told her to bring. "Take some." She opened her valise and searched through the contents, realizing too late that she was making a scene, that the press of bodies from the queue was now around her, that she didn't have enough for everyone.

Alex snapped her suitcase closed, pulled Estella from the ground and prodded her and Huette away from the crowd, just before a German patrol reached the boulangerie. Lena waited for them on the other side of the street.

Estella knew straightaway that she shouldn't have done it. But how could she not? How could anyone walk through Paris and see people so cowed, so reduced, and not want to give them everything one had?

"Why did you come back?" Huette asked as Alex marched them away, Lena behind them, far enough away, thank God, that Huette hadn't noticed her and therefore wouldn't start quizzing Estella about the likeness between them.

The lie came to her so smoothly that Estella almost couldn't believe it. "I work for a lawyer." She indicated Alex. "His French is awful. I'm his translator. He's American; you know what they're like with languages." She rolled her eyes dramatically and was so glad when her friend's face lit with some of her old spark and Huette giggled.

Estella felt Alex's fist, clenched at her back since the boulangerie, relax. She even caught the quick flash of a smile as he heard her say that his French was terrible.

"I'll bring food," she said to Huette. "Later tonight. Otherwise it looks as if it'll be stolen right out from under you."

"Everyone's hungry," Huette said sadly. "Except Renée."

"Why not Renée?"

"She has a German officer. She stays at the Hôtel Meurice most nights. Trading herself for meat. For dresses. For everything you can only get on the black market. Women aren't given ration tickets for tobacco. It's amazing what some people will do for a cigarette." The bitterness in Huette's tone was harder than a winter frost.

"Why would she do that?"

"It's the only way to live. The rest of us merely exist. In the winter, people skinned their cats for fur, Estella. Then we ate the cat."

"No," Estella whispered. She'd been in New York, crammed into a tiny room, but with enough to eat, clothes to cover her back, heat to keep her warm. "Have you seen my mother?" she asked at last, the words she'd been wanting but fearing to ask since she'd run into Huette.

Huette shook her head. "I used to see her in the queue for food. But not this week. Not last week either. Maybe not since last month. Perhaps she found another boulangerie?" Huette added hopefully.

"Perhaps," Estella said, unconvinced.

She heard Lena's heels tapping closer and Alex cleared his throat. "We're going to be late for our meeting."

Late? Estella nearly snapped at him. What did it matter in the face of what she now saw? Thin women cycling along, wagons attached to their bikes to make a kind of velo-taxi, a strapping German officer and a giggling woman in the back. Emptiness: empty shops, empty faces, empty streets. Most of all, empty hearts. But she remembered she was there to help Alex find a man who was one of those trying to stop the emptiness, to return France to what it should be.

"I'll come tonight," Estella promised Huette. "With coffee and chocolate. What else do you need?"

"Soap," Huette said hopefully. "Everyone smells."

"I have soap," Estella said. "You can have it all."

"And…" Huette hesitated.

"What?" Estella cried. "Anything."

"Could we go out somewhere? Like we used to. Pretend that…" Huette's voice trailed off.

"Of course. We'll go to La Bonne Chance," Estella said firmly. "That's if it's still open?"

"All the clubs are still open. The Germans, and their women like Renée, have time for fun." Huette kissed her cheeks then disappeared back into the street, just as Lena caught up to them.

From behind them came the sound of clip-clopping, like a horse. Estella turned to see two women hurrying along, baskets slung on their arms. Their shoes bore wooden soles, not leather. The clopping sound of the wood rang on long after they'd passed, and Estella now saw others similarly shod. But what stood out most were the women's hats and turbans, exuberantly decorated with all manner of embellishment: fox heads, feathers, flowers, cherries, birds' nests, ribbons, and lace in extravagant piles.

Alex saw her staring and said, "There's no leather for shoes, not enough fabric to make new clothes but I guess it doesn't take much to decorate a hat."

Estella smiled. How typical of French women to take the one

thing they had left and use it to the edge of ostentation, to say that, while their stomachs might be hungry and their bodies worn out, they would show that appearances still mattered; that a flare of their spirit could be found in their hats. The sight made her feel a little better; many were fighting back. She hoped her Maman was too; in fact she hoped Jeanne was responsible for making some of those hats. If all those women could remain resilient in the face of deprivation and fear, then Estella could easily do a simple thing like take Alex into the Village Saint-Paul.

Soon the three of them arrived at the Rue de Sévigné, at the house Estella had last seen on the night she took maps from a dying Monsieur Aumont. In the afternoon light of a summer day, it looked almost beautiful, a grand old Parisian dame whose elegance could still be seen in the long line of her body, in the way she held herself, but whose exterior was showing all the signs of having lived a long and difficult life. She saw the words Alex said he'd chalked on the wall—*maison habitée*. "Here," she said to Lena. "Look familiar?"

"My God," Lena said, shock written all over her normally unshockable face at the sight of the house.

Estella pushed open the carriage gates and led the way into the courtyard. "Whoever built the Gramercy Park house must have been here. It's a perfect copy."

"I told you Harry Thaw built the Gramercy Park house," Lena said.

Estella frowned. Harry Thaw could not have been here. She passed beneath the arched entry, waited to feel the same shiver she always had. But this time she didn't. This time she felt the house let out a breath, as if it had been waiting and hoping and doubting that she would return, as if it was glad to see her. As if it held something meant for her.

The courtyard garden was as scraggly as ever but the mint smelled like every Parisian summer she'd ever known. Inside the house, Estella ran her hand along the wall as she passed down the hall, just like Lena's, but without artwork, the paint coming off the walls in clumps of white powder. Alex took her valise from her. "Let's go," he said. "The longer we wait, the more I'm worried about…"

"Your man," Estella finished. "Let's go then."

Lena stared up at the staircase; Alex had forbidden Lena to go with them but she seemed not to know what to do with herself. Then Estella realized Lena was waiting for permission from Estella to go upstairs, as if Estella was in charge of the house. Which she supposed she was, if her mother owned it, as the *matrice cadastrale* suggested. "You can put your things in whatever room you like," she said to Lena. "You probably know the house better than I do."

Lena advanced up the stairs and Estella walked back outside with Alex.

"Just act as if you're showing me the sights," he said. "I know it's in the wrong direction, but start with the Place des Vosges, then we'll make our way across to the Village Saint-Paul. In case anyone's watching."

Estella nodded, fear returning and making it hard to speak the minute they were outside and in this unfamiliar, Brutalist version of Paris. All the romance, all sense of it being a place for love and lovers, a place where every stone, every window shutter, every streetlamp held a thousand stories, a place that didn't just belong to history, but a place that was history itself, had fled along with the French government, hiding out somewhere, waiting.

She put on her brightest voice, as if she really was just a simple tour guide trying to impress her American boss. German women in gray uniforms scurried along the pavement which used to be occupied by women in bright dresses with art portfolios under their arms. "Here is the Place des Vosges," Estella said. "Built in the seventeenth century, it is the loveliest square in Paris. The Queen's pavilion is to the north, the King's pavilion to the south. Victor Hugo once lived here, and, over there, the Paris School of the New York School of Fine and Applied Art once operated. It's where I trained for a year, before it closed due to the war."

"I didn't know that," he said in a low voice.

"Why would you?" she replied, pressing on with her faux tour of the Marais. "And this is a statue of Louis XIII; it's not the original. That was decapitated during the revolution."

"What else is worth seeing?"

"You must see the Church of Saint-Paul-Saint-Louis."

Two German soldiers, each on the arm of a girl whose dresses were not at all worn, whose legs shone with silk, whose cheeks were rouged, whose shoes were leather, walked past and nodded at them.

"Which way?" Alex asked Estella in English, his accent deepened to become recognizably American, the confidence he ordinarily carried subtly now dropped over him like a made-to-measure suit. His voice rang loudly, so perfectly the brash American that Estella had to remind herself it was just an act. But it worked.

"Paris is beautiful!" one of the German soldiers cried, nodding at Alex, taking him for the tourist he was pretending to be, his Americanness protecting both him and Estella. "Especially the women," the other soldier said, leering at Estella, and the girl on his arm gave his hand a slap.

"They're not bad," Alex said evenly.

Estella made her feet keep walking, even though her legs felt as flimsy as cotton threads. Once the Germans were well behind she attempted a joke. "Not bad? You're full of compliments," she said to Alex, but she heard the slight tremor in her voice.

"I wasn't talking about you," he said, grinning down at her. "You're the epitome of bad. Always asking questions. But you are an excellent tour guide. I would very much like to see the church you mentioned."

His riposte relaxed her a little and her legs began to function normally and her voice resumed its artificially gay tone. She led the way to the streets near the church and, once there, took the secret entrance into the Village Saint-Paul, the entrance nobody except those entirely familiar with the area even knew existed. She saw a flash of surprise on Alex's face when the narrow alley led them to a cobblestoned courtyard, surrounded by whitewashed walls that jutted in and out unevenly, creating more courtyards, passages; a twisting, winding maze that none of his spies would have been able to make sense of.

Once part of a convent, the area was now a slum of the worst kind. Both its decrepitude and the difficulty of finding a way in had kept the Germans away but there was less rubbish than she remembered, as if people had suddenly found a use for the old carriage wheels and wooden crates that used to be piled up high along the walls. If the winter had been as cold as Huette had said, she imagined they'd been burned to keep people warm. She shivered a little, despite the warmth of the sun, but kept going to the one old bookstore she remembered among the snarl of workshops, the bookstore she assumed must be the one Alex's man could see from the apartment he was hiding in.

"That's it," she whispered to Alex. The windows were shuttered over; the shop hadn't been opened in months and they were the only people in the courtyard.

She watched him scan the windows of the surrounding buildings, all the while shaking his head at the dust and dirt and disrepair.

"There's nothing worth seeing here," he said with disgust. "I'm going to the American Hospital to finalize those contracts. I don't need you to translate for me there. You can have the afternoon off."

He turned around and, at the first corner, said quietly to Estella, "Go on ahead. I know where he is."

"How?" Estella asked, bewildered that he would, from that cursory scan, have determined which building was the right one.

"A red geranium in one of the windows was pushed to the right-hand side. It means he's there and it's safe to go in and get him. I'll be back later."

"Can I help?" Estella asked.

"You already have. And please don't go and see your mother until I'm back. I need to make sure it's safe." He gave her the flash of a smile, then doubled back to the bookstore.

Estella left reluctantly, walking back to the Rue de Sévigné, skittish whenever a German soldier passed by. The streets sounded different and she realized she couldn't hear any birds, that the trilling songs which heralded summer were gone, driven away by what? Starvation? The after effects of the factory bombings?

All along the streets, she could see posters bearing a strapping German soldier looking down at a child, urging Parisians to put their trust in the soldiers, who wanted nothing more than to protect them. She was so glad to see the familiar battered wooden door of the house, and the *chasse-roues* missing chunks of stone from where carriage wheels had hit them, happy to vanish into the courtyard and feel the house open its arms to her and offer its protection.

She went straight to the kitchen and boiled three pots of water. While she waited for them to heat, she wiped out one of the baths with a set of old drapes that had fallen gracefully to the floor a long time ago. She heard nothing from Lena and thought it likely that, after their long journey, she would be asleep. She carried each pot carefully up to the bath, added cold water from the tap, then sank down into it.

Don't go and see your mother. She would do as she'd been asked, even though the effort not to walk to the Passage Saint-Paul was tremendous. Instead, she scrubbed her hair clean, then brushed out every knot and tangle she'd accumulated over the last four days, wishing it was as easy to brush out the knots and tangles that had twisted their way into her life.

In her valise, Estella found the gold dress she'd hidden at the bottom. Before she went to see her mother tomorrow, or whenever Alex said she could go, before her life changed irrevocably by hearing whatever it was her mother would or wouldn't say, she would take Huette out to enjoy one Paris night. She couldn't bear to sit in the house and do nothing but think of the inevitable meeting between herself, Jeanne, and Lena when she suspected she might discover a truth that would hurt her more than anything ever had.

She walked along the hall until she reached the last room facing the street. She remembered, from when she was younger, before she had access to the music rooms at school, her mother would bring her here to the house, to this room, which had once held a piano. Estella would practice her scales and Jeanne would listen, smiling only when Estella looked at her, mouth pressed tightly closed and hands clenched into fists whenever she thought Estella was concentrating on the instrument.

Estella pushed open the door now and gave an exclamation of delight. The piano was still there. And because she missed her mother terribly, because her city was critically wounded, because Huette was a shrunken version of herself, because the Jewish Marais no longer existed, because she'd just escorted a spy across Paris to retrieve another spy—an act she now understood, after feeling the intense fear curled inside every Parisian on the streets, could have been fatal if she'd been caught—she sat down at the piano and began to play a song her mother had always liked.

It was Ella Fitzgerald's "The Nearness of You" and it came to Estella's fingers more slowly and deliberately than she'd ever played it before, somehow fitting for a Paris night where sadness rather than light pooled beneath the covered streetlamps. As she sang the words— about the delight of simply being near someone you loved—she heard the door open, felt someone sit beside her on the piano stool and pick out the accompaniment to the song.

Alex's hands moved expertly over the keys beside hers and she could sense him next to her, back tall and straight, arms relaxed, sleeves rolled up, a natural pianist and then, quietly, too quietly for such a voice, he sang too. His voice, perfectly suited to the song, cast around her like an enchantment.

When they reached the end, neither moved; both stared at the piano, their hands resting atop the keys, hearing the gentle echo of their voices ring steadily through the room.

"You play well together." Lena's voice broke into the room like a cymbal accidentally struck mid-lullaby.

Estella jumped and she saw Alex's hands tense on the piano.

"I'm going out," Estella said, standing and moving away from the piano stool, crossing under the chandelier which spot-lit her gold dress like a single window in the city with its blackout curtain ripped off.

"Where are you going in that?" Alex asked.

"What's that supposed to mean?" Estella retorted.

"That came out entirely wrong." He held up his hand. "It's just that going out at night in Paris isn't as safe as it used to be."

"I want to see Huette. I can buy her a meal. I'm going to take her to Montmartre, to a jazz club we used to go to, so she can feel better about everything. She can stop thinking about lining up for food. And I can stop thinking about how much I want to see my mother. About the fact that, the minute I see her, everything changes. I'd like, for a few more hours, to have nothing change." The last sentence came out before she could stop it. She closed her mouth before she said any more.

"Lena and I will come too," Alex said.

"I don't need babysitters." She was speaking abruptly, she knew, in an attempt to relocate her defenses.

"I know that. But perhaps I've never been to a jazz club in Montmartre."

"I doubt that."

Alex smiled wryly. "Okay, I can't get away with that but I'm not offering myself as your babysitter either."

"All right." Estella acquiesced, and then the words tumbled out. "When can I see Maman?"

"Tomorrow I hope."

"If I'd had a choice, I would have put off the moment everything changed too." With that, Lena turned around and walked out.

Estella looked uncertainly at Alex. "Does that mean she's coming?"

"Give me a minute to get changed. Then I'll check."

He waited, seemingly expectantly, until Estella asked, "Are you going to get changed?"

"I thought you'd prefer me to wait till you'd gone but if you insist on staying. You're in my room," he said.

"Oh!" Estella hurried out, face bright red with embarrassment.

He appeared downstairs five minutes later, looking more handsome than a man had a right to be, especially when they'd been traveling rough for so long. Estella hadn't bothered to do more than put on her dress, rub powder over her nose, touch color onto her lips, and flick mascara over her lashes and now she felt she should have made more of an effort. But Lena would be the one on his arm; she'd simply be following along behind.

"Ready?" he asked.

"Where's Lena?"

"She's going to catch up on sleep."

"You can stay here with her."

"I know I can."

He didn't go back up the stairs.

"You're still coming with me?" she asked.

"Unless I'm cramping your style?" he replied impatiently. "Are we going to stand here and discuss this all night?"

Estella walked out into the courtyard, mint and jasmine potent on the air, the gentle warmth of a Paris summer night sliding like silk over her skin.

"Where exactly are we going?" he asked as he caught up to her. "Bricktop's? It'll be full of Germans."

"Of course you've been there. Definitely not Bricktop's. Somewhere decidedly cheaper." She smiled, remembering all the nights she and Huette used to spend out dancing and laughing, more sure than ever that Huette needed this chance to revive her spirits so she could resume the struggle again in the morning. "But a lot more fun."

CHAPTER TWENTY

On the way to Huette's, Estella asked Alex just one question. "Was your work successful this afternoon?"

"Very," he said. His words, and the slight loosening of the worry lines on his forehead, made her understand that his agent was safe.

"I'm glad."

At Huette's, Estella introduced Alex as her lawyer-boss who didn't speak French and handed over the bag of necessities that Huette seemed to regard as better than treasure.

"Cigarettes!" Huette crowed, hugging the tobacco to her. She pawed through the food and soap and chocolate and Estella watched her with tears in her eyes.

"Do you have anything left for the journey back to Lisbon?" Alex asked Estella in English.

"I kept the escape box. You said that was all I needed."

He sighed but thankfully didn't object.

"I brought you a dress too," Estella said to Huette, switching back to French. "I thought you mightn't have been able to buy fabric to make yourself anything new for a while. I've worn it before but it's only a couple of months old." She passed Huette the white dress she'd worn to her meeting with Elizabeth Hawes.

Huette beamed. "It's beautiful. Thank you."

"Then put it on, I'll buy you dinner and you can smoke as many of our cigarettes as you like."

Huette's smile grew larger. "Dinner and cigarettes and a dance with your very handsome boss sounds perfect."

Alex gave a splutter, which turned into a cough and Estella couldn't resist adding, "Oh, you don't want to do that. He gets rashes all over his face when women come too close. I think he's allergic to them."

As Huette dashed off to get changed, Alex said, "Next time, I'm going to make you something much less powerful than my translator."

Estella couldn't help grinning in reply.

Then they all walked to the club in Montmartre, Estella with her arm linked through Huette's, reminding herself to speak English with Alex, to not do anything to break his cover given that he'd forgone a night with Lena to help her make Huette smile. Before long, the convivial mood dissolved, the night marred by the sight of so many women lining the streets, calling out to Alex, selling themselves, easier to get than butter.

"Their husbands are prisoners of war," Huette said. "They have no money—remember we aren't allowed to have checkbooks like you probably can now in America—and they can't work during the day because they have to stand in queues to buy food for their children. This is what they do for money."

Estella looked at Alex, stricken.

At that moment, the doors to a nearby club opened, revealing a room full of German soldiers dancing with beautifully attired and not-at-all-skinny women.

"Collaborators," Huette said bitterly, nodding at the women.

And Alex's words—*which would you be, Estella, if you'd stayed?*— thundered in her ears as she saw starkly before her the choice that *les Parisiennes* were making every day—to starve slowly like Huette, or to smile at a German and put food on the table.

In the uproar of music that rolled out of the club and made it impossible for anyone to hear what they were saying, Alex whispered to Estella. "One of my informants works in one of Paris's two hundred brothels from nine in the morning until well after midnight. She turns nearly two hundred tricks in that time, every day—seven minutes per man. But she won't stop because the Germans tell her things when they lie in bed with her and she passes them on to my network and she thinks that the price she pays is worth it. That's why I had to rescue my man today; he looks out for her, collects information from her, feeds it to me and I take it to London and that's how we fight the war." He stopped speaking as the doors closed and the music quieted.

Estella shook her head and grasped blindly for Huette's arm, pretending that Alex hadn't said anything, that she was still as eager to take Huette out for the night as she had been earlier. God she was selfish! Why hadn't she said yes to Alex the minute he'd asked her to come to Paris to help him? Because she knew he could have told her that story the night he'd tried to convince her to come and she would have had no choice but to agree. But he'd withheld it, pressuring her, yes, but not blackmailing her with stories of horror, still giving her the option to stay safely in Manhattan if she'd wanted to.

It struck her then with absolute clarity that even though she knew so little about what he did, even though she'd hated him for it at first because it had killed Monsieur Aumont, Alex had to keep doing it. Every airman he saved was an airman who could drop bombs on the German army, every spy he helped out of a safe house in Paris was one more person who could pass on information to help rid Europe of the Nazis, every secret he couldn't tell her was one more secret safe from falling into the hands of those who already had too much power and were wielding it like a machete.

"I will *never* question anything you ask me to do again," was all she said, but she knew he understood because he said, "Thank you."

They reached the club at last and were swallowed up by the sound of the saxophone the minute they walked in the door.

"How have I never been here?" Alex asked, in English, holding the door open for Huette, gazing around at the jazz band, the dancing, the bar that still seemed to have wine at least.

"You were too busy slumming it at Bricktop's with all the beautiful people," Estella said.

"I made a mistake," he said to her. "All the beautiful people are right here."

Estella blushed brighter than a field of poppies.

It was his fault. He definitely shouldn't have said anything about her being beautiful. She'd darted away like an escapee in sight of the Spanish border. At first she stayed by the bar with Huette, chatting to the barman who seemed to know her. Then the musicians stepped down from the stage, kissed Estella's cheeks, dragged her over to a table and sat her down. They teasingly tried to slip an arm around her shoulders but she batted them away good-naturedly and each man sat back in his chair, crestfallen.

Then she passed out more tobacco, one of the men produced a bottle of black market whiskey and soon she was the center of their devoted attention, regaling them with stories of life in Manhattan, each one grander and more ridiculous than the last, taking everyone out of the misery that was Paris for a while. But Alex could see what it cost her, could see her eyes darting around, fearful of whether the Wehrmacht might enter the club, could see her solicitude for Huette and the way she made sure her friend ate a hearty meal, could see her talk doggedly on even though she must be exhausted by their long voyage to France because she understood that Huette and the musicians and everyone else wanted to listen to New York fairy tales and not think about Occupied Paris for as long as she would entertain them.

Alex didn't listen to Estella's words; instead he watched the men, smitten, each of them spellbound, aware of what he'd noticed the first time she'd walked into the Théâtre du Palais-Royal: her quality.

She was rarer than blue diamonds, so beautiful it hurt, and bolder than any man he'd ever worked with. More than that, she radiated joy. He could hear her laughing from where he stood, back leaning against the bar, unable to take his eyes off her.

Eventually he was drawn over to sit at the edge of the group, glad for once to not be thinking about his own work, glad to forget that he had an official reason to be in Paris which was tied to all the cruelties and predilections of men at war, happy to enjoy the calm before the inevitable storm. He pretended not to understand the flow of conversation around him, even though he knew more street French than a Marseilles dockworker and could understand all too well the ribald innuendoes the musicians flung across the table at one another.

After a time, he caught Estella's eye. The smile she gave him took his breath away. The saxophonist at his side saw it too and elbowed him, saying, "She don't give out smiles like that to just anyone."

How Alex ached for that to be true.

Estella knew she was probably a little bit tipsy but she didn't care. To see Huette laughing, to speak French was bittersweet and the whiskey also helped to dull the thought of how nearby her mother was—but still out of reach. Did Maman still have the gold blouse that matched the dress Estella wore?

"Play with us, Estella," Luc, the pianist said, the sound of her name bringing her back into the room.

"No," Estella protested. "Nobody wants to hear me."

"Estella, Estella," Huette began to chant. The rest of the band picked up the chant and, within moments, the entire table was chanting her name.

She saw, with both amusement and astonishment, that Alex had joined the chant too. He grinned at her across the table and she couldn't help laughing.

"*D'accord*," she said, holding up her hands, deciding it was better to give in than to suffer the embarrassment of them chanting her name. She pointed at Alex. "If I'm doing this, then you are too."

"Is that a challenge?" he asked.

"It damn well is," she said and the band members cheered.

"Your wish is my command," he said and mock-bowed.

"If only that was true," Estella said, shaking her head and smiling as he followed her and the band members up onto the stage and sat beside her at the piano. For laughs, she picked out the first notes to Josephine Baker's "Don't Touch My Tomatoes."

Philippe, the singer, whistled. "She's corrupting us."

Estella raised an eyebrow. "The first place I ever heard this song was right here from you."

Alex followed her lead with the accompaniment and she realized he knew the song too; being undercover probably meant he spent a lot of time in bars like this. Then she began to sing along with Philippe and Alex joined in, ad-libbing every now and again with variants he'd heard, he whispered, in Marseilles, in Toulouse, in some town near the Pyrenees. One of them made her laugh so hard she could no longer play and so he picked up both the melody and the accompaniment and embellished with a few riffs that the saxophone copied and which made Estella realize he was as good at piano playing as he was at everything else.

"You know," she whispered in the lull between words, "if your current occupation gets too much, you could always become a jazz piano player."

"Sometimes I think that might just be the ideal life," he whispered back.

At the end he began to play "The Nearness of You" again and Philippe let Alex take the floor because Alex's interpretation was so moving, each note a key struck on Estella's heart. He looked at her with a quizzical expression when she didn't join in.

"I can't," she said. "It's perfect just the way it is."

When he reached the chorus he whispered, "Please?"

In that moment of vulnerability, she caught a glimpse of the young man who lay behind what he'd become, the young man who'd wanted so much to save his mother that he became a kind of highwayman or pirate, the young man given no choice but to accept the largesse of the British government in return for his life, a bargain struck and most likely repented but one he was too parceled in now to ever extract himself from.

She nodded but didn't play. She let him keep the song moving through the room the way it had been, slow, tender, as touchingly beautiful as her vision of the boy-Alex collecting gun money for his father with one hand and stroking his mother's cheek with the other. But she sang with him, softly, letting his voice carry the melody, harmonizing with it in places, making her part in it be the synthesis between the sad and the lovely, the bridge that could take one from sorrow to *jouissance*.

By the end, her eyes were so full of tears that she could hear them in her voice, making it low and husky. As he played the final note, she turned her head away, not wanting him to see her so undefended, but he reached out his hand and gently wiped away the drop falling down her cheek. Then he took her hand in his, raised it to his lips and kissed it.

It was the most insubstantial of gestures, featherweight, but its force was staggering, sending a searing ache right through her center, an ache that made her want to lean in closer to him. An ache that made her want to feel what it would be like if his lips touched hers the same way they had brushed against the back of her hand.

CHAPTER TWENTY-ONE

Immediately after that, Estella fled, pausing only long enough to say to Alex, "I'm going back to the house. For once in your life, please don't follow me." She didn't wait for him to reply, just pushed her way through the cheering club patrons, flinging a hasty good-bye to Huette as she passed. She didn't slow her pace until she was several blocks from the club.

Why was she imagining kissing a man who was dating a woman who could well be her sister? It was madness, stupidity, the temptations of a Paris night in a jazz club, seduced by the saxophones, working feverishly on her already unsettled mind.

She'd go to her mother's. She didn't care what Alex had said about waiting. She'd collect her things from the Rue de Sévigné and be gone before he returned. It would be impossible to even look at him now without betraying everything she'd felt in the moment when he kissed her hand.

She walked on slowly, couldn't make her legs pick up pace, could only replay the way Alex's face had looked as he'd sung, could hardly believe how much it had affected her. Could feel the sensation of his lips blazing on the back of her hand.

Eventually she opened the door of the Rue de Sévigné house and jumped, hand on her heart, when she heard Lena's voice call out. "Alex?"

"No, it's me," Estella said.

Lena stood at the top of the stairs, her face troubled, and Estella wanted to tear off her hand. She might not have betrayed Lena in anything she'd done but, in every one of her feelings, she'd betrayed Lena far more deeply than if Alex had kissed her on the lips. She knew that meant it was time to have an honest conversation; she owed Lena at least that much.

She sat down on the stairs, looking up at Lena. "I've been holding on to the security of not knowing how we're related," Estella said. "Thinking it's better to be ignorant than face the hurt that knowledge will bring."

"You'd never have taken the apple if it had been offered to you?" Lena asked softly.

"That's just it. I probably would have." Estella studied Lena, this woman who was so much like her physically, but so unlike her in the way she didn't seem to know how to smile. As if that had been stolen from her a long time ago. "I'm going to see my mother. Before I do, I hoped you might tell me everything about how you came to be with Harry."

"Come with me," Lena said.

She stood and followed Lena up the stairs, to the end of the hall and to another hidden flight of stairs that Estella had never noticed, stairs which led past what must once have been the servants' quarters and out onto the roof.

When Estella's head emerged into the Paris night, she gasped. "How did you find this?"

"There's a staircase like it in my house. So I assumed there'd be one here. How was your night?" Lena asked as she sat down on the roof.

Estella sat down beside her and realized Lena had a shoebox under her arm. It was labeled with the name of the shop from which her mother used to buy all her shoes. Estella shivered at the thought of what might be inside. "I went to a jazz club," Estella said carefully.

"Did Alex go with you?"

"He did," Estella said.

"Has he told you about his mother? And father?"

"A little."

"I'm glad."

Why? Estella wondered. Instead she pointed at the box. "What's in there?"

"I found it pushed under the piano," Lena said. She passed it to Estella.

"You didn't open it?"

"I wanted to do it with you."

"Thank you," Estella whispered, catching Lena's eyes with hers. Lena let her hold her gaze, and gave her a smile in return.

Then Estella placed the box between them and opened it. On top was a dress, the first one Estella had ever made for herself, the stitches uneven, the buttons loose, the fabric worn. Estella hadn't cared about any of its imperfections and her mother had let her wear it everywhere, even through winter, simply wrapping her daughter up in tights underneath and coats over the top so she'd stay warm, never once telling her to take it off.

As she held the dress, a memory flashed: Estella and her mother walking through the Marais, stopping outside this house. The look on her mother's face was of such despair—not that Estella had been able to name it at the time, she'd simply known that sad was not an adequate way to describe what her mother was feeling—that Estella had wrapped her arms around her mother's waist.

Her mother had wept one loud sob and then, somehow, stilled herself, hidden away the agony and picked up her daughter, even though she was probably too big to be carried. "I just hurt my heart, that's all," Maman had said.

Estella now knew what she meant. Sitting here beside a woman who was most likely her sister, with a box of secrets and a scrap of dress in her hand, Estella's heart was hurting too.

She put her hand back into the box and withdrew a rolled canvas, a portrait of two people, a man and a woman. They were looking at one another in a way that suggested they were deeply in love. Estella frowned as she studied the portrait; she recognized the room the couple were arranged in. A window shaped like that in a church, a piano to one side, a view beyond of buildings that Estella had seen through the same window frame, sitting at that piano.

"They're in this house," she said slowly. "Who are they?"

"It's Evelyn Nesbit. And John Barrymore—you might have seen him in one of his movies. He was her lover before Stanford White and Harry."

Estella turned the canvas over. Written on the back in her mother's perfect handwriting were the words: *Mes parents, 1902.*

"Evelyn Nesbit and John Barrymore were my mother's parents?" Estella said slowly. "That's why Evelyn sold my mother the house for one franc?"

"And why your mother was brought up in a nunnery. Evelyn wasn't married. It's well known she had at least one abortion when she was with John and that she came to Paris ostensibly to recover. She must have decided to give birth though, one time, and your mother was the result."

My God. It was almost too much to comprehend. But there was more in the box.

This time, Estella pulled out a typewritten manuscript page and a pencil drawing which caught her full attention. It was done in her mother's hand. Maman had often sketched too, always in pencil, and this drawing was of two babies asleep. Two tiny babies, newborn.

"So there were two babies," Estella said.

"Do you know who drew it?" Lena asked quietly.

"My mother did," Estella said. "We are twins then."

"I never imagined, ever, that I would have a sister," Lena said so softly Estella almost didn't hear her.

"You don't have to call me your sister if you'd rather not," Estella said hastily. "You can just go on as before, as if I didn't exist."

"Why would I do that?" Lena asked.

"Because…" Estella's voice trailed off. It was some kind of strange gift. In that instant, she felt a new and precious bond. That of a sister. The sister she'd always craved. She put her hand over her mouth, knowing a sob just like the one she'd heard from her mother that day on the Rue de Sévigné was about to escape her and there was nothing she could do to hold it back.

"I know I'm probably a disappointment as a sister," Lena said and Estella watched two lonely tears drip from the corners of Lena's eyes.

Estella gave a half-laugh, half-cry. "Well," she said, "having never had a sister to compare you to, you can't possibly be a disappointment."

Lena gave a shaky laugh. "But none of it tells us who our father is."

"And it doesn't explain how you came to be with Harry. Even if Evelyn gave birth to my mother, and Evelyn was once married to Harry, how did it come to pass that my mother—who wouldn't have known Harry at all—left you with him?" It was the biggest and most terrible of all the questions. Because now that Estella had met Harry, she couldn't imagine anyone leaving a child with him.

"Technically she left me with his mother. I was always told I was the result of a relative getting herself into trouble and who Mrs. Thaw took pity on. But I've never known Mrs. Thaw to show pity to anyone. She adopted me and when Harry was let out of the asylum she gave me to him to look after; he was younger and therefore more fit to raise a child, apparently."

Lena took a long, slow breath. She lay back on the blue-black slate roof and stared up at the sky. "It's amazing to think that there could be something as beautiful as the night sky and that everyone owns it equally, as much as anyone is ever able to own something like that. Harry's the kind of man who, if there was a way to bottle the night sky and all the stars and the moon, he would."

Estella waited, knowing Lena had more, so much more, to say.

But instead of speaking, Lena pulled down her dress at the shoulder and turned away from Estella. She pointed to a mark on her skin, a scar. More than a scar.

Estella realized the thick ridges of white skin were letters: HKT. "Harry Kendall Thaw," she whispered. "He didn't do that to you, surely not."

"He branded me when I got my first period," Lena said matter-of-factly. "To show me that I would always be his."

Estella wanted to curl into herself, to make herself smaller than the tiniest star in the sky, to lose the ability to hear, to see, to think of that loathsome man who'd come to her fashion show and behaved worse than a madman because a madman could never be so deliberate. "And there was nobody who cared enough about you to make him stop," she said slowly. "Nobody to help you."

"No. His mother was as insane as Harry. By then I'd read Evelyn's memoir and knew how cruel he could be and why I had to let him do what he wanted. At least then I had a certain degree of freedom. If I refused, I'd lose even that. He threw a party for me the night after he branded me, announced that I should come out into the world, and he bought me a dress appropriate for a courtesan and paraded me in front of a roomful of salivating men."

I don't want to hear any more, Estella wanted to say. But all she had to do was listen. Lena had been made to do far worse things and here she was, still alive. The least Estella could do was allow Lena to talk because she suspected that nobody besides Alex knew any of this story. "How did you get the house in Gramercy Park? How did you get away from him?"

Out it all came.

The day of my coming out party, Harry opened the door to my room without knocking, as was his way.

"We're having a celebration tonight," he said brusquely, his overfed and over-wined bulk corseted tightly by a silk waistcoat, the buttons of which betrayed the strain. "Dress with care." He deposited a gown on my bed.

"Certainly," I said, the pain in my shoulder reminding me how much better it was to acquiesce. I sat down at the dressing table, my elegant room and my blight of an uncle reflected in the glass. So much silk: wallpaper, drapes, silk covers on the bed. An excess of gilding: the posts of the bed, the threads of the wallpaper, the Ormolu clock shining like an impertinent sun on the mantel.

I did everything that was required of me, making up my face and putting on the dress, which had a neckline low enough to show off the tops of my breasts. I strolled into the drawing room about half an hour late and drew the eyes of every man in the room. My "uncle"— Harry—smiled behind his glass of red wine and I knew I'd pleased him and that it might, if I was lucky, buy me a few days free time.

Once dinner had finished, Harry stood. "Gentlemen, let us retire for brandy. Ladies, please make yourselves comfortable in the drawing room."

The ladies rustled off, ready to make veiled and catty remarks about one another. Especially about me.

"Lena," Harry said. "You will serve us."

It was what I expected. In a house full of servants it was so much more extravagant to have the thirteen-year-old dependant do the work.

I followed the men into the smoking room and passed the cigars around. When I held out the box to one man, who I recognized from the newspapers as one of the Thaw family's biggest business rivals, Frank Williams—Harry always liked to keep his enemies close—he barked, "What's your name?"

"Lena."

"Lena? Your parents were not traditionalists."

"My parents are dead."

Frank shrugged. And with that gesture of absolute unconcern, I knew what I would do, if I could. The fact that Harry hated him only made it more perfect. I clipped the end of Frank's cigar.

"Speaking of traditions," Harry said, smiling magnanimously from his chair by the fire, "I have something for you, my dear."

"Oh, you've given me so much, Uncle," I said, so sweetly I could feel the honey dripping from my tongue. "I don't need anything more."

"What about this?" he offered, holding up a silver locket, intricately engraved and with his picture inside.

I was so familiar with his performance as the benevolent uncle who gave his burden of a ward everything she could wish for that I simply inclined my head so he could place the locket around my neck. It was heavy, like a millstone, but I smiled and drew a couple of tears into my eyes, as if I was overcome. Harry nodded.

"Let me have a look at that," Frank called from his chair.

I obliged, making sure to bend down close to him. I saw his eyes fix on my cleavage and I knew exactly what he wanted, and that the *plan I was just beginning to form might even work. "I do love jewelry," I whispered. "And men who buy it for me."*

He shifted uncomfortably on the chaise, crossing his legs. "Another brandy."

"Of course."

I waited on him expertly and, the next day, a locket larger than the one Harry had given me, edged with diamonds, arrived. It was from Frank. And from that moment on, I cultivated him, encouraging his gifts, the more expensive the better. It excited Frank that, no matter what happened in business, he was having the last laugh with Harry's prized possession. Occasionally, at parties in darkened rooms, I had to pay Frank for the gifts. But it cost him more than it did me. Every now and then, I showed Harry a ring or a brooch which infuriated him, but would lead to Harry buying me a larger piece and presenting it to me at a party in front of Frank.

It only took me six years to gather a collection of jewelry that, when pawned, amounted to a tidy sum. It wasn't quite enough to buy a house or to buy my freedom though. So I had Frank help me one last time.

I told him about a house in Gramercy Park that Harry always liked to walk past, covetously, looking at it the same way Harry looked at me. If I had this house, I told Frank, then he could visit me wherever and whenever he liked. And how that would annoy dear Harry.

Frank engaged a lawyer to look into it and found out the house belonged to Harry; he'd had it built when he was in the asylum in 1917 after ruining a poor young boy. It was in his mother's name though, because he couldn't transact business if he was mad. He'd obviously knocked down the original house and built his own replica of the Paris house. Back then I wondered why he'd never lived in it but I think it was yet another thing he wanted to own for the simple sake of possession. His dearest wish was always to possess Evelyn and, in imitating her house, he must have felt he'd regained some control over her.

Anyway, once Frank found out it was Harry's house, he was only too eager to steal it out from under Harry's nose. He gave me the additional money I needed, thinking he would have uninhibited access to me once I was installed there. The lawyer made Mrs. Thaw an anonymous offer, one too good to refuse, and Mrs. Thaw was happy to be rid of such an extravagant folly. As soon as I had the keys, I changed the locks and forbade Frank from ever crossing the threshold. His revenge was to slander me all over town. I didn't care.

As for Harry, I knew that, when I told him, there was nothing more he could do to me that he hadn't already done. It was a symbolic victory rather than a real one. But I took great satisfaction in hearing him throw a vase at the wall when I left.

When Lena had finished, Estella didn't speak. She realized that somewhere during the terrible story, she'd stretched out her hand and taken Lena's. They both lay staring up at the night sky and Estella knew that Lena's life had long existed in a night where nothing came after. Just more night, long empty stretches of darkness pressing in.

She gripped Lena's palm, offering the only kind of solace she could, knowing now why Lena had always been so reticent to talk about her past and about Harry, besides what was on the public record. She wished she could go back to that night in Café Society and speak to Lena with compassion rather than suspicion.

"I'm going to Maman's apartment now," Estella said. "I'll take you to see her tomorrow, if you still want to, after what she tells me. Putting it off isn't going to stop or change whatever has already happened in the past."

"No," murmured Lena. "The past can be a bastard like that."

Estella turned her head to see that Lena was smiling a little. "How do you do it?" she asked. "How do you keep yourself alive in spite of everything? How do you…fall in love when you've never been given love?"

"As loathsome as it sounds, my secret is a life lived in vengeance. I stayed alive because I wanted the satisfaction of seeing Harry's face when I walked out. Of meeting him again and having him know he lost. And as for love, well, I don't think I have any answers for you."

"But you and Alex…"

"Alex is as much of a mess as I am. Two disasters who clung to each other one night long ago. Since then, it's been convenient for us to be one another's date at parties when he's in town; it keeps the wolves away. But that's all it is."

"It must be love," Estella insisted. "He brought you here so we could find out something that might…"

"Make everything better? Like you said, the past can't be changed."

"But the future…"

Lena interrupted her again. "We're in the middle of a city that's given in to a bully. That's the way of life. That's what the future holds."

No it doesn't, Estella wanted to protest. Instead she squeezed Lena's hand. "I hope you're wrong."

Lena was silent for so long that Estella thought the conversation, their first moment of true intimacy, was over. But then Lena said so unexpectedly, "Maybe…maybe I am wrong. Maybe this," she indicated their joined hands, "is what the future holds."

To turn that little spark of hope, the first Estella had ever seen in Lena, into optimism, into joy, into belief that all human relations were not selfish and violent was suddenly Estella's most desperate wish. She reached out and hugged her sister. "I love you, Lena."

Estella knew as she spoke the words that *she'd* been wrong. How could she have wanted Alex to kiss her, how could she have reveled in the nearness of him, how could she have found pleasure in that moment of sitting beside him? Lena deserved for Estella not to covet the one good thing she'd found; the comfort Alex gave her.

Estella felt Lena's body shake. She let Lena go, offering a smile, which Lena returned, the tears in her eyes matching Estella's. *We* are *the same*, Estella thought now. *We both want this bond forged by blood to become something more, adamantine, lasting beyond forever, adding an unexpected brilliance to our lives.*

It was half an hour until curfew. Plenty of time to get to her mother's house. Indeed, the streets were still busy with prostitutes, and with German soldiers soliciting. Estella felt ill that Paris, her city, was given over to this kind of filthy commerce but she'd never had to survive on only her wits and who knew what she might do in order to stay alive? What Lena had done? She shivered.

As she walked, the warm air on her skin felt almost scalding. All her senses were heightened, raw, and she didn't know if it was because of the war, because of Alex or because of Lena. Or if it was because she was about to see her mother for the first time in so long.

At the familiar door, Estella rested her palm on the wood, then jumped back as it opened. Monsieur Montpelier, the slithering concierge, flashed his teeth. "*Bonsoir*," he muttered and Estella noted that he hadn't lost weight, that he didn't look hungry, that somebody was keeping him well fed and watered.

Collaborator. Huette's accusation, directed at the similarly well-nourished Parisians they'd seen earlier in the night, sprang to Estella's mind. She shivered. But who would care about anything Monsieur Montpelier might know?

"You are looking for your mother?" he asked with more solicitude than he'd ever shown her before.

Estella nodded.

"Upstairs," the concierge smiled, pointing. "You should go upstairs."

"I know the way," Estella retorted.

She took the stairs to the top floor, pushed the door open and snapped on the light but there was no power. She picked her way through the dark to the room she'd once shared with her mother. The bed was empty.

"Maman?" Estella called softly. No reply came.

Estella frowned. In the kitchen, there was little food. Dust clothed the table in a thin but noticeable layer, the cup on the table was filled with dried-out chicory. She returned to the room she'd once shared with her mother, lay down on the bed and felt the emptiness around her—the absence of her mother's scent—as she listened to the sound of her city under the boot of the Germans: unfamiliar, joyless, afraid.

Some time later she heard the front door open and she stiffened.

"Estella?" Lena's voice, followed by Alex's, calling more loudly, "Estella?"

She heard the sound of the light switch flicked uselessly, heard them moving through the main room. She heard Alex say to Lena, "Stay here."

After a moment, he stood in the doorway.

"Was she helping you?" Estella's words came out dully.

"I asked her to stop." His voice was wooden too. "But she made it very clear that she'd do it anyway, on her own, without British support, which is the most dangerous way. So I let her. I'm sorry."

Everyone was sorry. What good was sorry? But Estella knew how stubborn her mother was, refusing Monsieur Aumont's insistence that they not pay back the money they owed him, pushing Estella to go to New York, working from the time she was fifteen to support Estella.

If her mother had insisted, there was no way Alex would have been able to stop her.

Lena joined Alex in the doorway, then moved over to sit beside Estella. And Estella knew that she'd come with Alex to find her because she'd refused to be left behind. That she'd wanted to help. That Lena was as stubborn as Estella and their mother.

Estella slipped her hand into Lena's.

"Your mother was afraid someone was watching her," Alex said. "Perhaps she's moved to a safer place. I'll do everything I can to find out."

"If she's been taken by the Germans, what will they do to her?" Estella asked.

"They might take her to a camp…"

Rather than kill her. "Which is better?" she whispered. "A camp or death?"

Alex swore. But he told her the truth. "Death."

"Then if you find out she's been taken, that's what I'll pray for," she said.

"We need to go." He hooked a finger around the blackout curtain and peered out, hackles obviously raised. Then he cursed worse than Estella had ever heard him swear. "Quick," he ordered. "Down the stairs, before they come in. To the third floor."

Estella tried to hurry but it was as if grief had set itself in concrete inside her limbs, robbing her of nimbleness. As she stumbled down the stairs, she thought she understood why Alex had said the third floor, not the ground. One of the apartments there had a room that ran across and above the Passage Saint-Paul. They could get out that way.

"In here," Alex commanded, pushing open the door of the apartment and ushering both her and Lena inside.

Estella could see that it was yet another abandoned home; the old couple who used to live there had probably left for the Free Zone or to stay with other family in Paris to pool their meager resources.

But Alex didn't take them across the Passage. Instead he opened the window above the Passage. "Out here. Lower yourself down, keep your hands on the sill and then drop. It's not far enough to hurt you. Here," he held out his hand to Lena.

"Let Estella go first," Lena said.

So Estella found herself being bundled through a window un-ceremoniously, hands gripping the ledge, body hanging. Before she dropped to the ground, she heard running footsteps. A door crash open. An explosion, like a gunshot. Lena crying out. Terror dampened Estella's palms and she almost slipped. Then a panicked shot of adren-aline gave her the strength to hoist her head up high enough to see what was happening.

Lena lay on the floor. Alex stood in front, shielding her body. The concierge stood in the doorway, smiling toothily. A man in a German uniform had a gun knocked from his hand by Alex. Then Alex ran a knife viciously through the German's belly. The concierge fled.

Oh God! Estella remembered how insistent the concierge had been that she go upstairs. That Alex had said her mother thought somebody was watching her. The concierge, who'd always hated both Estella and her mother, was plump, most likely on the rewards paid by the Germans for feeding them information about anyone suspected of working against the Nazis.

"Lena," she tried to say but her mouth was dry from fear and her arms were shaking, unable to hold her head above the sill anymore. Her last glimpse of the room was of Alex picking up Lena, who was bloodied, insensate.

"Move!" he hissed at Estella as he slid through the window, using one arm to maneuver himself, the other arm wrapped around Lena.

Estella's feet hit the ground, the shock of landing jolting her out of her uncomprehending state.

Alex followed close behind, landing with a thud. "Dammit, dammit, dammit," he swore, feeling Lena's neck, leaning in to listen for breath.

Estella stood frozen, unable to move or to speak, unable to care that the concierge might now be telephoning for more Nazis with more guns.

Alex looked at Estella and shook his head.

"No." Estella's mouth made the shape of the word but it was soundless, a protest she could not voice.

Alex closed Lena's eyes. "I'll take her with us."

And he did, as best he could, struggling along the Passage Saint-Paul with Lena in his arms; lifeless Lena, her limbs swaying as they moved. But Estella knew, and she knew that he knew, they would move a lot faster without Lena and she also knew that he was bringing Lena for her. She led the way deep into the Passage, knowing the back door to the Église Saint-Paul-Saint-Louis lay right at the end and she prayed that whoever might be following them wouldn't know, would think the Passage a dead end, and would search for them out on the street instead.

They made it to the church. For the first time in her life in that sacred space Estella didn't turn her eyes to the beautiful altar of Mary and her baby with its columns of rufous marble slashed with white, its statuary, its gilded candelabra, the altar that bore the inscription *Regina Sine Labe Concepta*—Queen conceived without sin. Nor did she turn her mind to the continuation of the phrase: the exhortation to pray for us. Because who was praying for them? For Paris? For her mother? For Lena?

She wanted to scream at Mary, holding her infant child so serenely. The only people left in the world who still believed in the power of the dome above, in the three-storied transept, the grand organ, the Delacroix painting, the clamshells for holy water that Victor Hugo had gifted to the church, were people who still believed in hope, holding on futilely to ridiculous bibelots.

She could hear the noise of scuffle and shouting outside and she turned to Alex at the same time as he turned to her. She read the question in his eyes and she nodded. Gently, so gently it made Estella's throat constrict and the tears stream from her eyes, almost made her turn away because bearing witness was an agony beyond pain, Alex lay Lena down and crossed himself.

He kissed Lena's cheek and whispered to her:

"I am the soft stars that shine at night.
Do not stand at my grave and cry;
I am not there, I did not die."

His words fired a sob from Estella's mouth, too loud.

Then she bent down and kissed Lena's cheek for the first time, weeping. That flare of hope she'd seen in Lena's eyes as they sat on the rooftop, hands joined, was forever extinguished, put out just as it had begun. Far from making Lena's life better, far from bringing her answers, far from showing her that love trumped violence, Estella had only proven the exact opposite. The sister she had always wanted, and that she thought perhaps Lena wanted too, was irrevocably lost.

Alex reached out and took her hand. "We have to go."

She followed him out onto Rue Saint-Antoine, away from Lena, away from any sense of ever again being the person Estella once was.

CHAPTER TWENTY-TWO

But the streets held still more horror. The day hadn't yet taken hold, but the Germans had. As Estella and Alex stood in the main doorway of the church, peering out, Estella saw the French police, which was the worst thing of all—that her own people could do this to their fellow citizens—behaving like brutes. Hundreds of men, no thousands of men, were driven along by the police like animals, toward waiting busses. Few protested. The men of Paris were too cowed, too afraid. They walked with their heads down, in case the act of looking up was deemed a betrayal and thus punishable with violence. Red streaks of dawn fell across their faces like fresh wounds, or the unhealed scars of old ones.

Alex tried to keep his body between Estella and the doorway so she couldn't see but it was impossible to obscure so many men. "What's happening?" she asked in a shocked whisper.

"They're Jewish," he replied in a low voice. "It's another round-up."

"Where are they taking them?"

Alex's voice was so low she could barely hear it. "Drancy," he said.

"Drancy?" she asked.

"An internment camp."

A camp. A place Alex had said was worse than death. But there were too many for that surely? She looked up at Alex and he caught the question in her eye.

"I'm doing everything I can. But not right now," he said. "I'm not risking your life as well as…"

As well as Lena's.

"It's a hellish thing to admit but the confusion will help us get away," he said grimly. "You have to do everything I ask though. No questions. None."

The first time he'd told her that, she'd thought he was stony. But now he was darker and colder than the Seine in winter. If she didn't know him, she would have been terrified of him, transformed into the man who'd knifed another in an attempt to save Lena. She nodded.

They hurried along, winding through side streets and gardens and courtyards. He stopped at a bar and had a heated conversation with a man with a limp, who Estella recognized as someone he'd spoken to at the club and also in Marseilles.

When he rejoined Estella, he said, "The Rue de Sévigné is still safe. We can go back there."

Not long after, they pushed through the gates into the courtyard, then into the house. Alex disappeared up the stairs and closed the door to his room without another word. What was there left to say?

Estella climbed back onto the roof where she'd lain with Lena just a few hours before. She pulled her mother's drawing of the two babies out of her pocket and ran her hands over the pencil lines, thinking of Lena. A sister she wouldn't have known had she stayed in Paris, had the war not happened. A sister Estella suddenly missed more than her own mother because at least with her mother she had memories. With Lena all she had were possibilities that had been suddenly and savagely snatched away.

The only consolation was that the drawing meant Jeanne really was her mother, and Lena's. But it didn't solve the mystery of who her father was, nor why her mother had taken one baby with her, and left the other in America with the Thaw family. A wind blew up, almost tipping the box over and, as Estella went to rescue it, she realized there was one more thing inside. A photograph. She picked it up.

It was a photograph of her mother smiling beside a man who looked like a younger version of Harry Thaw. Estella froze. Then white-hot fury seared through her. She ripped the photograph and hurled the pieces into the street below.

Then she lay down and the tears came again, tears for Lena, tears for what she'd just seen in the photograph. Her mother had known Harry Thaw. She shut her eyes against that thought but behind her closed lids all she could see was Lena's lifeless face, and the look in her eyes when she and Estella had discovered that they really were sisters.

She must have fallen asleep after that because she awoke blinking, a midday sun beating down on her, burning her face. She put up a hand to ward it off, then she stood up and, as she did, the memory of the night before caused her to stumble. She needed to eat. To drink some water. Her stomach hurt with nausea and loss.

She climbed back down to the hall. A noise made her stiffen. The sound of someone being sick. A groan. Low voices. She stepped over to Alex's door and listened. She heard the sounds again. She put her hand on the door and turned the handle, furious.

Inside, the room was so dark after the sunlight on the roof that she couldn't see. She blinked a few times and heard Alex's voice mumble, "Ask her to leave, Peter."

A man materialized by her side, the man with the limp. Before she knew what was happening, he'd ushered her out and closed the door.

"Drunk away his sorrows, has he?" Estella asked sarcastically. What other reason could there be for the noises she'd heard than that Alex had gotten himself deeply and extraordinarily drunk? How like him, while she'd been mourning Lena, to go out and submerge himself in whiskey.

Peter didn't answer.

"Is this how he recovers himself the morning after a disaster?" she prodded again and this time she got what she wanted. A fight.

Peter took her by the arm and marched her down the stairs and into the kitchen.

"You don't know the first thing about him," Peter said, scorn drenching each word. "Alex Montrose is the best man I've worked with. I've been with him for five years and he'd lay down his own life for any of his men."

"After he's written himself off with whiskey so he can pretend nothing has happened you mean?"

"I don't know what happened last night but you're responsible for it." Peter spat the words at her like bullets. "You went to your mother's apartment when he told you not to. You led him smack bang into a trap that your mother had been smart enough to run from. You mightn't have noticed but a war is about people's lives."

"My sister died for this goddamned war," Estella blazed, "so I know very well it's about lives."

"It's about thinking of other people besides yourself." Peter stepped closer to her, and Estella stiffened, wanting to move away, hating this man for making her feel weak and vulnerable.

"He'll kill me for telling you but I'm going to so that you take that look off your face, as if everything you've done was innocent and he's the only one in the wrong," Peter raged on. "He went back this morning for Lena's body. He buried her in the garden outside. He sent out three men who should be doing something more important to find word of your mother. Only then did he let the fucking vertigo that's plagued him since he dropped out of a plane with a broken parachute and almost died, the vertigo that raises its ugly head when he's had more to deal with than he ought, ride over him."

He paused for a moment but the tongue-lashing wasn't over. "Think about it," Peter continued. "How much has he slept since you arrived in France? Who got you from Lisbon to Paris? Who got an agent with a broken leg over to the American Hospital in broad daylight and got him fixed up enough so he could be on an escape line, all within twenty-four hours of Alex being in Paris. It didn't just happen, Estella. It happened because he made it happen. He kept lookouts posted and gathered intelligence and found the safest way and the whole time he was passing on messages to the French resistance and you just thought you were all here for a holiday. And now he's upstairs so sick he can't move off the bed and it'll last until tomorrow night at least and he won't even be able to stand up because the room is spinning so much it'll swing right up and hit him in the head. But if you'd prefer to think of him as a selfish drunk, then go right ahead."

Sick? Alex couldn't be sick. He was invulnerable, unassailable. But Peter didn't look or sound as if he was joking. Estella tried to speak. She was unable to.

Peter walked over to the stove, boiled the kettle, made a cup of coffee, filled a glass with water and went to take them up the stairs. All the while, his words reeled through Estella's head as if she were the one with vertigo.

She hadn't thought of anyone but herself. She'd gone to her mother's when Alex had told her she shouldn't. Once there, she'd mindlessly gone upstairs as the concierge had suggested, never once considering the possibility that it was a trap, a trap that she'd led Alex and Lena right into. She'd let Lena send her out the window first. She'd spent the last year loathing Alex just because he'd been there when Monsieur Aumont had died and her life changed forever. And because he'd brought Lena into her life. But she couldn't dislike Alex for that, not anymore.

"Wait!" she called.

Peter stopped.

"You're right," she said starkly. "You have better things to do. Like stop a war from going too far. Tell me what to do and I'll do it. He'll hate it but he doesn't have a choice."

He stared at her and she didn't think he'd relent. But she stared straight back, not giving in.

"Just get him through it," Peter said eventually. "Make sure he doesn't move. Make him drink water. He'll be sick but distract him, make him keep it down. Do not let him sit up or stand up before he's ready. You'll be able to tell; look at his eyes. They'll be flickering if the vertigo's still there."

"Right," Estella said. "Give me that." She took the water and coffee from Peter. "He said we're safe here. Is that true?"

"Yes. Your former concierge was watching your mother. Alex knew it, and he went to the club with you to keep you away from her apartment. But I'm certain nobody has connected this house with your mother."

He went to the club with you to keep you away from her apartment. Again, she'd been wrong. Again she'd been selfish. But for Estella's actions, Lena's death could have been prevented. She'd all but killed her own sister.

Of course Alex tried to protest, as much as he was able. But Estella ignored him.

Alex cursed Peter and lay on the bed fuming, furious at Peter for letting her into the room, furious at Estella and, most of all, furious at himself. That he'd spent his whole life eliminating weaknesses and his goddamned body threw up one that he couldn't control. He knew he was lucky; that his insistence on being an operative on the ground brought with it physical risks and he'd gone for a long time without anything too bothersome happening. But just when he thought he'd recovered from the broken parachute and subsequent too-fast collision with the ground earlier in the year, he'd discovered this legacy of vertigo, which he couldn't control or predict. All he could do was lie on his back on the bed and watch Estella, through half-open eyes, as she busied herself with water and coffee.

He'd tried to sit the moment she walked into the room, which was a huge mistake. The floor came up to wallop him in the face and the nausea flooded him. He was sick into a basin right in front of her, unable to even take the basin to the bathroom and wash it out. He saw her do it and he cringed, wasting energy telling her not to, asking her to leave, demanding that she leave.

"I don't need a nurse," he'd barked once he'd recovered enough to speak.

"I can see that," she said sarcastically.

"I don't need you," he'd insisted, which of course wasn't true either.

"I know that but I'm all you've got." She sat down on the piano stool and folded her arms.

Alex tried to stay awake but it was too hard and he soon dozed off. He woke later to find her leaning over the bed, water glass ready. He shuffled his head up the pillow the smallest amount, just enough to allow him to drink, and even that slight movement nearly undid him. She lay a cold cloth on his forehead while he fought back the nausea, grateful for the damp cloth soothing away the clamminess of his skin, calming the nausea at last.

The trouble with lying in a bed so still and silent was that he had too much time to think. He thought of Lena, of Estella, of what had happened. Of how Lena's death was his fault. Of how he'd broken his vow never to do anything that involved his heart, which he'd thought was safely preserved in cynicism, hiding away behind meaningless affairs with willing women, always moving on after one encounter because it was the only way to not drag anyone else into the ruin he called his life.

The first time he'd followed his heart was back when he was fifteen and he'd made a stupid and dangerous plan to get his mother out of

Hong Kong, behind his father's back. But his father had discovered the ruse—he'd been told by someone Alex had trusted to help him—and Alex and his mother had been forced back to the house. His father had beaten Alex to within an inch of his life—his father was always very careful to go just far enough that he wouldn't die. He'd been in the hospital for over a week, with more broken bones than he cared to remember.

But his mother—he almost couldn't bear to think of it. His father had beaten his mother to within an inch of her life too and he'd told everyone they were set upon by street thugs, which was an entirely believable story in Hong Kong. His mother had spent a month in the hospital. That was when he'd decided to kill his father.

But his father had thought of that. He told Alex, "If you kill me, then your mother will die too. I've left instructions with *friends* to make sure she dies a painful, prolonged death if anything ever happens to me."

So he had to keep his father alive in order to keep his mother alive. He had to do what he was told and never let his heart rule his head again because the price of doing it once had nearly cost his mother her life. Just like the price of yesterday's fracas had been Lena's life.

He must have sworn aloud because his eyes flew open at the movement of someone, Estella, touching his arm ever so lightly.

"Alex, you're dreaming," she said gently.

He shook his head, forgetting that shaking his head was like hurling himself onto a violent and relentless carousel. He winced and tried to breathe normally, prayed that he wouldn't be sick in front of her again, that he could at least keep hold of a scrap of dignity.

"Have some more water," she said. "Here." She put the cloth on his forehead again and it was so cold he realized he was sweating, that he'd been dreaming, that he'd probably said things in his sleep that he didn't want her to hear.

This time, when he lifted his head to drink the water, the room still spun wildly, but it settled more quickly. "Thank you," he said, knowing he could at least be gracious despite the fact that he wanted her to leave.

And then she did something that he both wanted and didn't want. She walked around the bed and sat on the other side, leaning her back against the wall, a respectable distance away from him but still beside him on a bed. "I think you can leave me alone now," he said, trying to ask nicely rather than demanding as he'd done before. "I'll be fine."

"Yes, you look as if you're ready to shepherd me single-handedly from one side of France to the other all over again."

"Just France?" he replied, more weakly than he would have liked, hoping banter would convince her he was feeling better, even though he wasn't. "I think I'm ready to tackle flying one of those ships across the Atlantic."

She grinned. "Can you fly?"

"Yes."

"Is there anything you can't do?"

It was a teasing question but all he could think was, yes, there was a long list of things he couldn't do: he couldn't bring Lena back from the dead. He couldn't make everything better for Lena the way he'd wanted to, in some kind of strange apology to his mother for not being able to make her last years happy ones. And he couldn't reach out and touch Estella, not because the vertigo was stopping him, but because it would be the most dangerous act of all.

"Will you talk to me about Lena?" she asked.

"Talking is probably the only thing I'm capable of right now," he admitted.

He wriggled a little and she leaned over, propping his pillow slightly. He felt the room tilt as he raised himself the smallest amount, suddenly aware that he wasn't wearing a shirt. He wished he could ask

her to pass him one but he wouldn't be able to put it on by himself and
there was no way he was going to ask her to help him with that.

What do you want to know about her? he supposed he should ask. But
he didn't want to confine Lena to a series of questions and answers.

"I met Lena at a party in July 1940. I was on leave for a week and I
always go to New York when I'm on leave. We were at a masked ball.
I noticed her hair. I asked an acquaintance about her and he laughed
and said that he was surprised I hadn't met Lena before. That her
notoriety meant she was always at the best parties, invited as an amusement because she was easy." He winced. "Sorry, I should be sanitizing
this."

Estella shook her head. "Tell me exactly as it was. I'll know if you
change anything; you have a habit of scratching your left little finger
when you lie."

He laughed, then blanched because even that was still too much. "I
didn't know. I'll have to stop."

"Keep going," she said, wriggling down to lie her head against a pillow and resting her hands on her stomach.

"Lena had quite a reputation, almost as bad as mine," he confessed.
"I asked her to dance because she had hair I thought I'd seen once before. We danced together but we didn't really speak and at the end she
kissed me. And…" He realized he'd moved his right hand on top of
his left and was about to scratch the back of his little finger.

"You slept with her," Estella supplied. "You can skip that part."

"Thanks," he said wryly. Then he hesitated. "It wasn't what I
thought it would be. She was…cold. For her, it was an act of the mind
only."

"Because that's the way it normally is for you." Estella again filled
in the blanks he didn't know how to explain. "Like I said, I don't need
the details."

How to explain what he wanted her to understand without seeming as if he was bragging about his sexual prowess? "I just meant that I empathized; she thought she was ruined, not meant for the joys of life. She was doing it to forget. But her hair had reminded me of a magnificent woman who'd stormed into a theater at the Palais-Royal as brazenly as if she'd been spying for half her life and who'd delivered me papers with more flair than I'd ever seen in any of my counterparts." He stopped; he'd said too much.

"Surely you didn't dance with Lena because you thought she was me?" Estella asked, slowly. "You must have women in every port around the world; I don't believe I could have made such an impression on you."

You did. Instead he continued. "I knew after that first night that she couldn't have been you because the woman at the theater was so full of life; she hadn't had it crushed out of her the way Lena had."

Estella squeezed her eyes shut. "She all but told me that he raped her."

"Over and over. You've read Evelyn's memoir. He's a sadist. He locked Evelyn Nesbit up for two weeks and raped her too."

"I keep thinking that if Lena had been raised by my mother, none of this would have happened to her. That I'm the lucky one. It should have been me going out the window last. I should have given Lena a chance to live, just like, from birth, she'd given me that same chance."

"You're not responsible."

"And you haven't been lying here beating yourself up over it? Haven't been blaming yourself?"

He didn't answer because he couldn't, not truthfully.

"All I know for sure is that none of it was Lena's fault," Estella said quietly and he heard her voice catch.

He couldn't help it; he reached out and took her hand in his, holding it very gently so she could easily slip away if she wanted to but she let him and it was almost unbearable, to feel the touch of her skin on his. He lay with his eyes closed, thankful that he could blame his inability to speak on illness.

"Lena and I weren't lovers," he said abruptly, needing her to know that now. "I was never with her again, not after that first time. I cared about her though; nobody else did. So we became odd escorts for one another. If I was in Manhattan, we'd go to parties together because then neither of us would…" *Feel the need to go home with strangers.* He cut the words off. "I wanted her to find some sort of peace. A peace I could never give my mother. I know I pushed you to get to know her but I thought if anyone could make her happy, you could. It was stupid of me to even think that bringing the two of you together could make any kind of reparations for my mother."

"I didn't know," Estella said in a low voice. "I thought you and she were…an item."

"We weren't." Because she wasn't the woman who'd sailed into a theater and stunned him, the woman who took his breath away by just being near him. A woman who'd grown up with love, not with hatred; he'd seen the evidence of it in her mother's apartment, which was poor in material things, but there were mementos of Estella everywhere, testifying to a deep-held adoration of mother for daughter.

He shifted a little in the bed, hoping to turn the conversation and it did, but not in a way that was any better. As he moved, the medallion engraved with three witches riding a broomstick that he wore on a silver chain around his neck caught the candle flame, sending out a sharp glint of light.

"What is it?" Estella asked. Her hand reached out to touch the pendant, her finger grazing the skin of his chest in a movement so exquisite he could do nothing other than hold his breath.

When he thought he could speak, he said, "Three witches. *The Road to En-Dor*. Rudyard Kipling?"

Estella shook her head.

So he quoted:

"Oh the road to En-dor is the oldest road
And the craziest road of all!
Straight it runs to the Witch's abode,
As it did in the days of Saul,
And nothing has changed of the sorrow in store
For such as go down on the road to En-dor!

"It's a story about a witch who sees the future," he continued, "but who comforts those before they step out into danger. *The Road to En-Dor* was the name of a book written about one of the greatest escapes by a soldier in the Great War. So the witches are the insignia of my unit now. They keep all of us safe."

Estella didn't say anything, just returned the pendant to his chest, her finger again brushing his skin. "I'm glad you have something to keep you safe," she said.

Neither of them spoke after that. He was tired now, which always happened just before his head righted itself. He could feel himself drifting away into sleep and the last thing he thought before he went under was that if he died right now, he'd die happier than he'd ever been, knowing that a woman as extraordinary as Estella was lying on a bed beside him while he slept.

CHAPTER TWENTY-THREE

It was a long night, punctuated by Alex's nightmares, nightmares which told Estella that, whatever he'd done, whatever had happened to him in his past, he paid for it every day. That he cared deeply, too deeply, which was perhaps why he seemed so careless on the surface. Because Alex was good. He'd been more than good to Lena: solicitous, concerned, wanting to grant Lena the gift of a sister in an attempt to show her that love did exist.

For Alex to have been as careful as he'd been with someone as broken as Lena made him worthy of a great deal more admiration than Estella had ever spared him. So every time he murmured something in his sleep, she drifted over to the piano and played a song, quietly, gently, hoping the music would lull him back into peace and it worked, mostly.

Around midnight, when she was sitting at the piano, forehead propped on her hand, the things from her mother's box resting in her lap, crying a little for Lena, for her mother, for Alex too, she realized, she heard him say her name.

"Estella?"

"I'm here," she said, slipping back over to the bed and lying down next to him. In the dark, his eyes were open and she studied his face. "You were dreaming again," she said, the papers in her hands crackling.

"Bad habit of mine," he said mirthlessly. "What's that?"

She explained what she and Lena had found—everything except the photograph she'd ripped to pieces—and held up the manuscript page that she and Lena hadn't had time to look at. "It's from Evelyn Nesbit's memoir. But it's not in the copy Lena gave me. It's very intimate—I mean, I know the whole memoir is intimate—but this page isn't salacious; it's gentle, about her and John and their love. It even mentions the Rue de Sévigné as their sanctuary. And…" she stopped, unsure if she was reading more into it than was really there.

"Go on," Alex said.

"It mentions a gift from John that she couldn't keep. A gift she had to give away and that it broke her heart."

"Your mother."

"I think so. Perhaps that's why this page isn't in the published version. Sadism and murder aren't too sensational but giving away an illegitimate child is."

"When was Evelyn's memoir published?" Alex asked.

"I don't know. But the date on this manuscript page is 1916."

"The year before you were born," he said slowly. "Is that a coincidence? Does the writing of the memoir have anything to do with you and Lena?"

Estella frowned. "It's hard to see how."

Alex rubbed a hand over his face as if he was tired.

Estella moved to sit up. "Sorry, I should let you sleep."

"Stay," Alex said. "I was just thinking." He paused, as if turning something over in his mind. "Lena said Harry had the Gramercy Park house built in 1917. That was the year you were born. Which means he must have seen the Paris house before 1917. Did he find out about it from Evelyn's memoir?"

"But this page isn't in the published book. So that can't be it. And it says here that neither Evelyn nor John used the house after 1902 when she had my mother. So it was empty for years." She closed her eyes. Talking about Harry made her remember what Lena had told her about the things he'd done. She shivered. "Monsters," she said. "Why is the world giving way to monsters? Harry Thaw. Hitler." More pictures scrolled behind her closed lids: Huette starving, her mother's empty apartment, the police marching the Jewish men out of the Marais. Her eyes snapped open.

"Tell me something funny," she said suddenly. "There must be something you've seen or done that's made you laugh. Isn't there?"

He didn't reply immediately and Estella worried that he'd misunderstood, that he thought she was trying to make light of the last two days. But it was the opposite. She couldn't fully comprehend everything that had happened without knowing its counterweight, without remembering that there were other emotions one could feel besides grief and anger.

"Something funny," he repeated, considering. "How about this? A British soldier who escaped from one of the camps wrote in his report about two fellow prisoners. One of them had been there for almost a year; he had a photo of his wife stuck to the wall above his bed. The other man arrived one night and was given the bunk below. The first thing he did, in the dark, was to stick a photo of his wife to the wall too. When they woke up in the morning, they realized that they each had the same picture. That their wives were one and the same. That she must have got tired of waiting for the first man to come home so she'd married the second. What are the chances that they would have both gone to the same camp, been allocated to the same set of bunks? Fate has the best hand in this game called life, don't you think?"

"That wasn't funny," she insisted, shaking her head. "Oh God, it's so awful it's like the worst kind of bad joke where you keep waiting for the punch line." She gave a wry smile. "What are the chances? Maybe the same as the chances of me bumping into you and Lena in Manhattan."

"One of fate's better games," he said cryptically and she didn't know if he was being sarcastic or not.

He rolled onto his side a little, probably so that he didn't have to turn his head all the time to see her. Estella watched him breathe, watched him wait out the spinning that must still be in his head.

"All right?" she asked.

"Getting there."

"Well," she said, "since your funny story didn't exactly lift my mood, maybe you can tell me what makes you feel good about what you do."

"Every time an airman gets to the embassy in Spain, every time we get intelligence from a prison camp about a nearby airfield or other potential bombing targets or Nazi activity, every time a man escapes a prison camp even if only for a day, it makes me feel good," he said. "Victory in battle isn't one glorious fight. It's a million tiny wins, wins that nobody notices. But every man we get out of a prison camp, or who evades capture after his plane goes down, is a man we can send back in to fight. Every minute the Germans spend searching prisoner-of-war camps for tunnel spoil or escape equipment, or reading letters to find codes is a minute they're distracted from the main game. Every piece of intelligence we receive from prisoners about a strategic railway junction or munitions plant is another target the bombers can zero in on with accuracy."

She studied his face. Even in sickness it was resolute. "But nobody knows what you're doing. And the people you're saving, you don't know them. How do you put your life on the line for strangers who never thank you?"

"It's not for strangers," he said quietly. "It's for every one of those Jewish men we saw being marched off to Drancy. It's for every courier or *passeur* who's been betrayed to the Germans and tortured before being killed. It's for every one of the one hundred people the Germans shot in reprisal killings because they caught one person scratching a V for victory onto a wall. I know all of those people, Estella, and so do you. They're the people who gave their life for nothing unless I make it mean something. Like you should make Lena's mean something."

She stared at the ceiling. "How?" she whispered, so ashamed for ever having doubted his intentions.

"You'll find a way."

This time, she rolled over to face him. His dark eyes glinted at her in the blackness of the room. She felt again what she'd felt at the piano, that the sensation of being near him was more unsettling than flying over the ocean, that it left her lunging forward and back at the same time, wanting to be close to him but also wanting to pull away because whatever lay in the space between them was so powerful that, once she dove into it, there would be no recovery.

He turned his head to stare at the ceiling. "You can leave me now," he said gruffly and it was like a slap in the face.

"Peter said to ignore you until you could stand," she said weakly, knowing she'd somehow lost the power she'd had.

"I don't need a nurse anymore."

A nurse. That was how he thought of her. She rolled off the bed.

When she reached the door, she heard his voice.

"If anything happens, go find Peter at this bar." He gave her an address.

"What do you mean, if anything happens?"

"Goodnight Estella."

He closed his eyes, shutting her out. And Estella knew that she was the only one who felt it, that he had no interest whatsoever in moving any closer to her, of seeing what might happen if they were to touch.

Estella didn't sleep. Instead she lay awake and thought about Alex: the night she'd arrived at the theater and he'd been standing in the middle of a

group of admiring women, so debonair that he barely had to raise a smile
to get any of them to look at him. The man who'd followed her out into
the street to give her a jacket so she wouldn't be cold, who'd gone with her
to help Monsieur Aumont. The man who'd tried to find Lena a family,
who'd gone back for Lena's body and whispered the most beautiful poetry
over it. The man who'd never once laid a hand on Estella in any compro-
mising way, the man who frustrated her and made her laugh, who made
her feel more emotions in the space of five minutes than she'd ever felt in a
lifetime. The man who'd tried to save his mother despite the personal cost,
the man who was trying to save a nation without regard for himself.

My God, she thought, one hundred times or more that night: *I'm in
love with Alex. I'm so in love with Alex I can't see straight.*

That he didn't love her was so perfectly clear she had to close her
eyes rather than look at the fact. He wanted rid of her, done of her, had
wanted her only to help Lena and she'd failed at that. Yet…he remembered that night in Paris, the night she'd first met him, with talismanic
reverence. As if it stood for something more than two strangers exchanging a map of a prison camp.

By five in the morning, as the sun was stretching its lazy rays into
the sky, Estella could no longer stand it. She didn't know what she
planned to do: make a declaration, ask him to clarify his feelings, or
whether she just wanted to see his face but she stood up and walked
down the hallway to his room. She'd heard piano music playing inter-
mittently through the night, which meant he was at least able to stand.
But there'd been silence for the last hour at least.

She tapped lightly at the door. "Alex?" He didn't answer so she
stepped inside.

The bed was empty. The piano stool was empty. The room was
empty. His bag was still there; perhaps he was in the kitchen. She
sniffed the air for food or coffee, remembering he hadn't eaten in more
than a day, but she couldn't smell anything.

He wasn't in the kitchen. Nor the garden. Nor on the roof. Wasn't in the house at all. She could feel his absence just as she felt his presence, she now realized, acutely. She waited for an hour but he didn't return. Then she hurried upstairs. Dressed. Walked down to Rue Pigalle to the address Alex had given her and saw Peter polishing glasses. She almost turned away. The last time she'd spoken to Peter, he'd said she was to blame for Lena dying. She didn't know if she had the strength right now to withstand any more of his bitter truths. But she remembered Alex and that was enough to make her walk over to a chair and sit down. Soon Peter came over to take her order.

"Where is he?" she murmured.

"I told you not to let him out of your sight," he snapped. He lowered his voice. "He's gone?"

Estella nodded. "A bloody Mary please." Then, quietly, "I think he may have gotten tired of me," she admitted. She'd talked so much about her own problems, rather than about his vastly more significant ones.

Peter leaned down and winked lasciviously. "Alley's fine with me, love."

Estella found herself being shoved into an alley, wondering what the hell Peter was up to. When they got there, he began to bark at her again. "Tired of you? You're the only woman he's ever asked me to look after. You're the only woman he assiduously avoids speaking about. And that tells me two things—that he cares about you too damn much, and that makes you fucking dangerous."

Estella's mouth wouldn't work. She stared at Peter as if she hadn't been speaking French her whole life, as if she couldn't understand him. "What?" she managed in the end.

"And you're so fucking dumb you can't even see it."

She felt her hand lift to deflect Peter's aggression, a futile gesture but it was all she was capable of in that moment. She couldn't quite piece Peter's words together into any kind of sense. "Is Alex all right?" she asked, because that was the most important question. Had he gone of his own accord?

"You'd better hope he's all right." Peter smacked his hand against the wall. "Forget it. He wants me to get you out, I'll get you out. Stay out of trouble today and I'll fetch you tonight and get you out of this goddamned country and far away." Peter stalked back into the bar.

At the same time, two Wehrmacht officers with snuffling bulldogs turned into the alley and Estella could do nothing other than stride off as fast as she could, using her body's muscle memory to find her way. Her vision was blurred and her ears buzzed with Peter's words: *he cares about you too damn much.*

Why? Because she was Lena's sister and he felt he owed it to Lena to protect her? But, even as she had the thought, she knew that wasn't it.

Now she could clearly see everything she'd missed before: the fact that he'd only danced with Lena in the first place because he thought she was Estella. Standing shoulder to shoulder with him before the window of a flying boat, staring out at the blue sky. Sitting beside him on a piano stool in a jazz club laughing, and then longing. Lying next to him on a bed when he was unwell and him never once touching her, never once betraying anything of the reputation that went before him, always treating her with carefulness and restraint. She had thought it was because he barely tolerated her but that wasn't it: it was almost as if he couldn't bear to touch her because he was afraid of what might follow.

As she walked up the stairs of the house in the Marais, she no longer felt it settle over her like a gloomy day. It suddenly seemed bereft, as if it was missing the one thing that brought it to life: a pair of lovers.

Estella opened the door to Alex's room and she lay down on the bed, on the side where he had slept, a flood of want and yearning sweeping over her. His pillow carried the scent of him and as she rested her cheek against it, she knew that if what she felt wasn't love, then love must be so acute it couldn't be survived. Because what she felt right now was agony.

PART SIX
FABIENNE

CHAPTER TWENTY-FOUR

June 2015

Estella's funeral was held at the Church of St. John the Divine as per Estella's instructions. Antique French peonies, all in white, sourced especially from hothouses, overflowed the altar, spilled down the ends of the pews and scented the air with a fragrance Fabienne had always associated with Estella. So many people came that a crowd had to gather in the vestibule, all the seats long since taken.

Fabienne sat in the front row near her grandmother's coffin, all the people who'd worked at Stella Designs filling the pews around her. Fabienne's mother had been too busy to fly from Australia. Or too scared of seeing the ghost of Fabienne's father in the pictures of Estella adorning the church.

Fabienne made it through the eulogy with only one long and dreadful pause but she knew she owed it to her grandmother to honor her properly, and so she pulled herself together and continued to speak. "Estella told me the thing that most comforted her after the people she loved had died was a poem, which I'd like to read now:

"When you awaken in the morning's hush
I am the swift uplifting rush
Of quiet birds in circled flight.

I am the soft stars that shine at night.
Do not stand at my grave and cry;
I am not there. I did not die."

Fabienne's voice cracked on the last line and she swallowed hard to stop the sob that wanted to break free. "My grandmother might not be here with me anymore, bodily, but I know she did not die. Her legacy is sweeping. More than the soft stars or the birds in flight, she is walking the streets of Manhattan, of Paris, of any city in the world where women buy her clothes. She is in the button on a sleeve, the pleat of a skirt, the peony on the shoulder of a dress. She did not die," Fabienne repeated, knowing she had to finish or she would break down utterly, "and I'm so very glad that I was lucky enough to call her my grandmother, that my life was blessed by her presence. I'm so very glad that she lived."

Her hand flew up to her mouth as she stepped away from the microphone and the applause rang out, more beautiful than any hymn, for Estella.

Fabienne saw Will briefly at the wake in Gramercy Park.

He kissed her cheek. "Your eulogy was beautiful," he said.

Then she had to turn away and talk to and thank all of the other mourners, to laugh with her grandmother's employees over stories of Estella and her grandfather and their two desks, which had sat opposite each other in their shared office, a desk her grandfather rarely used, preferring to be on the floor of the atelier. Two desks that had been empty now for a year or more, her grandfather's for longer, and Estella's since she'd been too frail to go to the office anymore.

As they talked and reminisced, Fabienne felt the proof of her assertion that Estella was not in her grave, but here in the room in the hearts and minds of so many people. And in their souls, or in Fabienne's soul at least.

The most difficult moment of the day was when Kimberley, the designer who'd been in charge of the atelier for the last year or so, approached Estella. "What will you do with the business now?" Kimberley asked.

Fabienne shook her head. "I don't know."

All of it was hers—the business, the house in Gramercy Park, the house in Paris, the furniture, the archive of clothes, the paintings, the money. She had more things than she could even comprehend and she had no idea what to do with any of it. Because she lived in Australia and had a job in Australia and she could not imagine sweeping into the enormous void left by Estella.

Finally the guests left. Will had waved to her before he'd departed a couple of hours before, extracting himself from Kimberley who had either been exchanging design stories with him or who had seen in him the same things that Fabienne had. And Fabienne wasn't jealous, just sad. Kimberley would be so perfect for Will. She lived in New York for a start. And she was an artist.

Alone at last, Fabienne looked around the front living room of the Gramercy Park house, at the champagne glasses pinked with lipstick, at the plates and napkins and bits of food clinging to dishes and tables, at the coat someone had left on a chair, at the phone abandoned and beeping on a sideboard, at the detritus of celebration and sadness. Tiredness descended upon her.

She turned on her heel and walked out of the house, all the way to her grandmother's offices on Seventh Avenue. Stella Designs was one of the few fashion businesses that still operated there, clinging onto the long history of the street, which was now being swept away like litter as clothing factories were transformed into twenty-first-century capital-raising and technology businesses.

On the fourteenth floor, she unlocked the doors; everyone had been given the week off and she knew it would be quiet and peaceful. Perhaps there she might recapture the sense of what she'd said at the funeral, wouldn't feel the utter lack of Estella.

But Estella's empty desk only made the lack more visceral. There was the sewing box that had come with Estella from Paris when she was twenty-two years old, the photographs of Fabienne, her father, her grandfather, and Janie, her grandmother's best friend who'd died— was that ten years ago? Nothing lasted. Nothing.

Her grandfather's desk sat opposite, kept dusted and neat by Estella's secretary, Rebecca, who'd done the same with Estella's over this last year of disuse. More peonies, pink this time, sat extravagantly in Estella's favorite orb-shaped aquamarine vases, dragging France across an ocean and laying it down at Fabienne's feet. But it all looked wrong without Estella being wheeled to her desk or, if Fabienne was to look back a decade or so, without Estella walking into a room in that way she had, model-like, as if life was a catwalk and she would continue to parade on it forever.

Fabienne sat down gingerly in Estella's chair but it was too capacious and she jumped up, not wanting anyone to catch her, the impostor, unable to take Estella's place.

"Fabienne?"

"Jesus," Fabienne exclaimed, bringing one hand up to her chest and whipping around to the door. "Rebecca, you scared me."

Her grandmother's diminutive and young but extraordinarily organized secretary smiled. "Your eulogy was so lovely."

"Thanks," Fabienne said. "I thought I gave everyone the week off?"

Rebecca held a box out in front of her. "I came to get this. I thought I'd drop it off to you tomorrow but you're here so you should take it now."

"What is it?"

"I don't know. Estella gave it to me about five years ago. She told me to keep it for you until…"

She died. The words hung in the air. Fabienne stepped forward and took the box. "I'm going back to Gramercy Park," Fabienne said. "It doesn't feel quite right being here yet."

Rebecca hesitated, then put her hand on Fabienne's arm. "She told me to put fresh flowers in the vases every week. To make sure it was always welcoming. She said, one day, you'd claim it. When you were ready."

At the house in Gramercy Park, the mess was exactly where Fabienne had left it. She sighed and sank onto the couch, box on her lap, opening the lid and pulling out a stack of papers.

"Oh," she gasped as she realized what they were. Sketches, dozens of sketches, sketches Fabienne had drawn on scrap pieces of paper while lying on the floor of her grandmother's office, or sitting at her grandfather's desk, every summer in New York from the time she was old enough to hold a pencil until the time she stopped drawing. Estella had kept them all.

Looking over them now was like falling down a shaft and into the past, fashions and trends rushing past her: early noughties boot-cut trousers, baby-doll dresses, and colored denim; nineties khaki, slip dresses, velvet, faux fur. Some of them made her laugh at her sheer outrageousness at age six, others made her shake her head at her timidity, and in others she could see the lineage of her grandmother but also something more, a slight curve in the road that took her grandmother's sense of style to a place it had not yet ventured.

She sighed and put the sketches on the couch beside her, reached into the box again and pulled out a CD, which made her smile. When was the last time she'd seen a CD? She inserted it into the player.

A song, bluesy and sad and pining filled the room. Norah Jones, "The Nearness of You," Fabienne read in her grandmother's hand on the CD case. She picked up a handful of glasses then stopped as she caught the words of the song, a hymn to the breath-stealing charm of stepping into the arms of the person you loved.

The doorbell rang through the music and Fabienne glanced at the video screen, meaning to ignore it but it was Will. She opened the door.

"Hi," he said. "Sorry I didn't get a chance to speak to you before."

"It's okay," she said. "There were too many people. Come in."

He followed her into the living room, where Fabienne suddenly remembered the aftermath of the funeral still despoiled every surface.

"I gave Estella's housekeeper the week off," she said by way of explaining the plates and glasses and napkins and crumbs. "She was upset. I didn't really think through the mess that would be left after a wake."

"I'll give you a hand." Will gathered up a stack of plates.

"You don't have to do that. I was just about to start."

"It'll be quicker if I help." He smiled at her.

"Thanks," she said, feeling the hint of a smile curve her lips. She went into the kitchen to fill the sink with suds and water.

Will came in and out, ferrying plates and glasses and rubbish and the only conversation was her telling him where to put everything and him asking mundanities like: *Where's the bin?* And that was fine, the wash of water over crystal, the appearance of something clean out of the soap, the steady diminishment of dirty dishes was a problem easy to solve with a little hard work, the immediate satisfaction of their efforts apparent in the gleaming pile that now lay to her right and which Will began to put into cupboards.

"The housekeeper is going to kill me when she gets back and finds everything in the wrong place," he said.

"She won't mind," Fabienne said, aware of how dull she sounded, discussing dishes with a man like Will, Head of Design at Tiffany, used to beautiful things. "You don't need to do any more. I'm almost finished."

"There's some stuff on the sofa in there." He indicated the living room. "Do you want me to put it back in the box?"

Fabienne shook her head. "Those are things my grandmother saved for me. It's funny how much a piece of paper or a song can mean. I still remember what she was wearing when I sketched those pictures, or what she said when I gave it to her: *The color is very good, and I like the length of the skirt, but the sleeves are too short*." Fabienne mimicked her grandmother's voice.

"Show me?" Will asked.

Fabienne put down the dishcloth and led the way into the living room where the streetlights stippled the night time blackness of the park, visible through the windows, with gold, the greenery almost absent, hiding until the morning sun reappeared. Her grandmother's favorite Frida Kahlo painting, two women joined by a skein of blood, hung over the fireplace as it always had. The women seemed more tranquil now, Fabienne thought, as if their joined hands were gripped a little tighter, as if the bond implied by the vein that connected their two separate hearts had finally been achieved. She sighed. She needed sleep. She was imagining changes in a static painting.

She pressed play on the CD and the words—"The Nearness of You"—spilled back out into the room like the tears she suddenly found on her cheeks.

"Oh God!" she said as she slid down the wall and sat on the floor, wishing she could just stop crying, wishing she wasn't behaving like such a mess in front of a man who meant so much to her.

Will sat on the floor beside her, reached into his pocket and passed her a clean, white, perfectly pressed handkerchief.

"My grandmother would have loved you," Fabienne sniffed.

"I'd rather her granddaughter did," he said quietly.

Her head snapped to the right. "What did you say?" she asked, sure she hadn't heard him correctly.

"I said I'd rather her granddaughter did." Will reached out and touched her chin lightly. "I'm in love with you, Fabienne. Which is why I'm going home now. Because I want to kiss you—want to do more than kiss you—but not like this. Not when you're so sad."

Fabienne leaned her forehead in, pressing it against his, so aware of his lips not far from hers, of the quickness of his breath, of the nearness of Will Ogilvie. If he kissed her then she knew exactly where they would end up and she also knew that he was right; it would be an act of forgetting when what she wanted to have with Will was an act worth remembering.

He kissed her forehead gently and stood up. "I'm prescribing you a glass of whiskey and bed," he said, cheeks flushed like hers.

Fabienne did what he'd recommended, swallowing down the whiskey and climbing into bed, Will's words—*I'm in love with you, Fabienne*—accompanying her into sleep.

CHAPTER TWENTY-FIVE

Either cleaning was cathartic or Will's prescription had worked wonders because Fabienne slept for the first time in days, not waking until almost noon. She dressed, finished tidying and then stood in the house not knowing what to do. The box still sat on the sofa and she knew she could investigate its contents further but she also knew that it would be nice not to cry for at least a few hours.

So she picked up her sunglasses and stepped outside, crossing over to Fifth and walking along, dodging the tourists who all wanted to look up, as if Manhattan was a city of the sky, not of the ground. She passed a window full of her grandmother's clothes at Saks Fifth Avenue, and then found herself outside Tiffany & Co. At the same time, a cab pulled into the curb and a very handsome man wearing a suit stepped out, with a smile all for her.

"Fabienne," Will said. "That was good timing."

"I needed some air." She smiled. "I'm not entirely sure how I ended up outside Tiffany but diamonds do exert a certain lure, I suppose."

He laughed. "Since you're here, why don't you come in?"

"You're not too busy?"

"Not for you."

She followed him inside and across the shop floor to an elevator. He led the way to his office, stopping to say hello to a woman she assumed must be his secretary and asking her to hold his calls.

Then she stepped into a room that looked familiar from their tele-phone calls: one wall painted Tiffany Blue, his desk an absolute mess, covered with drawings, but everything else about the room neat and tidy.

"I see your creativity thrives in chaos," she said, indicating the desk.

"The running joke around here is that I don't actually need to de-sign a collection every year. I just need to dig deep into the piles on my desk and I'll find enough drawings there for a season," he said.

"Does that mean you've found your idea for the new collection?"

"I have, thanks to you."

"To me?" She looked at him quizzically.

"Turns out ideas put forward by beautiful women in hospital cafe-terias are the best kind." He smiled at her and she both blushed and beamed.

"Really? So you're using people you know as your inspiration," she said.

It was his turn to flush a little. "I am."

"Can I have a look?"

"Sure. Do you want a coffee?"

"That'd be great."

Will put his head out the door and asked, politely, she noted, for two coffees while Fabienne studied the drawings on his desk, not touching or moving anything in case its placement was somehow critical.

"This one is beautiful," she said. "I mean they're all beautiful. I just really like this one though." She pointed to a pendant, two joined pen-dants actually, one of milky white streaked with blue, like the sky in reverse, offset by a cabochon of black, dotted with stars.

He came over to see, standing so close that she could smell his af-tershave, that same blend of citrus and amber she remembered from Paris.

"That's azurite," he said, pointing to the blue and white pendant. "And the other—that's fossilized dinosaur bone."

"Really?"

"Here." He rifled through a box of jewelry, extracting a piece she could see was the replica of the sketch. "Spin around."

She did, lifting her hair off her neck and felt the pendant slide over her collarbones, felt his fingers securing the clasp at the back of her neck, felt his hands resting on her shoulders, realized the back of her body was only a centimeter from the front of his, that he must be able to hear the sound of her heart throbbing in her chest.

"It needs to be just a centimeter shorter," she said, turning to face him. "Necklines will be higher next season. This isn't a pendant you want hiding beneath your dress."

"No," he murmured, eyes fixed on hers. "It isn't."

The buzz of his phone made Fabienne almost jump to the ceiling.

"Sorry," he said, taking his hands off her shoulders, reaching down to press a button on the phone.

"Will, Emma Watson and her stylist are here to choose pieces for her film premiere. They've asked for you." A voice came over the speaker.

"Emma Watson?" Fabienne mouthed.

He raised an eyebrow at her. "Sure. Send them up." He hung up the phone.

"As in the gorgeous actress?"

He had the grace to blush a little. "Yes. It's my least favorite part of the job. Being nice to actresses because they show off our jewelry."

"Oh yes, it sounds terrible," said Fabienne mock-sarcastically. "And I can see why you're suddenly so inspired by people," she added teasingly. "I'd better go. I'm no match for Emma."

Will caught her hand. "You're more than a match for Emma. Can I see you tonight?"

"I'm flying out tonight. I'm going to see your sister, then I'm on a plane."

"Already?"

"I have to get back to work. I can't stay any longer or I won't have a job."

"So this is good-bye?"

Fabienne nodded.

"I've hardly spoken to you. What are you going to do about Stella Designs?"

The phone buzzed again and Will sighed. "Sorry."

"I'll let you do some work. I'll call you tomorrow, or whenever I'm back in Sydney." She picked up her purse. "Thanks for last night," she said, wanting to say more but his secretary's voice crackled into the room and she lost her chance.

The nurse let Fabienne in to the Ogilvies' apartment and showed her up to Melissa's room, which looked out over Central Park, the green splendor as rich as a bolt of silk unfurled before them.

"Fabienne!" Melissa said, delighted. "Come and sit down." She patted the bed and Fabienne tried to keep her face still, to not betray the fact that Melissa looked so much worse than the last time she'd seen her in Paris.

"I look awful, I know," Melissa said and Fabienne knew she'd failed. Melissa hesitated, then said, "Will didn't want to tell you; he knew you had so much to deal with already. But the doctors have said…" Her voice trailed off in a decidedly un-Melissa-like fashion, then she seemed to recover her resolve and her next words came out with typical candor. "All they can offer is palliative care."

Palliative care. A euphemism, Fabienne's mother had always said, for the last stepping-stone on the path to death.

Fabienne opened her mouth to speak but Melissa shook her head.

"I don't want to talk about it. Talking about it won't make me better. Tell me how you are instead," Melissa said, voice firm and Fabienne knew she meant what she'd said.

So Fabienne forced herself to swallow the words she'd wanted to say to Melissa. "I'm sad," she admitted truthfully, knowing there was no point lying to Melissa. "Lost. A little afraid. It's hard to imagine a world without Estella in it. I know I only saw her once a year but I spoke to her every couple of days. She's always been in my life and I feel as if my feet have been cut off and I don't even know how to walk anymore."

Melissa took Fabienne's hand in hers and Fabienne winced when she saw that Melissa's eyes were damp with tears.

"I'm so sorry," Fabienne said. "I'm an awful friend. The last thing you need is my misery."

Melissa shook her head and wiped her eyes. "No, you're not an awful friend. It's just that, when you said that, I realized how Will might feel when…"

When I'm gone. She didn't finish the sentence.

"Did you see Will last night?" Melissa asked instead. "I was asleep when he left this morning and didn't have a chance to ask."

Fabienne nodded. "I did. And he…" She paused. How to describe what last night had meant to her? "He helped me clean up. He gave me a hanky when I cried. He sat on the floor with me when that was the only thing I could do. It probably sounds silly but he did all the things that I needed on the night of my grandmother's funeral."

"Are you in love with my brother?"

God. If she could get through even one day without crying it would be a miracle. Fabienne felt the familiar ache in her throat and blinked, hard. "How could I not be?" she whispered.

"Come here." Melissa opened her arms and Fabienne hugged her, neither of them capable of saying anything coherent.

"It's the only thing I regret," Melissa whispered into Fabienne's shoulder. "That I never loved anyone. Not like that. Of course I love Will and I love you and I love my friends but…I've never fallen in love with anyone. I've been sick since I was twenty. The last five years haven't given me enough time off from feeling like shit so that I could fall in love."

Fabienne's tears only flowed all the faster and her heart, already scarred from the last week, seemed to break open again. She remembered Estella's words: *loving can hurt spectacularly, but it can also heal.* Maybe if Melissa had been able to find someone to love her…Fabienne let the thought die. Love didn't cure cancer. Whatever healing it had given Estella was of the soul or the spirit, not of the body.

"I'm so lucky," Fabienne said. "To have met you, to have met Will. But I live in Australia. I'm a mess right now. I feel like I should slink off and let him find someone else."

"I will never speak to you again if you do that." Melissa's voice was firm. "Take the chance that I can't have, that I won't ever have. You're made for each other. The way he looks at you…"

The way he looks at you. The words played over in Fabienne's head in the taxi on the way to Gramercy Park, played over again as she packed her suitcase, and as she called another cab to take her to the airport. When the driver arrived, she asked him to make a stop on the way and then, when she was just a couple of blocks away she texted Will: *Can you meet me on the street for just a minute?*

Sure, he texted back. *I'm on my way down.*

He was waiting with a quizzical expression on his face when the cab pulled in to the curb and Fabienne jumped out. She took his hand in hers and kissed him, softly at first but she knew she didn't want softly; her senses were even more acute these last few days and anything that lacked intensity felt like dust motes and feathers. She kissed him harder, her arms sliding up his back, his drawing her in. Someone wolf-whistled as they walked past and Fabienne stepped back, running a finger over Will's lips.

"Now you're wearing lipstick," she said.

"I don't mind at all," he said, forehead resting on hers, bodies touching, both of them breathing hard. "Why are we always doing this with a cab waiting and you on the way to the airport?"

"I know," Fabienne said. "But I couldn't go without telling you that I know it's crazy and impossible but I love you anyway and I wanted you to know."

"I thought I scared you away last night."

"Not at all."

"All I want is for us to be in the same city for a few days with no sadness and no taxis and no planes. And we'll make that happen, Fabienne. I promise."

"I'm going to hold you to that." She drew back reluctantly. "I should go."

He waited as she climbed into the cab, waited as the cab pulled away, waited on the sidewalk until she could no longer see him. As soon as he was out of sight, her phone buzzed. *You were right about the necklace. I shortened it and Emma Watson loved it. You have a good eye. Never doubt that. I love you. Will x*

The jet lag woke Fabienne up at two in the morning again. She lay in bed for half an hour then decided to get up and do something to tire herself out. She needed sleep if she hoped to function in any useful way at work. She finished unpacking her suitcase, which she'd been too exhausted to bother with when she arrived home, and stood with her grandmother's box in her hand, wondering if that was the right thing to do or whether it would only send her brain spinning.

She carried it back to her bed, pulled out the things she'd already found and put them to one side. A folder was next and inside it were a series of sketches, again Fabienne's, ones her grandmother had made up as part of the Stella line. Fabienne had been sixteen the first time her grandmother had plucked a sketch from the pile, asked permission to use it and had paid Fabienne handsomely for it. This had continued for about eight years; at every collection, one of the pieces would be a design of Fabienne's. Fabienne had always assumed it to be no more than nepotism, her grandmother indulging her, but she now saw that clipped to each design was a sales chart for the season and Fabienne's designs had usually been among the bestsellers. She vaguely remembered her grandmother telling her the same thing but she'd ignored it, once again thinking that Estella was trying to prop up Fabienne's ego so she'd consider coming to work for her.

She peered into the box for the next thing, a piece of paper, which she unfolded. It was Estella's marriage certificate. Fabienne frowned as she scanned the words. *Marriage Date: June 20, 1947.* 1947?

She knew she didn't need to check her father's birth date but she did anyway, taking out the certificate she'd carried around in her purse since she'd first found it: March 27, 1941. Six years before Estella and Fabienne's grandfather married. Fabienne thought back over the years, recalling that they'd never once celebrated a wedding anniversary for her grandparents; she supposed now, looking back, that it was strange but because they were in different countries and it would be impossible to celebrate together, it had never come up.

Her heart contracted then, a hard and sharp squeeze that made her lie down on the bed, both certificates held tight in her hands. Because if her father was born six years before her grandparents married, then it made the words on his birth certificate—*Mother: Lena*

Thaw, Father: Alex Montrose—so much closer to being true. Which meant that Fabienne had no right to anything her grandmother had left her—not the business, not the house, not the role of head designer. Nothing. It meant that Estella, her beloved grandmother, might not be related to Fabienne at all.

CHAPTER TWENTY-SIX

The next day at work, Fabienne drank copious amounts of coffee as she made her way through e-mails and phone messages and a stream of people in and out her office door. Mid-morning, her boss, Unity, came in and sat down.

"Good to see you're back," Unity said crisply, crossing her legs, her shimmery flesh-colored stockings reminding Fabienne of how much she hated flesh-colored stockings.

"It's good to be back," Fabienne said brightly, hoping a smile and a lightness in her voice wouldn't betray the fact that she was running on caffeine.

"How are the exhibition plans coming along? Charlotte seemed to have everything in hand while you were away."

"Yes, she did. She's been a big help," Fabienne said honestly because Charlotte had dexterously managed to keep all important decisions on hold for Fabienne while still making it appear as if they were making progress.

"I'd like to see a concept this afternoon. I'm worried about timing given it's your first exhibition for us and you've been away so much."

"I know exactly how much time we need and everything is in hand. But I'm also very happy to run through a concept today. It'll be rough though." Fabienne kept her smile on; the only alternative was to look utterly dumbfounded at the thought of having to present a concept that very afternoon, all the while knowing that a concept wouldn't normally be presented for at least another month.

"Good. Two o'clock. My office." Unity stood up, her white skirt suit unwrinkled and spotless. Jil Sander, Fabienne guessed. Sleek and Scandinavian-like and always serene.

Fabienne tried to stop her own hands drifting down to the wide-legged black tuxedo pants and jacket she wore, along with a white shirt that seemed to be sagging in deference to Unity's crispness. It was an outfit she always wore when she didn't have time to think, an outfit she always loved, but today it felt less polished than it should. She waited until Unity had returned to her own office and then scurried out into the hall to find Charlotte. "We have to put a concept together by two o'clock. No lunch for us today."

Charlotte rolled her eyes. "Maybe it'll keep her off our backs."

"I hope so," Fabienne said.

In Fabienne's office, they laid out the photographs of the dresses they'd already chosen and Fabienne began to sketch a plan, a narrative, a story, which placed each piece in an order, an order that she was making up as she went along, but at least it was a start. She always drew and re-drew the exhibition concept many times before she felt it was final and she hoped the first draft would have enough in it to satisfy Unity.

After a couple of hours of discussion and drawing, Fabienne stretched. "Great, I've got enough to keep me going. Can you do a timeline showing when we'll write the captions, when each piece needs to arrive from the loan museums, when we need to meet with the builders, when the programs need to be started, when we need to think about which pieces to pick for the website—everything. If she can see we know what we're doing, she might just believe us."

"Will do," Charlotte said.

"If you can get it to me by one, then I can make any changes in time. I'll re-draw this now," Fabienne indicated the concept sketch, "and we'll have enough."

Fabienne didn't step away from her desk for the next two hours. She planned and she sketched and she thought and she looked over the photographs of the pieces she and Charlotte had shortlisted in e-mail conversations over the last week. Then, at two o'clock, smiling, and feeling as if Unity might actually find it within herself to smile too when she saw what they'd done, she collected Charlotte and walked to Unity's office.

Fabienne began with a short introduction about the idea behind the exhibition and then led Unity through a narrative that wound its way from Lanvin's La Cavallini dress in both its incarnations—one with flowers and one with crystals—through Chanel's camellia corsages, to Dior's Venus dresses, a spectacular Worth embroidered and sequinned jacket, a sparkling Schiaparelli with so many paillettes one could almost believe there was no fabric beneath to support them, an early Stella Designs velvet dress with a white crystal-studded peony that was one of the first pieces her grandmother had ever shown, some Collette Dinnigan and Akira Isogawa and, of course, the Vanderbilt dress from Tiffany, set like an exquisite engagement ring with diamonds. At the end she stood quietly, knowing she'd done good work, that the exhibition would be a paean to the traditional *métiers* which had been intrinsic to the transformation of fashion from homemaker craft to art.

"I'm not sure," Unity said, "about the whole idea anymore. It's so brazen, all of this decoration. Do we want something so arrogant for your first exhibition?"

Fabienne carefully put her drawings down on the desk. "It's a way of honoring lost crafts," she said, voice level. "The handmade, the painstaking, the patient. All that's precious and might easily be forgotten in this modern age. It ties in perfectly to contemporary ideas about slow-movements, about returning to pre-internet and pre-machine days when things took more time, when we valued individual artistic endeavor just for the sake of beauty. Not money. It's an homage to a way of life that fashion has grown from, a way of life where the quest wasn't to own more, but to own a piece of genius. I think people will appreciate the chance to see a set of skills that have almost vanished, to contemplate what it would be like if fashion wasn't disposable, if we viewed what we wore as art rather than fad. You could step into any of these pieces right now and wear them out and you would not look as if you'd stepped out of time. These pieces are the opposite of ephemera; they're ageless."

Unity didn't speak. Nor did Fabienne. She'd said everything she needed to and she wasn't going to jump into the silence and babble like Charlotte was doing, making suggestions about replacing some of the more ornate pieces with something simpler.

"Perhaps you two should get your stories straight," Unity said. "You either want simple or you don't."

"We don't," Fabienne said firmly.

"I need to think about it," Unity said, standing up.

Charlotte scuttled out of the room and Fabienne was about to leave too when Unity stopped her. "I understand you and Jasper Brande are no longer an item. I'm sorry things didn't work out."

Fabienne shook her head. Was Unity offering friendly commiserations?

"He's joined our board of directors," Unity said smoothly. "I hope that won't be a problem."

Why? Fabienne wanted to shout. He was a sought-after board executive but why, of all the boards in town, would he join this one? "No problem for me," she said, matching her tone to Unity's, at the knife-edge of condescension. "I don't have anything to do with the board. That's your job." Then she left the office.

* * *

All she wanted was a glass of wine and bed, Fabienne thought as she pushed open the door to her apartment and deposited a pile of work on the hall table. If she woke again at two in the morning, then the paperwork would keep her occupied, although after today's meeting, she'd lost a little of her enthusiasm for her new job. She was just pouring the wine when her phone rang. She sank gladly onto the couch when she saw Will's name on the screen.

"Hi," she said. "How are you?" His face flickered out of pixels and into flesh and she put down the wineglass abruptly. "What's wrong?" He looked as if he hadn't slept or shaved since she'd last seen him on the sidewalk outside Tiffany.

"It's Liss." He paused and Fabienne could feel the effort it took for him to hold himself together. "She has a bladder obstruction. She's in surgery."

"Surgery? Is she well enough?"

"I don't know."

"Will."

The buzzer in Fabienne's apartment sounded. "Just a sec," she said and she reached out to press the button to let in whoever had buzzed. "It's probably just a delivery. Don't go anywhere. I'll be quick." She opened the front door and Jasper waltzed in, calling out, "Fab! How are you?"

Fabienne realized she had her phone in her hand, that Will could clearly hear Jasper's voice, could probably see Jasper leaning in to kiss her cheek. "Jasper, give me a minute," she muttered, turning away. "I'll call you back," she said to Will. "I won't be long."

"Okay," he said gruffly, hanging up.

"Why are you here?" Fabienne wearily asked Jasper who had sat himself down on the sofa.

"To see you. It's been ages. I heard your grandmother died."

Even though she was used to his dispassion, she still recoiled at his words. "She did," she said shortly.

He hesitated. "I know that before I would have just sent you a text. But I wanted to come and tell you I'm sorry. I miss you, Fab."

"Really?"

"Really." He shifted awkwardly, then caught her eye. "I miss you a lot."

And that was why she'd stayed with Jasper for so long. Because he could, at times, beneath the nonchalant and fun-loving exterior, be sincere and charming. But it wasn't enough. "I'm seeing someone else," she blurted.

"Is it serious?" he asked.

"Yes."

"Who is it?"

"No one you know. He lives in New York."

"How are you going to have a relationship with someone in New York?"

"I don't know, Jasper, but that's my problem. You have to go. That was him on the phone."

"Wouldn't life be easier with me here in Sydney than with some guy half a world away?" He smiled in a way that had always softened her, once upon a time, but it no longer worked.

"Easier maybe," she said. "But easy isn't what I want. I'd rather have every complication in the world knowing I could see Will even just occasionally. He's worth that."

"And I'm not?"

Fabienne shook her head. "I'm sorry."

"I've just organized dinner for you and me next week with Unity and some of the other board members."

"Why did you do that?"

"I thought it'd be good for you to meet the board. Schmooze a little. Having board members on your side is a good thing for your career. And you've always accused me of only thinking about myself. I wanted to show you I could think about you too."

"I can't come."

"You have to. It's work."

You have to. And in those three words, Fabienne saw the Jasper she'd fallen out of love with, the one who cared more about work and himself than anything else. "I have a phone call to make," she said.

He remained on the sofa, eyes locked to hers, waiting, she knew, for her to back down. But she didn't. Eventually he stood up. "Eight o'clock Thursday at Aria. Unity will expect you there."

"Good-bye, Jasper."

As soon as the door clicked shut, she called Will back. But he didn't answer. Nor did he reply to the two texts she sent him. In the end, she was thankful for the work she'd brought home because it stopped her from checking her phone every minute of the long and sleepless night.

The next few days rattled Fabienne. She spent a lot of time in the archives at the museum, looking through piece after piece, refining her list of Australian designers for the exhibition. But she had a peculiar sense that all she was doing was assembling, mustering an army of clothes rather than fighting for something that mattered; spending her time amid the brilliance of others, moving pieces on a chessboard that had long ago reached stalemate. Some of the designers on her list she had studied with, had thought of, once upon a time, as her peers. Most of them she hadn't spoken to for a very long time.

Every time she left the archive she would return to her desk and re-draw the exhibition concept, tightening the narrative, editing out all imperfections. And that was the only time she felt a glimmer of something more than pointlessness, where she smiled a little and fell out of the world for a couple of hours as she drew and drew and drew.

She texted Will and Melissa every day. She had one text from Will: *Liss isn't doing great* and then nothing. Of course he wouldn't even think of texting if Melissa really was ill. She prayed, even though she didn't believe in prayers, that Melissa would recover. Any god would surely see that Melissa was worth saving.

Thursday evening came around with the ridiculous dinner which she couldn't get out of because Jasper had invited her boss and it was therefore a work occasion at which her presence was required. She told him she'd meet him there, that she'd go straight from work and, on the way, her phone buzzed with another text from Will.

She's out of hospital, it said. *Settling her back in at home now*.

I'm glad, Fabienne texted back. *How are you?*

I've been better, was the reply.

I love you, she returned.

Thanks.

Thanks? Then she shook her head at herself. His sister had just undergone a serious operation and here was Fabienne expecting him to text declarations of love. She thought about calling him but she imagined that if he had time to talk to her, he would have called himself. A person in Melissa's weakened condition, undergoing such a surgery, would require constant care. All Fabienne could do was keep sending messages to both him and Melissa so they knew she was thinking of them.

At the restaurant, Unity and Jasper were laughing together at the bar. They'd be the perfect couple, she thought grimly as Jasper kissed her cheek.

"We're all here now so we can sit down," he said after he'd introduced her to the other board members.

She had the bad luck to be sitting next to Jasper and across from Unity so she turned her attention to the man on her other side and introduced herself.

"How does one become a fashion curator?" the man asked. "It's not the usual sort of job is it?"

"I don't suppose it is," Fabienne said, used to the question. "I studied fashion design and art history at university. Curating combines both my interests."

"Fab used to design a bit too," Jasper added and Fabienne winced. It wasn't something she cared to discuss among this group of people.

"You have to be very good to be a designer," Unity said faux-sympathetically.

"Fab's one of the best," Jasper said and Fabienne shot him a look. He almost sounded supportive, which wasn't a word she'd used to describe him for a very long time.

"There's that saying: those who can't do, teach," Unity mused. "Maybe it should be: those who can't create, curate." She laughed at her joke, as did some of the others who'd overheard.

Fabienne stabbed her sashimi viciously. *And what exactly is the saying about those who sit at the top of organizations doing nothing besides going out for dinner?* She swallowed the words and, as soon as she could, she excused herself to the bathroom. Jasper was waiting for her on her return, stopping her before she could reach the table.

"You're too good for them, Fab," he said. "Way too good."

"Why are you being so nice?" she asked suspiciously.

"Because I really do miss you. I'm just sorry it took you dumping me for me to work it out."

She sighed. "I'm sorry it did too."

He touched her arm. "I remember when you first moved in with me. You used to sew all the time. I'd go out cycling with the boys"—he held up his hands—"which I know I spent too much time doing, but I'd come back in the afternoon and you would've been drawing and sewing all day and you'd look so satisfied, as if you hadn't missed me at all. As if all you really needed was a pencil and a sewing machine to be truly happy."

"I remember that," she said. "Those were the good years."

"They were. And then you did it less and less—I know I used to drag you out most nights for dinners and corporate entertaining and maybe you didn't have time and that's why you stopped. But I look at you sitting there at the table and your face is so blank, so stiff. Nothing like your beautiful face when you'd spent a day making things."

An avalanche of memory almost made her stumble, those summer days when Jasper would be gone cycling for hours and she'd have the whole apartment to herself and she would, as he'd said, just draw and sew and forget to eat and feel a contentment like nothing she'd felt for a long time since. She'd wear the clothes and people would remark on them and she'd shrug and say it was just a hobby. There was nothing to lose if it was just a hobby. But then she'd worked harder, in jobs like Charlotte's, writing about others' beautiful clothes, or commissioning display cases for exhibitions, or putting together funding proposals and she'd stopped designing, had let the daily grind slowly wear away the thing she most enjoyed.

She leaned in to kiss Jasper's cheek. "You're a good man. Thank you."

"But Will is better?" he asked quietly, eyes fixed on her face.

"For me, he is."

"Then be happy." He smiled. "Go home. I'll tell them you're not feeling well. And I'll flirt hard enough with Unity so she forgets about it and doesn't hold it against you."

Fabienne laughed. "Have fun."

"I think I will." He grinned at her and walked away.

The minute she stepped outside the restaurant, Fabienne felt as if she'd taken off a dress she no longer needed, as if her skin—her self that she'd hidden for so long—had finally been revealed.

She took out her phone and telephoned the administrator she'd put in charge of Stella Designs. "I'm coming to New York," she said firmly. "I'm going to design the next collection."

PART SEVEN
ESTELLA

CHAPTER TWENTY-SEVEN

August 1941

"I was worried about you." Sam hugged Estella when she turned up at his apartment the night she arrived back in New York.

Janie, who'd hurried over after Sam had telephoned, sparked a smile too but Estella thought it wasn't quite the Janie-dazzler she was used to.

"You look sad," Sam said to Estella before she could ask Janie anything. "What happened?"

She told them about Lena. About her mother vanishing. But not that Alex had disappeared.

Her friends held her while she cried. They tried to soothe her, to say that her mother would be okay, that Lena would never have been happy on this earth. *But if only I'd been kinder, I could have made her last months so much happier*, Estella thought as she wept.

Eventually, she wiped her eyes and walked over to the window. "What have you two been doing?" she asked in a shaky voice. "I feel like I've been away for months."

Janie looked at Sam and he nodded. "You should tell her," he said.

"Tell me what?" Estella asked.

"I got married," Janie said, waggling her hand, now adorned with two well-sized rings.

"Married!" Estella cried. "But you only just got engaged."

Janie shrugged. "No point waiting around."

"I missed it," Estella said, hugging her friend. "I'm so sorry."

"You should be. I had to make Sam my bridesmaid; there was nobody else."

That made Estella laugh a little. "Did he wear a fabulous gown?"

"I wore a fabulous gown," Janie said. "I borrowed one of yours."

"I'm glad you did," Estella said.

"What are you going to do now that you're back?" Sam asked.

Estella shrugged. It was the one thing she hadn't been able to think about on the long journey home from France.

"I'm going to sleep," she said. "I'll think about it tomorrow."

"That's a good plan," Janie said. "You have the whole room at the Barbizon to yourself now that I'm living with my husband."

Estella fingered the keys to Lena's house that she'd brought with her from France. "I might stay at Lena's for a while."

"You won't want to rattle around in that big house all by yourself," Janie said. "Big houses are lonely."

The way she said it made Estella ask, "Is everything all right?"

Janie's face crumpled a little, like threads loosening and letting down a pleat of fabric. "I never thought marriage was like living with a stranger," she said.

"What do you mean?" Estella asked gently.

"Just that..." Janie bit her lip. "You meet someone, you date them for a bit and then you're supposed to marry them. But all I know about Nate is that he does something in a bank, that he likes his coffee black, that he prefers his brandy poured for him before he arrives home, that chicken is his least favorite meat and that he's an efficient lover, rather than a languorous one."

"I imagine efficiency has its advantages sometimes," Estella said but there was no smile in response.

"I had food poisoning the day after the wedding," Janie said. "I was so sick I couldn't get out of bed. Nate put his head in the door and told me to rest, then he went off to work. If we'd been at the Barbizon, you'd have looked after me. Or my bridesmaid would have." She raised a smile at last in Sam's direction. "It made me miss my mum. When you're sick, you want someone around who makes you feel better. Someone who loves you the way that only happens when you know a person really well."

Estella thought of Alex lying in the bed, how he'd let her run a cloth over his face, how he'd talked to her, how he'd fallen asleep beside her. And she knew, with absolute certainty, that what Peter had said was true. Because Janie was right. Even though she'd been the only person available at the time for Alex, she also understood that if he hadn't known her in the way Janie had said, then the awkwardness would have made the kind of conversation they'd shared impossible.

"Maybe it takes time," Sam said.

"Do you really think that in a year's time I'll be more comfortable vomiting into a basin in front of him?" Janie asked. "Or does he just want the smiles and the brandy and the roast beef?" She sighed. "It's not his fault; it's just the way the world works. The man goes out to work, the wife stays home, they spend a couple of hours at night together if they're lucky and they have sex when he wants it."

Estella hugged Janie, mourning the wise-cracking, vivacious, head-turning woman of a few weeks before. In her place was someone uncertain, someone stuck making coffee, someone bound for life to a man she knew less well than a foreign country.

"Go back to modeling," Sam said.

"Married women don't work," Janie said firmly. She straightened her shoulders, more like the Janie of old, the one who gatecrashed parties. "You haven't told Estella what you've been up to, Sam."

"I've been cutting mediocre clothes," Sam said. "We saved this for you." He passed Estella a clipping from *Vogue*.

Estella scanned the words. Babe Paley had written an article about Estella's designs. It said she was one to watch, that readers should do whatever they could to get their hands on one of her samples. The article was accompanied by a picture of Leo Richier, the cosmetics queen who'd come to the showing, wearing the black velvet gown out at a party.

"She telephoned the Barbizon looking for you," Janie said excitedly, pointing to Leo Richier. "She wanted to order the dress. So I boxed it up—I know you'd worn it once but nobody would ever know and you can just make yourself another one—and I took it around there and she paid one hundred dollars for it. She told me that she was friends with Babe Paley and then *voilà!*" Janie finished in the worst French accent Estella had ever heard, "this was published."

"Really?" Estella asked.

"And she gave me her husband's business card. Apparently he owns Forsyths department stores. He wants to place an order."

"Do you think he means it?"

"Of course!" Sam said. "Question is, what are you going to do about it?"

"As soon as I've worked that out," Estella said slowly. "I'll let you know."

Estella drifted around the house in Gramercy Park for weeks, hoping to find something that might tell her more about Lena. There was so much of Lena there, and yet there wasn't. Lena's clothes, her makeup, her jewelry sat unworn in her bedroom and, on the walls, an eclectic and arresting collection of artwork attested to her taste—the Frida Kahlo, a beautiful Tamara de Lempicka nude, a Dora Maar photograph called *Double Portrait* where one negative of a woman had been overlaid on the other. But there was nothing personal. No letters, no photographs, no keepsakes.

Mrs. Pardy had vanished somewhere too so the house was silent. Most days, Estella spent hours sitting in what had been, for those few months earlier in the year, the workroom. In the house in the Marais it had been Alex's room. The cathedral window was there, overlooking the park, the piano waited to be played; the only thing missing was the bed he'd lain in. Her workbench stood in that spot and she stared at its surface, then at the spot in front of the mirror where Janie should be, ready to be draped in ideas, ready to have sketches transformed into dresses just by the act of swathing her body in fabric. But of course Janie wasn't coming back; she was waking up every morning beside a man she'd married, was falling asleep beside him, was able to roll over and curl herself into his arms any time she chose. Even though love wasn't something she'd found there.

Whereas Estella was alone with no idea of who or what she was. No idea how she felt about anything. Not even sure if she had any feelings left. Unable to think about Lena, who was gone forever. Unable to think about her mother or Alex because they were gone too and she didn't know which of them she might see again. Unwilling to think about why her mother had kept only one baby, or who Estella and Lena's father was; he certainly wasn't the dead French soldier her mother had made him out to be.

Instead she concentrated on selling bolts of fabric because she wasn't able to draw anything worth making and she needed money to eat, to live. She sat in the workroom and watched her fledgling business being sold off, piece by piece. Occasionally she stared at the article from *Vogue*, wondering how it could be true when now, the design ideas that used to cascade over her, had entirely dried up. She prevaricated with contacting the Forsyths' buyer as she had nothing new to show him.

One day in late November, as she sat in the workroom, the clouds floated in a layer of gauze across the sun creating a half-light, a smoky, steely, blackout-blue that reminded her of the night she'd sat at the piano with Alex and he'd sung one perfect song. The night when Alex had kissed her hand and she'd seen something in his eyes, a hunger so potent that she hadn't been able to look away and so, for a few seconds, it had just been her and Alex and the gunmetal light and she'd never felt paradoxically quite so free, yet so tethered. As if there were no sky. As if everything had dissolved and they were enough, in that moment, for one another.

"Damn you, Alex," she said. "Where are you?" And Maman? Where was she?

In response, the clouds won, swallowing the sun completely. Despite that, the feeling of the night in Montmartre remained with Estella, the curious sensation of being both unleashed and grounded, and her hand reached out for her pencil and sketchpad. She flicked through the pages until she came to the sketches she'd drawn on the flying boat, dresses in all colors of the sky: dresses that floated, dresses that rained down hard upon a body, dresses that might make the wearer look as if they'd just stepped down from the stars. They were good, she realized. More than good. They were the best things she'd ever drawn.

She pressed the lead of her pencil onto a new page and began to draw. She stayed there for hours, drawing into dusk, not turning on the lights; it was hard to see but she almost didn't need to see, just needed her hand to keep moving over the paper, transferring everything in her mind to the sketchpad. Dresses emerged quickly, needing almost no erasures, proportions correct, details traced in precisely: belts that emphasized waists in exactly the right way, sleeves that fell just as they ought, peonies blossoming against shoulders, or tied out of sashes, or blooming audaciously up from a collar.

She took out her watercolors and daubed paint on to her designs, watching skirts swirl to life, seeing shadow and light play upon the fabric so that it became animate, as if one's hand—were it to reach out—would stroke silk jersey rather than paper.

She thought she heard the door open; she at least felt a cool rush of air behind her and she shivered a little but neither sensation made her turn around, nor at first did the voice that said, so low as to be almost inaudible, "Estella."

She lifted her head from the page for just a second then returned to her sketch. She was imagining things, so caught up in the feeling of that night in Paris that she'd heard Alex's voice in the room.

But she heard it again, louder this time. "Estella?"

This time, she turned around and saw Alex silhouetted in the doorway, watching her, the look on his face so tender and yearning that she felt her legs push her upright, her feet propel her across the floor. Before she had time to think about it, she ran to him. He moved toward her at the same time and, when she reached him, she felt him lift her up so that her legs wrapped around his waist. Her mouth pressed against his, harder and harder but still not hard enough, desperate to take in everything of him that she could before he vanished again.

For a few minutes they stayed like that, one of his hands under her hips, holding her up, the other on her back, clenching the thin fabric of her dress, her whole body aching, mouth unwilling to move away from his. Kissing, just kissing, trying to tell him what a fool she'd been, how wrong she was, how much she wanted him, how she hadn't stopped thinking about him and it almost felt like he understood because he didn't let go, but responded in kind, drinking her in. Then he walked a few steps forward and sat her on her workbench, still keeping her legs around him, now able to move both his hands up to her face, to draw away just a little, staring so far into her that she felt turned inside out.

"God, I missed you," he said.

"I thought you might be dead."

"And you cared about that?" he asked.

"I was terrified," she said.

He leaned his forehead against hers and she could hear his breath, as unsteady as hers, could feel his heart and her own beating too fast but in perfect accord. "I shouldn't do this," he said, pulling away. "There are so many better men out there for you."

Estella loved him all the more for his uncertainty, his unwillingness to taint her with what he saw as his checkered past, and his bizarre and incongruous present. "Alex, if you stop now I swear I'll be more annoying and prickly and irritating than you can even imagine." She smiled at him but he didn't smile in response to her jest.

"I've done some terrible things, Estella. My father was the world's worst man. You should be with someone who knows more about light than dark, more about love than hate. One day you'll look at me and you'll wish I hadn't let you kiss me. That's why I should stop now and walk away."

She could hear the effort it took to keep his tone even, heard the tiniest tremor as he said the words: *walk away*. "I don't care about any of that. I know who you are." She caught his eyes with hers as she spoke.

"If you hadn't run across the room to me there's no way I would have kissed you. Not because I didn't want to but because I don't want to drag you into the mess of my life. I should leave." He stepped backward.

Estella caught his hand. Instead of replying, she drew his mouth back to hers and kissed him even more deeply and at last she felt the subtle shift in his body as he let go of his doubts about himself. He stroked her cheeks with his thumbs then, after a time, his hands dropped to the hem of her dress, found their way beneath the fabric and slid along her thighs until they reached her hips. His hands slipped inside her knickers, caressed the skin of her buttocks as he drew her closer toward him and she could feel how much he wanted her.

"Alex…" She murmured his name against his mouth, before his lips traveled a path down to her neck and her fingers twisted in the fabric of his shirt.

Then his hands moved to the buttons on her chest and fumbled with them before he said, "How do you take this damn thing off."

She laughed. "Those ones are just decorative."

She undid the button at the back of her neck, lifted her dress over her head and sat before him, naked besides her knickers and he drew in a long, sharp breath.

"My God," he said. "You're so beautiful I almost can't look at you." He raised one hand to stroke, so gently, the skin of her breast, making her whole body shiver, making her hands tighten their grip on the front of his shirt.

"And I almost can't bear you doing that," she murmured.

He did it again and this time she gasped before he kissed her, hard but too fast.

"Wait there," he said.

She was about to ask him where the hell he was going at such a time when he unrolled a bolt of midnight blue velvet onto the floor in the corner by the fire, struck a match to the wood and paper waiting there, then returned to her, picked her up, carried her over to the fire and laid her carefully on top of the velvet.

"That's better," he said. "Not standing at a worktable, but here where I can lie beside you."

"You know that's one of my most expensive rolls of fabric," she said.

"Shall I stop?" he teased.

In response, Estella kissed him, unbuttoning his shirt, allowing her palms to run over his chest, to feel every scar, every perfectly defined muscle, every inch of his glorious upper body. She bent her head to him and kissed the skin of his chest, feeling his heart throb against her lips, and then she moved her mouth down over his stomach, past his navel, hands never once stopping her exploration of his skin. She reached his waistband and undid the buttons of his trousers.

"Estella," he said, lifting her head back up to meet his.

His lips lit fires along her neck and she felt her back arch, her head tip back. He shucked off his clothes with one hand as the other caressed her breast, then teased her nipple, then marked a path to her hipbone, her thighs, and finally between her thighs and she had to close her eyes from the rush of sensation through her body. He kept one hand circling languorously between her legs as he moved his mouth down to her ankle and kissed his way up her leg, from her calf to her knee to her thigh, finally placing his mouth where his hand had been and Estella was no longer able to breathe, was no longer able to do anything except cry out his name as everything except Alex evanesced.

It took her several long moments to regain her breath, to open her eyes and, even then, all she was capable of saying was, "Oh God."

He smiled and said, "Kiss me again," and she did, drawing him on top of her, drawing him into her so fully that it was his turn to close his eyes, to murmur her name against her neck, to grip one of her hands in his so tightly she knew that his world had just receded too; that all that was left in that moment was Estella and Alex and the feeling between them that she was unable, because the right words did not exist, to name.

CHAPTER TWENTY-EIGHT

Neither moved for a long time after, helpless to do anything other than lie body to body, kissing as they recovered. Eventually Estella rolled over onto her stomach, propping herself up on her forearms and Alex turned onto his side, leaning on one elbow, running his hand lightly up and down her naked spine.

"Well, that was even better than I'd imagined it would be," he said, smiling.

"Now you sound just like the womanizing man-about-town you pretend to be," she said with a laugh.

"Was I not supposed to enjoy it?" he asked, eyebrows raised.

"You were definitely supposed to enjoy it," she said. "But did you really...imagine this?"

He reached over and lifted her chin, kissing her softly. "If it won't get me into trouble," he said, "then yes. I have imagined doing this with you a thousand times." He laughed. "You're blushing! I can't believe that the normally audacious Estella is speechless and blushing."

She pushed him onto his back, resting her arms on his chest. "I've been a complete idiot," she admitted. "I had no idea. I guess that I mostly thought of you as the man responsible for turning my whole life inside out and back to front so I just didn't let myself think beyond that. And I always thought you and Lena..."

They were both quiet for a moment. "I understand," he said. "I wanted you to think Lena and I were together because it would keep you away from me. I'm just glad now that you feel the same as I do."

"You have Peter to thank for that," she said. "He gave me the worst tongue-lashing I've ever had in my life."

Alex winced. "Sorry about that. He's overprotective. We've been through hell and beyond together. The agent with the broken leg in the Village Saint-Paul was his brother. I think Peter's bluntness was his peculiar way of saying thank you for helping."

"I didn't know," she said. "And don't apologize. I'm glad he gave me a piece of his mind. Otherwise I might be in someone else's bed right now," she added, eyes sparkling with mischief.

"I don't think I can joke about that," he said, kissing her again, as if wanting to convince her that this was the only place she should be, a fact of which she needed no persuasion.

"Mmmmm," she said when he let her go. "There should be a law against kissing like that unless you want it to end up…"

But she didn't finish her sentence. He kissed her again, exactly like he'd done before, and she slid her body on top of his, running her hands over his chest, feeling his hands circle her hips, moving in time with him.

"What were you working on when I came in?" he asked later as he sat up to light a cigarette and lean his back against the sofa.

Estella stood and he watched her walk, naked and stunning and, for the time being, all his, and he had to stub out the cigarette because it was hard enough to breathe, watching her walk, let alone with his lungs full of smoke.

"These," she said when she walked back, passing him the sketch-book.

He held out his arm and she curled into his side, tucking her head into his shoulder. He kissed her hair and had the same sense of breathlessness; that she was the kind of woman who wanted what came after the act itself, that she wanted the slow embrace, the stopping of time on a winter evening after sex, when the light had long since faded but the air was still alive with what they'd just done, with the promise of doing it again shining like a full moon above them. When it felt as if they had all the time in the world to kiss and to touch and to never move apart for more than a moment, to never be clothed again. To be two people adrift from the world, castaways into love and desire.

He looked at each drawing and could see her in all of them, her body moving sultrily beneath the fabric, see the smile she might give as he slipped each one off her. "Are you going to put together another collection?" he asked, lighting a cigarette again, trying to do something with his hands which just wanted to touch her.

"I don't know," she said. "I haven't worked at all for the last few months. I've felt lost for the first time in my life. And then today, inspiration came. I haven't decided what I'll do with the designs though."

"I have something for you," he said, reaching out for his trousers, taking an envelope from the pocket. "It's why I came to see you. I went to Sam's apartment since I couldn't get into the Barbizon and he told me you might be here."

He passed her the letter and steeled himself for how she might react. But she deserved everything the letter granted her—the Gramercy Park townhouse, the paintings on the walls, the furniture, the money in Lena's bank accounts, which was a reasonable amount because Lena had carefully and assiduously invested the proceeds of Frank's and Harry's pawned jewelry—but he knew Estella would disagree.

As she read, he said, "She had me draw this up before we went to France. Now I wonder if she had some kind of premonition."

Estella reached the bottom of the letter and looked up at him, wide-eyed. "I can't accept any of it," she said. "I was the worst sister anybody could have had. Always pushing her away...It's like I've stolen the life she was meant to have."

He gathered her up in his arms, the pang he felt at seeing her pain unlike anything he'd experienced and he'd known all kinds of physical pain. If love hurt this much, it was a wonder anyone did it. But if love meant being able to hold so close what was most precious in the world to you, then love was worth anything.

"You have to accept it all," he said. "Because it's a gift Lena wanted to give you. She wants you to live your dream, just like she says in the letter. Otherwise her life really was a waste. This way you can make something of what she was. You owe it to her." He knew he was being unfair, in a way, but it was all true. Only Estella could redeem Lena's life, could transform all of the many hurts Lena had suffered into a legacy of tenderness, warmth, and affection, rather than waste and suffering. "She loved you," he said, kissing Estella's forehead. "She really did."

He felt Estella's body shudder, heard the fierce intake of a sob. He held her even more tightly, and she clung to him, as if his presence made her feel better. He felt such a wave of adoration and disbelief that, of all people, she would seek comfort from him, that he couldn't speak. They sat there for a long time, bound together, the solace of one another's presence a thing beyond understanding.

When Estella pulled back, he wiped away the tears from her cheeks.

"I feel..." she started.

"Guilty?"

"Yes."

"Don't. You should feel guilty if you don't do anything with these drawings." He gestured to her sketchpad. "Make them for Lena. It's what she'd have wanted."

She nodded. "I will. I'll name this collection for her."

"It's perfect," he said.

Neither spoke for a moment and then she asked, "Where were you?"

He hated the answer he had to give. "I can't tell you. You know I can't."

"Did you find my mother?" she whispered.

This time he thanked God for what he could say. "Yes. She's alive. She's moved though. I can't tell you where."

"I don't suppose I can write to her?"

"Not yet."

"How long are you in New York for?"

"That I can tell you," he said, smiling. "I have a month's leave. And I plan to spend as much of it with you as possible. I plan to kiss you whenever," he leaned over and kissed her neck, then her breast, gently at first, then hungrily, "and wherever I want." He moved down to kiss her stomach and then looked up at her.

"Don't stop," she whispered.

"I don't intend to," he said.

When they'd finished he rolled her into him, her back pressing against his chest. "Let's go to the Hudson Valley," he said. "Away from every-thing. We can just be together."

When she didn't reply he added, "You can work out there, if that's what's bothering you. I don't mind what you do so long as you come."

"You really want to spend your entire month of leave with me?" she asked and he could hear the incredulity in her voice.

He turned her over to face him. "I love you, Estella."

The look on her face was one of such astonishment he couldn't help laughing. "I was hoping for a thank-you at the very least."

"It's just that I can't imagine you...falling in love with me."

"I know it sounds crazy and not what happens in real life—it's something you see on the silver screen—but the minute you walked into the Théâtre du Palais-Royal and spoke to me, I felt something more than I'd ever felt for anyone in my life. And it's never gone away."

"I can't believe I wasted all those months disliking you for things that weren't your fault. But I intend to make up for it," she said smiling, "because I love you too. So much."

"Thank God," he breathed and he kissed her.

She let the kiss linger then pulled back. "Let's go to Sleepy Hollow," she said. "I won't be able to work there though. I need Janie to model for me and Sam to cut for me."

"They can come too," he said and even he could tell that his voice sounded not quite thrilled with the prospect.

She laughed. "Yes, because having them in the house while we spend an entire month naked is just what you had in mind."

He groaned. "You can't say things like that," he whispered. "A month naked with you is more than I can bear thinking about." He paused. "But, realistically, I have work to do too. Safe work, I promise," he said as she looked askance at him. "Just a few government meetings. So why don't we spend a week there with just the two of us and then they can come out and you can do your work. I don't mind." He stopped, but then made himself say it. "Are you sure that you and Sam…"

"Sam is my friend. A very good friend, but a friend nonetheless. I promise."

"I believe you," he said. "I just feel as if he'd be more suitable for you."

"I don't want suitable," she whispered. "I want this. And thank you. I don't imagine many men would be willing to let two virtual strangers share their hard-earned leave with them."

There wasn't a thing in the world he wouldn't be willing to do for her. He couldn't believe his good fortune, that of all the women in the world, the one who was the most extraordinary had somehow fallen in love with him. He couldn't even speak, felt sure he might actually cry so he just held her fiercely against him so she couldn't see his face, couldn't see that he was about to break down into sobs of joy, of gratitude, of wonder that life could be so damned good.

But she knew, she knew everything about him it seemed because she reached up and touched his chin with her hand, drew it down, looked directly into his face and saw him as no one had ever seen him before. Still she kissed him, still she said, "I love you, Alex."

They finally tore themselves away from their makeshift bed long enough to get in a car and drive to the Hudson Valley. They talked the whole way there and Estella felt the opposite of what Janie had felt about her husband; that she knew Alex better than anyone, even though there was so much about him, facts and figures, that she didn't know. But all the important things were absolutely known.

"How old *are* you?" was one of the questions she asked as they drove.

"I had my twenty-seventh birthday while we were in Paris."

Twenty-seven. It was so young. "I remember you once said you'd been doing this for six years," she said, taking his hand. "It's not the kind of thing most people start doing not long after they turn twenty."

"I started working for the British government the day I finished law school. Which is why I've hardly spent any time in New York over the last six years. Just short trips, on and off. Enough to keep my cover of Americanness. I've mostly been in Europe."

"Well," she said, knowing he probably wasn't able to tell her any more, "we'll have to make sure we celebrate your birthday properly when we get there."

Which meant they barely said hello to his housekeeper when they arrived, just ran up the stairs to his bedroom, at the door of which Alex gave her a wicked grin. "This will be our first time in a bed. Even the womanizer that I'm supposed to be usually manages to find a bed for these things. Which must mean it's you leading me astray."

Estella laughed. "We have been in a bed together before. In Paris."

He drew her in close and kissed her forehead, her cheeks, her neck. "That was torture," he said. "I was sick enough anyway and then to have to lie there and pretend to feel nothing with you sitting on a bed beside me just about killed me."

"Now you can feel whatever you like." She led him over to the bed and touched the scar just above his right temple with her fingers.

"That one's from the parachute drop," he said.

She kissed it. Then she touched the scar line on his chin, which was almost hidden by stubble.

"A skirmish with a double agent in Marseilles," he murmured.

She kissed that one too. And so on, down his body, as she undid each button on his shirt and on his trousers, as she eased him onto the bed and learned the history of his body, what each scar meant. She let her fingers and her lips touch the remnant of every wound and he gave her its provenance, then she moved to the skin in between, letting her mouth tell him how much she wanted him, how much she trusted him, how much she couldn't bear to be separated from him.

With each kiss, she heard him whisper her name, and then say it louder, and then louder still until he eventually pulled her head up toward him, and she saw the desire unmistakable in his eyes, heard him say, "I want you so much, Estella."

She let him roll her on to her back where he did to her what she'd done to him, marking her skin with his mouth, repeating to her everything she had told him with each one of her kisses.

PART EIGHT
FABIENNE

CHAPTER TWENTY-NINE

July 2015

At half past nine, Fabienne walked into the atelier where she'd asked everyone to gather. This was it. Her one chance to convince them she had what it took to sit at Estella's desk. She'd arrived in New York just yesterday and had spent most of the hours of the night thinking of what she would say.

As soon as she appeared, the noise of the workroom quieted. The spreading machines stopped their work of laying out fabric, the graders halted their resizing of the pattern pieces, the cutters turned off their blades, the machinists took their feet from the treadles. And as Fabienne looked around at the faces in front of her, many of whom she knew because they'd worked for her grandmother for years, she felt the tightness in her stomach relax. She'd spent so many summers on the factory floor, being shown by the seamstresses how to sew, by the finishers how to trim, by the cutters how to cut. They used to buy her gifts, bring her cookies, ask for her to sit beside them while they worked. Remembering that, she smiled. Perhaps she had always belonged here; perhaps Estella's business was as much in her blood as her grandmother had always said.

"I know the last few weeks have been shocking," she said. "We all knew Estella was old, but I think most of us had hoped she was also immortal."

A murmur of assent rippled around the room.

"One of my fondest memories is of Estella telling me about the early days of this business. That she had a workroom set up in her home in Gramercy Park and Janie, who we all miss terribly, would stand in the center of the room, looking amazing in anything Estella put on her. My grandfather would, in his gentle way, teach Estella everything she needed to know to help her transform her sketches into things that could be worn. When she told me those stories, I thought it was so romantic; that she and my grandfather had met over a shared desire to make beautiful but wearable clothes, that their love for the things they made had eventually transformed into love for one another."

Fabienne paused and breathed as deeply as she could. She was not going to cry today. Today was all about fresh starts. Nobody in the room moved; they watched her, intent, and she believed that they were also imagining Estella and Sam and the wonderful way they had always worked together.

"Estella had so much love to give," Fabienne continued. "For a long time I thought that everything she said to me, everything she did— making up one of my designs for each collection for instance—was a simple act of love. But while Estella was a loving grandmother, she was always a businesswoman. She had to be; she quite literally started with nothing, leaving Paris during the war with only a suitcase and a sewing machine. And out of nothing, she made this." Fabienne gestured to the room they all stood in, the factory at 550 Seventh Avenue that had been the home of Stella Designs for seventy years.

"So I know that, when she asked me to take on her business, it was because she thought I could do it. I can't let any of this go. What, then, was Estella's life for? Why else was she brave enough to move countries, to make the kind of clothes women had needed for so long but had never been able to find? Her legacy should not stop here. And I don't intend to let it."

She had more to say, but the uproar of applause that followed her words meant that she would need to say it another time. And she finally and truly understood that everyone at Stella Designs had, like her grandmother, been waiting for Fabienne.

It was a thought that both thrilled and terrified her. She had two months until the spring/summer collection had to be launched to prove that she was worthy of their trust.

Over coffee the next morning, sitting in the front room at Gramercy Park, looking out over the lushness of the park, Fabienne read about herself in the *New York Times*: "Fashion Matriarch's Granddaughter to Take Over Stella Designs."

Fabienne smiled. How Estella would have rebelled at being called a matriarch. Like dowager, it was a word Estella had always felt did not apply to her.

Fabienne's phone rang and she answered it with a huge smile. "Hi!"

"Seems like you made quite an impression yesterday," Will said, lightly enough, but she could tell that he wasn't himself.

"Are you okay?" she asked. "I was going to call you this morning to let you know I was here. It was a bit of a last-minute decision to come. Do you want to grab some lunch?"

"Lunch would be just the kind of mundane thing I would love to do right now," he said wistfully. "But Liss is…not expected to last the week. I keep going to call you and then I don't know what to say…" He stopped, but not before Fabienne heard the sound of his heart breaking in his words.

"Will…"

Neither spoke and Fabienne knew it was because he couldn't, and nor could she. She also knew why he'd telephoned, rather than used FaceTime. He hadn't thought he'd be able to hold it together.

"Can I visit her?" she asked.

"She'd love to see you. But she might seem confused. She's not eating. She can't get out of bed. Her hands…Her hands are blue. She looks…"

"Melissa always looks beautiful," Fabienne said firmly. "I'll come tonight after work. I have something for her. Is she at home?"

"Yes. Home is the best place for her now."

"Will?"

"Yes?"

"I love you."

She heard a sharp and sad intake of breath as he hung up the phone.

That day at work, Fabienne outlined more of her plan. The line, while still strong, had drifted a little from its origins over the past couple of years since Estella had been too frail to spend any time in the office, leaving much of the work to designers who had certainly tried their best, but who also wanted to make their own mark. Fabienne wanted only to strengthen her grandmother's mark.

She spent the day in the archive, looking through sketches, finding ones from the very first showing Estella had ever done in the Gramercy Park house, a showing Fabienne hadn't ever known about. She now understood, as she read over a short piece from *Women's Wear Daily*, that this showing was what Estella had been referring to when she'd told Fabienne she'd once made a mistake and that it had been her biggest learning experience.

In the archive were a couple of photographs and a clipping from *Vogue* with a picture of Estella looking so young and so beautiful that Fabienne shook her head. How was it possible for Estella to really be dead, she wondered anew. Another photograph showed a group of people: Janie—gorgeous Janie who'd taught Fabienne to carry herself with grace—and Sam, her kind and loving grandfather.

Grandfather. Her mind recalled the birth certificate which named two strangers as her grandparents, and the marriage certificate which seemed to confirm that her father couldn't have been Sam and Estella's child. Fabienne closed her eyes as if she could draw the curtains over those hurtful thoughts.

When she reopened them, her eyes fell onto a line of text in the *Vogue* article: "*The first showing of Stella Designs at Lena Thaw's home in Gramercy Park.*" Fabienne drew the page closer. Was she so tired from the flight and from throwing herself straight into work that she was hallucinating? The page was a facsimile, a poor quality copy but, even so, the words Lena Thaw were distinct enough, as was the wall in the background with the Frida Kahlo picture above the fireplace. It was definitely Estella's house. So why did the article say the house was owned by Lena Thaw, the same woman whose name was on her father's birth certificate?

Fabienne pushed everything back into the folder and took out her phone. She typed in Lena Thaw, just as she'd done months before, and again the meaningless search results came back. Then she opened up the New York Public Library's website and clicked through to the digital image collection. This time, when she typed in the name Lena Thaw, she found two pictures. Both looked to have been taken at parties. Both showed a woman who was Estella, except the caption called her another name entirely. The second of the two pictures, from the social pages of the *New York Times*, showed Lena/Estella in July 1940 dancing with a man. The caption read: "Lena Thaw and Alex Montrose."

So they *were* real, these people who, until now, had just been names.

The only thing to do after such an unsettling discovery was to work. Her mind was too jumpy to focus on Stella Designs so she took out the dress she'd started to make for Melissa, opened her grandmother's beautiful old sewing box and sat down at the sewing machine, the very one Estella had brought with her from Paris in 1940. It had always stood on its own special desk in Estella's office and it still worked as well as ever. For the next two hours, Fabienne did nothing besides cut and sew. She too needed to work on her cutting skills but she felt certain she could do a good enough job on this piece.

When it was done, she smiled. It was good. And it had helped her to forget. She put the dress aside and threw herself into drawing, using the sketches from Estella's very first showing as her inspiration. At six o'clock, satisfied that she had the start of a collection before her, she picked up Melissa's dress and caught a taxi to the Upper West Side.

Will answered the door looking even worse than she'd expected. He hadn't shaved for days and the skin below his eyes was stained dark with fatigue. He wore a crumpled white T-shirt, jeans, and bare feet.

"Come here," he said, holding out his arms.

She stepped into them gladly, felt him take a shaky breath and knew he was fighting to control his emotions. "I missed you," she whispered into his shoulder.

"I missed you too," he said feelingly and they stood for a long moment, holding one another.

Eventually, he let her go. "I know the last time I saw you I promised the same city, no taxis, and no sadness," he said. "But I'm already breaking my promise."

"Two out of three is better than zero," she said. "Let's go see Melissa."

He led her through to Melissa's room and, even though Fabienne had willed herself not to react, it was almost impossible. Melissa was shrunken, thin, her body so slack it was as if her soul had already escaped and all that was left were the physical remains. Fabienne saw Melissa's hands resting on top of the covers, saw the telltale blue of circulation shutting down and she knew from her mother's work that death wasn't far away.

Melissa's eyes flickered open. It took her a long moment to rouse enough to comprehend where she was and who was in the room and Fabienne's chest compressed as she saw the realization flood Melissa's eyes—as it must every time she awoke—that she was, as yet, still alive.

Fabienne kissed Melissa's cheeks, enveloped her in a hug. "I brought you something," she said, furiously staring at a spot on the wall over Melissa's shoulder so that her eyes would not cry. "You said you were bored of nightgowns so…" Fabienne passed Melissa a wrapped present.

"What is it?" Melissa asked, sounding as ebullient as she always had.

"Take a look," Fabienne said as Will sat down on the other side of the bed, eyes on his sister, expression so wretched that Fabienne wanted to lay his head in her lap, to stroke his hair until he fell asleep, to comfort him even though she knew he was beyond comfort.

Melissa's fingers struggled with the bow, eventually working it off so that the paper fell away to reveal a gold dress. Not just any gold dress. An exact replica of the one they'd been standing in front of at the Met the evening they'd first met. The dress Melissa had said was fabulous.

"It's probably not as good as the original," Fabienne admitted. "I'm rustier than I'd thought. Even so, I think it'll be almost splendid enough for you."

"Are you kidding?" Melissa's voice was thin. "It's much too splendid for me."

Fabienne blinked hard. "I'll help you put it on."

"Turn around," Melissa commanded Will.

He did as he was told and Fabienne lifted Melissa's little body toward her, helped her take off her nightgown, and drew the gold dress over her head. Then she took a brush out of her bag, redid Melissa's hair, propped the pillows, leaned her back against them and dabbed some gloss on her lips. "Perfect," Fabienne said, smiling. "Don't you think?"

Will turned to face his sister and the look on his face made Fabienne's throat ache and her heart crack just a little more. Oh God, she was going to cry, even after all the promises she'd made. But it was okay because Melissa was the first to break, a tear sliding down her cheek. Then Will, holding the tears in his eyes but they shone with a telltale brightness, and then Fabienne too as Melissa held out her arms and gathered them both to her and nobody moved for such a long time, holding on in an embrace that Fabienne would remember all of her life.

After an hour or so, Melissa fell back asleep. Fabienne and Will watched her for a few minutes, then Will said, "Fabienne, I'm not going to be much use for a while. I feel like I've strung you along—you could be out with someone right now, not sitting here."

"You heard Jasper that night, didn't you?" Fabienne asked and Will nodded.

"Jasper's my ex," she said. "In fact, he's the reason I'm in New York. He reminded me what I used to love. Not him," she said gently, "but fashion design. Sketching. Drawing. I have a collection to launch in less than three months' time. So I'm here because I want to be; I have work to do. But I'm also here for you and for Melissa, and I don't expect anything from you. Not until you're ready. I'm happy to wait."

"Really?" he asked, eyes shining again and Fabienne couldn't sit on the other side of the bed any longer. She moved across and slid her arm around him.

"Really," she said. "Take as long as you need."

"I'm terrified I'm going to mess this up," Will admitted. "That all we have is bad timing and I'm going to look back on this in a few months and know it was the kind of love I should have done anything to hold on to."

"It is that kind of love," Fabienne said. "And that kind of love can wait for as long as it needs to."

She reached out to wipe away the tears that sat in the hollows below his eyes. Then she kissed him gently on the lips. He responded with a kiss so soft and tender that it hurt and she felt the most staggering, sweeping sensation rush over her and her grandmother's words—*loving can hurt*—rang in her ears. It did hurt, loving Will. It hurt so much she almost couldn't stand it. Because he was in pain beyond anything and bearing witness to that was almost worse than feeling her own pain at Estella's death.

She swiped at her own cheeks. "Before I end up a blubbering mess," she said, "I should go. I'll come every night just to sit with her. Just to see how you are."

"I love you, Fabienne," he said.

"I know," she whispered before she left. "I know."

In the taxi on the way back to Gramercy Park her mind whirled. Melissa was dying. She and Will wouldn't be together, not properly, for a long time. Not until the grief had diminished somewhat. She had a collection to throw her thoughts and energies into. And she had a mystery to solve. A box of secrets to reopen. *Yes, Mamie*, she thought. *Loving can hurt. It hurts so much that you aren't really mine. But who do I belong to? Who did my father belong to?* Maybe she should find out. Perhaps her love for her grandmother could stretch to taking in the secrets Estella obviously wanted her to know.

PART NINE
ESTELLA

PART NINE
STELLA

CHAPTER THIRTY

December 1941

The week of doing nothing besides talking and loving and kissing passed too quickly until one glorious late morning, when the sun shone like springtime and Estella was lying on one of the bamboo sun loungers that sat on the river side of the house on the wide verandah. She was alternating between sketching and gazing out at the view, so beautiful on a winter's morning, sun gilding the water, the sky, the trees. The cypress trees, backdropped by the river, were like ball-gowns, the intricate ruffled effect of the leaves like exquisite lace adorning the silk of the water.

She felt Alex come up beside her, irresistibly handsome in bare feet, rolled chinos, a white shirt with sleeves pushed up and the top button undone, felt him watching her for a few minutes and then he leaned over to kiss her so deeply that she didn't hear the sound of a car pull up in the driveway, nor footsteps clatter across the verandah.

"You two look like honeymooners." Janie's voice made them jump. There she stood, hands on her hips, grinning. Sam gave Estella a wave and Alex a look that Estella couldn't quite interpret but it seemed reserved rather than friendly. When Estella had telephoned them and invited them to come, she hadn't really explained about her and Alex. She knew it would be obvious the moment Sam and Janie arrived, and it was.

She hurried over to embrace them both, kissing Janie's cheek, so relieved that Janie had come—she hadn't been able to promise anything when they'd spoken on the phone but Nate was away on business so she'd hoped she could swing it. She kissed Sam's cheek too, knowing that Alex was watching her and she smiled back at him reassuringly to remind him that she'd chosen him, was not interested in Sam, that there was no need to worry. Estella understood it wasn't jealousy; that because of Alex's past, he believed he didn't deserve her and that she would leave him one day because of it. But she would never do that. He smiled back at her as if he was starting to believe it.

Alex organized lunch on the verandah, dragging out coats and lighting a fire to keep them warm, and they sat in the sunshine and drank champagne. Estella relaxed as Alex drew Janie out, had her talk about Australia, what she missed and what she didn't. She watched Sam slowly warm to Alex as Alex showed him the library and a collection of books on modernist art which Sam pored over, eventually returning and saying, "You know, at this rate, we might never leave."

Janie collapsed dramatically into a bamboo lounge, glass of champagne in hand. "Damn right."

Estella walked past Alex, brushed his hand with her fingertips and whispered, "Thank you." She saw his eyes darken and knew what he was thinking, but she also knew it would have to wait until their guests retired.

And so the afternoon passed in a kind of charged and expectant manner, both of them enjoying the company of Sam and Janie but both of them making any excuse to sit next to one another, to make some sort of bodily contact, whether it was leg pressed to leg, or brushing a piece of hair away from a cheek, or their fingers touching as they passed a glass or a dish, not needing to speak because they knew exactly what the other was thinking.

After evening had fallen and they'd agreed that the work would start tomorrow, that Alex had meetings to go to, that Estella and Sam and Janie would take over the sunny sitting room on the ground floor, Estella sank onto the sofa beside Alex, tucking her legs up, resting her head on his shoulder, feeling his hand drop down to stroke her hair languorously, with promise, and she couldn't look at him because seeing what was in his eyes would be too much.

"How's Nate?" she asked Janie, a subject Janie had studiously avoided.

Janie was more than a little drunk so she answered the question with what sounded like truth. "It was his birthday last week; I wanted to get him a surprise. I went to Bloomingdale's and stood in the store for an hour, but there were too many things. Then I went to the bookstore because he likes to read—I'd studied his bookshelves to understand his tastes but I couldn't see a pattern and I didn't know what he'd already read. So I asked the clerk for a recommendation and he sold me a book. When I gave it to Nate, he said it was fine but I haven't seen him read it yet. I was at a luncheon earlier in the week and I asked one of the women how long it takes to really know your husband and she laughed and said that sometimes it was best not to know."

Estella dared to look at Alex and he glanced down at her and she knew he thought the same as her: it wasn't marriage that made a person knowable.

And Janie must have picked up something of what passed between them because she said, "I thought love was all about finding someone who'd give you a ring and say those three words but now I can see that I don't have any idea what love is."

"Janie," Estella said, hurrying over to her friend.

Janie stood up. "I'm drunk and going to bed." She disappeared inside.

"Is she all right?" Estella asked Sam.

"She's bored. And lonely. This week will be good for her. Thanks for asking us to come up." Sam smiled at her. "I hope we're not interrupting."

"Never," Estella said, moving across to him and squeezing his hand. "Besides, who else is going to cut the way you do? I can't trust my designs to any pair of scissors. And I've missed my friend," she added, so that he knew she didn't think of him as just a pair of scissors.

He kissed her cheek. "I look forward to having you boss me around again tomorrow. Goodnight," he said, and nodded at Alex who said goodnight also.

With that they were alone on the verandah, the velvet night air cool but soft and gentle around them, and it was only seconds before they were in each other's arms, kissing as if they'd never before kissed, his hands stealing up beneath her top to unhook her bra, to run his palms over her breasts, her nipples, her hands searching beneath his shirt for the muscled skin of his back, feeling how fast his heart was beating, loving that she could do that to him, that she could make his breath ragged, his body tense with desire.

"We need to go upstairs," she whispered.

"I'm going to miss you tomorrow," he said, then added, "Will you marry me?"

"Pardon?"

"I asked you to marry me," he said, looking down at her, his face no longer inscrutable, his eyes no longer empty, the hands that couldn't stop touching her telling her that he wanted her, the heart beating strong and fast in his chest telling her that they were meant for one another, his soul telling her that he loved her beyond anything.

"Yes," she said. "Yes, I'll marry you. And we'll live happily…"

"And lustily…" He grinned.

"Ever after."

* * *

When Alex arrived home the next night, it was to find Janie draped in an impossibly beautiful gown, Sam brandishing his scissors and threatening to cut off Janie's toes if she didn't stand still and Estella, his fiancée—God, how was it possible to believe that?—laughing, which was one of the best sounds in the world. He stood in the doorway for a moment, seeing her in a different light, in her element, working with her friends and he suddenly understood that she needed them, needed her designs, as much as she needed him; that without her work she wasn't Estella.

She turned, as if sensing him, and the smile on her face was a wonderful thing. She walked over and kissed him and he couldn't let it be just a brush of the lips because he hadn't seen her all day and it went on for so long that Janie said she'd get Sam's scissors and cut them apart if they didn't stop.

He reluctantly drew away. "I missed you," he whispered.

"I missed you too," she said.

"How was your day?" he asked.

"We have a plan," Estella said, her eyes sparkling. "Don't we?" she said to Sam and Janie who chorused in unison, "Sure do."

He laughed, so infectious was her enthusiasm. "Which is?"

"I'm not doing another show for society ladies," she said emphatically. "I've thought of a better way. The Barbizon is full of the kind of women I want to buy my clothes—drama students, musicians, secretaries, models, artists; they're women who value good design, who can't afford couture and who need clothes they can work in. So I'm going to do a showing there, just for the Barbizon girls. They can place their orders before anyone else and they'll feel special because they'll have something nobody else has. Of course my plan is that they wear the clothes to work or college and other women will ask about them and want the clothes too. I telephoned Babe Paley at *Vogue* and she's going to come to the Barbizon with a photographer and write another piece. I hope that'll get the orders flowing from the stores. And I called Forsyths and arranged to see them when the collection is ready." She finally ran out of breath. "What do you think?"

"It's brilliant," Sam said.

Alex nodded. "It is," he said. "Perhaps I should go off to work more often if this is what happens when I'm not here."

"None of this would have happened without you," she said and it was another one of those moments of absolute communication, moments he knew must be strange to witness so he broke off eye contact with her as Sam cleared his throat.

"Now to get enough pieces made in the next month," Sam said.

"We'll do it," Estella said.

"Sounds like you'll be busy," Alex said.

"Do you mind?" she asked.

"Not if it makes you look so happy." He heard Janie sigh and saw her turn away.

"How about champagne?" he suggested to make Janie feel better. "And food."

"And an early night," Estella said wickedly and he laughed, knowing exactly what she meant.

Estella went back down to the city one night and invited out as many of the girls from the Barbizon as were available. She talked to them about what they did at work all day, found out how they moved, what they did after work, how their clothes let them down. She learned that she'd been too bold in her first showing, that just because she loathed the ubiquitous shoulder-padded victory suits, other women clung to their familiarity. That women still, above all, preferred dresses. That it was still forbidden to wear trousers in the public areas of the hotel. So she would include less of the trousers and blouses, a fresh spin on the victory suit, and lots of dresses, done her way, not the Parisian knock-off way.

The next day she returned to the Hudson Valley and sat down at her desk with pictures of her sky dresses. Then she re-sketched each picture, transforming them from something to look at but never to touch into something that demanded to be touched and worn, with enough flair to attract any set of eyes. Dresses that were not just fine but adroit too.

Each day Estella gave Sam her sketches and he cut them in the most economical way, talking with her about what adjustments she might need to make so they could be produced more cheaply. Each day she fitted the models onto Janie, and then Sam re-cut, narrowing seams to reduce the difference in lengths between the edge of the fabric and the seamline so that the bias cuts, which allowed for stretch and comfort, would sit well against a body, using all the tricks that Estella, whose talents had always lain more with sewing and sketching, hadn't yet figured out.

"You know," she said to Sam, "I feel as if I owe you far more than I'm ever going to be able to give you. Even giving you full charge of a thriving workroom, if—no, when—," she corrected herself, "we get Stella Designs up and running seems a poor reward."

"Working with you is reward enough," he said cheerfully.

Janie nodded emphatically. "This is the best fun I've had in ages. The worst thing is," she added, suddenly pensive, "I don't even miss Nate."

"Why don't you start dating again?" Estella asked suddenly.

Janie stared at Estella's reflection in the mirror as if she'd just gone mad. She wore a dress that matched with a demure little jacket for work and which, when the jacket was taken off, transformed into a flirty number with a peephole cut from the back—a first-date dress when you wanted to get to second base, Janie had declared on seeing it.

"I'm married, remember," Janie said.

"I mean dating your husband," Estella said, sitting back on her heels, removing the pins from her mouth and sticking them into the cushion on her wrist. "Fall in love with him. Make him fall in love with you. Go out. Seduce one another. Learn everything there is to know."

The clearing of a throat in the doorway made them turn. "There's someone here to see you, dearie," Mrs. Gilbert said. "I've put him in the front parlor. I couldn't get his name from him. He's a little..." Mrs. Gilbert paused. "Unusual."

Estella stood up. "I'm not expecting anyone. I should only be a minute," she said to Janie and Sam before she followed Mrs. Gilbert to the front parlor.

Waiting for her there was Harry Thaw. Estella felt the same chill pass over her that she'd felt the first time she'd met him at Lena's house but she didn't let it show, just fixed her eyes on him, knowing he couldn't hurt her now. All the hurts he'd inflicted were in the past. Done. Buried. Forgotten.

"You've taken Lena's leftovers, have you?" he asked with that awful smile. "Her house, her lover..."

"Mr. Thaw," Estella said sharply, "I didn't invite you here. I have no interest in seeing you. And I certainly don't wish to talk to you about Lena. You've wasted your time coming."

"I don't think I have," he said, sitting down in a chair, crossing his legs, smoothing out his trousers. "A brandy would be just the ticket."

"I'm not getting you a brandy."

He laughed, a wolfish sound. "It's not for me, my dear. It's for you. But if you'd rather hear my news unfortified by drink, then so be it. I thought the time had come to fill you in on the details of your parentage. Yours and Lena's."

Estella didn't reply. She didn't enter the room, but stood in the doorway. She didn't drop her eyes away from Harry Thaw's face even though the effort of holding them there made her head throb.

"Here you are," he said, holding out a piece of paper. "Your birth certificate. The only mistake your mother made was recording your existence. I suppose she wanted you to have the option of American papers. But it also means that the truth she tried to hide from you is incontrovertibly recorded in ink on paper. Say hello to your father." Harry's smile hadn't left his mouth throughout his terrible speech. In fact it had grown larger, rapacious, a lunatic gleam brightening his eyes. "Say hello to Daddy."

If she made sure she never looked at the piece of paper Harry proffered her, then it wouldn't be true. "That's impossible," she said, keeping her head as high as she could, wishing her voice had come out more loudly.

"I'll read it to you, shall I? Let's see. City of New York. Certificate and Record of Birth. Name of Child: Estella Bissette. Sex: Female. Color: White. Father's Name: Harry Kendall Thaw. Mother's Name: Jeanne Bissette."

"It's a forgery."

Now he laughed. That same awful laugh she remembered from the encounter in Gramercy Park. "Perhaps if I explain *how* it's possible. You might be aware that Evelyn Nesbit published a memoir in 1916. When I heard it was forthcoming, I asked the publisher if I might see the manuscript; money can buy anything, you know."

"Not the things that matter," Estella interrupted. "Not respect, not decency, not courage."

"You're as impertinent as your sister Lena. You have that in common at least."

She knew he was goading her, daring to speak Lena's name in her presence, but she couldn't stop the involuntary stiffening of her back and could tell by his laugh that he'd noticed.

He continued to speak, standing up, gesticulating as if he was giving a fine performance. "There were a couple of pages in the manuscript that I didn't think anyone needed to read. Pages in which she prattled on about John, their Parisian love nest and a precious gift he'd given her, one that she'd had to leave behind in the Convent of Our Lady in Paris. She was a drunk and a morphine addict by then so who knew if it was true? But I'd never believed in her 'appendectomies.' So I asked the publisher to remove those pages and I went to Paris. I wrote the Mother Superior a check to repair the chapel and she confirmed that she'd presided over Evelyn's lying-in and had taken the child, who was still at the convent. Which was very lucky for me."

Estella's legs began to tremble, then her arms, her hands, her whole body. She wanted to sit but she couldn't. She had to make herself stand and listen.

He walked closer to her as he spoke. "I should have known all along that Evelyn was the kind of woman who would dare to have a child in secret. She was never duly grateful for everything I'd done for her and I did *everything*."

The emphasis on that one word made Estella shudder. She knew he was referring to the murder of Stanford White, which, in the newspaper article Alex had shown her, Thaw had claimed was prompted by jealousy over Evelyn and White. "You can stop now," she insisted, but of course he didn't.

"So I thought it would be fun to take out my revenge on Evelyn's child. And what a lovely child she was, your mother. She thought I was so charming. Shall I go on?"

"You may leave," Estella said while she could still speak. If only she'd never seen that photograph of her mother smiling beside Harry. Then she could believe that the certificate was a forgery and he was telling her a fanciful story. "I think you've done what you came here to do."

"I certainly have, daughter."

Nausea rose in her throat, a nausea so overwhelming she didn't know how she was going to stop herself from being sick right in front of Harry Thaw. She cringed as he swept past her, almost retched as he leaned in to kiss her cheek, then ran, hand over mouth, to the nearest bathroom where she heaved over and over into the basin.

A spasm of self-disgust and loathing gripped her and she knew then, that no matter how sick she was, the shame of Harry's words would never leave her.

CHAPTER THIRTY-ONE

L isten to this!" Janie's face was white too when Estella groped her way back to the parlor.

A voice on the radio spoke words that Estella could hardly take in: *"At 7:48 a.m. today, Hawaiian time, the Japanese air force and navy attacked Pearl Harbor, Honolulu, and other United States possessions in the Pacific. It is expected that the United States of America will make a formal declaration of a state of war very soon."*

"We need to pack," Estella said hoarsely, her throat raw from the attempt to purge Harry Thaw. "We're going back to the city."

"Are you okay?" Janie asked as she took in Estella's face.

"Sit down," Sam said. "It'll be all right. Maybe it's a good thing for France if America joins the war."

"It won't ever be all right," Estella said dully.

"Who was your visitor?" Sam asked as if he'd suddenly realized there was more to Estella's current state than the news of America readying for war.

"I don't want to talk about it. *Ever*," she added as Sam started to speak.

She threw armfuls of clothes into her suitcase, gathered up needles and pins and ribbons and fabric and wished she'd never been born. How could her mother have slept with a man like Harry Thaw? The worst kind of man, demonic, a man to whom the word evil truly applied because he showed no remorse, continued to hurt people and took great pleasure in doing so. He'd raped his own daughter for God's sake. What did that make Estella, daughter of the devil himself?

Her body shook as she packed. She couldn't unthink the awful knowledge that if Alex had thought his own father was bad, then he would think Estella's diabolical. *My father was the world's worst man*, he'd said. *One day you'll look at me and you'll wish I hadn't let you kiss me. That's why I should stop now and walk away.*

Oh God! She tried to swallow the sob but she felt Sam's and Janie's eyes on her and knew she hadn't succeeded. Her whole body ached, as if her soul had been ripped away. If Alex knew the truth, there was no possible way he'd want to marry her. His father might have been awful but he'd never raped or murdered or been committed to a lunatic asylum. *Harry* was the world's worst man. And insane to boot. Which is why *she* had to walk away. It's what Alex would do if he discovered Harry was his father.

And then there was the shame. The horrible engulfing shame that her mother was the kind of woman who would fall for Harry, and then, knowing what he was like, would leave Lena with him. The blood in Estella's veins was beyond tainted; it was putrid. She couldn't look at Alex and not feel that shame ruin everything they had.

She felt Janie and Sam watching her as they loaded the car. Felt their concern, their dismay; knew they assumed something had happened between her and Alex and she let them think that because then she wouldn't have to explain.

At last they were ready to go. Alex would be home soon. Estella asked Janie and Sam to stay outside, said that she'd join them as soon as she'd spoken to Alex. And then she waited to tell him she could never see him again.

He knew something was wrong the instant he arrived. "Why are Janie and Sam in the car?" he asked, walking over to kiss her. He stopped when he saw her face. "My God, what's wrong? You look so ill. Is it Pearl Harbor? I have to go back to Europe but…"

Estella stood up. Even holding her hands clasped in front of her couldn't stop them from trembling. Her voice was high-pitched, strangled; she didn't even sound like herself but then wasn't that reasonable, given she was no longer the Estella he'd fallen in love with, the Estella he'd wanted to marry.

"I can't marry you," she said. "I'm sorry." *Don't cry*, she told herself. *Please don't cry*. Make him believe you don't want him, make him believe anything so that you don't have to tell him about Harry. So that you don't have to see the look on his face when he finds out who your father is.

"What did I do?" he asked, desperate. "I know I promised you a month and I'm sorry I have to go back but I can't stay, not now."

Estella wanted to cry. "It's not you," she said. "It's not the war. It's me. I…" How could she say it? How could she lie and not have him know it? But she had to, for Alex's sake. If Harry was insane, then mightn't she be too one day? Or her children? For God's sake, her mother was the kind of person who would give Harry a baby. *That* was insane. Everything about Estella was born out of disgrace. And to have to admit that to Alex, to witness the love leach from his eyes the minute he learned of her sordid parentage was more than she could bear. She could never say those words aloud: *Harry Thaw is my father*. But nor would it be honest to let things continue with him all the while keeping her deplorable secret.

So she forced herself to say it. "I made a mistake. I don't…" She couldn't make herself say, *I don't love you*. "I don't want to be with you," she finished. "Not anymore."

She walked toward the door, willing her body to hold up for just a few moments longer. Her heart seemed to stop, and her breath too, and the room shifted into blackness. *A few more steps*, she told herself.

Get out of the house before you blight Alex, the best and bravest man there was—the love of her life—any further.

"Estella," she heard him say, his voice bereft.

It took all of her willpower not to turn around, not to hold him as she cried and said *I'm sorry, I'm sorry*, over and over again. Because in the sound of her name, she heard all his doubts made manifest: that she would leave him one day. That he didn't deserve her. That he thought it was why she was going.

No, Alex, she thought as she walked down the front steps to the car. *I'm leaving because you deserve so much more than me.*

"Wait!" she heard him call as she opened the car door. She made the mistake of turning around, of seeing what she'd done to him. He was annihilated.

And she almost turned back. Almost gathered him up in her arms and smoothed her hands over his face, restoring to it the brilliance she'd been so lucky to witness. But then she would have to tell him and that would destroy everything they'd shared. At least, this way, she saved him from the burden of her shame.

PART TEN
FABIENNE

CHAPTER THIRTY-TWO

July 2015

Once Fabienne was in her pajamas, she took out the next piece of paper from the box. It was a letter, signed by Jeanne Bissette, Estella's mother.

April 21, 1943

My dearest, dearest Estella,

I've been told you're well. Alex, the man who's offered to make sure you receive this letter, tells me that you're in love, that you have a child. But as I look at his face, I can see that he loves you too.

I hope you haven't turned him away because of me, but I suspect you have. I know something of Alex; I know that he's worked to make sure I'm protected through this war, to make sure I can help the French people in my own small way, just as he does, but in much larger ways.

I know you've met Lena. Lena. When I think of her I want to die. Except that would be one more selfish act. I had to choose one of you and who can ever say that I made the right or the wrong choice? Here is the only explanation I can give.

I first met Harry Thaw in December 1916. It was a cold and bitter winter. I was fourteen, had grown up in a convent, knew nothing of the world. Harry charmed the Mother Superior, gave her money and asked to meet me as he was an old family friend of Evelyn Nesbit's. Mother Superior, knowing nothing of who Harry Thaw really was and convinced by his solicitousness, allowed him to meet with me several times over the course of a week in the convent drawing room. We drank tea. He gave me a diamond ring and a diamond bracelet. He was the first man I'd met properly and his goal was to charm me. Charmed I was, having no model against which to compare him to other men.

The last time Harry Thaw came to the convent, he convinced me to leave with him for a day. I'd seen so little of Paris and there he was, prepared to show me. I was thrilled by the thought of seeing all the monuments.

At first he was considerate, taking me to the Eiffel Tower and the Arc de Triomphe. We stopped at a booth to take a photograph and then had lunch. He bought me one brandy, then two. Then more. I was drunk and feeling unwell so he took me to the house on the Rue de Sévigné, John and Evelyn's love nest, which he knew hadn't been inhabited for fourteen years. He bade me lie down on the bed until I felt better. I don't need to tell you what happened next.

When I woke up, it was evening and he'd gone. I had to find my way back to the convent and, as I did, I remembered something Harry had said each time he'd visited me. That Evelyn owed him. I understood that I was the final payment in what he considered her debt to him.

After a few months, I also understood there was a consequence to what Harry had done, besides my own shame. Mother Superior noticed that I'd washed no rags for too long and I told her what had happened. Not about the violence. Just that I'd made a mistake with

Harry. It would have been impossible for a nun to believe somebody could be so evil.

She wrote to the Thaw family, requesting they take responsibility for Harry's actions. Harry's mother said they would take the child. They would pay for my crossing to New York, where I would give birth, pay for the lying-in home and my passage back to France so long as I promised never to speak about what had happened. She promised—and this is the only reason I agreed to it—that the child would be protected from Harry. I had no idea that Harry's madness comes from his mother; I thought she was a kindly woman helping out a girl her son had ruined. If I'd known anything about her, known she would give the child to Harry one day, I would never have done it. I thought the child would grow up with wealth and have everything I couldn't, as an unmarried fifteen-year-old, give it. I thought I was doing the best thing.

Mrs. Thaw didn't keep her promise, as you know. She wanted the child in order to prevent blackmail—I didn't know, but after Harry returned to New York, he'd kidnapped a young boy, his rage obviously not having been sated by his actions with me. Harry's mother had endured months of her name being dragged through the newspapers. She didn't want me, the daughter of Evelyn Nesbit, Harry's former wife, making any claims of rape which would be too good for the newspapers to ignore and would jeopardize his chance of once again making a plea of insanity and escaping incarceration in jail over what he'd done to the boy.

Mother Superior went with me to New York; she felt guilty for having put me in Harry's path in the first place. She was as surprised as I when I was delivered of two babies. She'd met Harry Thaw's mother by then—I hadn't—and I think she had her doubts about her. Not strong enough to understand that leaving a child with her would be a dangerous thing to do but enough for her to make sure that the Thaws didn't know anything about the second child. Mother Superior made sure to register your birth; she told me American papers might be useful one day.

We couldn't take both you and Lena. Harry's mother had been promised a child that she would pass off to the world as a symbol of her extraordinary charity—she'd told everyone she'd benevolently come to the aid of a poor fallen distant cousin in her time of need. Adopting this child would enhance her family's reputation at a time when everything Harry did destroyed it, meaning their business associates wouldn't desert them, their companies would remain profitable, the wealth they'd grown used to would be secured. She would have made it impossible for the Mother Superior and I to leave Manhattan without first relinquishing a baby. It wasn't until much later that I discovered she'd given Lena to Harry.

I held Lena for a short time. I placed you both in a crib together for long enough that I could draw you together, so I had something of her to keep. I couldn't choose which child to leave and which child to take with me because how does anyone make such a choice? Mother Superior did that. And I'm so glad to have had you, Estella. Every day I wished I could have kept Lena too.

I said good-bye to Mother Superior when we reached Paris. I told her I would find a job and care for the baby. She gave me some papers that Evelyn Nesbit had left with her when I was born. A rolled canvas—a painting of Evelyn and John—and the deed to the house Evelyn had bought on the Rue de Sévigné, a house she and John had used, a house I never wanted because everything about it made me think of Harry Thaw. That's why we never lived there.

So that is my story. You are your own woman, Estella. If you let the facts of your birth stop you from being who you are, then Harry wins again. And that would be a legacy I couldn't live with. Be brave. Love well and fiercely. Be the woman I always knew you would be.

Fabienne reread the letter twice. Then she flipped open Evelyn Nesbit's memoir to the typewritten pages that had been taped into the book to be sure she had everything right. Evelyn Nesbit, chorus girl and femme fatale, had fallen pregnant to her lover John Barrymore, had had a baby in secret, and that baby was Estella's mother. Evelyn Nesbit's lunatic ex-husband, Harry Thaw, had discovered the fact fourteen years later and, in what appeared to be a pattern of calculated and rage-fueled acts, had gone to Paris, found the baby who was then a young woman, raped her, and Estella was the result. As was another baby: Lena. Estella had a twin sister called Lena. Lena's name was on Fabienne's father's birth certificate.

"I need a drink," Fabienne muttered, as her eyes fell on the death certificate that was the next piece of paper in the box. Lena had died when she was just twenty-four.

She mixed herself Estella's favorite, a sidecar, and took several healthy sips, her mind reeling through the facts. If her father's birth certificate spoke the truth then there was some good news: Fabienne *was* related to Estella. Estella was her great-aunt. And Estella's twin sister, Lena, a person she'd never heard of, was actually her grandmother. Her grandfather, according to the birth certificate, was the mysterious spy called Alex Montrose, and it seemed likely that the medallion Estella had worn around her neck all her life was his. Why?

But the first lines of Jeanne Bissette's letter said that Estella *had* had a child. Which surely, judging by the date of the letter, must have been her father. So the birth certificate was wrong, perhaps.

Another sidecar provided no further illumination and Fabienne didn't feel as if she could deal with any more discoveries. If what was left in the box was as explosive as what she'd just found out, then it might be best to wait until after the collection was done. She had enough to deal with right now without excavating any more skeletons from the seemingly enormous closet of her grandmother's past.

* * *

Melissa died one week later. Will's text was brief. *9:05 this morning. RIP Liss.*

Fabienne stared at her phone. How did anyone respond to a message like that? *I can take the day off, come and see you?* she replied.

Thanks, but I have stuff to do. I'm okay. x

The news swept away every scrap of creativity she'd found since coming to New York. So she went down to the factory floor and worked with the manager of the atelier, draping fabric on wooden dolls as Sam had taught Estella to do, seeing what variations could be made and whether or not they were an improvement on the original sketch.

That evening, as she was leaving work, her phone buzzed. *The funeral is on Wednesday. 11am. St. John the Divine. See you then.*

The funeral was sadder and lovelier than even her grandmother's had been. The sense that Melissa had been taken before her time was palpable, from the age of the assembled crowd, right through to the image on the screen at the front of the church, of a beaming Melissa sitting in bed in her gold dress, Will's arm around her, smiling too. Fabienne had taken it. It made Fabienne think of Estella, and of Estella's sister, who'd also died far too young.

Will spoke beautifully, hauntingly, and everyone in the church was sobbing by the time he'd finished. At the wake, just as at her grandmother's, there were so many people that she didn't have a chance to do more than kiss his cheek and say hello, but she felt him hold her a little more tightly, and for a little longer than he'd held anyone else, felt him inhale as she bent her head up to his, heard him whisper, "Thank you."

Fabienne left after an hour. She caught a cab downtown, took out her key, opened the gate to Gramercy Park, and went inside, sitting down on one of the benches not far from the statue of Edwin Booth, enveloped by the canopy of green from the trees. She closed her eyes, turned her face up to the sun and thought about Melissa, and about Estella. Around her, the sparrows twittered in the birdhouses, and when she opened her eyes they locked onto Estella's home, now hers. The Parisian-inspired mansion that had its own double in the Marais far across the ocean, cut off, just like Estella and Lena had been separated for so much of their lives. Seeing the house, she had an idea, along with a stronger sense of peace than she'd ever experienced in her life, as if everything might turn out the way it was meant to.

She stood up and caught a cab to Will's house. When he answered the door, his eyes were red and he was unsteady on his feet. "Drink?" he asked, holding up an almost empty bottle of red wine.

"Sleep," she said firmly. "Come with me."

She led him into the living room and told him to sit on the sofa. He complied, leaning his head back, closing his eyes, suddenly so vulnerable, so at odds with the man in the suit at the office of his fabulous job as Head of Design at Tiffany & Co. that Fabienne's throat tightened.

"I'm going crazy," he said. "Drinking too much. Like my father. I can't…"

I can't rush into anything like he did as a way to ease the pain, she knew Will was thinking.

So she went upstairs, found his room, took the pillow from the bed, a pillow that smelled so much like Will's aftershave that she had to stop herself from drinking it in, and went back downstairs. She placed the pillow on the sofa.

"Lie down," she said softly and he did.

She found a throw rug and tucked it around him, realizing he was already asleep. She took a key out of her pocket, wrote down the address of the house on the Rue de Sévigné, and added a note, telling him that her grandmother had always said Paris was the best healer of wounds. He should go to Paris and stay in the house, she wrote.

Take some time. Recover. She'd miss him terribly, but she thought that, staying here, surrounded by memories of Melissa, mightn't be the best thing for him.

Then she kissed his cheek and whispered, "Sweet dreams," before she let herself out the door.

All too soon it was only a few weeks until the launch of Fabienne's spring/summer 2016 collection. She read the newspaper with her morning coffee, smiling; Will had returned from Paris the day before. They'd talked on the phone most days and he was sounding more like himself. He'd even told her that Paris had inspired him and he'd managed to pull together the new Tiffany collection in its entirety.

Her smile faded when a headline caught her eye: "Matriarch's Granddaughter Feeling the Pressure."

She read further and realized that the matriarch in question was Estella and the granddaughter was none other than Fabienne. A disgruntled employee who Fabienne had had to fire a few days earlier for taking one of the samples home and wearing it out to a party, thus showing the entire world the design before it was launched on the catwalk, had decided to spin a little story for the newspapers. And the newspapers weren't holding back:

The fashion world remembers the buzz and bravado of Xander Bissette's only collection for Stella Designs, which had seemed to signal a true and exciting changing of the guard. But the excitement was short-lived when he followed his heart to the Antipodes and was never heard from again. Fabienne Bissette is, of course, his daughter but it remains to be seen whether she's inherited any of her father's and her grandmother's considerable skills or if she's just riding on the coattails of the Bissette name.

She turned the page.

Will's face smiled out at her from the newspaper. She read the accompanying article about his return to work after a period of mourning for his sister, about the highly anticipated new collection he'd designed in Paris and which would be unveiled in the Tiffany catalog in a fortnight. The journalist raved about the éclat he'd added to the already solid Tiffany name and the certainty that his next collection would cement his reputation as one of the world's greatest jewelry designers.

One of the world's greatest jewelry designers versus *riding on the coattails of the Bissette name.*

She was thrilled for him. But when she sipped her coffee, all she could taste was its sharpness. She hated herself for what she felt, jealous of everything they'd said about Will and ashamed of everything they hadn't said about her. But it meant only one thing: she had to work harder than ever over the next month. Everything had to be perfect. She had no time to do anything else.

Her phone rang and she answered before she'd registered that it was Will.

"Hi," he said, his voice almost back to the way she remembered. "I haven't seen you for too long. Can we go out tonight?"

Yes, was her first thought. But the words that came out of her mouth were, "I can't. I have too much to do right now."

He didn't reply straightaway. "Did you see the paper this morning?"

"Yes."

"You've never ridden on anyone's coattails."

"I have to prove myself, Will. So that everybody else believes it too. I can't let Estella down. I just can't."

He was silent again and she hoped to God he would understand what she meant. She tried again. "I need some time. To focus only on the collection."

Time. It was all they ever seemed to need from one another. Time to mourn. Time to work. Never time to be together. But right now, she couldn't do her work well and spend time with Will. One of the two things would suffer. "I have to get to the office," she said.

"You gave me time when I needed it," he said then. "So take as long as you need. I just don't believe you need as much time as you think you do."

PART ELEVEN
ESTELLA

CHAPTER THIRTY-THREE

December 1941

Janie and Sam tried to keep up a light banter on the way back to the city in the car Janie had borrowed from Nate and which Sam was driving. But after half an hour of no response whatsoever from Estella, her friends stopped trying and let her be silent. At last they reached Gramercy Park and Estella waved good-bye, flew out of the car and up the steps and nearly dropped her bag when she ran into a man on the doorstep.

"My sincere apologies," he said, holding out a hand. "I'm Newt Fowler. Miss Thaw's attorney."

"I thought Alex Montrose was her attorney," Estella said warily.

"I believe he was. But she engaged me to help her with a particular matter. Can we go inside?"

Estella unlocked the door, snapped on the lights and led him into the front room. She asked him to sit but she stood by the fireplace, beneath the Kahlo painting.

"News of Miss Thaw's ah, death, was a little delayed in reaching me," he said, settling back into the chair, propping a briefcase on his lap and snapping it open. "She'd given me instructions to locate a Miss Estella Bissette, which I very much hope is your name"—Estella nodded—"and to pass on this letter. I've been here every day for the last fortnight at various times in the hope of catching you. She was very clear in her instructions; I wasn't to post it."

He held out a letter and Estella reluctantly walked over to take it from him. What now? What more could happen on this awful day? It wouldn't be good news, of that Estella was certain. Letters never were.

"Thank you," she said. "I'll show you out."

"It's not quite so simple. I need you to read it while I'm here because there are some papers she had hoped you would sign after doing so."

Estella unfolded the letter, the man's intent eyes upon her, and read words that she almost couldn't believe.

Dear Estella,

This is the most presumptuous letter I've ever written in my life because it assumes two things I can't be certain of. One, that I may die. And two, that you're my sister. The second I truly believe and the first, well, let's just say that I've always had a sixth sense when it comes to the future.

I've asked Mr. Fowler to give you this in the event of my death. Perhaps you'll never read it. Strange as it sounds, I hope you do. The reason I vanished right before your first showing was because I was pregnant. Even though I'd only slept with Alex one time, and I was very careful to wear a diaphragm, fate played yet another trick on me.

Of course I haven't told Alex anything about it. He once told me that in the field you're stronger if you're not leaving behind someone you love. And I knew he'd love a child. I thought maybe I'd tell him after the war was over. Or maybe I'd be too much of a coward and never would. I don't know.

All I knew was that I couldn't raise a child. How would I know the first thing about it when my only role model was Harry Thaw?

And I was terrified that, if Harry knew I had a child, he'd take it from me somehow and he'd do to it what he'd done to me. It seemed safer out of my hands.

I gave it to Mrs. Pardy to look after until I could work out another solution. But I always knew what the best solution would be. For you to take the child. Raise it as your own. And maybe one day you can tell Alex that he has a son. I think he'd like to hear those words from you.

All my love
Lena

"What?" Estella whispered when she reached the bottom of the letter and looked over at Mr. Fowler, sitting calmly on the chair as if they might be about to have aperitifs rather than shocking disclosures.

"Here are the adoption papers," Mr. Fowler said. "If you'd like to take on the responsibility Miss Thaw wants to confer on you, all you need to do is sign here." He pointed to a place on a sheet of paper and held out a pen.

"But Alex is the father. I can't adopt the child. It's his."

"Miss Thaw understood that his work precluded him from caring for a child, at least while the war continues. She had me insert a clause that if Mr. Montrose would like to raise the child as his own after the war then it would revoke your rights. I rather think she hoped you might raise it together." Mr. Fowler looked at Estella over his glasses. "Is there any chance of that, do you think? Simpler all around for everyone if so."

After what she'd just done to him, she'd be lucky if Alex would ever speak to her again. And the roiling shame of Harry's disclosure still sat trapped in her heart, a place where it would stay, never to be confessed to Alex. "There is no chance of that," Estella said despairingly. "Alex doesn't know about the child?"

Mr. Fowler shook his head.

"Excuse me." Estella stood up abruptly and strode over to the nearest telephone. While she couldn't bear the thought of talking to Alex after what had just passed between them, he needed to know he had a child.

Mrs. Gilbert answered. "Hello, dearie," she said. "You've just missed him. He left for Newark an hour ago."

"Newark?" Estella said stupidly.

"Back to London again. Doesn't expect to return for a long time, he said. I'm just closing the house up now."

"Do you have any way to get a message to him?" Estella asked desperately.

"I don't. I never do." Mrs. Gilbert's puzzlement told Estella that she didn't know what had transpired between Estella and Alex.

"When he calls, when he gets in touch with you, can you tell him I have to speak to him urgently. It's important. Please."

"I would if I could, dearie. But I don't expect to hear from him at all."

Estella hung up the phone and stared at Mr. Fowler.

"I take it you're not interested in the child," Mr. Fowler said, putting the papers back into his briefcase.

"Of course I'm interested in the child," Estella said. "What do I need to do? Where is the baby? When can I see it?"

Mr. Fowler held up his hands. "One thing at a time. If you sign the papers, there is one thing you must agree to. Miss Thaw was adamant that in signing this contract you would commit to never telling the child who its true parents were. That you would be the child's mother. And whomever you marry would be the child's father. Mr. Montrose is the only one with the power to revoke that, of course, should he choose to tell the child he is its father."

"But I can't do that!" Estella cried. "Of course the child deserves to know who its real mother and father are. Why would she say that?"

And as soon as she'd asked the question, Estella knew. Lena was as ashamed of her history as Estella was. She wanted to give the child a clean past, not a notorious mother who'd grown up as a plaything for cruel men.

Mr. Fowler held out his pen. "Those are the terms of the contract. If you want to adopt the boy, his parentage is not to be revealed to him by you."

A little boy. How lovely. Estella's heart thudded, already letting in love for a baby she'd never met. She couldn't refuse the child just because Lena was wrong in her ultimatum. Estella had to take him, had to care for her nephew, had to give the child a chance to know Alex someday in the future.

Estella signed her name.

"Mrs. Pardy will bring the child here in a fortnight," Mr. Fowler continued. "I'm allowing time for you to think about it, in case you change your mind. Better to do it now than later."

"I won't change my mind," Estella said firmly. "He's my nephew."

"Even so, it's part of the agreement. If you're serious about this, a fortnight should be sufficient to prepare the house for the arrival of a child."

A child. Alex and Lena's child. A child Alex didn't know about, wouldn't know about unless Estella could find a way to get a message to him. "What's the boy's name?"

"I believe it is…" Mr. Fowler consulted some papers "…Xander. I'm sure you can change it if you want to."

Xander. "No, it's perfect."

The next day, Estella's mind was not on poor Janie who she stabbed with a pin half a dozen times before Janie said, "Out with it. What's going on?"

Estella, crouched on the floor, looked up at Janie and shook her head, as if that would make the news settle, make it become real rather than a strange dream she had yet to make any sense of. "Alex and Lena had a child," she said slowly. "And it's arriving here in two weeks. I've just adopted it."

Janie's eyes widened so much that Estella thought they might pop like buttons out of their sockets.

"Get your purse," Janie commanded. "We're going out for a drink."

"It's ten in the morning."

"It might steady your hand," Janie said, attempting a joke but Estella couldn't make herself laugh.

Not long after, they sat at the nearest bar and Janie ordered two sidecars. "Tell me."

Estella did. She told her the whole damn mess. What had happened in Paris. What Harry Thaw had told her. What the lawyer had said to her the night before. That she had no way of letting Alex know he had a child.

"I need another drink," Janie declared when Estella finished. "Two whiskeys. On the rocks," she called to the bartender. "A sidecar is too diluted for a conversation like this." Then she lowered her voice. "You shouldn't be ashamed about Harry. You didn't do those things. He did."

"My mother slept with him!" Estella cried. "How could she? Then she gave him Lena. I don't know who I dislike the most right now. At least Harry has the excuse of lunacy. My mother's only excuse was poor judgment."

"Why don't you write to her? Maybe there's an explanation for everything."

"There is no possible explanation for it," Estella said, sipping whiskey to stop her throat constricting with a noose of sadness and shame. "I can't write to her anyway. I don't know where she is."

"Maybe you could let Alex decide if it's a problem for him or not," Janie said, reaching out to hold Estella's hand.

"Do you know what it feels like to wake up and remember that Harry Thaw, a murderer and a rapist, is my father? To know that my mother gave him my twin sister to look after? I want to die every time I think of it. Harry Thaw is a million times worse than Alex's father. I can't bear to see the pity in his eyes if he were to find out. I can't bear to tell him that my mother left Lena with him. Can't bear to have him think that I might pass on Harry's lunacy if we ever had children of our own. Harry's mother had it. Harry had it. What if I get it? I won't tell him."

"So it's better just to hurt him instead?"

Estella withdrew her hand from Janie's and finished her whiskey. "I would give up my soul not to have hurt him. But to stay with him and hurt him each day over a lifetime would be so much worse than having us both suffer one catastrophic hurt right now. Enough about me." She put down her glass. "Did you take my advice?"

"Not yet, no." Janie's bravado fell away.

"Start dating your husband," Estella said firmly. "Find out who Nate is. Really get to know him this time. The pressure of marriage is off; you're already committed. Relax and enjoy whatever it is you have. See what it might turn into. If it turns into even half of what I feel for Alex…" Estella broke off. An unhelpful segue. One which only made her light a cigarette and pretend the smoke had made her cough and choke, rather than the emotion.

Janie scrutinized her. "Maybe I will take your advice," she said. "Nate's back tonight. Although I suspect that no matter how many dates I go on with my husband, he'll never look the way you do right now talking about Alex." Janie lit a cigarette too. "I almost envy you," she said wistfully. "To know that love really exists. Do you think you'd rather have that knowledge, or have never had it because it would mean never…"

"Never feeling like this?"

Janie nodded.

Estella tapped her cigarette on the ashtray. "I don't know. Every moment of every day, I remember the first time I really kissed him. It was ecstasy. But he also tried to stop that kiss from going any further by saying to me, 'It's not fair to you, given who my father is.' He was ashamed of a father who was merely a bullying criminal. Mine is a psychopathic, murdering rapist." She stopped, struggling to speak through the tears that were pressing in yet again. "What Alex said reminds me of why I had to leave him. But he would never have said it if we hadn't kissed. Without one memory, I wouldn't have the other. So I can't wish that it never happened. But I wish it was so very different."

Neither spoke. Janie gave a cold stare to a man advancing on them with a round of drinks in his hand and he scuttled away. Then she stood up. "I'm going to go home and invite my husband out for a drink tonight," she said. "Maybe you're right. Maybe what I have is worth making something of."

After Janie left, Estella sipped her drink. There was something to be thankful for at least: Xander. She would do the best she could for her nephew, for Alex's son. She would make sure that Xander knew only love and not pain.

For the next two weeks, Estella lost herself in making clothes for the showing she had committed to holding at the Barbizon in March, changing the fabrics to accommodate the rationing she imagined was headed America's way now that the country had gone to war. Men's cotton shirting, jersey, lightweight wool. A crisp silk faille that she bought for a special price from one of the mills after the restaurant that had ordered it for tablecloths ran out of money, would be perfect for a dress Estella had in mind; it would sit off the shoulder, showing elegant collarbones, the sleeves twisted, a wraparound bodice atop a mid-calf flared skirt. Just two pattern pieces, so it was cost-effective, with the nipped waist and emphasis on the shoulders that women were used to, but it was the women's actual shoulders now accented, not false padding.

In between such coups, she counted down the days until the baby would arrive. The morning it was due, she flew across to the door the minute the bell rang only to find Janie on the doorstep. Janie looked different somehow, happier, lighter, smiling properly.

Janie strode in, and before she'd even removed her gloves and her hat, she spoke. "I talked to Nate. I asked him what made him happiest of all and he talked about how he used to play baseball and how he loved the feel of the leather ball hitting the wood of the bat. I asked him to take me to a baseball game and so we went and had hotdogs and he explained all the rules and it was fun because he was having fun; because he was happy. So I told him that marriage was my dream come true but so was modeling. That I just couldn't sit at home all day. That I'd only work for you, if you'd have me. That it would make me happy, the way baseball did for him. Then we went home and made love and he wasn't quite so efficient." Janie grinned and Estella actually laughed, shocking herself that she was still capable of happiness.

"I'm so glad," Estella said. A happy Janie was a sight to behold. It was like the hot sun of Australia blazing in and making everything brighter.

"Shall we get started?" Janie asked.

Estella shook her head. "Not today. The baby's coming today."

"Tomorrow then," Janie said briskly. "I'm coming at nine in the morning. Mrs. P will help with the baby, I'm sure."

All Estella could do was nod at Janie transformed, purposeful. It made her want to be the same. She kissed Janie's cheek. And she remembered, for just one short moment, the feeling of discovering what was breathtaking about love, rather than what left her empty of all air.

Not long after Janie left, the doorbell rang again and there stood Mrs. Pardy with a nine-month-old baby in her arms. A glorious little boy, chubby and fat and so delightful that Estella immediately said, "Look at you!"

Xander smiled at her and waved his plump little arms about.

"Can I?" she asked Mrs. Pardy.

"Of course. He's seen so few people in his life but he's such a curious little mite. Every time he meets someone new, he wants to explore them."

And explore he did. As soon as Estella took him from Mrs. Pardy, Xander's hand squeezed Estella's cheek, a finger popped into her mouth, another poked her in the eye and she reached up just in time to stop one traveling up her nose. She laughed. "Well, you're as much trouble as your father." It came out so impulsively and so true that she couldn't unsay it.

"Come in," she said to Mrs. Pardy to cover the sudden emotion. "I shouldn't have left you standing on the doorstep."

Mrs. Pardy studied her. "If I didn't know any better, I'd say you were nursing a broken heart."

Estella hugged Xander tighter. He wriggled in her grasp, looking at her with dark brown eyes so much like his father's that Estella knew she was going to cry.

"We need tea and pastries," Mrs. Pardy announced. "You get to know the little fellow and I'll be back in half an hour with something to make you feel better." She patted Estella on the arm and made her way to the kitchen.

Which left Estella alone with Xander, with Lena and Alex's son.

She sat on the sofa, the child on her lap, facing her. Xander smiled at her and she smiled back through a mask of tears, knowing she'd just fallen headlong in love. That if she couldn't have Alex, Xander was the next best thing.

CHAPTER THIRTY-FOUR

Each day, Xander spent time in the workroom lying on a rug or bouncing in his bassinet, cooing at Janie, cooing at Sam when he came in every evening after his paid work had finished. Mrs. Pardy took him every now and again, out for a walk, or to put him to bed, but he spent most of his time with Estella, happy to watch, to be adored. And Estella found herself smiling all the time now because Xander loved to receive her smiles. They made him shriek and grin and bubble over with happiness.

At last they had enough samples. The showing was set for early evening, when the women of the Barbizon had finished work for the day, in the first-floor lounge which had a stage to accommodate the concerts and plays that the actresses and musicians of the Barbizon often performed. There was no decoration, just wooden balustrading that ran around the room, the palm trees wafting fingers of leaves in the corners, the black-and-white tiled floor. And the women, chatting and laughing and eager to find out what they were about to see. Estella had given each of them an order sheet and told them they were the first to ever see the clothes. She sat with them in the audience, studying their reactions to her creations, knowing their faces would tell her everything she needed to know.

Janie glided onto the stage, wearing sample after sample, starting with playsuits, perfect for running around the squash courts in the basement and for moving straight into the dining room for dinner, followed by cotton bathing suits for the Barbizon swimming pool that came with matching wraparound skirts to assuage the scruples of the matron.

Then they moved onto dresses, the off-the-shoulder silk faille called Freedom receiving rapturous applause, which made Estella's mouth curve into the beginning of a smile. The Stars and Stripes—a navy jersey with thin white horizontal stripes fashioned into a dress with a flared skirt, stitched with one large box pleat at the front and back to make the skirt fuller and the waist more defined, and a red star affixed over the heart—had the women scribbling on their order forms. And the Bastille Day dress, a red cotton skirt fitted to a white sleeveless collared top with a sash of navy blue to draw in the waist stirred more cheers. Every piece was finished with a peony in red, white, or a silvery blue.

The show ended with a dress meant for the most special occasion. It was a triumph of architecture, and she'd based it on the dress she'd made for herself the night she went out to meet Alex at Jimmy Ryan's and had first seen Lena. Sam's cutting had achieved what Estella had imagined on paper: backless emerald green jersey with a long sash that created a halter-neck, crossed over the bust, then wrapped over the hip to tie in an arresting flounce, like a peony flower, at the left hipbone. No fastenings, which made it cheaper to produce. Estella had called it I'm Lucky because, sitting at the Barbizon out of a war zone, they all were.

At the end, the applause was thunderous. The order sheets totalled two hundred pieces. Two hundred pieces of clothing to make in just two weeks because that was when she'd promised to deliver.

She used Lena's money to rent a proper workroom on Seventh Avenue, near 550. It didn't take any effort at all to persuade Sam to leave his job and take charge of the workroom. She employed two women, for one-month contracts, and Janie said she'd come in every day for fittings. Babe Paley from *Vogue*, who'd come to the Barbizon showing and had spoken to some of the women who'd ordered the clothes, came in to interview Estella about her unorthodox approach to selling. Babe brought in Louise Dahl-Wolfe to take photographs of Estella at work and promised an article would be published the following month.

At the end of the fortnight, there was a stack of garments on the worktable. Sam's eyelids looked as if he needed Estella to pin them open, and Janie was opening a bottle of champagne.

"We did it," Estella breathed.

"We sure did," Janie crowed.

Sam gave Estella a hug.

"Thank you," she said to him.

"Thank *you*," he said with a grin. "That was the most fun I've had in ages."

"Let's hope they come back for more though," Estella said, frowning.

Janie passed her a glass of champagne. "Enjoy the moment. Worry about that tomorrow. Celebrate what you've done."

Estella nodded. "To Lena," she said, holding up her glass.

"And you," Sam toasted.

As Estella drank champagne with her friends in her workroom, she prayed that she could keep it for the six months she'd rented it for and beyond. Prayed that Stella Designs would be welcomed with open arms by the women of Manhattan.

The orders came in slowly and steadily from the friends of the women at the Barbizon. Forsyths department stores ordered the entire line and Leo Richier, the owner's wife, was seen out in both the Stars and Stripes and the silk faille. Then the *Vogue* article ran and six department stores made appointments to view the collection.

Estella ran into the workroom, grabbing Sam's arm and hauling him away from the worktable, eyes shining, holding out the letters. "Appointments!" she shrieked. "With the buyers from Lord & Taylor, Saks, Best & Co., and Gimbels."

"Really?" Sam said, reading over the letters and grinning too. "Hooray!" he shouted, taking her by the waist and twirling her around. They both began to laugh and the women in the workroom stared at them.

"We're in business," Estella declared.

"You were the only one who ever doubted it would happen." Sam kissed her cheek.

As he released her and she looked around at the seamstresses, so like Estella and her mother and Nannette and Marie had once been, she felt her smile collapse. This is what her mother had wanted her to do, had urged her to do when she'd put her on the train out of Paris almost two years before. And she'd done it, but she couldn't write to tell her mother, didn't even know if she wanted to write and tell her mother, didn't even know if her mother was alive.

But, standing in her own workroom at last, Estella knew that, despite everything, all she wanted was for her mother to survive. And Alex too. How long would it be before she heard anything of the fate of either of them?

One year passed by. How could it be March 1943, Estella wondered as she opened the door of the offices at 550 Seventh Avenue, offices with a sign in silver lettering that read Stella Designs Incorporated. She walked through the front reception, where a receptionist dressed in Stella clothes greeted her. She peeped into the salon, which was decorated with an Art Deco chaise, three chairs, coffee tables, and photographs on the wall of Janie wearing Stella Designs.

Then she walked into the workroom where thirty women sat

around tables, the chatter rising up like optimism as clothes were cut and sewed and embellished and finished, as deliveries came in and went out. Sam stood in the center of it all, making sure everything was perfect. He waved to her as she walked over to her worktable, placed right beside the window, and looked through the designs she'd begun working on for the summer collection.

On her desk sat a letter from Elizabeth Hawes, inviting Estella to take her place in the Fashion Group as Elizabeth was stepping down. Estella had received it a week ago but hadn't yet replied; did she really know enough, was she really successful enough to sit beside those other women who were far more expert than she? Beside the letter was a photograph of Xander, who'd fitted into Estella's life like a button into a buttonhole. It didn't take him long to look for Estella, to search for her in a room, to recognize her, to prefer her to all others. It didn't take him long to call her Maman, because that was what Mrs. Pardy called her, despite Estella's protests that she wasn't his mother.

"You're more like a mother than anyone he'll ever have," Mrs. Pardy had replied firmly.

He needs a father too, Estella didn't say, but knew the truth of it. She hadn't heard anything from Alex, didn't know where he was. The war had only gotten darker and dirtier and more dangerous. *Stay alive*, she prayed every day. *Stay alive so I can bring Xander to you when it's all over. And you too, Maman.*

Xander spent his mornings with Mrs. Pardy and his afternoons with Estella, toddling around tables, picking up pins, playing with buttons, doing everything that was probably unsafe but he emerged at the end of each day unscathed. His hair had grown in dark like both his mother's and his father's and he, hauntingly, had Alex's dark eyes and Lena's fine bones. The smiles and the happiness and the laughter were all Xander's own.

Manhattan had been told, via Babe Paley and Leo Richier, people

Estella had trusted to clarify the situation if it was gossiped about, that Xander was the son of a relative who had died. It was a risk she had to take because she couldn't run a business and be an unmarried woman with a child; nobody would have dealings with a woman thought to be so unchaste. Luckily, Estella had been so very obviously not pregnant at her first showing in 1941, which coincided with the birth of the child, so society had no choice but to believe her.

That day was going to be a little different from usual because she'd been invited to attend the American Fashion Critics' Awards. She, Sam, Janie, and Nate all intended to go and have a damn good time. She'd decided to wear the emerald green backless jersey dress that had won her so much success from the Barbizon showing. She'd made Janie a dress from tulle—tulle was cheap, off-ration, and underused, perfect for Stella Designs—in a bright yellow, sunny like Janie. It was strapless, showing off Janie's figure to full advantage, with a love heart neckline, ruched horizontally through the waist and flaring out into a full and long skirt so that Janie looked every bit the princess she was.

Estella left the office just after lunch and actually had her hair styled properly, eschewing an updo, but allowing the black length of it to be rolled into glossy curls that even she had to admit were rather spectacular.

Sam collected her and even though he'd cut the dress and seen it a thousand times, he still whistled. "You look beautiful," he said, kissing her cheek and she smiled, knowing Sam would say that no matter what she wore. He'd proven himself over and over to be her true friend, and every day she was grateful that she'd had the good fortune to catch a boat with him to New York.

"You should start dating again, now that the hard work is done," she said as she stepped into the cab with him. Over the past year, they'd all been working so hard that she suddenly realized Sam's love life, which had always been steady but fluid, never fixing on any one woman for too long, had become nonexistent. "Otherwise I'll feel like I'm ruining your life."

"Estella, you've done the exact opposite of ruin my life."

He sounded like he meant it but she told herself to be sure to give him some space at the party so women could approach him without Estella getting in the way.

They arrived at the Met at the same time as Janie and Nate, and when Estella saw the way Nate was eyeing his wife, she knew Janie's dress was definitely one she would put into production. She slipped her arm through Sam's and walked through the doors of the museum.

The first person she saw was Alex.

The shock was so acute that she stopped walking and the person behind ran straight into her.

"Sorry," she heard Sam apologize because Estella was incapable of speech.

Alex—it was most certainly Alex—stood across the room looking devastatingly handsome in his tuxedo, laughing with someone, jaw more stubbled than it should be, as if he'd only arrived in the country that afternoon and had come straight to the party. Indeed, his eyes looked tired and his face harder, as if he'd seen things that had changed him. Given everything he'd witnessed in the past, Estella dreaded to think what more he could have seen to make him look like that.

Sam followed her gaze across to where Alex stood. "Oh," he said.

"I didn't know he was in Manhattan," Estella whispered.

At the same moment, a blonde in a white dress in the bustle style that Estella hated slid her arm through Alex's. He looked up at the same time and saw Estella. The shock on his face seemed to be as acute as it had been for her and he actually stepped on the toe of the blonde, who pouted. Sam turned Estella around and led her in the direction of the bar.

"A large sidecar," she ordered.

"Estella! *Bonsoir*." Babe Paley kissed her cheeks and nodded at her glass. "You look as if you plan to have a good time."

"I do," Estella said cheerily as if nothing at all was the matter and she was simply at a party to enjoy herself.

"Let me introduce you to some people," Babe said. "Sam, you don't mind if I borrow Estella for a moment do you?" As she asked it, Estella realized that Babe thought she and Sam were an item.

Sam must have had the same realization because he grinned at Estella. "See you soon, lover," he said as he waved her off, which at least made Estella laugh. That was a good thing because, for some reason, Babe was zeroing in on the blonde who was staring up at Alex with simpering adoration. They reached the group far too quickly for Estella to properly compose herself.

"Eugenie, this is the woman I told you about. Estella Bissette, who created my dress for tonight," Babe said to Alex's date.

"I'm sorry I haven't heard of you." Eugenie's faux-apologetic smile was flashier than a billboard. "I don't want to offend you by saying that but I'm just so used to my Parisian designers. Of course with this horrible war on I can't get my hands on anything remotely fashionable and I keep telling Daddy to convince all his Senate friends not to ration anything and to let us all have the dresses we want but he just laughs as if I haven't a clue."

Estella could have sworn she saw Alex wince at Eugenie's use of the phrase "horrible war" just as Estella herself had winced. But she was keeping her eyes firmly fixed on Eugenie and not on Alex. "*Enchantée*," she said, being as French as possible for reasons unknown but feeling it was essential to keep herself together.

"Oh, you're French!" beamed Eugenie, as if that had elevated her opinion of Estella considerably. "What on earth are you doing all the way over here?"

"Making mischief and beautiful clothes," Alex interjected, clearly having recovered himself and using the suave tone Estella hated, his on-show voice, the one he'd used at the Théâtre du Palais-Royal, the one he used when he was working, which she hoped he must be tonight as it would be the only possible reason for him to escort a woman like Eugenie to a fashion party.

Which was entirely unfair. He was allowed to date whomever he chose.

He leaned over to kiss her cheek, which she supposed he couldn't get out of, his lips touching her skin as quickly and lightly as possible but it still made her feel as if he'd actually run his hand over her cheek, along her neck and all the way down to her stomach.

"Well, definitely the latter," she said. "I leave the mischief to you."

He laughed and instantly looked more like the Alex she knew, guard let down by her smooth rejoinder.

"You two know each other?" Eugenie interrupted, her voice a notch higher than before, head turning back and forth between them, stepping a little closer to Alex as if that would give her the right of possession.

"Eugenie is Senator Winton-Wood's daughter," Babe interjected. "She's interested in fashion and is spending a month at the *Vogue* offices. We're educating her in American fashion. Perhaps I could bring Eugenie to your showroom tomorrow so she can see what Stella Designs is doing?"

"*Certainement,*" Estella said magnanimously. "*J'ai hate de vous voir a demain.*" Of course she wasn't looking forward to seeing Eugenie tomorrow but she owed Babe at least that small favor.

She opened her purse, searching for the distraction of a cigarette, and then put one in her mouth only to discover that Alex was leaning across to light it for her. It was such an ordinary gesture, something men did for women all over the country every day. But now it seemed the most intimate of gestures, the way he had to move closer to her, the way he had to watch her, the way both her face and his flared in the light, the way she had to be silent until she'd inhaled, and was then able to turn and exhale the smoke away, hoping her hand wasn't shaking, wishing she could exhale away every last piece of attraction she felt for Alex.

"Excuse me," she said to Babe and Eugenie.

As she walked away to find a bathroom she didn't need, she heard Eugenie call out a garbled mix of French words that she assumed were supposed to mean *lovely to meet you*, but which made no sense at all. In the bathroom she sat in a chair and smoked her cigarette slowly, wishing she could stay there all night.

She finally took herself back to the party and this time she ran straight into Harry Thaw. But rather than quail, Estella suddenly realized he could do no more harm. He'd revealed the secret. She'd lost Alex. There was nothing left for Harry to destroy.

"Well, if it isn't Harry Thaw," she said in a loud voice that was meant to carry. "Who are you going to shoot tonight?"

The maniacal smile froze on his face as every set of eyes turned their way. He clearly hadn't expected her to be so openly combative. There was an imperceptible and clearly hostile movement of the crowd toward Harry.

He tried one of his laughs, but Estella now saw it as the action of a bully who didn't know how to fight the strong, a madman who assaulted the young, a coward who'd been allowed to get away with too much. She didn't intend to let him get away with anything more where it concerned herself and Lena. "You're standing in a room full of women. I know better than anybody how you molest and abuse women. So unless you want me to start documenting every despicable thing you've done, I suggest you leave the room, and leave every woman who crosses your path in the future, alone."

For one long minute, she and Harry stood with gazes locked. But this was her patch. Here, she was the strong one. He had no more power over her.

He was the one to look down at the floor.

"Good-bye, Harry," Estella said. She knew it would be the last time she'd see him, that he wouldn't come back for more, not now.

He walked away, the wall of the crowd opening to let him through then closing behind him, circling Estella, offering her, not Harry, their protection.

Before Estella had time to recover, the room was called to order. Everyone was asked to take their seats. Sam, with a worried look on his face, escorted her to their table at the side of the room.

"I'm fine," she whispered. And she was. The worry of when she'd next see Harry had gone. She'd met him again and she'd survived. She had other things to think about now. Like Alex's back, directly in her line of sight, held rigid, leaning over occasionally to smile politely at whatever Eugenie was saying. Eugenie seemed to have no trouble finding excuses to pat his arm, or to dangle her cleavage in front of him.

Speeches followed, mildly interesting. Then Babe took the stage, diminutive and delightful, and everyone clapped because Babe was impossible not to like.

"This is my favorite part of the evening," she announced. "We have a new award to give out, for a designer who has caught the eye of the fashion world, a designer we believe will be back here again next year, will be the name on the lips of every woman on Manhattan's sidewalks. One whose clothes you must all rush out and buy tomorrow because, by next year, you'll need to spend twice as much on them. Someone who has shaken us up, someone who brings an unerring sense of style to clothes women actually want to wear. Estella Bissette, come up here right now and claim your award."

Estella shook her head. "Did she just say my name?" she whispered to Sam but she knew Babe must have because Sam was whooping and leaning over to kiss her cheek, grinning and saying, "Stand up! Go get it! You earned it."

Somehow she rose out of her seat. The sound of clapping rang on and on, several people pushed back their chairs to congratulate her as she walked past. Her path took her directly by Alex's table and she felt as if she'd been knocked sideways when he pushed back his chair too, stood, hand grazing the bare skin of her back as he leaned down to whisper in her ear, "Congratulations. I'm so proud of you."

Then she was on the stage, listening to Babe telling everyone more about Estella and her designs, one hand straying up to the ear into which Alex had spoken, hearing again the low murmur, that voice she'd never heard him use with anyone besides her: *I'm so proud of you.* And after that, so low she almost didn't hear: *God I miss you.*

Babe held out her hand to Estella and welcomed her to the microphone. Estella knew exactly what she would say.

"This award should go to my mother, who taught me everything I know. She put a needle in my hand when I was four years old, along with a piece of fabric and she told me to make something; it only needed to be simple. I made what I thought was an exact replica of a Schiaparelli evening gown. I don't think it was quite what she had in mind." She paused for the laughter, saw Alex smiling too.

"Nobody stands on a stage and receives an award because of what they alone did. It's always because so many other people helped more than anyone will ever know. Without my mother's devotion and dedication to me, I wouldn't be standing here today. Without my friends Janie and Sam I wouldn't be standing here today. Without my sister Lena I wouldn't be standing here today." She heard a squall of whispers at this official acknowledgment of Lena as her sister. "But, as well as being functional and technical, any kind of art is an emotional thing. It comes out of what you know and what you experience; what you feel. So there's another person I have to thank. To the man from the Théâtre du Palais-Royal, thank you from the bottom of my heart."

With that she turned to leave the stage, knowing that to have done anything else would be dishonest; without Alex, an entire part of her would not exist.

The rest of the night was a whirl, a blur. She danced with Sam for a while, laughing, spinning, twirling, trying out every crazy move they could think of. She drank many sidecars. She had her photograph taken by a dozen newspapers and magazines. She sat at a table to talk to Babe but people kept coming over to congratulate her and she started telling her story about being a sketcher and sending copied designs to America, and the euphoria and the whiskey made her put it together like a funny tale and more people gathered to listen and soon she realized there was quite a crowd assembled around her, that she was sitting in a circle of peers and they cared enough to listen.

It struck her speechless momentarily and she lost her train of thought, which meant that somehow the next sentence came out in French. She shook her head and laughed. "I don't even know what I'm saying."

It took some time for the crowd to disperse and, when they did, she stepped out onto the roof of the Met, breath stolen away by the view: New York City laid out around her like the most intricately patterned fabric, sequinned with light, embroidered with skyscrapers, a shining button of moon at the very center. She smiled, felt like shouting out because there was so much joy in her. She'd done what she set out to do when she left Paris. She had her own fashion label. She'd won an award for it. So why then did it still feel as if something was missing?

Because it would be nice to have Lena beside her, to show Lena that the world was still capable of good things. Because she didn't know if she could ever forgive her mother; acknowledgment and forgiveness were not quite the same thing. And because she wished there wasn't a man in the same room whose very soul she'd once held in her hands, like the loveliest and most precious gift of all, but from whom she was now hopelessly and irrevocably estranged.

Alex watched her for a long time. That smile; it hit you like whiskey straight from the bottle, making every part of you feel instantly alive. Those eyes: like the argent light of the early morning hours when he'd left her in Paris the night after they'd learned too much about the other and he had, against all reason, fallen more in love with her than ever. Her body: he could see the tanned skin of her back where the fabric had been cut away, the gentle curve of her spine and her slim and lovely arms. The only thing he wanted to do was to step up behind her, place both his hands on her skin, kiss her neck, watch her eyes close, feel her lean into him and then she would turn and he would kiss her the way he kissed her every night in his dreams.

But he didn't do any of that. Instead he walked up behind her and said her name and saw her stiffen, every inch of her body instantly alert, saw her hands grab the rail, the joy flee from her face. What he wouldn't give to not be the cause of that; what he wouldn't give to be the reason she smiled rather than the reason she tensed.

"How are you?" she asked disinterestedly.

"Fine," he said.

"How long are you back for?"

"Just a week. Government meetings. Eugenie's date pulled out at the last minute and her father asked me to chaperone her." He hoped she'd hear the subtext: *I never want to be with any other woman besides you*.

She turned around and looked at him and her next words were like a slap because he'd thought he was doing a good job of hiding everything he'd seen in France over the last year. But she saw everything.

"It looks as though it's been rough," she said quietly. "I'm sorry."

How to respond? How to even speak? How to tell her that every night he went to bed with nightmares in his eyes even before he closed them?

He'd been asked to liaise with America, to help the United States Department of War with a unit they'd set up to operate as MI9 did. But he'd said no and, after this, he was going straight back into the field, that place of living on one's wits, where there was only danger and risk, where there was no chance to think of anything other than surviving. He couldn't tell her any of it, couldn't say that her country was ruined. Couldn't tell her about all the people—not murdered because that would be the better option, but tormented, hoping to die yet unable to because their enemies wanted them to suffer. How to describe any of this and keep his eyes dry, his voice smooth, his face clear?

"It's worse than what we read in the newspapers then?" she asked, reading everything he hadn't wanted to say into his lack of response.

He nodded. "Just last week I saw a cattle train filled with Jewish children being taken to a camp." He stopped abruptly. He'd said far too much.

She let out a long breath. "And yet the world still turns indifferently. I still make dresses. We all stand around here and drink champagne."

"Stopping those things won't change what's happening."

"I know. But it seems wrong that we leave it all to a few people like you to take on the burdens that the rest of us are unable to face. Thank you."

Goddammit! He was going to cry. He could feel a tear leaking into his eye, welling up from a place he'd long thought had turned to drought and he busied himself with finding a cigarette and lighting it, turning away from her as if the wind was bothering him when in fact there was no wind at all.

"Your mother's alive," he said abruptly. "I haven't seen her. I just know she's back working the escape line. Not in Paris though."

Estella froze at the news, tears the only part of her that moved, running freely down her face. She swiped at them before he could reach out to stroke them away with the pads of his fingers.

"Thank God," she breathed at last. Hands visibly shaking, she opened her purse and pulled out a cigarette, then fumbled some more, uttering a "Damn," which made him realize she didn't have a lighter.

It meant he'd have to do it again, even though lighting her cigarette earlier had almost undone him. At least then they were surrounded by people but now they were alone together and he had to rely on his willpower, which he was finding, despite years of tempering, wasn't as great as he'd always thought.

He flicked the flint, saw the flame leap, saw her eyes flash, saw her curve her lips around the cigarette, saw her eyes fixed to his and as much as he wanted to look away, it was impossible to break that gaze.

"Thank you," she said softly. Then, studying his chin, "You have a new scar."

His heart leaped when he remembered the last time she'd traced each scar on his body. But he didn't refer to that night at his home in the Hudson Valley over a year ago. Didn't mention their last awful encounter because it hurt too damn much and her leaving him was what he'd always expected would happen anyway—that she'd wake up one day and realize she could do so much better than a peripatetic spy with a checkered past who all of Manhattan thought was dissolute at best. He didn't want to hear her repeat those awful words—*I made a mistake*—not now, not when he was feeling so bloody tired.

He was about to thank her for what she'd said in her speech but then she said the most peculiar thing. "I need to see you. There's something I have to show you. For Lena's sake. Please?"

For Lena's sake? What the hell was she talking about?

"Gramercy Park. At nine tomorrow morning." Then Estella spun around and disappeared into the party. He saw her cross the room and speak to Sam who led her onto the dance floor and she was, in a few minutes, smiling a little.

Alex had a sudden and awful feeling about what she would say to him in the park tomorrow. For she certainly hadn't smiled at him the way she'd just smiled at Sam.

CHAPTER THIRTY-FIVE

The next day, Estella could hardly concentrate. She'd known that she couldn't tell Alex about Xander at the party. It would be so unfair to him with Eugenie there, not to mention everyone else around, and, besides, she'd been unprepared, hadn't known what to say. Not that she was any better prepared now. Thank goodness for Sam, who came over to the house to distract her. She could hardly brush her own hair, let alone look after Xander, so when Sam said he'd take Xander to the park early, would roll a ball with the little boy and give her some space to get dressed, she nodded.

At a quarter to nine, she was ready.

Alex arrived early, set himself up by an apartment building in the northeast corner, pretended to read a newspaper and watched the park.

Twenty minutes later, Estella appeared and his whole body contracted with pain. That she could look so goddamn gorgeous should be a crime. She was clearly flustered, her hair undone and loose, her dress buttoned incorrectly. His bones ached the way they did when something ominous was about to happen.

He saw Estella open the gate to the park with her key, saw her cross over to a man sitting on a bench, his back slightly turned to Alex, shielding something on his lap. Alex could tell that the man was Sam and the thing he was shielding was a child.

Estella sat down next to Sam and Sam looked up from the bundle on his lap, as if reporting something in the way parents did about their child. He saw Estella laugh, saw Sam put his arm around Estella's shoulders and kiss the top of her head. Three people looking for all the world like a family.

Alex's heart squeezed so hard he knew it had finally been wrung dry. He had to get out of there before they saw him. He'd received her message loud and clear—that she had a family and that Alex should forget all about her.

He never would though.

Estella reached out to take Xander from Sam. As she did so, the wind caught Xander's hat, blowing it away. She whirled around to catch it and saw a man hurrying down the street, away from the park, a man she would have known anywhere.

"Alex!" she screamed as loudly as she could. "Alex!"

She raced out the gates but by the time she reached the corner, he was gone.

"Oh no!" she cried.

Then she heard Xander, toddling over to her, say "*Maman?*"

That one word made her suddenly see that she'd been wrong. Everything that she'd thought mattered, didn't. Xander was the loveliest, happiest, most beautiful child regardless of the fact that he shared the same blood as Harry Thaw. With love and patience and kindness Xander's principal family—Estella and Mrs. Pardy and Janie and Sam—had made sure that Xander would never be like Harry. Xander was his own person.

And the realization Estella had had at the party about Harry Thaw was incomplete. Yes, there was nothing left for Harry to destroy but she herself was destroying her future with Alex—the man she loved inestimably—before it could truly begin. The scruples and the shame should belong to Harry, not to her. Rather than protecting Alex when she'd lied to him and told him she'd made a mistake, she'd handed Harry Thaw another despicable victory.

She scrubbed her eyes with her hands. She'd never catch up to Alex. He knew better than anyone how to throw off a pursuer, how to hide. And she doubted he'd be back in Manhattan again for a long time. But that didn't matter.

As soon as this damn war was over, she was going to take Xander to Alex and she was going to tell Alex how she had made a terrible mistake. Not in loving him, but in pushing him away. She was going to tell him that she still loved him. That she wanted to marry him. That she hoped, with every filament of her body and soul, that he loved her too.

So long as he survived the war.

Please God, she thought, *you couldn't be that cruel. Please let him live. Please let me give him the gift of Xander. Please let us be together at last.*

Alex ran into Estella's mother by accident in Marseilles. He'd never met her; Peter was the one who organized the minutiae of the safe houses. But when he saw a woman who looked enough like Estella, before he could stop and think, he reached out a hand to her and said, "Is Estella Bissette your daughter?"

She looked at him blankly and he knew she was doing what she'd learned to do. To answer all questions with a "no" in order to keep out of trouble. He gave her his code name and only then did she follow him to a café where they sat down in the back, watching the German soldiers. They spoke in French because at that moment he was French, an essential munitions worker on his lunch break.

She stared at him across the table with eyes like Estella's, although less brilliant and more haunted by what she'd seen.

"I know your daughter," he said.

"How is she?" Jeanne asked.

"Happy," he said. "But sad about you."

"You're the one who's been passing on her letters. You care for her."

He didn't bother to reply. He knew it was written on his face; everything he felt for her. But also the heartbreak and the loss. Still, he tried to deflect. "Estella is a friend. She loves another man, Sam, and has a child with him."

"She's found out about Lena?"

He nodded again. "If you have a letter, something I can take back to her, it would make her so happy to hear from you."

And so she began to write, two pages of small, neat writing. When she was finished, she handed it to him.

"You should read it," Jeanne said.

He shook his head but she only said, more urgently, "You should read it."

So he did. He read of how Harry had raped Jeanne too. And Alex knew, he goddamn well knew, how stupid he'd been. Thinking Estella had left because of him. She'd left because she couldn't face herself.

He closed his eyes and remembered how sick she'd looked that afternoon in the Hudson Valley when she'd told him she was sorry. He was sorry. A thousand times sorry. If only he'd not given up and run back to Europe. But now it was too late. She'd married Sam. She had a child.

"I'll make sure she gets it," he said in a voice barely controlled as he opened his eyes.

"Thank you," Jeanne said before she left.

That night, he heard from Peter that one of his *passeurs* in Marseilles had been taken, tortured, and killed. He knew straightaway who it was.

It took three months for that letter to pass through hands Alex trusted and to find its way to New York and to Estella.

She opened it with surprise when she saw Alex's familiar handwriting on the envelope. She tore it open. Inside was a short note, as well as another envelope, addressed to her in her mother's hand.

Alex's note said: *I'm so sorry, A.*

And she knew that it meant her mother had died. All she could do was read her mother's letter and cry, *I'm sorry, Maman, I'm so very sorry.*

CHAPTER THIRTY-SIX

It was early 1945 before Estella could take a ship to Europe. She had no real idea where to find Alex, but she had to start somewhere. She thought—or rather hoped—that he might have kept using the Rue de Sévigné house. But how long should she wait there praying she was right before she gave up and had to try somewhere else—but where else?

She and Xander arrived in Le Havre and took the slow train through a broken country to Paris. Once there, carrying a valise in each hand, Estella led Xander to the house in the Marais. She stopped at the portal, one hand resting on the wood, and she had the strangest sensation that she could feel the house breathing, but shallowly.

She held Xander's hand and entered the courtyard. The notes of a piano cried out through the window. There was only one person in the world who played the piano like that.

She tightened her grip on Xander's hand, pushed open the front door and climbed the staircase. Xander began to chatter. The piano stopped.

She kept walking along the hall, halting only when she reached the doorway of the room in which she'd once nursed Alex. Seeing him again after so long, alive, so very handsome, unchanged but for a deepening of the lines on his forehead, was so overwhelming that she had to hold on to the doorframe with one hand, the other hand clutching Xander's even tighter.

"I have someone I'd like you to meet," she said to Alex.

Alex's hands remained on the piano. He wouldn't look at her. "Your son," he said in a voice so expressionless she knew it held more feeling than any sob ever could.

"No," she said quietly. "Your son. Yours and Lena's."

"What?" A whisper, so soft, like a tear in the fabric of the air around them.

"You have a son. Lena fell pregnant after you were together. I've been keeping him for you; I knew you wouldn't want him to grow up alone."

"What?" he said again and Estella almost wished he would revert back to the expressionless tone of before because his voice was now so loaded with emotion, so close to the brink of breaking that she wondered if she could bear to hear him speak like this and not hold him in her arms.

"This is Xander," she said, willing Alex to lift his gaze to meet hers. "*Your* son."

Xander was watching Estella, slightly fearful, able to tell that something wasn't right with the adults in the room. "Maman?" he said.

Estella blushed. "He just calls me that," she said. "Because I've been looking after him. He's too young to explain anything to just yet."

Alex lifted his hands from the piano, stood, and took one step toward them. He stopped as Xander pressed himself into Estella's side, wary.

Alex crouched down, halfway across the room, so he was at the child's eye level. "Hi, Xander," he said. "We have the same name, sort of. I'm Alex, short for Alexander."

Estella bent down too. "Alex is my...friend. I told you we were coming to meet my friend."

Xander smiled shyly at his father and Estella saw Alex's eyes—so like his son's—bloom with tears, saw his jaw working as hard as it could to keep his face still, untroubled, so he wouldn't frighten the child.

Alex held out his hand. "It's nice to meet you, Xander."

Xander looked at Estella and she nodded. Then he walked over to Alex and slipped his hand inside his father's.

"Can I give you a hug too?" Alex asked. "I'm a bit sad, you see, and a hug would make me feel much better, I think."

And Xander, lovely, sweet child that he was slid his arms around Alex's neck and gave him the softest and most gentle hug. It destroyed Estella. Her sob was so loud that Xander turned back to her, a troubled look on his face, as if he thought he'd done something wrong when of course he'd done the one perfect thing.

Estella saw that the dam had broken in Alex, that the tears were now flowing freely down his cheeks. That a child, a small and tiny child, could have so much power.

"Thank you," Alex said, voice raw, to Xander. "That's better."

Xander reached out a hand to touch one of Alex's tears, to pat it away. Then he grinned at Estella, as if to say, *See, I helped*.

"Good boy, Xander," she managed to say.

"You did this?" Alex asked. "You've been looking after my son. For how long?"

"Three years," she said. "I tried to tell you I had him. That's why I wanted to see you in Gramercy Park. But you left before I had a chance. And since then I haven't known how to find you."

"I thought..." Alex paused, drew in a shaky breath. "I thought Xander was your child. Yours and Sam's. That you'd married Sam."

"If you'd hung around to ask," she chided gently. "But I was so awful to you..." She couldn't continue; the memory of her telling Alex she couldn't marry him hurt too much.

"After I saw you and Sam and the child I thought you didn't want to be with me because you'd fallen in love with Sam."

Estella shook her head. "No. I found out that...Harry Thaw is my father." She managed, just, to not look away as she spoke.

Alex stood up then and so did she, straightening slowly, eyes fixed on one another. "I know," he said. "Your mother asked me to read her letter to you. I think she wanted us to understand that it doesn't matter who your father is. Or where you come from. What matters is what we make of it. And we've both made so much of everything. Except for one thing."

"What?" Estella breathed the word out quietly in case what she hoped he would say and what he actually said were two different things.

"This." He slid his arms around her waist and up her back, drawing her to him. "Us." Then he turned to Xander who was gazing up at this strange performance with wonder. "Xander, would you mind if I kissed your Maman?"

Xander shook his head. No, he didn't mind at all.

And nor did Estella.

Later, after they'd shared a riotous dinner with Xander, after they'd bathed him together, dressed him together, after Alex had told him a story about a young boy who grew up in a land far away and who had to battle pirates and thieves, after they'd tucked him into bed and they'd both kissed him goodnight, Xander's arms snaking around Alex's neck the same way they did around Estella's, Alex led her to the room with the piano. Actually, led is not an accurate description. He shut the door to Xander's room and they stumbled, arms wrapped around each other, mouths locked tight, hands raking desperately at clothes until they found the sanctuary of the bed in the music room.

Once there, Alex took his mouth away from hers. "I need to see you. So I can believe you're really here."

"I'm here forever," she vowed.

He didn't kiss her again, even though he wanted to so much it hurt. Instead he kept his lips a breath away from hers, because watching her was bliss. It meant he could see the moment her breath came faster when he undid the buttons on her shirt, could see the way her eyes darkened as his fingers grazed the nape of her neck, could see her cheeks flush as he slipped her skirt off, could see her mouth open when he traced a slow and sensual line along her collarbone, down the center of her chest, across to one breast and then the other. It meant he could see the desire written in the most discernible of languages on her face as his hands came to rest at the top of her hipbones.

"I love you, Estella," he said.

"I love you too," she said. Four words he'd never thought she'd say to him again. Four words he now believed he would hear every day for the rest of his life.

They shared three months of bliss. Later, that's how Estella would think of that time. Even though it was February, they opened the windows of the house on the Rue de Sévigné to let in the air and the sunlight. They had men, wounded soldiers who could no longer fight out the dying weeks of the war and who had moved across from Germany, eager for work, come in to paint and repair and restore. They watched the house unfurling, which was like watching a rose blooming, the petals of beauty finally released from the tight bud they'd been trapped in for so long.

Alex had to fly back and forth to London. Estella and Xander went with him and, when they were in Paris, he had meetings there too and Estella had appointments with Printemps and La Samaritaine to show them her samples and to organize for the grandes dames of the Parisian stores to stock the Stella brand.

In between all of that, there was the simple joy of sitting in the Place des Vosges and watching Xander run, of playing the piano together,

Alex and Estella in perfect harmony, Xander hitting the keys whenever he felt like it, keeping everything new and unexpected. And then there were the nights when Huette would come to watch Xander and Estella and Alex would go to the Théâtre du Palais-Royal.

Estella would wear the gold dress, which hadn't dated a bit, for the sake of nostalgia and something more: to see the pulse in Alex's throat beat faster when he saw her, to feel him draw her in as close as she could possibly be, to have him whisper in her ear, "God I love you"; to have to resist the temptation just to stay inside, in bed, naked together, but to feel that same intensity passing between them at the theater; to feel the impossibility of even looking at him or the almost unbearable sensation of his hand on her leg, or his fingers caressing her wrist, knowing what would come later when they were at home together.

Until the day Alex came to her with a frown on his face and she reached up to smooth it away.

"I have to go away for a few days," he said. "Tonight. To Germany. I can't take you with me."

"We can survive a few days apart, I'm sure," she said lightly, knowing that, sometime soon, they would have to return to New York and resume a more orthodox life where they didn't see one another quite so much.

"I handed in my notice," he said. "This is my last trip. I'm going to be a boring Manhattan attorney and we're going to have summers in France and…" He stopped and looked at her so intently, with so much love, that her breath caught. "The life we'll have, Estella," he said.

"The life we'll have," she repeated. And she believed it, believed their life together would be extraordinary, unforgettable.

Until the next morning when Xander climbed into bed next to her and she heard something clinking.

"What's that?" she asked sleepily.

Xander opened his pajama shirt and there, resting against his chest, far too long for him, was Alex's medallion. "Daddy gave it to me yesterday," he mumbled as he snuggled in to her. "Said it would keep us safe while he was away."

And Estella felt it, felt the explosion, the moment Alex ceased to exist, felt his soul kiss her forehead—oh, too lightly—as it flew past and all she could do was clutch the medallion in her hand, draw Xander closer, and scream: *No, no, no, no, no.*

PART TWELVE
FABIENNE

CHAPTER THIRTY-SEVEN

August 2015

A fortnight after the piece in the *New York Times*, Fabienne came into the office early, as was her habit, and smiled at Rebecca who was already at her desk, studying something intently.

"What's that?" Fabienne asked, setting down a coffee for Rebecca.

Rebecca pushed a robin egg blue magazine over to Fabienne. "The Blue Book," Rebecca said. "The Tiffany catalog. I've been sent one every year since my mother bought me a Tiffany key for my twenty-first birthday. Look at this. It's so beautiful. And it has your name."

Fabienne read the title on the page: "*The New Tiffany Collection: The Women I Have Loved.*" And then, underneath in smaller font, the words: *Dedicated to the women who have made an unforgettable impression on him, our Head of Design Will Ogilvie defies you not to find something in our latest catalog that is worthy of celebrating the uniqueness of the women you love.*

A magnificent pendant, made of polished white stone, the skeleton of a seahorse suspended in the center, sparkled on the page. *Just as a fossil survives for millions of years, its story caught in the bones it leaves behind, so too can the love of a lifetime survive beyond time. Fabienne pendant, $110,000.*

"What's wrong?" Rebecca called, puzzlement plain in her voice as Fabienne tore her eyes away from the page and raced into her office.

She slammed the door shut and picked up the telephone. What a fool she'd been. Yes, she wanted her collection to be a success. To put everything she had into a business that was one of the loves of her life. There was nothing wrong with that. But there was another love in her life.

She'd been so busy wanting to please Estella's ghost, her father's ghost, the newspapers, everyone, that she'd forgotten the only person she had the power to make happy was herself. And she wanted to do that with both Stella Designs, and with Will.

She dialed Will's number.

"Hello?" His secretary answered. Fabienne asked for Will but was told he was in a meeting. She left a message.

Then she paced for ten minutes before picking up her phone and sending him a text. *Can you meet me at Momofuku Ssäm Bar at 8? I need to talk to you.*

Then she walked, with a newfound confidence in herself, down to the salon for the final fittings and spent the day watching models don her samples, tweaking, perfecting, having resolutely left her phone on her desk so she couldn't check it every five minutes. When at last the final model was done, Fabienne returned to her office, picked up her phone, and thanked God that Will's message, brief and impersonal as it was, had at least contained the word *yes*.

She dashed home to shower and change but, finding nothing in her own wardrobe to suit her mood, she opened the closet in the spare room in which her grandmother had kept, in defiance of proper curatorial practices, several Stella Designs gowns that she couldn't bear to part with. One was a brilliant green dress, probably too much for Momofuku; it was the dress Estella had worn the night she won her first Fashion Award and Fabienne felt that she could do with some of the bravado that the dress must still hold in its seams.

She slipped it on, thankful that she and her grandmother had always been about the same size. Then she made up her face and stepped out into the night.

Momofuku wasn't far from Gramercy Park so she walked, nerves increasing with her pace, as she drew closer to Second Avenue. She pushed open the door and saw that Will was already sitting at a table, the tiniest frown on his face, and she hoped it wasn't because he was about to say something that would hurt her.

"Hi," she said. She pulled out her chair and sat down.

"Hi." He looked up from the menu. The restaurant was so dark it was difficult to see if he was still frowning but he certainly hadn't smiled.

It would be best to launch straight in, Fabienne thought, before she lost her courage. "I'm sorry," she blurted. "I'm sorry I've been so busy. I had to do it though, to learn something about myself. I've realized I need to design the collection for me, not for the media or the skeptics or to preserve the legacy of Stella Designs. I have no idea how you feel anymore after Melissa, after being away, after me burying myself in work but I'm going to say this anyway because, if I don't, I'll regret it for the rest of my life. And too many people live lives of regret, or don't live long at all."

She took a deep breath. He hadn't shifted his eyes from her face but neither had his inscrutable expression altered. "I love you, Will. I want to be with you. I want you."

A waiter appeared, smiling brightly, asking if they were ready to order. "We've changed our minds," Will said abruptly and stood up.

Fabienne stood too, even though her legs didn't want to. In fact her whole body would rather just stay in the chair and order a warm sake, anything other than step out onto the street with Will, have him shake her hand or, worse still, kiss her politely on the cheek, thank her for her sentiments and say he didn't feel the same way. She could feel her jaw tense as she followed him through the door and along the footpath a little, where he finally turned.

This is it, she thought. *Grit your teeth, nod, say that you understand and do not cry*. Not until he's walked away.

But instead he reached for her hand. "Your place is closer."

Fabienne shook her head. "What do you mean?"

He drew her in to him and whispered in her ear. "I love you, Fabienne. And I want you too. So much."

As the desire kindled by his words tore through her, she understood.

Later, in her bed in Gramercy Park, Will kissed her gently and she smiled up at him. "I have no words to describe how good that was," she said.

"I don't either," he said, kissing her again. He rolled off her onto his back, gathering her in his arms, resting her head on his chest, stroking her hair.

"It's not exactly how I thought the night would turn out," she admitted.

"Why?" he asked. "You don't regret…"

"No!" she exclaimed, interrupting him. "No regrets at all. In fact," she grinned wickedly, "I'd quite like to do it again very soon."

He laughed. "I think we can arrange that. How did you think the night would turn out? I suppose you thought we might actually eat dinner. Sorry about that."

This time she laughed. "I'd take this over dinner any time. No, I just didn't know how you felt anymore. But then I saw the Tiffany catalog today…"

He leaned over the side of the bed, searching around on the floor for something, locating his trousers and removing a box from the pocket. A Tiffany box. "For you," he said.

She tugged at the ribbon. Inside the box sat the Fabienne pendant, the fossil within its smooth whiteness seeming to suggest that there were always layers of beauty, even inside something long dead, that wonder and awe would always survive.

"It's the most stunning thing I've ever seen," she said.

Will took the pendant out of the box and she lifted her hair while he placed it around her neck. She turned around to show him and he smiled. "It's very distracting that you're naked right now," he said. "I hadn't really thought about how it might look on you without clothes."

"I can always put my clothes on," she teased.

He took her hand. "You're perfect just the way you are."

Later, as Fabienne walked back into the room with the omelet she'd made for their dinner, she saw him looking at her grandmother's box, which was opened on the bedside table, the piles of paper she'd already read sitting beside it.

"What's all this?" he asked, propping pillows up for them to lean against.

"The answers to the mysteries of the past," she said, filling him in on what she'd learned so far about her grandmother. "I think there's one more letter in there. I wasn't sure if I wanted to read it but now I think I do. Do you mind?"

"No. Let's see what it is."

So Fabienne put her hand into the box and withdrew the last piece of paper, a letter written in her grandmother's elegant hand. Then she began to read aloud.

My dearest Fabienne,

I put this at the bottom of the box deliberately. If you hadn't been strong enough to read everything else, then you wouldn't possess the resilience of spirit that you need to read this. I think you do; but I know you often doubt yourself.

You'll know by now that Xander, your father, was my nephew rather than my son. That I had a twin sister, Lena Thaw, whose existence I knew nothing of until 1940. And you've seen in the letter from my mother how that happened.

The more difficult thing to explain is Alex, Xander's father. I met him one night in Paris at the Théâtre du Palais-Royal and even though I didn't realize it at the time, I fell in love with him as he fell in love with me. But circumstances took us our separate ways. When he met Lena in New York two months later, he assumed she was me. They spent one night together. Xander was the result of that one night.

After many, many months, I saw Alex for what he was. The bravest, most admirable man I'd ever met. I loved him in a way I didn't know it was possible to love: unfalteringly, unrestrainedly. There was nothing in the world like the love we shared.

But he worked for MI9, a British spy agency. On his last act of duty, the car he was in drove over an unexploded bomb. It was set off and everyone was killed. Including Alex. My world ended.

But I had Xander to look after. Thank God. If I hadn't had Xander…

A couple of years after Alex's death, gently and kindly and unfailingly, Sam was there. He'd always been there. I didn't fall in love with him the way I fell in love with Alex, spectacularly and breathtakingly and all at once. My love for Sam crept up on me by degrees, no less real for taking its time to reveal itself. He understood about Alex and he never wanted to compete, never wanted to be anything other than who he was. And what a life we had together.

I hope you forgive me for never telling you any of this. Lena forbade me to. She thought she wasn't worthy of a child's love and so *she wanted Xander to think of me as his mother, not her. And he was only four when Alex died so his memories of Alex were lost. Which is why I registered Xander's birth properly. I just wish Xander had had the courage you had: to ask me about it.*

Even as I write this, I miss you so much, Fabienne. You are Alex's granddaughter in every way. And I hope you, some day soon, find a love that melds the two I had. So I repeat my mother's words to me, as they are the only legacy worth passing on: Be brave. Love well and fiercely. Be the woman I always knew you would be.

CHAPTER THIRTY-EIGHT

On the day of the showing of the new Stella Designs collection, the house in Gramercy Park sparkled like the doyenne it was, wearing its history proudly. Tiny lightbulbs scattered along the floor of the hallway lit up a path into the front room where the show was to be held. In honor of Estella's very first collection, Fabienne had decided to take Stella Designs back to its origins, back to the fearless and practical designs her grandmother had conjured up in a makeshift workroom in the Gramercy Park house, designs that had stood the test of time and looked even more spectacular now than they had back then. Fabienne wore the black velvet gown, the finale of Estella's original showing, a dress that was anything but cowardly.

She'd realized, as she thought about Estella's letter over the past two weeks, that her generation *was* far too cautious, that everyone she knew protected their hearts and their egos because they'd never had to face protecting their lives, like her grandfather Alex had. It didn't matter a bit if people thought her collection was terrible. She was proud of it and she knew her grandmother would be too. Estella had survived failures and Fabienne knew she could do that too.

And now, in the room at the back of the house, which Fabienne had set up as the models' changing room, everyone was ready. Fabienne smiled and said to the models, "Let's go," and a cheer greeted her words.

She stayed backstage for most of the show but, before the finale, she crept into the front room and took her seat next to Will. He leaned over and kissed her in a very unchaste manner and Fabienne saw the light of a dozen cameras flash to steal the moment.

He grinned. "Sorry, but you're too gorgeous not to kiss."

"Never apologize for kissing me," she said, smiling too.

Then the final dress, in bold, gold silk, sashayed onto the runway, accompanied by a spontaneous and resounding burst of applause. As the audience stood to pay tribute, Fabienne felt the ghosts of all of those from the past—Evelyn Nesbit, Lena, Sam, Alex, her grand-mother Estella and Xander, her father—cheering her on, embracing her, blessing her, before finally stepping away and loosening their grip on the present.

Thank you, she whispered to them, so softly that nobody would hear, but she knew they would. And with that, she tucked them, these people she'd loved, people who'd made her what she was, into the album of her heart, safe at last. And she took Will's hand in hers.

AUTHOR'S NOTE

Harry Thaw, Evelyn Nesbit, John Barrymore, and Stanford White were real people. Harry Thaw really did walk into the rooftop theater at Madison Square Garden and shoot Stanford White out of jealousy over Evelyn in front of a crowd of people. Both Stanford White and Harry Thaw are reported to have raped Evelyn Nesbit, and Harry Thaw was also accused of kidnapping Evelyn, locking her up, whipping her and abusing her. What horrified me most about this story was that Harry Thaw was never prosecuted for anything he did to Evelyn Nesbit, or the other women he reportedly abused and injured. He was only prosecuted for the murder of Stanford White and then later for assaulting another man.

Why were the women he hurt not offered justice? Of course, the answer to that lies in a long history of women feeling too scared and ashamed to report such crimes and the legal system failing to recognize those acts as crimes. What I wanted to do in this book was to look at what kind of legacy it leaves for women if a man is able to terrorize them over and over again and is allowed to get away with it without punishment. Of course I can't begin to know, but I wanted to try to understand. Even though I'm writing historical fiction, it seems to me as if much hasn't changed; men in power are still able to say or do demeaning and disgraceful things to women and get away with it.

While the people are real, some of the experiences I've granted to them are invented. It was widely speculated that Evelyn Nesbit had fallen pregnant to John Barrymore—whom she attested to have loved—more than once and that those pregnancies were either terminated or could even have resulted in a live birth. What I've done is to extrapolate and imagine, as is the novelist's prerogative: *What if?*

On a lighter note, many other characters in the book are real people, including Elizabeth Hawes, famous American designer and author of the memoir *Fashion Is Spinach*, and Babe Paley from *Vogue*. Many of the events in the book have their basis in fact, including the exodus from Paris in 1940, the SS *Washington*'s encounter with a German U-boat, and too many more to mention! Similarly, the buildings my characters inhabit are real, such as the fascinating Barbizon Hotel for Women, the London Terrace where Sam lives in Manhattan's Chelsea district, and the Jeanne d'Arc Residence. Estella's house on the Rue de Sévigné is an amalgamation of some of the *hôtels particulier* in the Marais district in Paris. MI9, the British Military Intelligence agency Alex works for did exist: it was formed in late 1939.

ACKNOWLEDGMENTS

As always, biggest thanks go to Rebecca Saunders at Hachette Australia, publisher extraordinaire, who, when I telephoned her in late 2015 with a barely formed idea of writing about the fashion industry in the 1940s, said: *Write it. That's a book I want to read.* I did write it, and the whole way through she was supportive, encouraging and, as always, perceptive in her editing. Her belief in the book made me believe in turn that maybe it wasn't too bad, that maybe somebody would read it, and perhaps even enjoy it.

The rest of the team at Hachette are also fabulous. From sales to marketing to publicity to editorial, I am very blessed to work with such amazing people.

In writing this book, I am indebted to the wonderful Margaux, my tour guide through Your Paris Experience, who walked me around and talked me through the Marais district in Paris, and the historical fashion district of Paris—the Sentier. She took me to the Atelier Legeron, where I was able to watch women making the flower and feather decorations for couture dresses, as Estella does in the book. Margaux also introduced me to the beautiful Théâtre du Palais-Royal, which I knew, as soon as I saw it, had to go into the book.

My sincere thanks also go to Matthew Baker from Levys' Unique New York for a fabulous tour of Gramercy Park and surrounds and to Mike Kaback for an illuminating tour of New York's Garment District.

I've always said I love a dusty archive and in writing this book, I am hugely grateful to Jenny Swadosh, Associate Archivist at the New School in Manhattan for access to the Claire McCardell fashion sketches collection and the André Studios collection of sketches, and for pointing me in the direction of the alumni newsletters which alerted me to the existence of the Paris School.

The National Archives in Kew has a treasure trove of information about MI9, which I used extensively.

I also read many books as part of the research process, among the most helpful of which were: *MI9: Escape and Evasion 1939–1945* by Michael Foot and J. M. Langley; *Fleeing Hitler: France 1940* by Hanna Diamond; *Avenue of Spies* by Alex Kershaw; *Paris at War: 1939–1944* by David Drake; *Les Parisiennes: How the Women of Paris Lived, Loved and Died in the 1940s* by Anne Sebba; *1940s Fashion: The Definitive Sourcebook* by Emmanuelle Dirix and Charlotte Fiell; *Fashion Is Spinach* by Elizabeth Hawes; *Claire McCardell: Redefining Modernism* by Kohle Yohannan and Nancy Nolf; *The American Look: Fashion, Sportswear and the Image of Women in 1930s and 1940s New York* by Rebecca Arnold; *Fashion Under the Occupation* by Dominique Veillon; *Paris Fashion: A Cultural History* by Valerie Steele; *Forties Fashion: From Siren Suits to the New Look* by Jonathan Walford; *Women of Fashion: Twentieth Century Designers* by Valerie Steele; *A Stitch in Time: A History of New York's Fashion District* by Gabriel Montero; *American Ingenuity: Sportswear 1930s–1970s* by Richard Martin; and *Ready-to-Wear and Ready-to-Work: A Century of Industry and Immigrants in Paris and New York* by Nancy L. Green.

The quote on page 134 about beautiful clothes and French Couturières comes from Elizabeth Hawes's book, *Fashion Is Spinach,* and is reproduced here by kind permission of Dover Publications. The headline of the newspaper article that Alex shows to Estella on page 148 is borrowed from the June 26, 1906 edition of *The Washington*

Times. The poem that both Alex and Fabienne quote from is called *Do Not Stand at My Grave and Weep*, by Mary Elizabeth Frye.

My family get as excited as I do about my books, and there's nothing better than taking my kids to a bookshop and having them shout, at the tops of their voices: *Look Mummy! There's your book!* Ruby, Audrey, and Darcy, I adore you. To Russell, who always takes every opportunity to tell everyone he meets about my books, thank you for your unfaltering support.

Finally, a book is nothing without its readers and I have the best, most loyal, most enthusiastic readers in the world. Thank you to everyone who has ever read any of my books. I hope you enjoyed reading this one too.

ABOUT THE AUTHOR

NATASHA LESTER worked as a marketing executive for L'Oréal, managing the Maybelline brand, before returning to university to study creative writing. She completed a Master of Creative Arts as well as her first novel, *What Is Left Over, After*, which won the T. A. G. Hungerford Award for Fiction. Her second novel, *If I Should Lose You*, was published in 2012, followed by *A Kiss from Mr. Fitzgerald* in 2016 and *Her Mother's Secret* in 2017.

In her spare time Natasha loves to teach writing, is a sought-after public speaker, and can often be found playing dress-up with her three children. She lives in Perth, Australia.

For all the latest news from Natasha visit:
natashalester.com.au
Twitter @Natasha_Lester
Instagram @natashalesterauthor
Facebook.com/NatashaLesterAuthor
#TheParisSeamstress

THE PARIS SEAMSTRESS
READING GROUP GUIDE

CREATING
THE PARIS SEAMSTRESS

Natasha Lester

I have quite a selection of books on fashion history in my office, as it is a particular interest of mine. Once I had the idea for *The Paris Seamstress*, that it would be a book about the birth of the ready-to-wear fashion industry in the 1940s, I began to look through some of these books. I also ordered some new ones—of course! One day, as I was flicking through a book on 1940s fashion, I came across an illustration of a gold silk dress.

Probably, to anyone else, this gold silk dress would simply be another dress. To me, it was a scene. I could immediately see my main character, Estella, making this dress and wearing it out to a jazz club in Paris. I could see her sitting in the atelier in Paris, sketching the dress, designing it, conjuring it up from the excitement she felt at first seeing the bolt of gold silk.

Immediately, I sat down to write the scene: Estella dancing around the atelier draped in gold silk, then creating a dress from the silk. As I was writing the scene, I felt true excitement about the story.

In that one scene, I got such a sense of Estella's character; I *knew* her almost instantly. I also knew this would be the first scene of the book, that it would open the story, and that it would lure people into Estella's world. It's one of the most exciting parts of writing when that happens, and now it's become a really important part of my writing process: to find the opening scene that encapsulates the character, that allows me to be in her mind, that makes me feel her as a person rather than words on a page.

Of course, it's all very well to have an opening scene, but you also need another 100,000 words or so! Everything was going along just fine until I reached about 80,000 words. I had written myself into such a tangle that I had no idea how to unravel the knots. I put the book away and went to Europe to research, imagining I'd come back and the thinking time would solve the problem.

It didn't. The plot was as tangled up as ever.

I had mysteries with no answers, or no possible way to get the answers into the story without a whole lot of explaining and info-dumping and taking the reader out of the world of the book. I also didn't quite know all the answers myself!

Nevertheless, I sat down to redraft, thinking that as I neared the place where I had become stuck, the solution would present itself. It didn't. I began to panic.

Then, in August 2016, I watched the documentary *Crazy About Tiffany's*, about the iconic Manhattan jewelry store. At the time I thought it was just an amusing diversion and had no idea that it would spark an entirely new direction for *The Paris Seamstress*. Up to that point, it was purely a historical novel, with all the action taking place in the past.

That night, I woke up with scenes practically writing themselves in my head, and those scenes were set in contemporary times—2015, in fact. One of the characters was the granddaughter of Estella. (No, Estella had not had a granddaughter until that moment.) The other character was a man, and his job was the head of design at Tiffany & Co., a character clearly brought to life by the documentary I'd watched.

It ended up being the most productive sleepless night that I've ever had. I got up and wrote everything down, thinking that I would look at it in the morning and either laugh aloud or still be excited by it. Fortunately, it was the latter.

Most importantly, I realized I now had a way to solve my plot tangle. By making *The Paris Seamstress* into a dual narrative, I could use the contemporary narrative to unravel some of the answers to the mysteries without it becoming an info-dump for the reader, which is the way it had been heading.

One of my favorite parts of writing this book was traveling overseas for research. Who wouldn't want to go to Paris and New York and places in between all in the name of work?!

Here are some of the most vital places I visited during my trip:

THE THÉÂTRE DU PALAIS-ROYAL

I organized a private tour guide to take me through the Sentier, Paris's historic fashion district. I met my guide at the Palais-Royal, which backs onto the Sentier. There, I made the most wonderful discovery before the tour had even officially started, which inspired one of the opening scenes in the book.

As we walked through the Palais-Royal, a man sweeping the pavement outside his cafe beckoned my guide over and began to chat with her. I understood they knew one another. He passed my guide a key.

"Would you like to see the Théâtre du Palais-Royal?" she asked me. The man had given her his key to the theater upstairs.

"Sure," I said. If I'd known how spectacular the theater was, I would have reacted with a little more excitement!

We went in the back entry and it wasn't until later that I saw the entirely unprepossessing main entrance. You would never know what lays inside. It's an intimate, bijou space, with amazing flocked velvet wallpaper, lots of gilt, and a stupendous chandelier. As we walked in, I knew straight away that it would have to appear in my book. In fact, an entire scene came to me as I stood there, staring.

It was one of the most marvelous moments of serendipity. It cemented my belief that you must go visit the cities you are writing about because these discoveries can't help but make a book more authentic and more real. I also recommend that if you ever go to Paris, you go to the theater—it's one of the city's hidden treasures.

ATELIER LEGERON

Before my research trip, I had imagined that the titular seamstress in my book would be a traditional seamstress, sewing clothes by hand or machine. Atelier Legeron, however, is the only independent artificial flower-maker left in France, and as soon as I saw what artificial flower-making was all about, I knew that was what Estella must do.

There are seven traditional métiers in haute couture, including flower-making, featherwork, lace, and embroidery. If you look at a Chanel or a Christian Dior dress you'll see that they are often adorned with flowers (and Atelier Legeron flowers, at that!). I had never once thought about where or how those flowers were made, but I was lucky enough to sit for a whole morning and watch the process in detail.

Atelier Legeron has been in Paris for centuries. It occupies a set of mazelike rooms, all of which serve a different purpose—dying the petals, stiffening the fabric, storing the flowers, making the flowers, etc. It is an incredibly labor-intensive process, and many of the women have been working at the atelier for decades.

Sadly, it is becoming a lost art. For instance, the man who makes the heavy iron cutters that the seamstresses use to cut out the petal shapes is very old, and, once he dies, there will be no one left who knows how to make the tools. I know haute couture is worn by very few people, but watching the way the flowers were made and the traditions that are preserved in the atelier made me appreciate these clothes as works of art. It was an incredible experience.

LE MARAIS

The Marais area of Paris is wonderful. I went there specifically because one of the settings in my book is a hôtel particulier, and there are many of these still surviving in Le Marais. These are former nobles' homes, which present as a set of wooden doors to the street. The doors—which themselves enliven a novelist's imagination—open onto a courtyard, and then the town house is set behind the courtyard. They are magnificent and look as if they hold secrets worth excavating.

I visited several of these, but I also walked the streets of the neighborhood, as it was where I intended Estella to live. And it's in walking the streets that you make fabulous discoveries.

One of those discoveries was the Passage Saint-Paul, a tiny street near the Place des Vosges with an apartment vaulting over the passage. The street looks as though it's a dead end. But if you venture right to the end, you come upon a back entrance into the Église Saint-Paul-Saint-Louis, which is a typically magnificent Parisian church.

As soon as I walked down the street and discovered the hidden gem of a church at the end, I knew it would have to be the street upon which Estella lived. The shadowy nature of the street and the secret entrance to the church also inspired a scene in the book, which is what the research was all about!

NEW YORK'S GARMENT DISTRICT

I went to New York prepared to find a slightly less romantic version of the fashion industry than what I had found in Paris. But did this turn out to be true?

I once again organized a private tour guide, this time to take me through New York's historic Garment District. Incongruously, the

Garment District is located right next to Times Square, which you might think is the last place to find the remnants of a historic fashion district. But on the streets leading away from Times Square, there are massive skyscrapers that used to house clothing factories.

Most of those properties are now occupied by businesses with more contemporary concerns, usually to do with money. My tour guide pointed out the high windows of many of the buildings and showed me photographs in which you could see steam rising out of those windows, right up high off the streets, steam from the irons that once pressed the clothes. This alone was a beautiful and romantic notion, that above the busyness of the streets, little clouds leftover from making clothes floated out of windows.

My guide also took me to the infamous 550 Seventh Avenue, which is where some of the action in *The Paris Seamstress* takes place, and which housed many iconic New York fashion brands.

So yes, it was very different from threading my way through the mazelike rooms of the Parisian atelier, but there was still that same sense of history and that same sense of loss, especially as much of what is left of New York's fashion district are just monuments, plaques, and stories.

THE METROPOLITAN MUSEUM OF ART

Anyone who's been to the Met knows what a fabulous collection of historical fashion it holds. I went along knowing that the exhibition then showing was called *Manus x Machina*, Latin for "from hand to machine." What I didn't know was that I was about to experience another wonderful moment of research serendipity.

The exhibition was all about honoring the traditional haute couture métiers. As I walked into the Met, I was once again presented with beautiful dresses adorned with stunning, handmade flowers. If I hadn't already convinced myself after visiting Atelier Legeron in Paris that Estella should practice flower-making, wandering through an exhibition devoted to that craft surely convinced me.

The exhibition was wonderful for filling in some of the detail of the métiers, how long they have been practiced, and what some of the key traditions are. And, as an extra bonus, there were lots of beautiful clothes to look at!

PARSONS SCHOOL OF DESIGN

One thing that is very important to me when researching is to spend time in archives, looking at primary source material. I knew that the Fashion Institute of Technology (FIT) had a collection of illustrations by Claire McCardell, one of the first ready-to-wear designers based in New York in the 1940s. I thought these would be an excellent research source for my book.

But when I got in contact with FIT, whilst they tried their absolute best to help me, unfortunately my visit coincided with their students' final exam preparations. Thus, the students had booked out all of the available places in the archive on the days I was to be in New York! But archivists are always the most helpful people, and the person I spoke to told me that Parsons School of Design, which I'd never even heard of, had a better collection of Claire McCardell fashion illustrations than they did and that I should get in contact with them.

So I did, and they were only too happy to accommodate me.

I spent one glorious day sitting in the archives, poring over Claire McCardell's fashion illustrations. What amazed me the most about her illustrations was that she was able to show an incredible amount of detail with only a pencil. Because she was designing ready-to-wear, she needed to draw and produce garments quickly, so her sketches show only what is absolutely necessary. But she annotated each sketch as well, and I was able to see how important it was to her to identify precisely what fabric she wanted, what type of buttons she needed, or the belt buckles she wanted to use. All of those details were marked up on each sketch.

GRAMERCY PARK

I'd always known that Gramercy Park was to be one of the key settings for the novel.

My tour guide gave me an amazing rundown of the history of the area. Gramercy Park is both a neighborhood within Manhattan and the name of a park in the midst of this neighborhood. It's one of Manhattan's few private parks, meaning that if you don't have a key, you can't get in. Luckily, I was able to get into the park and have a look around. It's beautiful, as are the town houses surrounding the park.

We spent a lot of time walking the perimeter of the park, examining each of the town houses, discussing the architectural details and the history of many of the buildings that surround the park. Without that tour, I don't believe I would have been able to bring Gramercy Park to life in an authentic way.

There were many, many other things that I researched in New York. Estella lives with her friend Janie in Manhattan's infamous Barbizon Hotel for Women, a building with more history than any library! Estella's friend Sam lives in London Terrace, which, at the time, was a relatively new set of apartments in Manhattan's Chelsea neighborhood. Of course I visited the apartments and the Barbizon and took lots of photographs. Alex has a home out in the Hudson Valley, so I spent a day looking at many of the historic and beautiful mansions there, especially those near Sleepy Hollow.

It's always a pleasure and a privilege to be able to access archives and histories and photographs and other materials that other people might not have the time or the inclination to look at. Without fellow history lovers, people who collect the photographs and the sketches and the stories, my book would not be the same. It was a truly wonderful experience to visit both Paris and New York to research *The Paris Seamstress*, and it was a trip I will never forget.

For photos and more, please visit my website at natashalester.com.au or follow me on Instagram @NatashaLesterAuthor.

QUESTIONS FOR READERS

1. When Estella is sitting in a lifeboat in the middle of the ocean, she reflects that clothing has "power beyond the fabric and the thread and the pattern"—that clothing can give you courage, or comfort, or transform you into a different person. Do you have a piece of clothing that transforms you, that makes you feel different, or that you choose to wear for certain occasions? Discuss the special meaning behind some of the clothes described in the book.

2. The idea of bravery and courage is at the heart of the novel. At the Musée de l'Armée in Paris, Fabienne wonders if people are still capable of being as selfless now as they were during the war, of acting for a greater good rather than acting only for themselves. What do you think? Has contemporary life diminished the concept of bravery, and are heroes now defined in a different way?

3. Estella's mother makes a very difficult decision when she decides to leave one of her babies with the Thaw family. What other choice could she have made? Was another choice possible at that time in history? How did you judge her for the decision she ultimately made?

4. Estella works as a copyist in Paris, copying designs at fashion shows and selling the illustrations to American department store buyers. Were you surprised to learn that fashion's history of copying stretches back so far? Was there anything else that you learned about the fashion industry in the book that surprised you? Was there anything you hadn't previously known about the industry and its history?

5. In the author's note at the back of the book, the author says that she wanted to look at the long and difficult legacy left for women when men are allowed to do terrible things, over and over, and without punishment. Have things changed in contemporary life? What do you think of the idea that while sometimes historical fiction shows us how far we've come, sometimes it also shows us how far we still have to go?

6. Fabienne argues with her boss at the Powerhouse Museum that fashion should be seen as art rather than a fad. Is fashion art? Is haute couture just a senseless waste of money, or can it be compared to purchasing a painting or a sculpture? Do you "consume" fashion—buying seasonal pieces and then not wearing them again once the trend has passed? Discuss your own attitude toward fashion, and the attitudes of some of the characters in the book.